PRAISE FOR GEORGE SZANTO

"Szanto . . . is a real writer." —*New York Times*

"Exquisitely rendered." —*Gabriola Sounder*

"Szanto has a deft hand with characterization." —*Times Colonist*

"Genuinely heartbreaking . . . Vividly described . . . Szanto is acutely, almost painfully, sensitive to the world outside his front door." —*National Post*

"Memory is one of the rare privileges of age. With compassion, wise humor, and a poet's eye for the telling detail, George Szanto has given us a sort of Pilgrim's Progress from one man's intimate story to a dazzling meditation on history and nature." —Alberto Manguel

"Szanto writes with wonderful lucidity, never leaving the reader, always circling back to the essence of things." —Susan Crean, author of the award-winning *The Laughing One: A Journey to Emily Carr*

WHATEVER LOLA WANTS

a novel

GEORGE SZANTO

BRINDLE & GLASS

Brindle & Glass Publishing Ltd.
brindleandglass.com

LIBRARY AND ARCHIVES CANADA CATALOGUING IN PUBLICATION
Szanto, George, 1940–, author
Whatever Lola wants / George Szanto.

Issued in print and electronic formats.
ISBN 978-1-927366-35-6

I. Title.

PS8587.Z3W43 2014   C813'.54   C2014-902771-0

Editor: Leah Fowler
Proofreader: Heather Sangster, Strong Finish
Design: Pete Kohut
Cover image: RetroAtelier, istockphoto.com
Author photo: Bob Meyer

We gratefully acknowledge the financial support for our publishing activities from
the Government of Canada through the Canada Book Fund and the Canada
Council for the Arts, and from the Province of British Columbia through the
British Columbia Arts Council and the Book Publishing Tax Credit.

The interior pages of this book have been printed on 100% post-consumer
recycled paper, processed chlorine free, and printed with vegetable-based inks.

1 2 3 4 5 18 17 16 15 14

PRINTED IN CANADA

For Kit, for all the past and all the future

FAMILY TREES

MAGNUSSEN-BONNEHERBE

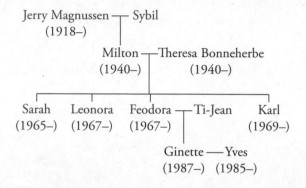

```
Jerry Magnussen ──┬── Sybil
    (1918–)        │
                   │
          Milton ──┬──Theresa Bonneherbe
          (1940–)  │      (1940–)
                   │
  ┌──────┬─────────┼───────────────┐
Sarah  Leonora  Feodora ──┬──Ti-Jean      Karl
(1965–) (1967–) (1967–)   │             (1969–)
                          │
                 Ginette ──── Yves
                 (1987–)    (1985–)
```

COCHAN

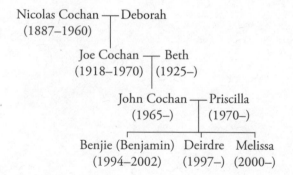

```
Nicolas Cochan ──┬── Deborah
(1887–1960)      │
                 │
        Joe Cochan ──┬── Beth
       (1918–1970)   │ (1925–)
                     │
           John Cochan ──┬── Priscilla
             (1965–)     │    (1970–)
                         │
   ┌─────────────────────┼────────┐
Benjie (Benjamin)   Deirdre    Melissa
 (1994–2002)        (1997–)    (2000–)
```

CARNEY

```
Maurice Feyerlicht ──┬── Barbara
  (1895–1965)        │  (1899–1974)
                     │
   ┌─────────────────┴──────────┐
Bobbie (Roberta)    Annette ──┬── Edward Carney
  (1926–)         (1920–1959) │   (1918–1959)
                              │
                   Carruthers Carney
                       (1949–)
```

CONTENTS

PRELUDE

SPRING EQUINOX

2003

Lola sat down next to me. I like it, her here at my side.

I've been watching Merrimac County and the surrounding country-side for near to three years. The people down there—families, lovers, a few enemies. Mostly a peaceful part of the planet.

Lola was studying my profile. I could feel it.

I survey my patch of world from some middling white clouds over Mount Washington in New Hampshire. Clouds are easier than vacant ether. Ether's like the open sea; on clouds you get your bearings better. I take in a solid chunk of geography, from the Connecticut shore and most of Massachusetts up to the Laurentian Mountains in Quebec, from the central Maine coast, Boston, and Cape Cod across to the other side of Lake Champlain. Mount Washington isn't some Olympus but it gives me pretty good perspective. Haze, the oncoming blizzard, a dazzle of sunlight? I look through them all.

Lola can't see like that. She's a God, higher caste than me. Gods can't observe what's happening in the down below, just as they don't remember the names and places from the lives they've lived. But we lesser types, we Immortals, we can; compensation, I suppose. It's as if Lola's so nearsighted, time like distance goes all blurred and glazy.

"Ted?" She smiled now. "Is the week up?"

"Just about," I said.

"You ready?"

"I am."

She nodded. "I could see it."

"Oh? How?"

"Something in your eyes. Like you're looking far away. Where they are."

I nodded, glanced for a moment over an edge of cloud, a slanted glimpse down to the west, and turned her way. She was still studying me, her lovely face so near.

She spoke softly. "Will you tell me?"

It pleases me, her wanting to know like that.

o

1.

In maps of the down below, the straight border of northern Vermont is broken by an extension of Merrimac County, a fist-shaped bump of woods, fields, and two streams, reaching fourteen miles north into Quebec's Eastern Townships. This acreage, depending where your sympathy lies, was rescued from Quebec in 1790 for freeborn Vermonters by the patriot Ethan Allen and his Green Mountain Boys, or stolen from the very bosom of Lower Canada by Allen the land venturer. Map lines show the border jagging up, around and down again. From where Lola and I sit, those demarcations don't exist.

One chunk of Merrimac land, two extensive properties. The western piece belongs to John Milton Magnussen, direct descendant of Jack Magnussen, whose Tory cousin was smithereened while trying to blow up a Green Mountain gunpowder cache. Milton and his wife, Dr. Theresa Bonneherbe, moved into the family farmhouse there, Magnussen Grange, their base for thirty-four years. And out again after her stroke, to an easier house at the edge of Burlington.

The other place, the old Fortier Farm, was bought five years ago by John Cochan. Cochan had come to explore the land and there found his ideal site, the place to build his city of tomorrow. The hills, fields, and waters flowed well; the geology that gave them shape was ideal for his hopes and purposes.

Milton and Theresa exchange equinox tokens twice a year, over breakfast. Once, they had celebrated the solstices too, with long hikes in the woods, December on skis, June smeared with bug repellent. Since her stroke two years back—the first year of the new millennium, and Theresa understood a treacherous revenge had been inflicted upon her—they've honored the days, summer and winter, spring and fall, at dawn with a glass of fresh orange juice, sunset with fine cognac.

Milton helped Theresa get dressed, aid she loathed but couldn't do without. He'd learned to plait her long white hair into a single braid. She allowed this, her affection and her impatience near equal. Now she lunged her wheelchair along an invisible path toward the stairs; Theresa at this precipice daily scared the shivers out of Milton, but she permitted no assistance. Deftly she rolled onto the platform of the electric haul-ramp, clamped the chair in place, and clicked to DOWN. With a taut whine the cables lowered the platform to the entryway below. Milton followed.

She released the chair. "Silly motor gets slower every day."

Her disability reduced her, angered her, but her voice sounded clear, the tiny sibilant slur undetectable, unless one had known Theresa before, a tall strong woman with a commanding ring to her speech. He'd never see or hear that Theresa again.

Her chair rolled along the hallway and its book-lined walls, past the sitting room and more shelves of books, by the dining room into the large white kitchen where only cookbooks, and birding and insect guides, were allowed. Beyond the windows lay the garden and the seven acres of their new home. Mount Barton rose in the distance. Left from the kitchen, the door to her study stood closed. She gave Milton a twitch of a grin. "I need to go in there."

"You're going to work on equinox morning? Come on, Tessa."

"For one minute."

He scowled. "Okay." He opened the freezer—"Sixty seconds"—and took out the coffee beans.

She muttered at him but without rancor, wheeled to the door, turned the knob and glided in. Built out into the room, five stacks of bookshelves. Journals and magazines lay heaped along the wall, newspapers in piles on two chairs. File cabinets, more files by the side window in half a dozen boxes. No typewriter, no computer. A trail of bare floor led to her desk.

From a drawer she took a package, her equinox present for Milton, wrapped in newsprint and decorated with flower shapes cut from the Sunday comics. He'd like it but it wasn't enough. She could never thank him fully for his fundamental gift, bringing her back from where that lance out of hell had sent her to. The hospital announced she was done and over. "They gave me up for dogmeat," she'd told Milton weeks after he had found her tottering at the edge of her mind.

Now she fingered the paper flowers. She turned the chair and darted back.

"—fifty-six, fifty-seven—"

"I'm back, be reasonable. Here, this is for you." She reached out the package.

"When I've got breakfast on, Tessa. What, you want to destroy order everywhere?"

"Depends on the kind of order," she growled.

He smiled. She was only half joking. He heated the scones he'd made yesterday evening, poured coffee and the orange juice. "Good wrapping, Tessa."

"Feasie did it. Made the flowers too." Their daughter Feodora, the married Noodle, had also located the present, driven into Burlington for it, all the way from the Grange.

Milton opened the package. A handsome book, *Nature in Winter*, animals and insects hibernating, sketches by the author, descriptions of their sleep patterns, their waking processes. Milton flipped through it. "I'll start it this afternoon." He bent down and kissed her dry lips. "Thank you." She stroked his cheek.

His present to her, wrapped in a bookstore bag and tied with September morning-glory vine, was *A Ton of Cure*, by C. Carney.

"Who's he?"

"Heard him on the radio. It's a collection of lectures he gave, about catastrophes stupid people cause." Milton laughed. "I thought, Now that's Tessa's kind of reading."

She nodded, a small drop of her head. How about a guide for avoiding fiascos in the first place? "Thank you, my dear." She reached out her arms.

He bent to receive the hug. He was a large man with a barrel ribcage and a breadth of shoulder. Water-combed white hair scraggled down his nape and over his plaid collar, linting dandruff. A lined forehead and gruff black eyebrows softened to round cheeks, a thin mottled beard trimmed at the sides extending his small chin halfway to his open-necked plaid shirt. Theresa kissed his fingers.

They spent the late morning outside. He walked behind her along trails converted for the chair. New snow was coming, the radio had announced, a late-season storm, twelve-plus wet inches predicted on a thousand-mile front. And after the storm, real spring? The sap flowing again, the new pale green. How many more springs will Tessa live to see, and how many for him? It was a late spring when he'd met Theresa, she radiant and elegant, so strong, and she'd loved him instantly. Of all the men she could have had, why me? The wonders of the world.

"I feel the storm on my skin," Theresa said. She took his hand and gently squeezed it.

The afternoon she spent in her study, reading her new book. The disaster specialist Carney described twelve catastrophes and explained how this devastation in Alberta need not have happened, how that calamity in São Paolo could have been avoided. For a too-often-corrupt society gone wrong, no good purging the symptoms. You have to doctor the whole disease.

Theresa couldn't agree more. Helping a single person here, another there, rescuing them one by one, believing you can correct systemic mayhem piecemeal, what a dump of swan shit. Milton often thought like that, that personal acts of decency could save people, that endless charity could improve people. Hundreds, thousands of hours to save a toe here, an earlobe there. And yet, thankfully, helping only her was precisely what Milton had done.

She studied the face on the back cover. Handsome fellow, C. Carney, around fifty. Wavy hair, solid chin. The beginnings of an idea played about in Theresa's mind. More reading, and Theresa decided. The first flecks of snow whisked down.

Later, before the fluttering fire, Milton poured cognac into their glasses. Outside, fat snow swirled. She spoke at the amber liquid. "To C. Carney."

It gave Milton a sentimental satisfaction to see her so involved, a glimpse of how she'd once been. "Glad you're liking the book," he said.

○

"I'm glad, too," I said, so quietly I didn't think the words came out aloud.

"Why?" asked Lola.

I smiled, and shrugged.

She slanted her head and again examined my face. "Ted? Can you really see all that down there?"

It continues to amaze me, that Gods have become so separated from the down below. Blind to it, so to speak. "Yes," I said, "I see it pretty clearly."

"You aren't just making it up?"

The ever-repeated question. Curious to hear it being asked up here. "Which would you prefer?"

She remained silent for a couple of seconds. "I—don't know." She stared down. Saw nothing. "Tell me some more."

"Okay. There's John Cochan. From the landholding to the east."

○

7

2.

That equinox afternoon John Cochan drove to the cemetery. I watched him stop the car, his Silver Cloud, twenty feet from the tombstone. He stared through the windscreen out to sheets of whipping snow. Leaving the engine on, he got out, walked past other headstones to the gravesite. He tried to come every second or third day, had over the many months. Not coming would be betrayal. Crystals stung his face, a couple of inches of white already on the ground. He'd not bothered with overshoes.

In his work John Cochan's basic instinct, survival on the highest level, depended on speed. His primary purpose, immense success, demanded it. Both survival and success had been the reason for his five-day foray to Lexington, a suburb of Boston, base of Intraterra, headquarters for the US side of operations and parent company of Terramac, the city Cochan's vision would build here in northern Vermont. His junior partner for Terramac, Cal Fenton, had been in the midst of setting up an unfriendly putsch down in Lexington; fatal mistake for Cal Fenton. From Lexington, Cochan had set in action the scheme to eliminate Fenton, a distant end-run winding through Intraterra's Canadian headquarters, Montreal home to the corporation's legal mazes. Fenton didn't know fish about Montreal. Last night Cochan had caught the late Boston-to-Burlington flight, then back to Richmond by car. The commercial plane took longer but he preferred it to an Intraterra chopper. By midnight Fenton had become history.

Cochan should have driven to the cemetery right from the airport. But he'd felt thoroughly drained. He could have come first thing this morning. But the calls from Montreal began at seven-ten.

He stood by the stone. He took off his glove and brushed a rim of flakes from the granite. He bent over, careful not to step on the snow over the casket under the soil. With one finger he cleared tiny white drifts from the inset letters. And from the dates. 1994–2002. He subtracted, as ever, the first date from the second, as if to take life from death. His eyes filled.

If he hadn't brought Benjie to Vermont it wouldn't have happened. If he hadn't bought the farmhouse, made it their home, all would be different. If he'd moved them into Richmond a year ago . . . Simple as that.

Not simple, Johnnie, Priscilla would say. Nothing is simple. And she was right.

Right, wrong, what's the difference?

Four months back they'd left the farm behind, no way to go on living there. They had a house in town now, on the Common, a large house. Benjie would have loved it. Johnnie came back to the house last night, to Priscilla, to Deirdre, Benjie's first sister, to Melissa, his second, not yet two. For an hour last night, one relieving hour, Priscilla had loved him as of old.

He stood, stroked the stone, squeezed his eyes shut.

Back in the Rolls he sat in silence, engine running also silent. He slid his fingertips along the steering wheel's gleaming wood. He loved this motor car. Not as one loves, say, a woman, even a good friend, all quirks and demands, but as one loves what is smooth, dependable, ongoing. The engine of the Rolls was the finest integration of mechanical parts he had ever let his eyes delight in, his fingers caress, his mind comprehend. Its balance of space and function, its power, soothed weariness away.

But no soothing his despair. Not from the gravesite, nor from last night's dream. A dream from the pit of dreams, a thick dark dream passing beyond forests to flat stretch-scapes beside a wall of water. From the distance, muffled by the roaring wall, surely he'd heard Benjie's call, help me . . . At first far off, then closer, close by, the wall thin as breath. Help me, Daddy . . . help . . . If a way could be found, whatever way in the universe, Johnnie would embrace it. He had cried out, "Benjie, where are you? Ben—?" Far away, dim in the wet dark . . . help . . . "Where? Where!"

Priscilla had awakened him, stroked his arm, his shoulder. "Johnnie." He grabbed her wrist. "Why'd you do that, I'll never find him, I'll—" "It's no good."

He squeezed hard. "Damn it, damn!"

"Shhh. You'll wake the girls—"

He slumped his face into the pillow.

Priscilla whispered, "Johnnie." Three-four-six times. She stroked his hair. He lay motionless. She drew his head, no resistance, to her breast. Her eyes filled, and flooded over.

He lay back flat, staring at the ceiling. The moon floated across the skylight. Soon she drifted back to sleep. Somewhere he'd find the dream again. But the worst of it, and so his anger, was she'd said it right, what good—?

He turned the car about and drove from the gravesite. By the cemetery gates he stopped.

For four years the purpose of his life had been Terramac City. Terramac, conceived for Benjie, for Benjie's generation. Terramac would be dedicated to Benjie the day of its completion. An electronic city, a city in harmony. The city of the future, a manageable and managed environment. A whole and integrated city.

An econovum: first projected, soon to be real. If it's crazy to dream, call me mad.

A few had laughed. At first. Funny guy, that John. And what's an econovum, anyway?

Funny to think life otherwise? Conceive an environment free of pollutants, of stink and damp? Free of pests, human and insect? Yes, he would create the consummate environment.

But the econovum question was one he enjoyed. Econovum, born out of a meeting with Sven Zimberg and Edgar Latier, Columbia and the University of Toronto respectively. Three dozen years back they had built influential careers by evolving what the world came to call ecological thinking and strategizing. Publicly funded research was their game, private-sector consulting their scheme.

John Cochan had outlined his dream. "I'll finance young scholars. They'll invent ecologies managed from the bottom up and the top down."

Latier puffed his dead pipe. "How d'you mean, managed?"

"An environment nothing gets into except what we bring to it. A pristine environment, built right."

Zimberg with his right pinky dug in his ear. "Environments aren't built." He showed his teeth with pleasant disdain. "They grow."

"That's been the practice. But now we construct."

"A kind of condo Disneyland for humans to live in, you mean? Nothing is real?"

"No. Far more real than the odious reality we live in every day. And no rot, no pests."

"A robot ecology, then?" A testy smile from Latier.

"For the first time, gentlemen, a fully human ecology."

"How big?" Zimberg checked for the results of his mining.

John Cochan smiled. "A small city, nineteen-twenty thousand."

"Can't do it." Latier shook his head. "You want to work with— with— I've got to neologize. You're looking to create an econovum. A wholly new system."

"An econovum? Econovism?"

"Ridiculous. No such thing."

John smiled. "Then you're not interested?"

Latier puffed his pipe loudly, and stood. "Not my line of work."

Zimberg rose, hitched up his jeans, shook his head. "Won't hold water."

"Too bad, Cochan."

No no no. Too good. Couple of academics, boots laced so tight to the past they couldn't walk into tomorrow. But they'd brought John a gift, a name to accommodate his project: Econovism. A whole splendid new thing. Of course environments get created, perfected managed environments; John had witnessed their creation. Among other places, in Idaho, sixty miles out of Boise. Thousands of acres. All for potatoes; potatoes pure and simple. No bugs. No weeds. Nothing in the soil except what the farmers put there. One hundred percent potatoes. Vaunted potatoes, potatoes indispensable for exemplary McDonald's fries the world around. Enough insecticide and the farmer held full control. Perfect potatoes. Of course Terramac was a universe light-years beyond potatoes. But the principle was similar. An environment entirely created by man the planner. When magnitude beds with quality, what grandeur is conceived.

QUALITAS ET COPIA, COPIA IN QUALITATE: motto of Intraterra, stainless letters a gleaming crown above the portals of its Lexington headquarters, embossed in silver across the brow of its stationery, announcing with pride the achievements of the young revolutionary multibillion-dollar enterprise. John Cochan, surrounded by superb talent tried and experimental, stood tall among the upstart giants of American techno-industry.

He'd made the right choice, Merrimac County in northern Vermont, near to the Intraterra offices in Montreal, close as well to Lexington, each less than a helicopter hour away. A few miles from Richmond, the county seat, a town of fifty-five hundred souls just south of Ethan Allen's bump. Johnnie had gutted the Fortier farmhouse, and remade it: newly wired, plumbed, insulated, walled, and glazed. And because it would have been out of place to put up some eye-scathing cement and glass headquarters in rural Vermont, he bought the one-time Methodist church, a white-clapboard Revolutionary War building two minutes from Richmond Common, and transformed it into Intraterra North, the Vermont branch of his international operations. He became part of the community. High-quality talent here, good local labor. The smoothest stonemasons, the most inventive carpenters. Mohawk steelworkers, their balance fine-tuned. Ever-creative financing on both sides of the border. And bi-national insight into legal problems; though Intraterra's staff of lawyers was unsurpassed, Terramac would be further valuably served by local Richmond attorneys. And protected too by an independent Montreal law firm. Thirty months ago John had met with Leonora Magnussen, daughter of John's neighbors Milton and Theresa, licensed locally in Vermont, long practicing under Napoleonic code in Quebec, a partner there at Shaughnessy, Vitelli, Goldman, and St.-Just, specialists in cross-border law.

"And why me, Mr. Cochan?"

Behind her teak desk lady-lawyer Magnussen had sat, trim and ironic. Standing to shake hands she'd towered over Cochan by three inches. Skinny, skinny, and such a narrow face. But well-lashed clever gray eyes. He'd answered her with partial truth: "Your family's commitment to Merrimac County is longstanding. Your knowledge of property and community is complex and deeply respected— Yes, yes," he said as she raised her hand, perhaps to protest. "I've done my homework. It's in your nature to respect the positions of all parties."

She smiled lightly. "With some small preference for my clients."

"Intraterra's interests are substantial. And they're not, I believe, antagonistic to those of your family."

"Tell me about your project, Mr. Cochan."

For an hour he did. Richmond and the county would do well by Terramac City, with clear economic spillover in all directions— southwest to Burlington, into the ski country around Mount Mansfield to the east, across the border to New Hampshire, up into Quebec as well. For decades to come, hundreds of jobs created, a powerful new tax base for education funding, healthy futures for the county's kids. And a lot of fun living, too.

In her office on the thirty-second floor at One Place Ville Marie, Leonora listened. She had privately researched the Terramac City project, and John Cochan too: the prospects and plans floated before the Vermont Commissioners, the contractors and tradesmen consulted, the preliminary community responses. She had read of his earlier achievements, recorded and celebrated on the multi-tentacled Internet. Three points became obvious. First, John Cochan was committed to twin goals, grand-scale variable-service projects with the highest of environmental standards that however did not sacrifice prodigious profit. Second, Terramac's early critics were conservative and confrontational, the kind who'd condemn replacing a log bridge across a stream with rough-hewn planks. Third, for better or worse, Terramac would increase the value of the Magnussen land five- to eight-fold. "Your project sounds intriguing, Mr. Cochan."

"Glad you think so. Good to have you aboard."

"So I'm sorry. I can't represent you."

"Excuse me?"

"I agree with your intentions. But I won't take you as a client."

In her voice, something more. "And yet?" John smiled, tight but open.

She echoed his tone. "As a concerned citizen, I could advise."

"I look forward to that advice, Ms. Magnussen." For possible Montreal lawyers he had three other options: no problem. He stood. Again they shook hands. If all worked out, one day he might make her a small present, a unit in Terramac City. A two-bedroom place, say.

As well as lawyers, John Cochan needed the law. He had called on the Sheriff of Merrimac County, Henry Nottingham; a well-balanced man, John had heard. On first hearing the Sheriff's surname, John found it amusing. "Call me John," he told the Sheriff. "They call you Hank?"

Cochan recommended the Sheriff start an investigation company, his own business, on the side. Not in any conflict with his public role, that would always come first. But through a private company John

Cochan could keep the Sheriff on retainer, just in case problems arose, the kind best solved by someone with Hank's knowledge of the county, his sense of equity. So Merrimac Investigative Services was born, Rebecca Nottingham as President, Jed Larsen for assignments outside the Richmond area.

Where snow touched the hood of the Silver Cloud, it melted. On the windscreen the flakes, big, slow, softened to a blurring curtain. White down covered the rear window.

John Cochan sat inside the tent of snow, invisible to the world. Please, Daddy, can we go camping, you and me? He didn't go camping with Benjie. Please, Daddy, take me down to Terramac! He didn't take Benjie to Terramac. Under the snow he saw the boy's face, waiting for an answer. Tears drained, thick and warm, along Johnnie's cheeks and into his mustache.

○

Lola's stare seemed searching far away, as if she herself actually saw John Cochan at the cemetery. I leaned toward her. "Are you okay?"

She nodded, still gazing somewhere beyond.

"Shall I go on?"

"Please," she whispered.

○

3.

All equinox afternoon Sarah Bonneherbe Magnussen Yaeger looked forward to the evening. Staying over in Durham was a good thing, she'd spent the night any number of times after late parties or if the weather was bad. Nothing for her to go home to anyway.

No, not quite right. Back in Boston there'd be their apartment. With Driscoll down in Washington tonight the apartment made few demands.

But she'd rather be here, delightfully illicit, at Nate's place in the woods. She too had a place in the woods, other woods, and a pond. Far away, up north, on her parents' land, where she went once a season.

○

"Milton and Theresa's other daughter?" A large smile, at once protective and wanton, came across Lola's face.

"The eldest," I said.

14

"Ah."

Lola intrigues me. When we first met I'd talk with her just casually, a quick clean phrase or two, and then be gone. It's how in the main I deal up here, with Gods and Immortals both.

Of course I'd noticed Lola long before we spoke. She's stunning—a narrow face and oval eyes, green splintered with purple. Even while she lived they called that face divine. Her flowing chestnut hair when bobbed for her film *Northern Heat* sold for a thousand dollars a hundred-hair strand. When she died it was long again, falling like a polished brown shawl across her shoulders. In her early days here, each dress she wore fitted like a second skin and her form was our open secret. These days she wears flowing garb; more comfortable, she insists. When a breeze drapes her bodylines, she's a glimpse of ancient perfection.

The Gods stick mainly to their own kind, small cliques like those at the Near Nimbus. I've been over there a few times—my need to explore, though I despise God-sighting. Over several trips I've seen the God Maynard, the God Wang, the God Greta, the God Wilhelm, the Gods Jack and Bobby, the God Joan, the God Pierre, the God Edsel, the God Mfebe; not all together, of course. Once early on, the old God Solomon passed by, and twice the God William. But it's not my kind of place, the lighting turns the guests all pink and white, even the God Mahatma. Mostly I go to Patrick's Power Place; it's where some Immortals meet. In the down below you'd call it a café but up here we don't have food or drink. I tell stories to my Immortal friends. Here too they want stories to laugh at, to be surprised by.

A few earth months back Lola took to dropping by and listening. At the start we'd scramble to make space for her—she is after all a God. But soon she blended in. She had a smile for everybody. And for me a sunny extra thank you.

Last week she'd come by as usual, to listen. I was telling them about John Cochan's son, Benjie, the five ways he teased his sister Deirdre. I finished. My Immortal friends drifted away. She sat beside me. "That was a good story, Ted. Though kind of mean."

"What?" I gave her a friendly scowl. "Mean? Me?"

"You told it well."

I hitched my robe higher on my shoulder. "Thanks." In the down below they'd call the material linen. Close. It's magenta colored.

"I think when I was alive"—her voice had sounded so hoarse—"it would've made me sad."

"Yes." A strange thing for her to have mentioned, since the passions die with our arrival here. How Lola, a God, could make reference to earthly moods, I didn't understand.

She'd turned to me then as on impulse. "Ted?"

"Yes?"

Against a white high-cloud sky her thick hair glowed, burnished bright. She raised her head. Her eyes, lilac in that light, held mine. "Would you tell a story? Just for me?"

I embraced her request the moment it left her lips. "What kind of story?"

"One you feel is right. One you've never told before."

I remember nodding. "Let me think on it." But even then I'd already known. "Let's meet a week from today."

"How long's a week?"

"Long enough for me to see what I can tell you."

"Oh." Impish. "Got an idea?"

As if she saw inside me. "Sure." Then over the last week I pulled together all the bits and pieces I'd recently discovered, a story that's converging just now. How could I guess that it might become a story? Simply, I could feel it. The people down there, slipping closer together, a bit more day by day, near-ready to touch. The battle for and against Terramac City. I sensed shifts and clashes that bring on passion and anger, care, violence, hate, kindness. My listeners always enjoy that sort of thing. Milton and Theresa, Johnnie Cochan. Onward with Sarah.

○

Sarah and Nate had been a kind of outlaw couple since late summer, not proclaiming themselves although a few people knew. They went well together, improved each other.

They'd met a couple of years ago. While working for the Ag School at the university, she interviewed for a lab tech position at the Center. Associate Director Dr. Nathan Vicacz asked, "What do you like best about your present job?"

16

"Oh, the tests. With the animals."

"Tests?"

"You know, blood and piss and shit."

He laughed. "Routinely getting your hands dirty."

"But it's never routine. Each one's different."

"Know the cow by its patty? Fascinating."

"In its way."

"So why quit, why apply for this job?"

She felt and knew her answer. "I want to figure out things people don't understand yet."

He hired her. They were a team of three. The Director was often away. Sarah and Nate had lunch together most days, brown-bag style. In the winter they'd eaten beside the heater, soon as it warmed out they sat on the grass. They talked about their lives. They talked about the lab, her brain teeming with notions. They speculated. They wrote two papers together. The second one was accepted by *Formicidae*. Nate without telling her put her name first.

"Why'd you do that?"

"It was your idea."

"Our idea."

He shook his head. "My context. Your discovery."

She was pleased. "Thank you."

The Director resigned, moving on to bigger things. Nate was promoted to Director, Sarah to Associate. A month later they hired a new technician, Helen. Rank, though, was a function only of experience and seniority; the project belonged to the team. Each had specific tasks but sooner or later everyone did everything for the babes. To be part of a team, for the first time in her life, was Sarah's greatest pleasure.

Nate and Sarah had celebrated their promotions by taking each other to a fine lunch, two good friends committed to their work. They toasted each other with cold Sauvignon Blanc. They told stories both of them knew, they laughed, they ordered more wine. That afternoon the babes, their ant colonies, would take care of themselves.

Nate leaned across the table. He faked glancing about to make sure no one could hear. "Your promotion has made you even more exquisitely beautiful than usual."

"You're drunk." She laughed. "Me too. But I love you for saying that."

"And now you can't take it back." He smiled, mocking light. "And I'll make it worse. I love you, Sarah."

She swirled the wine in her glass and stared into it. "I—was wondering."

He nodded. "Now you know."

"I'm glad to know."

He touched her fingers. "Hello, Sarah."

She gazed at his face and found she was wonderfully happy. "Hello."

It began with that ease, stirrings from gentle to mighty, secret pleasures large and tiny. It changed their outer lives only a little. Did they really love each other? Passion there surely was. The tickle from a glance. A warmth draping over them as he touched her cheek, as she covered his fingers. The surge of loss as she drove back to Boston. Friendship too, the generosity to understand quickly, the full trust to dare explain herself as herself. Each would say, Yes, love it is. And to the other, I love you. The difference was, Nate Vicacz believed it all the time. Sarah Yaeger wasn't sure. She was escaping a husband.

This equinox evening, this wintry night, carried weight, fueled coincidences. Driscoll Yaeger would leave at the end of the afternoon for a long-fizzling crisis meeting tomorrow morning in Washington. Helen the lab tech and Sarah's confidante was having a small party, just a b.y.o.b. get-together, people were told. Sarah knew otherwise. Plus, unexpected, a blizzard sweeping eastward would hit New Hampshire by late afternoon. Lots of reasons for Sarah to stay over.

Around three, large snowflakes began floating down. An hour later, winds whisping the snow, small drifts had formed. Sarah turned from the window. "Go home, Helen. I'm leaving soon too."

"Well—"

"Take a long bath. It'll do you ultra-good."

Helen laughed. "Gee, Sarah, how come you know so much?"

"Maturity."

"You'll feed the babes?"

"Yep. Anything I can bring?"

Helen grinned. "Just Nate." She left.

Sarah didn't feed the babes directly, they took care of themselves.

But someone had to spread nutriment around in the glass tanks. The set of base experiments was simple enough, a three-year study funded by the National Science Foundation to determine shifts in social behavior in ant species found in southern New Hampshire if the climate heated up four degrees. The Center had set up, in a double Quonset hut at the edge of the university campus, two tanks each seventy by sixteen feet, ten feet high, and had transplanted into them an ecosystem of meadowland, bog, and brush, including a variety of other insect life, as many bacterial forms as they could isolate, and a range of local springtails.

Central to the project were the babes, originally two colonies of black predator ants in each tank. In tank A they had multiplied to five, in tank B to four. The team fed the ants the Bhatkor diet, a blend of egg, honey, agar and water, and organic matter that couldn't reproduce in the tank: mealworms, cockroaches and crickets, mosquito corpses by the hundreds of thousands, decaying leaf matter.

The telephone rang. Sarah said, "Granite State Insectological Center."

"I'm impressed, your tongue getting around all that."

"Hi, Driscoll." He rarely called here. "How's Washington?"

"I'm still in Boston, I'm not going. Everybody there's got the flu."

"Oh. Sorry."

"Yeah, me too, I need to kick some ass. It'll be next week."

She made light. "Well, look, I'm sorry. Specially since I won't be back tonight."

"Oh?"

"I told you. Helen's party. Her number's there if you need me."

"Under what?"

Sarah sighed, and told him.

"Well, I can't remember all your friends' names."

She waited. "There's fish frozen."

"I'll probably eat out."

"Get somebody to join you." Someone female preferably. But Driscoll no longer knew how to make himself appealing, and least to women. "Somebody to talk to."

"I'll see."

He wouldn't. He spent his time with people who could help him advance. Except, at the Boston office, he was already number one. "I'll be home tomorrow night. If the roads are passable."

"Here it's freezing rain right now. Wish I was in Washington. See you tomorrow."

"Okay. Bye." She waited for his click and set the phone down. She stared out at the swirling snow. So? Nothing had changed. She'd told him a week ago she planned to spend the night at Helen's, repeated it this morning. A storm was raging out there, she couldn't get home safely even if she wanted to. Dammit, nothing would undermine her evening. And night.

She put on jacket, toque, mitts, and went out to the storage shed. The wind blew sharp shards against her face. Snow, inches deep already. The radio had said a foot was coming, maybe fifteen inches. Back inside she divided up four sacks full of ant goodies, confirmed the modulated thermostat settings, checked the lamps to guarantee late winter daylight for her babes, and set the backup generator.

She drove carefully to Nate's place, a log house. Over a dozen years he'd added on, first a wing, then a garage, then a rear deck, then he covered and insulated it, then closed in the garage and made it winter-proof. Three summers ago a second story went up over the central house and garage. In each room, his collections. In the wing, butterflies. In the one-time rear deck, beetles. An earthworm farm in the garage. Upstairs, his research records and a bedroom. A wife had moved out when the garage insulation arrived.

Sarah now kept some clothes here, including her purple silk dress— a birthday present from Nate back in August, a sunny afternoon, a striking match to her gray-green eyes. She'd put it on for him, felt her belly glow, wore it for the half hour before they made love. This evening after they made love, though it was a summer dress, she put it on for the party. And her long down coat over.

Nate's car crept forward, four inches already and mounds of drift. The party began slowly, not till nine did everyone arrive. At nine-thirty Helen, with partner Dan at her side, raised her glass. Dan clinked it with a fork. The room grew silent.

"We have some announcements," Dan said.

"We have some news," Helen said.

They looked at each other, nodded, turned to their guests. "We're pregnant!"

Delight, cheers, ribald comments, congratulations. These two, Dan and Helen, had been trying to have a child for four years. Due mid-October. Yes, all was well, just a little nausea.

Nate put his arm about Sarah's waist. She drew in to his chest, rested her head against his neck.

Again Dan's fork pinged the glass. "Quiet, quiet. So the kid's birth present will be—" A pause: "A married mother and father!"

"You're all invited," said Helen.

More cheers, mocking boos, back-slapping, kisses. Champagne appeared. Bad jokes, like those driving the farthest needing the most booze to keep warm.

Sarah and Nate left. For our own celebration, Sarah thought. Their secret, more open all the time. More visible, less outlaw. The wind howled. Inside the warm car, in the down coat, in her silk dress, she shivered. Would she like to be pregnant? Not tonight, she'd taken care of that. Here was Nate, warm beside her, soon warmer inside her. What more could she want?

She woke at quarter to six, the windows laced with ice. Helen, Dan, a baby. When Driscoll might have wanted a baby, she'd been miles from ready. After a couple of years she started thinking, Maybe yes. But then Driscoll said, Not yet. No, never a child with Driscoll now. With Nate?

She got up just after six-thirty, Nate heavy with sleep. Just as well, she wasn't ready for sex again just yet. She showered, got coffee going, watched the news. Locally the storm was the big story, fourteen inches and still coming down. The phone beeped. Answer? At Nate's at seven twenty-two in the morning? The signal stopped.

She poured herself more coffee. A shame the babes couldn't fully feed themselves, she'd like a day snowbound, Nate had extra snowshoes, they might—

Nate came into the kitchen. "It's for you. It's Helen." His brow had gone crinkly.

She picked up the phone. "Hi. Congrats again."

"Sarah? Your husband just called, he—"

"What'd you tell him?"

"That you were on your way to the lab, the storm was bad, it'd take you a while to get there."

"Bless you. What did he say?"

"You should call him."

"Something wrong?"

"He didn't mention anything. He sounded sort of funny."

"Okay. Thanks, Helen." She set the phone down.

"Everything all right?" Nate stood beside her in his dressing gown.

She liked the morning this way, domestic. "He asked me to call." She sipped her coffee.

"So? Go ahead."

"From the Center. We have call display." A half hour later Sarah dialed her apartment. Driscoll did sound weird. She'd be in Boston before evening.

By the time she arrived he was dead. Only her sister Feasie would come to the funeral. Sarah had said to her, "If I'd been home, he'd still be alive."

○

"But what happened to Driscoll?" Lola stepped toward the edge and leaned over.

"I don't know yet."

"I guess he didn't AA." She shook her head. AA, that's to Achieve Ascension.

"A less than Immortal type," I noted. "Let alone a God."

"Ted—" She took a deep breath and turned to me. "Why am I one? A God?"

I stared at her. I'd never heard a question like that. I sometimes think odd thoughts when I'm organizing a story, but to question a thing so basic? Not possible. "What do you mean?"

She waited. "I don't know."

"Then why're you asking?"

She shrugged. "It was sort of floating around. Inside my head."

Strange, this. Gods don't ask for explanations. The very definition of being a God is to live in an eternal infinite realm, *eir*, of self-pleasure,

22

large or larger. How could a God even think of thinking beyond self-pleasure? Becoming a God means, precisely, dwelling within the ultimate reward. There's not even a pretense of any other mode of experience. Even if, say, a God could fear a thing, or suspect some unhappiness—which they can't, so this is pure surmising—then such a moment would be understood as the pleasure of fear, the pleasure of unhappiness. The past, an imperfect time, is completely forgotten, as are the complicated people one lived among in the down below—one's dealings with them so imperfect their very names and faces have gone absent. In Lola's mind, a place where uncertainty could float? It made no sense. "But how'd the question come to you?"

"It was eerie." She squeezed her eyes shut. "When you were talking before, I thought, Why is Ted an Immortal, and I'm a God?"

Here was dangerous ground, wandering close to the border of what one is. I felt a sudden shiver. Could she step out of her God-realm? I wanted her close, yes. But not by putting her at such risk. She could hardly become an Immortal. And mortality was done with.

"How did we evolve to what we're seen as here?"

"Lola—" I can't say what came over me: I took her hand. "I have no idea."

Though her question did come close to another I've at times considered: What in fact is the process of deciding who becomes a God, who an Immortal? In fact, who decides who gets to AA altogether? I do know that about 99.9999 percent of us in the down below never pass beyond our graves. Let's say there are about six billion people down there. If an average worldwide lifespan is sixty, one-sixtieth of the world population dies each year, or one hundred million people. Of these, one in a million, or about one hundred people, AA annually. Mostly we demise and get forgotten. A few of us are obvious and become Gods, but most here are Immortals. Myself, one day I died, and AAed, and found myself here. So I get to be around forever, a sweet yet curious privilege. Why me? I can only guess. We AA because of something we did down there. They say it all depends on how long we're going to be remembered, and by how many. But by what device can anyone tell that in advance? In the down below I wrote stories for a living. I never made huge amounts of money.

I should amend some of this. They say for almost everyone, Gods and Immortals, it's the pre-departure that defines us. Heroic leadership, or resplendent singing, or a theory that holds the world together for a while, or curing some terrible disease, or privileged martyrdom, that kind of thing gets one to AA. They also say a very few of us have managed to AA some time after the demise moment—a celebratory posthumous biography, a momentous re-evaluation of one's work, fabulous underground word of mouth that bursts to the surface, deserved sainthood. Myself, I don't know anybody who got up here like that.

None of which explains Lola's questions. But I had to draw her back from them. Which I did, walking away from the cloud's edge, the pleasure of the touch of her hand against mine.

Yes, pleasure. Unusual, and we Immortals are different from the Gods in that way. We too function in the eternal infinite realm, *eir*, but under normal circumstance we feel relatively little pleasure. Immortals are content with the privilege of going on forever, having no responsibilities. Still, by doing certain important things, the pleasure sensation can arise. For me, by telling stories I get pleasure. I've been doing it even up here because I found I could. And I've observed how others get a jolt in their own pleasure-sphere by listening. Now with Lola here—

"Why so silent?" she asked.

"Why're you so full of questions?" I grinned at her, playful-hard.

She didn't take to the tease and pulled her hand away. "You're not being serious."

"Yes, very." I felt a sudden growing melancholy. Which is impossible, since passion dies with our arrival here. "More than you can imagine."

She found my eyes with hers, and held them, the left, the right. Her earthly beauty, undiminished, filled my chest with pain. She said, "I should go back."

I forced myself to nod. Technically she was right.

"See you tomorrow?" She spoke softly.

A smile must have made its way to my bobbing face. "I'll look forward to that."

She took my hand, squeezed my fingers, and was gone.

What, what were we doing? We function by the laws, and one of the most ancient says Gods and Immortals must spend a minimum of two parts in three of time space with their own kind. It's a law so old no one's ever needed to invoke it. What God would want to pass time space with Immortals? And why would a God let an Immortal spend time space with her?

I drew myself over to an edge of cloud and watched the happenings below. Tomorrow I'd tell her what I saw.

o

4.

C. Carney worked his Ram between snow-covered shoulders of the back-country highroad toward his appointment, a consultation with Dr. Theresa Bonneherbe Magnussen. She'd written that she needed help with a potential catastrophe, she'd like some guidelines. So maybe she hadn't made her mistake yet. He had called her.

"Sorry," her secretary told him. "Dr. Magnussen doesn't speak on the telephone. Shall I set up a meeting?"

"What does she want?"

"I'm afraid I don't know."

Carney took a curve, banking against ice. Woods on the left, ahead the lake, then Burlington stretched along the shore. Clients normally blurted out the problem in the first minute, but Magnussen hadn't even come to the phone. Why did he agree to meet her? On all sides white ground, blue sky, black trees; the world simplified to three basic shades.

For the last week he'd lived mostly with filth-laden orange, a methane fire out of control thirteen miles north of Median, New Hampshire, a town he knew well. At two-fifteen equinox morning he'd gotten a call from Mrs. Staunton, embodiment of the communication center at Carney and Co. She had the Median town manager on the line. It took Carney just three minutes to turn the man's bombast to a squeaky "Please! Help us."

Carney headed up jobs these days only if they looked to be some new kind of disaster, or a disaster so immense he had to be there himself. Methane fires weren't all that dangerous. But the others were dealing with disasters elsewhere. So Carney drove through the jaws of a spring storm so thick he was less than eighty yards from the fire before he saw smoke. Municipal solid waste in a litter dump the size of three football fields, and the most obvious precautions hadn't been taken. All they'd needed to do was let the methane release properly by covering the waste with adequate soil, simple as that. Now the peripheral temperature had reached 600 degrees Celsius and the local firemen had no idea how to handle it. "Thanks for coming," said the chubby town manager, reaching out his hand. Then he said, "We're in trouble, aren't we."

Carney studied the fire, getting as close to the filthy flames as he dared without face mask and body protection. The town manager trailed him. "Well," he said, "what's it going to cost?"

Always the first question. Never, How can we be sure no one gets hurt here? or, What can we do to keep this from becoming a long-term disaster? "It's a standard project. My costs, billed to you, plus twenty-five percent."

"And how much will—"

"I'd figure $3 million. Maybe more."

"That includes your share?"

"Nope."

"Oh my god . . ."

In the end the man agreed. They always did, they had no other choice. Carney's team arrived, seven men and six women. In fifty-two hours the fire was old news.

The road approaching Burlington had been well sanded. Carney turned onto the campus, found Brentfern Hall, parked the Ram, stared down at the ice-free lake. A glorious day. He'd been tempted to drive over in his Jag and would have if Bobbie'd come with him, she liked open cars. And good booze, good jokes, good talk, good work. He sniffed a laugh. And good men. She'd had a good man who became the sadness of her life when he died. A good woman, Bobbie, infinities more than an aunt. Like an older sister. A grand friend.

Theresa scooted her wheelchair away from the second-floor window. She recognized Carney from the back cover of *A Ton of Cure*, wavy dark hair thick in back, straight nose, wire-rimmed glasses. A shorter man than she'd figured, slighter. What, was tall and stocky better? She shook her head, positioned herself behind her desk, and for a moment agreed with Milton, that this meeting was a bad idea: keep the anger in the family. But son Karl was no help, nor Feasie and Leasie, the Noodles. Let alone Sarah. Maybe Theresa should have sounded out the Noodles anyway. But Leasie was too caught up in too many hours of too high billing. And Feasie? Practical, yes, but the woman thought only in domestic terms. The ways our kids can fail us.

The office of Theresa Bonneherbe Magnussen, Bullfinch Professor of Ethical Studies, when Carney found it, seemed merely paper in chaos. Between piles of journals and stacks of books a narrow path of visible floor space led from the window to the desk, from the desk to the door. "Mr. Carney! Welcome." Theresa, sitting straight in the wheelchair, stuck out her left hand, fine-boned, the fingers worn.

Carney took the hand, her grip firm. "Good to meet you."

"What do they call you?"

"Carney, when they're being polite."

She held Carney's eye, her cheeks drawn, her stare fixing him at the far end of a shared line. She nodded. "Be with you in a minute. Sit. Toss those exams on the floor." She turned to her desk and wrote in pencil on a pad of paper.

Carney lifted the exams from a cracked leather chair. He set them on bare floor—

"Not there! How d'you expect me to get out?"

He shifted them to a double stack of books. She wrote on, nodding to herself, a thin woman, her white ponytail falling halfway down her spine. Before setting the appointment he'd checked her out. An on-line *Christian Science Monitor* interview noted that among her more satisfying activities had been her work with the Women's National Fencing Team, first, one of its stars until stopped by a hip injury, then as a coach until her stroke. The interview had highlighted her demand for doubt and change, for a little anarchy, for a more unstatic order to daily life. "There is no single core to human hope." "Each sentient being becomes his own maker." "The fear of mortality drives the hardest bargain." "We'll let no social contract keep our dreams from slashing lies." He sensed in Theresa Magnussen a woman who, in the realm of philosophy, contended with issues similar to those Carney confronted day by practical day.

Mounted on the wall above the entry door hung a brown trout, taxidermized, dust-free, a handsome fish. Just caught it might have weighed eight pounds. Carney saw a broad stream, a rippled run at the head of a long pool—

"You fish?" Theresa was watching him over her shoulder, eyes gleaming.

Carney smiled. "Never leave home without my fly rod in the car."

Theresa nodded. "Before my stroke Milton and I'd fly in, camps in Quebec or Labrador. Or drive down hundreds of miles of logging roads, pitch a tent, slide the canoe into the lake, fish for hours. Days."

"Sounds right." What an indignity that wheelchair must be.

She spun about, nodded twice. "I liked your book, Mr. Carney, a lot. Your five levels of preventive tactics is dead-on." She sniffed a laugh. "Lots of good stuff there, the asides too. Especially enjoyed the little subsections, like the Two-Handed Ear Grab."

A metaphor Carney had used to describe a maneuver for getting an environmental transgressor's attention. "Thanks. I always accept compliments."

"You write like a man who's been there. I appreciate that." Her chin suddenly dropped as she added, "Ever hear of John Cochan?"

"Familiar," Carney said. "Can't place the name."

"Called Handy Johnnie by those who like him because they think he is. And by his enemies too 'cause he holds tight to where his hands grab on."

"You're not his friend."

"My existence, Carney, is plagued. John Cochan is my nemesis. A horror, like his father. The man used to be Cochan Pharmaceuticals, the drug king killer. But now it's way worse, and it's not just my personal problem. He's creating an unnatural catastrophe. He calls it a city, Terramac. It's a city arising where no city should be."

"Where?"

"For a while there it looked like he'd given it up. He was building it for his son but the boy died, an accident. Sad. Cochan was torn up, I hear. Didn't want to believe it 'cause that'd make him a bit human. Except now he's started up again. He has to be stopped. I need your help."

"And"—Carney raised fire-frizzed eyebrows—"what would that be?"

She leaned toward him. "Ever feel fear, Carney? Real fear?"

Carney's brows dropped. "I get scared from what people do to each other, and to their world. But I don't call that fear."

"A shame. Fear's good. Makes you think out your life. We ought to venerate fear. It concentrates the mind."

"Maybe. But it can also freeze the mind."

"It can grasp the mind. Then you react and it gives you strength. First to think, then act."

"Except there's better ways to concentrate. Like, say," Carney smiled, "through work."

"Work? Real work's the result of concentration, not its cause."

"Well then, how about concentration coming from, say, laughter." Carney was enjoying himself. The woman had an intriguing mind.

Theresa's head shook hard, vibrating a half-dozen times. "Laughter dissipates, it covers up, lets you live with whatever is."

"What about laughter that brings you hope. And helps create community."

"No no no. You laugh, you accept deception."

All interesting enough, but time to move on. "Excuse me, Dr. Magnussen, but what does this have to do with John Cochan?"

She scowled. "Be afraid of him." She whispered, "Keep his Terramac from happening."

"How?"

She tilted her head. "You're the expert. You're the one who knows that what most people accept as normal can be horrendous when you look at it up close." Her eyes focused on his left one. "How? Investigate him. Do whatever it takes."

o

"Tough dame."

My echo-memory realized Lola had said something. "Yeah."

"Hey. You okay?"

I let myself smile a little. "I guess."

"What's the matter?"

I looked at her lovely face. Words, once spoken, once heard, cannot be retracted. What to say to her, how deep into my confidence to take her? "Carney's my son." The words came out before I could censor

29

them. I want to think I told her because I'm an honest storyteller. But more likely I used it to try to draw her closer.

"Oh wow," said Lola.

I nodded.

"That's why you're following all that down there."

"No." I laughed a little. "It's weird. He just wandered in. I didn't know it would happen."

"You didn't?" She raised an eyebrow, sniffed a laugh. "Okay then. It is weird."

She left soon after, back to the other Gods.

I sat alone with my thoughts. Like about that notion, weird. One of the advantages of death-by-accident in your late thirties is that you don't lose your looks to time. I've got a sharpish Roman nose and strong chin, thick brows, my hair's all there, I'm a bit gangly. Carney's hair is thick, he's wiry, still in good shape. Like I am now, only alive. I'd guess I could tackle him down. Occasionally I've checked in, to see what he's up to. One of the Immortal privileges. So it's eerie to be forever thirty-eight, and watch my son turn forty, fifty, this year fifty-two.

Weird, too, is Lola's fascination with all I've told her. What do the mortals in my down below mean to her existence? When she did return, I figured I'd ask her.

Then some days later there she was, dressed in rich burgundy, a smile and delight in her eyes. "What's happening down there now?"

I told her about Carney meeting Theresa. But after the equinox there'd been little new. I feared that if I had nothing more to tell her she'd go away again. But I couldn't lie. "Except for that meeting, not a whole lot."

A pout took her lips. "Really?"

A few new patterns were beginning to form. Not ready yet to be reported. "Mostly people going on as they were. The same old stuff."

"Oh." She hugged herself, as if she were cold. "Okay." She looked back in the direction she'd come from. "I guess I'd better go then."

But my brain had heard something . . . the same old stuff . . . Of course. "Do you know anything about the old stuff?"

"About them? Down there?"

30

"You bet. Interested?"

It took her only two seconds to decide. "Okay." The mischief was back. Which made me wonder. "Lola?"

"Yes?"

"Those people down in Merrimac County, are they important to you?"

"I think—Yes."

"Why?"

She thought for a few seconds. "I wish I could tell you." And after a few seconds more: "I don't know."

I believed her.

"Just, they matter." She beamed at me.

She could make me her slave.

PART I

THE PAST

1959—2003

· One
AS THE TWIG IS BENT

1. (1959)

The telegram arrived in the middle of Bobbie's performance. Ginsberg stuck it in his pocket. For a while he forgot it. She was such a success, they loved both her and the stuff she was reading. He whispered to Gary, "She's given up the control's why it works."

Gary nodded. "Shifting it." They leaned back and watched.

She sat slumped in an overstuffed armchair and continued her paced pattern, silent and unmoving between poems, staring down the audience as they gazed at her, thirty seconds, maybe a minute, then she'd read again. She spoke. "This is from a new group. Sonnets. The only one that's nearly ready. There'll be ten. Called, 'Vomit Cycle,'" She read:

VOMIT 3

Then comes the pus.
Its nylon smothers us.
It sticks on our skin,
We're girdled in.

Pus glows on his skin.
The state he's in.
It kisses my lip,
Oozing acryl. I sip.

Pus pees through our guts.
What it touches it rots.

Try to sink it in gin.
Try to ice it in shit.
Sniff. Shoot. Score. Plastic spew.
We piss pus when we screw.

Lola wrinkled her nose. "Yuk."

"They say you had to be there," I replied.

"Where?"

"San Francisco. The scene."

"Who is Bobbie?"

"Carney's best friend." I grinned. "My sister-in-law."

"Oh. Her. Is she important to Carney's story?"

Important? No one more so. "Such impatience. Why don't I tell you? Then you'll know."

She gave me an "I'm sorry" smile, and pretended to glance over the edge.

○

Again Bobbie's silence. She stared out at them, her large brown eyes unblinking. Her darker brown hair covered her forehead, cut off in a hard line a half inch above her eyebrows. She stood. "That's all." Her brown sack dress hung to her knees, in front from her tits, behind from her ass. She walked off the makeshift stage.

The applause came hard. Cries of, "More, Bobbie! More!"

She reappeared, suddenly grinned, and Ginsberg saw the sister he should have had. The audience's shouting fell away. She said, "There isn't any."

"Go write some!" yelled Gary, and people laughed.

She sipped bourbon. She'd arrived in San Francisco seven months back. And fitted in. First place she could say to herself, Here is home now. She missed her sister, Annette, sure, and her nephew, Carruthers. A little bit Annette's husband; they sometimes talked easily, sometimes less so. Her father maybe but he was out of his head and if he ever came back in she had no idea what he'd be like. Her mother? Maybe she loved her mother but she sure didn't miss her. Nobody else. Here they all knew why she couldn't have stayed in Median. They'd all come from the same kind of place, Topeka and Dracut, Cincinnati, Medicine Hat, Amesville. The bourbon wasn't much good. Surely Kenneth had better taste than this; why the hell did he serve this crap.

She searched for him among bookshelves and displays. Never mind, if she wanted better bourbon she'd return to Median, to some Dennis who prided himself on his bourbon, needed his dentist's salary to pay for it. Go all the way to New Hampshire for better bourbon? Too late for that. She held her nose and chugged it down.

Ginsberg hugged her from behind. "Good," he said. "Friggin' good."

"Friggin'?"

"Should I say 'fuckin' to a lady who says 'fucking'?"

"Is that what I am, a lady?"

"Half," he said, and looked her up and down. "Less and less," he added.

She patted his scraggled cheek. She wondered what he'd be like in bed. She wondered the same about half the men here. Half of the other half she already knew about. She knew she'd never go to bed with Ginsberg, she wasn't his sort of attachment. She'd tried it the other way herself, with Carla and a couple of times with little Martha but didn't get off on it, she preferred men. She smiled. Female after all. Not feminine, thank god. The girls in her dorm tried to feminize her, makeup and satin; but for whom? Those little boys who arrived on Saturday afternoons from Brown, Yale, Dartmouth? Ridiculous. Which left only the professors. "Is it them we're after?" she'd asked her roommate Libby.

Libby blushed. "Bobbie, really."

Libby was truly clever in the bio lab, a smasho mind at work. But also so pretty, tease-curled hair and bitsy nose and bright red lips. For whom? Herself? More of a challenge to try a professor. Bobbie had been attracted enough to one, her history man. At the seminar table he was so wise and smart from the button of his jacket up. She'd wondered what he'd be like below the table, behind the zipper. She asked for an appointment, dressed feminine, met him in his office. She couldn't get him to touch her first, so she touched him. In ten minutes he was all in love. Lucky he was married or he'd have been on her the whole semester. This way, if he didn't accept her schedule, she'd write his wife a letter. She decided not to tell Libby about the history man, Lib would go all pink-cheeked and then distant and envious. Hard to live with envy. Might even drive Libby to drink. Bobbie laughed. No, never; Libby couldn't handle half a beer.

Over her time at Mount Holyoke, the most critical hour of her life was hearing Robert Frost read "Birches" and "Nothing Gold Can Stay" and "Fire and Ice," pieces of magic she spoke in silence as he read. But she was born too late, the last basic truths had already been written early this century.

She was expelled for anti-anticommunist rabble-rousing and in the fall enrolled at the University of New Hampshire, graduating a year late with a degree in economics and history. She came home, taught a year at Median High, and lived with her parents, her crazy father locked in his room, her mother's money taking care of them both. Her older sister, lucky Annette, married the writer who made enough so his wife could do exactly what she wanted: paint. Annette was getting to be real famous. And he took care of the boy.

Bobbie, writing poems nobody cared about, spent time down in Boston in coffee houses with her friend Mark, listening to men in dirty jeans and sometimes women too pretty for words read poems, the men, likely as not, returned vets who'd seen the black torments of war but didn't truly know how to write about agony: that had all been dealt with by the poets of the Great War.

Back in Median she met Dennis the dentist. He too was married so he was safe. She liked him enough, delighted in driving him out of his mind with what she knew about sex or invented. Except a year and a month of Dennis was enough, despite his giving her whatever she wanted if money could buy it; good bourbon and her first taste of cannabis. Not clothing or jewelry. Dennis was schizzy, too often not all there. Bobbie wondered what happened when he wasn't all there while drilling into cuspids and extracting molars. To his torment she took off for New York to live with Mark, but not usually in his bed because he was too much her friend. She met his city friends, they remembering the war in Korea, Pusan and Inchon, and Heartbreak Ridge; others still guilty with the relief of not having been there, still others that they'd missed out on the last great adventure of their times.

Dennis came to New York to take Bobbie home but Mark hid her. Dennis went back to Median. A few months later Bobbie got a letter from Dennis: "In the prison of my days I am my own warden," which turned out to be a copy of his suicide note.

She lay in bed with Zed, smoking shit. He tried to arouse her with palm, mouth, fingers, but her mind was held by those other Vomit poems she said she hadn't written. They were done and they were right but her stomach ached when the words came out. Writing them was a wrenching blast of fire, and now what was she supposed to do, publish them? Useless words and impossible to read, who would print such pain-filled, wonderful crap? Lawrence, ten minutes after she'd finished reading, said sure he'd bring them out in his chapbook series, especially the "Vomit Cycle" if the rest were as tough as what he'd heard, he liked that, that was good, good. But Lawrence said that to everybody. But if he really printed them? Did she dare allow her name on the little book? *The Vomit Cycle and Other Poems* by Roberta Feyerlicht. Not even her sister, Annette, would approve. And Annette's husband—? Bobbie snickered.

Zed thought he'd finally got her.

Except she turned her back to him and laughed outright. Maybe Annette would love the poetry. And Edward? They were artists, in their special way. But so normal. Craftsmen. Zed whispered a small perverse not-tried-in-a-while suggestion into her ear and she figured, Why not.

After a waste year in New York—not completely wasted, she wrote her poetry—one day she'd packed up and driven across the country with Mark and his friend Louis in a 1947 Oldsmobile they'd bought together and arrived in San Francisco, and when they sold it, they had enough to live on for a couple of months till they found jobs: Mark a night watch-man in a paper factory and Bobbie an assistant to the director of a YMCA youth group, two dozen nice, ready-to-learn-other-ways kids, thirteen to sixteen. Through Mark she met Jack; they got on because they'd each escaped from the old New England ways, she born in Median, he less than a hundred miles south down in Lowell. Through Jack she met Gary and Lawrence and Josephine, and Kenneth. First name friends. Only Ginsberg was Ginsberg, nothing else; he intimidated her like he could see her innards.

Of course it was Ginsberg who convinced her to read at the Six Gallery; nobody else could have turned her into a performer, she who liked being in crowds where she could stay impersonal, invisible, didn't have to deal with more than one other person, a single person at a time.

She slept. In her dream she heard a buzz. It didn't fit her dream so it couldn't be in her dream. Before she pulled her eyelids apart she recognized the doorbell. She slid Zed out, got up, pulled on her muumuu, opened the door. Ginsberg.

"Come in."

He nodded, and did. "You okay?"

"Yep." She turned her head on a slant and felt her hair sticking to her scalp. She saw Ginsberg wasn't okay. "What's the matter?"

He handed her a telegram. "This came for you."

She took it. It was open. At the bottom she saw her mother's name. She read the words: Annette and Edward killed, plane crash, terrible. Carruthers despondent. Come home.

On November 17, 1959, Bobbie Feyerlicht, age twenty-four, caught the night flight to Boston, the bus to Median, full circle, to raise her nephew, Carruthers Carney.

o

I stopped, not sure what to tell her next. It's always best to be selective.

Lola said, "I didn't like that pus poem."

I could feel her disapproval. I searched my notes. "Try this, then."

She took it and read.

FLOW

A leaf hears the dark breeze, feels the bat's squeal cut.
The leaves whisper, a breath shakes their arms.
A wet branch cracks, breaks, hangs.
The trunks tell each other. Now the sap knows.
Juice seeps to the bottom and below.
Into roots and soil, into the waters, a thick flow.

The sap tells, the soil confirms, the waters understand.
They lie steady.
The flow tells the larval nymphs, the snails, the fish, the
    breathing lands.
They make ready.

Roberta Feyerlicht
(February 3–16/03)

"That's the kind of thing she's writing now," I said.

"That's better," said Lola. But her mind was somewhere else.

"What's up?"

She waited maybe ten seconds. At last she said, "Will you tell me something, Ted?"

"Anything I know." Almost anything.

Again she held back, as if afraid to speak. "How do you do it?"

"What?"

"See their stories."

"Like I told you. I look down."

"But they're not there any more."

"What's not there?"

"The stories you're telling me."

"But I can see them."

"But how? I understand if the story's happening just about now. Like what all those people were doing around the equinox. But you've just told me about what was going on in 1959. Can you see 1959 down there?"

An insightful question. No, it had never occurred to me before, how I can see events that have gone by. Like I've never asked myself how I was able to walk. "You know, I'm not sure. But when I look, there they are."

"What're you looking at?"

"Them. Many of them."

She shook her head. "I don't get it. It's like you seeing into their minds, knowing from the inside how they're thinking."

"Yes." I've always been a little proud of that, seeing their thoughts.

Again she remained silent. I could almost feel notions crossing her mind. "Maybe it's because Carney's your son." She thought for a moment. "Can you see others in the past?"

"I—" I shook my head. "I don't know." Obviously I could see some, but others not. "Like who?"

She considered my question. "Like, maybe you can see what happened to the poet lady in 1959 'cause you're sort of related to her. Can you," she searched, "can you see what happened to anybody else in 1959?"

I closed my eyes. Bobbie I saw clearly, back in Median with Carney. Somewhere else back there I had a sense of amorphous forms, a lot of dark movement— Far over to the right, some color, something taking shape, someone there. I focused in. A woman. I recognized her; from where, I don't know. "Beth Cochan," I said, eyes open, staring at Lola.

"Who?"

"John Cochan's mother." I'd never tried this before, consciously trying to check out past moments in the lives of people.

"But, Ted, how's that possible?"

I shook my head and closed my eyes again. Still there. Beth Cochan.

"Is she doing something? Saying something?"

○

2. (1959)

Beth Cochan believed her great success—seven major papers by the time she was thirty-one, three of them on tropical coleoptera, a worldwide reputation in pharmaceutical entomology—grew from what she called her induced insight. Which is to say, she reflected on the objects of her research while under the influence of marijuana or hashish. Toying in her lab, eyes closed, her mind watched the apparently chaotic flow of distinct particles, contemplated their movements, saw invisible conjunctions turn into sudden obvious connections, and transformed these links into necessary patterns. She would then direct her experimentation toward her discovered loci. Time after time her "guess" proved correct. So correct, she had felt at the start of her thirty-first year, it was a duty to turn her research onto the source of her inspiration, cannabis itself. To reward the generous weed by crowning it with popular legitimacy, a recognition of its powers to inspire, salve, and possibly cure.

She could find cures for whatever conditions she chose to study, she knew this clearly. Sam Ulrich, Vice-President and Director of Research for Cochan Pharmaceuticals, CochPharm, also recognized her brilliance. But too often he was bent on blocking her, keeping her from pushing her experiments to their conclusions.

Beth knew the potential for the good that cannabis could bring to the world. But the US government forbade all trials; it made use of cannabis illegal. Because cannabis turned people into potheads, insane reefer loony maniacs, dangerous to America because the commies would turn them into enemy agents, undermine the moral fabric of the United States.

Such a stupid argument.

But Beth Shapiro Cochan needed to experiment. Hers was life-saving work, every day more probable that the cure for rheumatoid arthritis lay hidden in the hormonal transformations she induced in her allomyrina. "Without cannabis the transformations aren't powerful enough!" she shouted at Sam. "I need experimental quality cannabis! We're working in godforsaken Sherbrooke, Quebec, Canada, for pissake! How can the US feds control us here?"

"Because," Sam repeated, for the fourth time, the tenth, ever calmly, "the corporate center of CochPharm is Cambridge, Mass."

"It makes no sense, Sam, no scientific sense."

"Legal sense is what's at issue," Sam reiterated.

Beth found her cannabis, Beth always found what she wanted. For thirty months she experimented. Clear progress. Her allomyrina, fed on cannabis in a formula never to be revealed, took sleek and furious flight. Onward to mammals. The syrup called A-17, taken intravenously, later orally, transformed her rats, scraggly, arthritic, their leg and neck joints in agony, into silken, sure-footed, sunny creatures, all their painful shuffling evaporated. Undeniable success.

Time to test the drug on humans. But for this she needed specific permission. Already then she'd grown too distant from her husband, Joe, he the Chairman of the Board of CochPharm, to ask him for help. She went to see Sam. "I have to do this."

"You're crazy."

"Sam—"

"And you must think I'm crazy too." Sam stood behind his desk, his face and bald scalp gone red.

"We're none of us crazy—"

"Beth. Listen. Let me be basic here. Marijuana is illegal. Importing it, buying it, possessing it for whatever purpose, is a felony. You've been able to get away with your tests because all of your animals are in cages, they can't meander over to a cocktail lounge and blab away, 'Hey, I had this high the other day, outasight.' Right now CochPharm hides that secret here behind our walls. But you want to work with human subjects? Who live lives outside your lab? Who talk to their neighbors and their spouses? No, Beth. No."

"Sam, my whole purpose in doing this work is to show people the great good that marijuana can do. I want people to see it as an honest and helpful drug."

"You'll go to jail. And so will I."

"Sam. I need sick human beings to try it on, people with palsy, with arthritis, with the worst migraines you can imagine. I can't continue my work without testing it on sick people."

"Okay, Beth, let's say you succeed brilliantly. Where would you publish your results? *The New England Journal of Goddamn Cannabis Medicine?* Get serious. And worry about CochPharm. What good would the most successful testing be for CochPharm, where's the profit? We'd never patent let alone manufacture what your findings might prove, never."

"If I could show how remarkable—"

"The US Narcotics Bureau would close us down. Yes, even in Sherbrooke, Quebec!" Sam Ulrich shuddered. "Forget it, Beth."

"This is the essence of my work!"

They argued for half an hour. Finally Sam, as a friend not as Research Director, said he'd take it to the board. "Okay?"

She nodded. "Thank you."

The board heard Sam. They listened as well to Beth. They showed themselves more than adamant. "No way," said the board.

What choice for Beth? Was there a legitimate lab anywhere that would take a woman whose research called for illegal substances, unlawful inquiries? A woman who for nearly three years had not, after such promise, published a single paper?

"Go home, Beth," said the board. "Be there for your boy."

○

Very strange, seeing all that, telling Lola about Beth Cochan.

Lola said, "Is that all?"

All. I knew there was more, but I couldn't find it. Yet, or ever? "That's all for now."

She shook her head. "How do you do it, Ted? Is it your memory?"

"Well—it can't be. I have no memories of Beth Cochan." But how can she even be asking about memory? Gods can't experience memory. It's just a word.

"Is it, maybe, Beth Cochan's memory?"

"How do you mean?"

"Can you see her memory? And Bobbie's memory?"

I blinked. *I had seen Bobbie's memory.* That's how I could tell Lola about Bobbie in San Francisco. I had seen what Bobbie remembered. How remarkable! Lola had figured out something I hadn't known! I wanted to hug her. I only smiled broadly. "You know, I think you're right. I did see Bobbie's memory. Lola—thank you!"

She grinned as if I'd just rewarded her with a lollipop. "Good! You're welcome."

Again that urge to hug her, just the friendliest of hugs . . .

"And Beth Cochan's memory too. Two memories so close together."

Then my belly tightened. Now Lola was wrong. Because I knew I couldn't be seeing Beth Cochan's memory because I knew, without knowing how, that Beth Cochan was dead. I'd have to figure that one out.

I closed my eyes again, maybe find Beth again. No. She wasn't there. I'd try again later.

Later too I couldn't locate her. But I did see John Milton Magnussen. In his mid-twenties. In London. Deep under the ground.

And from about the same time, Theresa's memory.

○

3. (1963)

Milton had told his sister, Bev, about meeting Theresa on the boat, the *Princess Isabella*, second day out of New York, heading to England and France. Lots of students on board. Theresa would be working at the Hotel Boniface in Lyon after her fencing tournament in Paris. They'd spend the afternoon together tomorrow when he passed through, six hours between his train from London and the connection to Freiburg. He wanted to give her a small present. Bev said she'd take him to London's Silver Vaults.

"What're they?"

Back in the nineteenth century, Bev told him, silver dealers from

45

Hatton Garden stored their goods overnight in underground vaults there. Then dealers began to open these subterranean warehouses to the public, and the Silver Vaults sold retail ever since.

Bev and Milton descended, grim fluorescent light overhead, lines and lines of shops along the alleyways, all displaying silver: candlesticks, samovars, cutlery, picture frames, rings, tea sets. The next shop, silver animals: rabbits, mice, beavers, a dozen different insects, a silver cockatiel, cats, dogs of all breeds.

"Down this way." Bev led him to a store displaying smaller, less expensive items, necklaces, broaches, earrings. She knew how little money he had.

A necklace, he figured. Both intimate and general. The bald clerk laid out a dozen and more on the glass countertop. Milton examined each, his eyes returning to a delicate silver chain, links so tiny and interconnected it looked like a slender snake slithering across his palm. From the chain hung a small stone framed with silver, a bloodstone, green jasper with bright red dots spattered anarchically. Her birthstone. March 23. He'd sneaked a look at her passport.

"Chalcedony quartz," the clerk said. "Named heliotrope, reflects sunlight brilliantly."

"Can you try it on, Bev?"

Bev opened the clasp, took an end of chain in each hand, and brought it around her neck. The bloodstone glowed soft green against her skin, whitened by the fluorescence overhead. She attached the clasp without a problem. She raised her chin. "How's it look?"

"Good." He nodded to the clerk. "You have a little box to put it in?"

Bev undid the clasp.

He paid. Her birthstone. It would be for Theresa only. Until the boat had sailed away, taking her on to Le Havre, leaving him on the dock at Southampton, he hadn't understood how deeply smitten he was. Three days ago. Her absence had left him acutely alone. Even with Bev appearing as planned outside the Immigration Hall to take him in hand.

He pocketed the package and they left the shop.

"You know," Bev said, "in India they grind bloodstones into powder. You drink it down in water. It's an aphrodisiac. It gives you strength. They say."

Strength is what he'd hoped for on the boat. He'd noticed Theresa the second day at dinner, the chair at her table in the dining room back to back with his own. At one point she'd pushed backward, tapping his chair. He'd turned. She'd grinned, said, "Sorry," stood, and walked away. A tall woman, a couple of inches shorter than his own six feet. But elegantly curved. Had he been brave enough, he'd've gotten up and followed her out and demanded a mock apology. Instead he merely watched as she left the dining room, hair just down over her collar, light tight red sweater, straight khaki skirt to her knees, low heels. All evening that image tickled in his memory. Coming in to breakfast, he saw she was already seated, her back to him. He took the chair directly behind her and sat, careful not to tap hers. After a sip of coffee he pushed backward. As their chairs touched he turned, just as she did. "Revenge." He smiled.

She looked puzzled, then tittered.

A strange sound to come from between such lovely lips. He introduced himself: "Milton. Magnussen." He reached out his hand.

She stood, looking down on him, suddenly at attention, saluting, heels clicking together. "Theresa. Bonneherbe."

He stood. "At ease, Lieutenant Theresa."

She clasped her hands behind her back and took him in. At her height she could rarely look up to a man's face. Most of the guys she'd dated had been shorter, too often a big deal for them. In Milton Magnussen she liked what she saw: a man maybe a couple of years older, thick black hair parted in the middle, a sturdy forehead, bulky eyebrows, gentle brown eyes, generous lips, close-shaven cheeks and chin, face more round than long, a broad, strong body. Only the small chin marred his face. She would suggest a beard. What? Oh dear, already making plans . . .

So their conversation began. They spent most of their waking time together over the rest of the voyage. They learned about each other's lives. Agreement about films and wine, books and skiing, roaring fires and pizza, the poetry of Archibald MacLeish and e.e. cummings, Oscar Wilde and W.B. Yeats, and the pleasure and irritation at having a single sibling. She knew nothing of farming, he not a thing about fencing. They described their set-in-stone plans for their European summers—he first to England to spend a couple of days with his sister, then to Freiburg to improve his German so he could read Goethe, Heine, and Rilke in their own language during long winter evenings at the Grange; she a few days in Paris, then to Lyon for her fencing tournament, next to a hotel a few miles north of Lyon where she would work and live in French. And afterward? She to Harvard University, a Ph.D. in philosophy; he back to the Grange, to help his father farm the land as his father had helped his own father. Lives to be lived.

He would disembark in Southampton. They met before dawn as the *Princess Isabella* glided into the harbor, up to the dock. There at the rail he kissed her, their first time.

"It's been fun," she said.

"And funny," he said.

They both laughed at the same moment.

"Will you have any time when you pass through Paris?" she said.

"A few hours."

"Want to spend it together?"

He said, "I'd love to," and it sounded in his ears, I love you.

Theresa drank Paris down in huge gulps, using her greed for it all to drown away that other undeniable thirst—lust was not too strong—for Milton Magnussen. It must have already been there when they were both still on board the ship, but hidden away in some mental gap. Hiding on its own or hidden by her? Whichever, it had leapt out and screamed at her as the *Princess Isabella* steamed away across the Channel: And what if he gave you the wrong train time? Or if he decided to spend more time with his sister? Or if he fell and broke his leg and couldn't travel? She couldn't tell him the hotel where she'd be staying in Paris because she didn't have it yet. How could you be so dumb!? She had stared back toward Southampton, and her eyes welled. The closest thing to an address she had for him was the university in Freiburg. Maybe he just didn't want to see her again. A shipboard friendship, hardly a romance? But hadn't he known how much more she must be feeling when she kissed him there at the rail? Come on, Theresa, be fair. You hadn't known, how could he?

He hadn't known. Likely he didn't care. Clearly he didn't. But she'd be at station when the train arrived, 11:25 in the morning.

She took Paris literally by stride, walking everywhere in her uniform, short-sleeved blouses, khaki skirt, white socks, and sneakers. The Arc de Triomphe, the Champs-Élysée, the Grand Palais, and the Musée du Petit Palais. The Seine from the Palais de Chaillot, the Eiffel Tower, the Palais Bourbon, the Musée d'Orsay. And finally on Wednesday, Gare du Nord.

She woke early, lay still for a while, glancing about her narrow room. It was a tight five-floor walk-up, hers on the fourth, a hard climb the first time with her backpack and the case for her foil, mask, and padding, compact enough but clumsy on the thin stairs. And no help from the concierge, a sharp-nosed woman with thin gray scraggle on her head. Now Theresa washed, combed her hair, the light blue blouse? The white skirt definitely . . .

She lay back on her bed. Would he be on the train? Did he really want to see her again? As much as she wanted to see him? Not likely. She had it bad. Hadn't happened to her like this before, not even with Simon, good in bed and a nice guy but she'd never before felt this—this longing. Love? Just, right now, a huge desire. She pictured Milton as best she could, black hair, sturdy forehead, broad strong body. Funny. Kind. Generous. Taller than her so one day when she wore high heels she'd be almost as tall. One day? Leaping ahead, are we? Today is the only day. Ten to ten. She stood, straightened her skirt, brushed her hair again, glanced in the mirror. What she saw was what he'd get. Walk to the Gare du Nord, get there early, trains don't arrive early but you never know. She left, passing the concierge and her ever shifty glance.

She paced the grimy platform from 10:48 to 11:27. She saw the engine pulling into the huge hollow gray-black station and positioned herself to be parallel with the first car, likely not Milton's, she didn't expect him to travel first class. Though it'd be a good joke. She noted a luggage cart, no porter. She climbed up. The train wheezed steam, and stopped. A couple of minutes and the platform filled with passengers. She couldn't see him, couldn't make out distinct faces. Her glance panned the approaching people, bits of color on the gray platform. No

Milton. The last of the passengers were already halfway down the train's length, still coming on, no Milton. He wouldn't be here today. Or ever. Maybe he'd missed— "Hello, up there!"

She spun around so quickly she nearly fell off. He raised a hand to her, she grabbed it. "Hello, down there. Thought you could get by me, did you? Ha."

He laughed. "You coming back to solid land?"

"Catch me." She jumped, he caught her by the waist, she bounced, her face to his face, she threw her arms about his neck and they kissed; all unplanned. "Mmm," she said after a few seconds, "we're starting up where we left off."

"A good place." He brought his arms around her and held her. "A very good place."

Her face against his neck felt right. "I'm glad you're here," she whispered. She pulled away. "Oh! Where's your luggage?"

"I shipped it through. To Freiburg. It'll be transferred to the other station. I don't have to do a thing. I just paid somebody."

"Oh." Of course he was going on to Freiburg. "And when's your train?"

"Tonight. Seven-thirty. I'll claim my luggage when I get there." He opened his arms wide. "So you see? Nothing to carry. Except"—he reached into his jacket pocket—"this." He handed her a small cardboard box. "For you."

"What is it?"

"Take it. Then I won't be carrying anything."

She took it. Very light. "You sure there's something in here?"

"Open it."

She did. Beneath a layer of tissue paper, on another layer, a delicate chain with a pendant attached. She recognized the stone and a flush took her. How could he have known she'd lost her bloodstone in her first semester? How for that matter did he know this was her birthstone? Coincidence all? She took out the chain. The stone dangled. "Thank you, Milton."

"It's okay?"

"It's wonderful." She stood on her toes and gave him quick light kiss.

"Put it on."

She handed him the chain and stone. "Will you?" She turned, her back to him. She felt his forearms on her shoulders as he draped the chain and stone around her neck . . . She turned.

"It suits you," he said.

"Come on, let's get out of this grim place."

They left the station. He said, "What've you been doing since you got here?" just as she said, "How was the time with your sister?"

"Okay," he said. "She'll come to visit me."

"And I've been walking. All around the town."

Was he hungry? They found a perfect small café, sat at a sidewalk table, ate a sandwich au jambon, drank a beer. They walked all afternoon, down Strasbourg and Sebastopol, past Le Marais, down to the river. They talked all afternoon, more stories of their lives, their families, their hopes. She showed him the favorite bits of Paris she'd found, la Sainte-Chapelle, Gothic logic and intent pushed to its limits, stained-glass medallions exquisite in color and design; the magnificent capitals in the Salle des Gens d'Armes of the Palais de Justice; the walk along the Seine by the Jardin des Tuileries. At the end of the afternoon they found another quintessential café, ordered a bottle of wine and a croque-monsieur. They talked of what they would each do in their lives, knowing without knowing they were testing each other's futures to find a means for bringing these together. This fall he'd help his father at the Grange, later take courses at the University of Vermont, probably the Ag School. She had to get her doctorate specifically in philosophy before she could do anything else. Why? Because if you want any clout in this world you have to doctor other people's inferior philosophies—as much as most people have a philosophy in the first place. At Harvard she'd get her credentials, her union card, so to speak. In moral philosophy. She was going to doctor people's souls? She didn't know if she believed in a soul in any standard sense, but there was an aspect of people's bodies—because after all mind is body—which housed the source of their ethical stances.

They had finished the wine bottle. Their hands held each other's across the little table. Milton was saying, "Over the summer we—" when suddenly Theresa whispered, "Oh no!"

"What?"

She glanced at her watch. "It's nearly eight. You've missed your train."

He grinned. "I know."

"Oh Milton. I'm sorry."

"Don't be. I don't have to be in Freiburg till the day after tomorrow and there's a morning train. At nine."

She squinted at him. "Did you plan this?"

He shook his head. "No. Honest. It just"—he shrugged—"seems to have happened."

"What'll we do? I don't think I can sneak you into my hotel, the concierge's a monster."

"We can get a hotel."

"Without luggage? With passports with different names on them?"

"Then we'll keep on walking."

They walked all night, they talked all night; they held each other tight. Paris never closes. Before dawn they found their way to Les Halles, the great fruit and vegetable market, already bustling with farmers in from the fields, the freshest tomatoes and lettuces, artichokes and carrots, seven varieties of beans and four of peas, and onions and scallions and early potatoes and more, and more. Another perfect café, hot onion soup and fresh bread. A banquet.

They walked along rue de Rivoli to the Place de la Bastille, down the rue de Lyon to the Gare de Lyon. Over the summer he would come to Lyon to be with her, she would visit him in Freiburg. "After that . . ." They would talk of such things over the summer.

He exchanged his old ticket for one on the present train. He bought a book for the trip. They found his platform, his car, his seat. They went back out onto the platform. Milton said, "Luckiest thing, each of us from our private parts of the world getting on the same boat."

"Not luck. We made it happen."

"We did. We organized it. Together. We created the possibility."

A call from the conductor for all passengers to be on board. Theresa and Milton kissed, then just held on to each other. A squeal as the train began to move. Milton squeezed her tight, let go, jumped onto the rolling car. He turned and waved, blowing her another kiss. She waved back as the train pulled away. Her eyes were wet. Her fingers found the pendant, the bloodstone, hanging on its chain. She stroked it lightly. She cried half her way back to her hotel.

○

I stopped there, for two reasons. First, because they were newly in love. I knew what would happen, at least in the short run—their meetings over the summer, their wedding in the fall. No doubt wonderful for Milton and Theresa, but watching the early stages of love can get cloying. Second, and more importantly, something else was going on at the same time. Someone else's memory, and the corner of my eye had caught it.

"You saw a lot back there," said Lola. She looked wistful.

"A bit."

"The memories of both of them."

Lola was right. "Yes." I'd blended them in my mind.

"Is there more?"

"Let's leave Milton and Theresa for a bit. There's another memory from back then . . ."

○

Beth Cochan put the phone down. She watched Johnnie bounce a ball against the wall of the garden shed down the grassy slope. She tossed back the last half inch of her schooner of Tanqueray and didn't pour another because it wasn't noon yet. She called, "Johnnie!"

Johnnie walked slowly up to the house. "Hi."

"Your present's waiting. At my lab."

After a couple of seconds he said, "Please, can you bring it?"

"You want it?"

He nodded again, hesitant.

"We have to go get it."

He looked away from her. "What is it?"

"You'll see." She laughed lightly.

He thought for a while. "Can we just get it and come right back home?"

They drove in her open-top red and white Bel Air through hazy spring sunlight down to the lab in the old factories. The city had redone the mill yard, Joe Cochan had told his son, since textiles were in deep decline. Johnnie saw rolls of wool sliding down a steep brown hill. The city gave us a first-rate deal, Joe had said, half rent for a decade. So Joe, six years back, had moved Cochan Pharmaceuticals from Montreal over to Sherbrooke. He'd gutted the old weaving and cutting and sewing sweatshops and built laboratories. A lab for Beth too, as well equipped as the others, best of its kind in North America. CochPharm filled up a quarter mile of mills.

Johnnie hated going inside, through the new pine doorway down the long white corridor to his mother's lab. Nothing really scary, logically he knew this, no chemicals making smells, nobody cutting up monkeys. "Dogs and cats! And juicy rats!" the kids shouted at him. His teacher Mrs. Strong made them stop shouting. She wasn't on his side but she did say clearly, "Be mature, fourth graders are mature." No cats or rats in his mother's lab.

A year ago, he'd made himself get brave about the insects. He had hated crawly spiders and their sticky webs, old webs filled with dry, dead bugs and new webs perfectly shaped, the huge spider in the middle. He hated sow beetles and ants and all those little bugs you could feel creeping up your bare back and into your hair, those and the slimers, worms and slugs with their goober trails. But bugs were what his mother worked with. All over the place in big cages in her lab. She thought they were great. And Johnnie admired his mother. So he had taught himself to like the bugs. Well, not really like, just get along with. The beetles were kind of okay, and the bees he'd actually come to think were nearly all okay. He could handle them now, let them crawl over his fingers and hands. His mistake had been to brag about this to his friend Alan.

Alan's eyes went wide. "On your hands?"

"Sure."

"Liar!" Alan shivered.

Johnnie wasn't insulted. The bees liked him, he knew this. And he could control them. "I'll show you." He swore Alan to secrecy about what he'd see.

Next afternoon they took a bus down to CochPharm, ambled past the secretary—"Hi, Johnnie!" "Hi, Miss Judy!"—along the white corridor to the elevator and down to his mother's lab. If she was there he'd ask her to help. She'd let him play with two or three bees, some of the ones not in sterile caging. If she wasn't there, so much the better. He'd

54

get a dozen out, show Alan this was the real thing. Johnnie didn't lie. Not usually and really not now.

The lab was empty, not even his mother's assistant around. Great.

"It's cold here," said Alan.

Johnnie led Alan past the centipede caging, the termite nests, the earwigs. To the big bee enclosure. Hundreds. Buzzing. Crawling on the wires. They looked longer and thinner than three weeks ago. They must've grown.

Alan said, "Wow!" and looked impressed.

Johnnie felt an instant of doubt. He didn't want to mess up some experiment here. He'd take just a few bees for only a couple of minutes, then put them back. Only Alan would know but he'd sworn he'd never tell. Johnnie rolled up his sleeve, unlatched the mesh door, slowly reached his hand in, his arm to his elbow. He brushed the side of the cage with the edge of his palm and a dozen bees fell into the cup of his hand. He brought his arm out, and closed the door. He was careful like he should be. The bees buzzed. A couple flew a little and fell back into his hand.

Alan stared, kept away from the hand, said, "Gee, Johnnie, be careful."

"It's easy. Here." He reached his arm toward Alan. Alan jumped back, stepped away. Johnnie followed, slowly. Now Alan knew Johnnie wasn't a liar. Alan was scared. Johnnie walked faster. Alan was running! Johnnie followed—

From the corridor just outside, footsteps, two people, and he heard his mother: "You rotten louse! You goddamn louse!" And his father: "Stop it! Stop it now!" And his mother: "How can you get it on with that thing?! How?" And his father: "Beth, for pitysake—" And his mother: "She's a shit-crawling roach!"

Alan stared at the door. Johnnie's feet wouldn't move. Who was a roach? He could barely see the bee enclosure across the lab, it was that far away. The lab door opened. He stuck his hand and all the bees into his pants' pocket.

Beth spotted them. He could see she was upset. She shouted, "What're you doing here?"

Then Johnnie screamed. And again, again. And again; he drooped to the ground, clutching his thigh and groin.

Beth rushed to him. "What? What?!" She turned to Alan. "What's going on?"

Alan, white, crying, "The bees—"

Johnnie screamed again, "Aaiieeeeee!" His hand in his pocket? Beth pulled it out. Her wasps! Four, five— She pulled his pants off, his underpants. She counted quickly. Three bites visible, thigh, penis, scrotum—

Did he need a birthday present so much, was it worth all this? But they always gave him good presents. A tenth-birthday present would be special.

His mother said, "You'll be fine, Johnnie."

He said, "I'm a little scared, just a bit."

It'd be good for him to go into the lab again, she knew this. "It's a great present," she said. He didn't respond. She said, "There's no risk." And asked, "Even if there were, isn't it worth some risk to get a great present?" She smiled, she knew he could be brave.

The wasps were long gone, she'd told him so. They passed through doorways. The corridor. The elevator. She pressed the down button. The doors opened. He stood still. Get what on with what thing? He'd asked her that later. Only once. She'd given him a silent stare, turned, and went away. Now she took his hand and stepped inside. He had to follow. The doors closed.

She felt his reluctance. She could understand it. But she had to rid him of those fears. From long past. She patted his short black hair. His ears stuck out too much. He was a good-looking boy. Except for the big ears. Could she find a cure for floppy ears? Sam should have given her a chance. Half a chance. She could've found a cure for anything.

She would let Johnnie's hair grow, make the ears less rabbity. Much more handsome.

The doors opened. Subdued light, a kind of brown-orange. She walked toward dark double doors, pulled one open, stepped inside.

He'd not been here since the wasps. Before the wasps he'd been afraid of bugs of all sorts but he'd taught himself to be brave. After the wasps the fear returned, doubled, tripled. Bigger than ever, little creeping oozy biting things in his nose and under his fingernails, scratchy things in his underpants. Could he be brave now? He felt the chill beyond the doorway.

"Come on," she said.

Dark, and little cages. Humid like thin cold steam. The floor looked slimy.

She stopped by a package a couple of feet high, maybe three feet wide, covered in brown paper. She turned on a lamp.

He heard a tiny click. "Aren't you cold?"

"No," she laughed brightly, "never in my lab."

He pointed to the package. "Is that it?"

She smiled. "Open it." He reached— She slowed his wrist. "But gently." If he liked it, played with it, she'd reward herself from the refrigerator, her secret stock.

He heard more clicks. He undid the tape and the paper fell away. He drew in his breath and pulled back. The biggest bug he'd ever seen. A stuffed bug.

She stroked its thorax, ribbed shiny brown, a loving touch. "Allomyrina dichotomous. See its wing cover, how it's divided into two parts? That's dichotomous. Like the first leaves out of a bursting bean seed." She ran her fingertips along the shell. "It's a coleoptera, from Taiwan. Feel it, Johnnie, it's soft." She reached for his hand. He drew it away. "It's cloth and plastic, fur, it's soft. Here." She pulled him toward it, the insect of her one-time successes.

His shoe slid along the floor. He had to touch this monster. Yes, it was soft. The body, even the wings. But the legs were hard, hairy.

"Here, look at the front legs."

Not legs but fingers, like pincers. Antennae like the horns of a buck deer. Hairy too, and damp. He pulled back. More little clicks. His throat had gone tight.

"I had it made for you. It's stuffed just like Marmalade Bear. Don't you love it?" Damn, she'd failed. She saw the fear in him, pleading to flee. She wanted to scream, For shitsake, it's not a wasp! At least he had to see the trouble she'd gone to. If he knew he'd understand. She was working with the allomyrina again, all they'd let her work on—

"Can we go?"

His question perforated her good nature. Anger spurted: "Johnnie!

It's not a wasp!" She took him by the elbow. "Over here. I want to show you something." She part-led part-drew him to three cages on shelves against the far wall.

He wouldn't look. He closed his eyes. He heard a light flip on.

"There." She held his elbow with one hand, his shoulder with the other.

He must not open his eyes.

"What do you think?"

Could it be so terrible? The clicking again. Soon as he opened his eyes she'd take him home. He lifted one eyelid— Both lids tore open, he leapt away, the back of his throat screamed, "Yee—yeeeee—hee—!" He couldn't get his eyes closed, couldn't turn away. In the cage, a foot away, two dozen of those bugs, feet clenching the grill, bodies over three inches long. Their horns penetrated the grill half an inch out. They'd gore him to death from mouth to crotch! His knees gave but she held him standing.

○

"Now there's a woman the world would be better without," Lola said. "Torturing that little kid."

"Consider it done," I said. "She's long dead."

"Good." Lola gave an exaggerated look around. "Then whose memory were you seeing?"

I thought for a moment. "Maybe—Johnnie Cochan's."

"Yeah. I expect he'd remember those bugs." She nodded slowly. "I hate her."

"Hate?"

"Actually, I think I don't like the kid much either."

"Johnnie? Why not?"

"I'm not sure. Maybe— No, forget it. Tell me some more."

A quick glimpse, another memory, around the same time—

Terrible. I couldn't tell her. That year, 1963, in the fall, was when Lola died. "Uh—want to hear about Carney, growing up? He called himself C.C. then."

"Hope he had a better time than Johnnie Cochan."

Two

SO GROWS THE TREE

1. (1968)

C.C. admired Rabbi Grossman, but the man sure could take a three-tiny-point sermon and drag it out over forty minutes. Okay, it was done, and C.C. moved to countdown phase. Thirteen minutes from end of sermon to end of service. He'd timed it five weeks in a row. Even the announcements just before finishing took the same amount of time, no matter how many there were. They'd reached the Mourners' Kaddish. Good.

Charlie was likely out front already in his screamer Chevy, waitin', waitin'. He'd promised to leave the dance for a few minutes, pick up C.C. "Why d'you go to temple anyway?" Charlie'd once asked him. Charlie knew C.C. didn't believe in the whole God business, neither of them did, both felt brave for saying so. Out loud. Mostly to each other. "For my grandmother," C.C. had said. "She likes to have somebody go with her."

Which was true. And Barbara Feyerlicht had no one else to be that kind of company, no one from the family. Her husband, Maurice, C.C.'s grandfather, had died three years ago and Gramma was still in mourning; she didn't stand up for the Kaddish anymore, after the first year you only stand on the anniversary of the death. Bobbie wouldn't be caught dead in the synagogue, and anyway she was out at some anti-war rally. C.C.'s mum had always gone to the synagogue with Gramma, when his mum came back home here to Median, that is. But she was gone too, eight years gone, and Gramma would never stop mourning for her. For his father too, Gramma always added. But C.C. knew it was different, Dad wasn't Gramma's flesh and blood. Though Gramma had loved him a lot, she always said.

Strange. Each year C.C. remembered them, his own father and mother, a little less. He could still hear their voices, how their words sounded different from the same words when Gramma or Bobbie used them, and he could see their faces. But each year he had to look harder at the photographs, re-inscribe the images in his brain. Did he miss them? Of course, he'd say to anybody who asked. Except who would ask a question like that? And what did missing mean anyway? Charlie had parents and they were always on his ass. If C.C.'s parents were still alive, would they be on his ass too? No way of telling. Because the one thing C.C. knew about his parents, they'd be different today than they'd been the day the plane crashed. And he was different, too. How? He could barely remember the little kid he'd been, the one whose parents died. Nearly half his lifetime ago they'd died.

Bobbie replaced them. Sure, no one can replace your parents, he knew that. But Bobbie was great, day in and day out great. Even when he did something that got her pissed off at him. Because she had a way of being pissed off that said she understood why he'd come back late or hadn't gotten the trash to the curb in time or left for school without breakfast again. It was like she'd been in those places herself.

Now they were singing *Ayn kelohaynu*, so just a couple more minutes. He'd already told his Gramma he wouldn't stay for the *Oneg Shabbat*, all that sweet tea and dry cookies and talky non-talk after the service. He'd explained that Charlie was waitin' for him, they were going to the dance in the high school gym. Gramma didn't mind driving home by herself, she just didn't like to arrive at the synagogue alone. Leaving her here would be okay. If she'd asked him to go back home with her before the dance he'd do it, but he'd resent it. That'd only give him at best an hour there, hardly enough time to be with Julie, not nearly enough to make it sound natural instead of forced when he would ask her to come with him and Charlie and whoever Charlie picked up—Charlie always picked up some girl—for pizza at the Rat Kitchen Grill.

And now Rabbi Grossman's benediction was taking forever, more words, slower words, must be half an hour since the sermon. C.C. glanced at his watch. No, right on time, so predictable. Though three years back C.C. wouldn't have thought that. Studying for his bar mitzvah he'd gotten to know Rabbi Grossman pretty well. Before, C.C. had asked Bobbie should he even get bar mitzvahed? Getting bar mitzvahed because he went to the synagogue with his Gramma wasn't a good enough reason. He figured Bobbie'd be on his side, saying it'd be dumb to do all that, but instead she'd said, "It's your decision. Think what your parents would've suggested. You asked me, I'm giving you a context to think in." Bobbie was good at contexts.

But he truly didn't know what his parents would have thought. He could still see them clearly. Mostly. Whenever she was in Median, his mother used to go to the synagogue with Gramma, and C.C. went with them. His dad didn't go much because his dad wasn't Jewish and when he went it was to be with C.C.'s mother, that's what C.C. figured. So in the end he settled on Yeah, sure, why not. He didn't want to disappoint his mother and definitely not Gramma. Bobbie wouldn't care one way or the other.

Rabbi Grossman had agreed to teach C.C. his haftorah, that segment of the bible that was read out on the Saturday closest to C.C.'s birthday. But the rabbi insisted on teaching him something else as well. "When you turn thirteen and are bar mitzvahed, Carruthers"—the rabbi calling him by the name his parents had given him, it had been his father's father's name; at least he didn't use his Hebrew name Chaim—"you are officially a man, an adult man. And what is the most important thing a man must be able to do?"

C.C. had a few answers but figured Rabbi Grossman had an idea or two on the subject so said only, "I don't know."

"Ah," said the rabbi. "A grown man must be responsible. And be able to defend himself and his loved ones from the many dangers in the world. If you want me to teach you your haftorah, you must also let me teach you self-defense. I'll teach you judo." Rabbi Grossman had learned judo in the army when he'd been a chaplain. So C.C. learned shoulder locks and arm locks, hip throws and hand throws; C.C.'s favorites were the floating drop, the body throw, the elbow drop. After six months C.C., twelve and a half years old, just over five foot three, could throw an attacking Rabbi Grossman, forty-plus, nearly two hundred pounds, tumbling the man over either shoulder according to the line of assault.

"Amen," said Rabbi Grossman, and then, "Shabbat sholom." The members of the congregation turned to each other, shook hands with those nearby, wished each other a very good Shabbat. C.C. kissed Gramma on the cheek, filed out to the foyer with her, said goodbye. Her look might have spoken disappointment as she turned and headed for the reception hall but C.C. knew she was fine, quickly she'd be gossiping with friends.

He opened the door and headed down the steps. Yep, Charlie right there, waitin', double-parked, the Chevy engine revving. And at the dance, Julie, not waiting, not specifically, for C.C., so he had to get there fast. He jumped into the passenger seat. "Hey, Charlie. Let's roll."

"Hey, man. Got yourself godded?"

"Nope. Got out just in time."

Charlie loosed the clutch, goosed the gas, and the Chevy leapt forward, burning rubber. "Ready ta rumble?"

"Damn right." He waited before asking, "Uh, is she there?" He knew she would be, she usually went to the Friday night dances no matter which club sponsored them. This dance was sponsored by the mountaineering club and she was a member. But he had to be sure.

"Yep."

Another moment. "Is Stanley?"

"Nope." Charlie turned a fast left, sliding C.C. against the door. Charlie laughed.

"What?"

"If you were a girl you'd be a g.d.d.h."

"I suppose," said C.C. Very good news, Stanley not at the dance. He'd still have danced with Julie even if Stanley'd been there. Stanley didn't live in Median, he came in two-three times a week to see Julie, figured he could arrive whenever he wanted and Julie'd be there for him. Maybe he was right. C.C. sat next to Julie in both English and history. They talked a lot and he knew she liked him, laughed at his jokes and occasionally asked for his advice. At the school dances he'd danced with her only a couple of times because Stanley was usually there, and when they danced it was always to something fast, never touching. Stanley made her dance slow dances with him, holding her tight. Which irritated C.C., and she looked uncomfortable. But he didn't say anything to Julie, that was her business and right now he had to accept that.

Then yesterday, leaving history, Julie'd asked, "Going to the dance tomorrow?"

"You can bet on it," he'd said, knowing she would, she was in the mountaineering club.

Then she'd put two fingers on his forearm lightly and smiled up at him with her dark-blue eyes and said, "Good." She turned and headed off to chemistry.

Charlie drove fast, peeling around corners, hot to get back to the dance. "Got yourself a boss dolly yet?" C.C. asked.

"Workin' on it."

"Who?"

"She's new. Amanda. Haven't seen her around. But one classy chassis."

"And you left her to pick me up. Man, you're the best."

"Damn right. And don't forget it."

"How's she look? Julie, I mean."

"Good. Real good."

"But?"

"Not my type." Charlie liked them stacked.

Julie was slender. Nicely shaped. "I wonder if she knew Stanley wouldn't be there." He had told Charlie about her touching his arm.

"Oh, she knew. She wouldn't'a razzed your berries if she knew he'd be on the scene."

C.C. considered that. Then he said, "I think he's a dangerous asshole."

Charlie glanced over. "Huh?"

"Yeah. I think he could hurt her."

"You mean, like, physically?"

"Maybe." C.C. thought about it. "Maybe that too."

"Why would he?"

"Like I said. He's an asshole."

Charlie slowed, pulled over to the curb, stopped, and faced C.C. "Okay. Listen. He's big. And not big in the jets department. And older than her. And not going to school."

"Right. Doesn't he work in that car-parts plant in Concord, and—"

"Does that make him an asshole? Anyway, you should be friggin' glad he's on night shift or something so she can dance with you."

"Okay, okay."

"Okay what?"

"Just talkin'-worryin'."

"Cool out. And remember this. If he's dangerous for her, he's real dangerous for you."

"Yeah. Okay."

Charlie turned back to the wheel and started a slow roll. He said, "Maybe you want to shuck that coat."

A little cool to wear only a shirt but at least his hair was long enough, it covered the back of his neck and sat thick on top of his head. Kept heat from getting out, he'd learned that in biology. Anyway Charlie'd park close. C.C. pulled off his sport jacket as Charlie spun into the lot, near as he could to the gym. C.C. wondered about that, if he should worry about Stanley being dangerous. Maybe. Not tonight.

Charlie stopped the Chevy. "Let's get in there and kill 'em."

They got out. C.C., at five-nine and a half, had a couple of inches over Charlie, the tallest he'd get, no way for him to know this yet. But Charlie was fuller in the shoulders, the chest, and had a thicker neck. Both wore black chinos and light-colored shirts, open at the neck. They headed for the door, muffled music inside. "Ready?"

"Been ready since I bugged out twenty minutes ago."

C.C. opened the door and a blast of sound hit them, the DJ whacking some hard-edged rock cut C.C. didn't know. The floor was a mass of streaming surging bodies, guys in shirts and slacks, girls in miniskirts or granny dresses, everybody shoeless on the gym floor. Charlie and C.C. dropped their shoes, C.C. wondering if he'd ever find them again, good loafers, had to wear them to synagogue. A place a thousand miles away. He looked about.

Too many people, too much sweat. He walked the perimeter, looking at faces on the floor. No Julie. He knew maybe a quarter of the people here, mostly the juniors, his class. He waved to some, some waved back. Most of them liked him, many had voted for him for class president, he beating out the big new quarterback by a handful of votes. He saw Ella, Jacquie, girls he'd had a couple of dates with, Lauren too, a movie and then some back seat bingo in Charlie's Chevy while up front Charlie and his girl kept busy waiting for the submarine races to start. Fun, but none of them he wanted to spend a lot of time with. They must have felt the same about him, they didn't come bugging him—well, Ella, two times. But that was done with.

The cut ended, the DJ announced an intermission. The lack of music, filled with talk and laughter, seemed suddenly ominous. He searched. No Julie. Also no Stanley.

"Hi."

He turned. She was grinning, her lips and her blue eyes. She'd tied her hair, long, a sort of dirty blond, to the left side and it fell down past her throat. "Hi," he said.

"You walked right past me."

"I was looking for you. On the dance floor."

"I know. You were concentrating."

"Searching." Hard.

"And?"

"I couldn't find you. But you found me."

"I've been looking for you."

The best news. "You been groovin'?"

"Some. I'm helping with refreshments."

"Where?"

She pointed. "Over there. Left of the DJ. Want something to drink?"

"Cool."

She chuckled at his joke, took his hand, and walked him through the full gym, kids waiting for the DJ to come back, talking, laughing, a few with their arms around each other. The pressure on his hand from hers was dizzying. She wore a yellow scoop-necked minidress and her feet were bare. She had pretty toes. She stood behind the drinks counter. He bought an orangeade. She put a straw in the bottle and handed it to him.

"Want one too?" he asked.

"Can I have a sip of yours?"

"Sure," he said, and passed it back to her.

She raised the bottle, put the straw between her lips, pursed them around the straw, and sipped. Then she handed the bottle to C.C., her eyes on his the whole time. He took it, noted a tiny stain of lipstick on the straw, and sipped.

She watched him and smiled, less serious than with her grin from minutes ago, more earnest. She said something.

C.C. saw her lips move, then smile again. The most gorgeous

creature in the gym. In the city. His lips could practically taste the fleck of lipstick from the straw. More. More what, C.C.? More lipstick. He felt himself grinning. She said something again. Why couldn't he hear her? He walked around to the end of the counter. She joined him there. "What did you say?"

"I asked if you wanted to dance."

Music. Newton-John singing, I honestly love you. "Yes. Let's." This time he took her hand, his left, her right. They joined a hundred other couples on the floor. Their hands stayed connected, raised a bit, his arm came around her back, hers to his shoulder. They danced, moving slowly, she looking up at him. Her face came up to three inches below his. Was she standing on her toes? He looked down, past her small breasts and slim waist, past her hips down along her legs, yes only the pretty toes touched the ground. He pulled her in close to him, her head now on his collarbone, he supported her while they danced, his face in her hair. He hoped beyond hope she wouldn't notice how hard he'd gotten. No sign from her. Good. They danced. Afterward he could remember Roy Orbison singing "Pretty Woman," and the Beatles with something, maybe "Yesterday." They danced till eleven, closing time. They danced fast sometimes, sat out a few, too loud to talk, looked at each other, grinning.

After, no question, they'd all go to the Rat Kitchen for pizza, Charlie with Amanda, a busty funny girl, Julie funny too when she got going, a little like the Julie he knew from history and English, the same only more. Just past midnight. Julie had to be home by twelve-thirty so Charlie drove her and C.C. to her home first. They got out, C.C. walked her to the door. They stood facing each other and at the same instant their faces drew together, their lips touched, their arms came around each other. They kissed, and kissed again, until at the back of C.C.'s brain he heard a voice calling, "Let's get rollin'!"

C.C. said, "Can I see you tomorrow?"

Julie let her face drop. "I can't tomorrow."

"Maybe Sunday? We could go for a walk."

"I—I don't think so, C.C."

"Oh." He squinted at her. "Did I do something wrong?"

She shook her head quickly and put her finger to his lips. "No. Really. Nothing." She glanced at the door. "I have to go in."

"Maybe next weekend?"

She gave him a small smile. "Maybe."

"But I'll see you in school."

"Sure. Of course."

He took her hand. "Good."

She squeezed his fingers. Released them, reached for the door handle, turned it, stepped inside, one finger to her lips, blew him a kiss, and closed the door.

Back at the car he didn't see what the rush was for Charlie and Amanda, all wound into each other as they were. No g.d.d.h. was Amanda. She'd said she lived just a couple of blocks away and C.C. had to talk to Charlie so when they drove off C.C. was puzzled, Charlie driving in the wrong direction. "Charlie—" But by then he'd figured it out, they were going the right way, Charlie was taking C.C. home first. Damn.

○

"What's g.d.d.h.?"

"Goddamn door hugger."

"Oh."

○

C.C. found it hard to go to sleep, in his brain and anatomically. He knew the two were connected, he'd gone hard lots of times long before he'd sensed and now resensed Julie's lips pressing warm and soft on his. But lying in bed he couldn't make his erection go away, infuriating, he didn't want to think of her like that. She was way more than that, he wanted to remember dancing with her, her breasts and head against him as she ran her fingers slowly up and down his spine, as he pressed his lips against the top of her hair, as she stood with her toes on his socked feet, damn he should have taken off his socks, left them with his loafers. He got up and took a cool shower, which helped. Back to bed. He hoped he hadn't wakened Bobbie by running the water. But if she guessed his thinking, she'd understand. Somehow she just knew these things.

Right after his bar mitzvah, after his judo training—first-rate idea, she'd thought—she sat him down. "Okay, my friend the man, time to talk about sex." They talked for nearly an hour. It wasn't as if she

67

explained a lot he didn't know, more how she filled in spaces between patches of information he'd picked up at school from stories and boasts, and who did it with whom and how. They talked about why sex could feel so good, and where the dangers lay, not only pregnancy and diseases but how sex could mess up your mind if you didn't do it out of pleasure or love, if both the people involved didn't do it for closeness to each other. Stuff way beyond the mechanics of locker room bragging and fretting. At the end of the hour he'd said, "Thanks, Bobbie, that was good." And she'd said, "It's a start." Puzzled, he'd said, "We'll talk some more?" "You with me, you with others. It's a lifetime project." She'd chuckled. "Me with others too." So that when he was alone he thought, fuckinamazin. Bobbie too. Of course. He knew she dated guys but till right then he'd not really thought about Bobbie in that way, old as she was. A lifetime project.

Tonight, years after their sit-down, everything he'd understood— yeah he was smart, coolest guy on the block—tonight made full sense. Physically speaking. And no sense at all.

The weekend, all that free time he could've been with Julie, turned into unending gloom. Call her? She'd said she wouldn't see him. Or couldn't, he didn't remember which. Because she'd be spending time with Stanley? Maybe just with her parents. He could at least talk with her on the phone. Saturday afternoon, he called. Nobody home.

His despair deepened. He had to dispel it. Think of something else, someone else. Talk to Bobbie. But Bobbie was gone for the weekend. Read a book. Couldn't talk to Gramma, not about this. Watch television. Nothing worked. Julie's face hovered smack in the middle of his brain. Last resort, his cello. He'd been taking lessons for five years. He'd never be great at it—he maybe had talent, but not enough commitment. Still, he enjoyed playing, loved the rich smooth-textured sound he could produce, and he'd get caught up in a long moment, committed to a thing that seemed as much part of him as outside him. He opened the case, removed the bow, the handsome deep-brown instrument, sat, tuned it. He drew the bow across the strings. Lush tones flowed from its hollows, fascinating him as much today as when Bobbie had, years ago, bought him its smaller brother. How had she known he'd take to it? Bobbie knew these things. He would play as if Julie were in the room, listening, watching his hands, his fingers, as he concentrated on creating opulent crescendos, sweet legatos, light allegros.

For a while it worked. He was moved into another realm. He liked to think of these moments as Moments, larger than either the music or his mind, embracing them both as he played, certain beyond question of himself, of his very breathing. But after barely an hour the Moment faded, leaving him alone, again unsure. Maybe the gloom weighed a little less.

In the evening he went to a movie with Charlie. He wanted to talk about Julie but Charlie was full of Amanda, fastest tongue in the northeast, they'd almost done it but then she freaked and he didn't want to frost her so in the end she'd only done him. Still, it was fuckin' unreal.

Wrong to mention Julie to Charlie tonight. Not how he wanted to talk about Julie, or even think about her. Except sex nothing but sex had been running around his brain despite what he wanted to think he wanted. Yeah, he could hear Bobbie saying that. Sunday afternoon he called Julie again. No, her father said, she's out, won't be back till tonight, too late to call.

During the week it didn't get any clearer. In English and history she was always talking to somebody else. Until Wednesday when he saw her in the hall by herself, walking toward him before she saw him. So he stood still and smiled, and she saw him at last and smiled right back but just for a couple of seconds, then she dropped her eyes. He said, "Can we talk?"

She said, "About?"

"You know."

She nodded. "C.C.—" But she half turned, looking at the wall now.

"Okay, we don't have to talk."

"I shouldn't have—" Her glance dropped to the floor, then arced back to face him. "I'm sorry about Friday evening."

"I'm not. But about everything since, I am."

"I like you. I had to find out. But—there's Stanley, my friend from—"

"I know who he is."

"He was upset."

"About?"

"Me. With you. At the dance."

"Give me a break, Julie." Did she tell Stanley? Or had somebody else?

"More than upset. Angry. He had to work, he said, and here I was tuning him out."

"Julie." This wasn't any Julie he knew. "You don't belong to him."

She said nothing.

"Does he think he owns you?" He was being firm with her. He had to be. Owning someone: Bobbie's notion.

She said nothing but her eyes blinked hard a couple of times.

And now he had to ask, "Do *you* think he owns you?"

Her head shook, a couple of tiny twitches.

"Great." The world was real again. "Want to go for soda?"

She stared at him. "I do. But I can't."

"Why not?"

She looked over his shoulder. "It'll make Stanley angry again. I don't want to do that."

"How would he even—" But Stanley had friends everywhere, here, at the dance. Or Julie had friends—less than friends—who envied her. "Oh, Julie."

Now she caught his glance again. "That's why I said I was sorry."

"What could he do?"

She shivered a little. "I don't know." And more controlled. "I don't want to find out."

"Julie?"

"Yes?"

"Be careful. Please."

She nodded, and walked on.

He turned to watch her. She started to turn, stopped herself, walked on.

He told Charlie. Charlie said, "She's cute but she's square. Lots of classy cuties out there."

"Yeah I know, but—"

"Amanda's got a cousin comin' to town, she says she's a blast, Tina I think."

"I don't want to get into—"

"Let's say we four head out to the passion pit. Couple of good flicks. What say?"

What say. Say, what the hell. Say, sorry, Julie. He said, "I'll think about it."

"Well don't think too long 'cause Amanda needs to fix Tina up for Saturday night and I got to find her somebody or she'll get some asshole who I don't want in the rod with me'n' Amanda, catch?"

"Call you tonight."

By evening C.C. was so pissed at Julie he called Charlie and told him, Sure. Charlie said Amanda said Tina'd be a hot date. By morning he felt stupid for letting Charlie lead him around and tried to get out of the hot date but Charlie reminded him he was owed one—hell, more than one—so it was on for Saturday with Terri, her name wasn't Tina, C.C., better remember that.

The rest of the week was a total and complete drag. He saw Julie in class but they didn't talk. He called her at home. Her mother went to get her, the mother came back apologetic, Julie couldn't talk just now.

Saturday evening C.C. and Charlie picked up Amanda in a loose granny dress and Terri in jeans. The granny dress had a low V-neck. The jeans below a plaid blouse were loose, baggy, over a skinny young woman with short curly hair and a smile that tried. Not a total spaz but gettin' there. C.C. and Terri in back, sitting and talking, where you from, what d'you do there, when'd you get here, how was the trip. In front it was Charlie, one hand on the wheel, and Amanda on the driver's side of the seat. Off to the Sky-Glo Drive-In. Hook the speaker to the front window. Lights out. The first half of the double feature was *Planet of the Apes*; not what Charlie had told C.C. it'd be about, but Charlie and Amanda didn't care. A quarter of the way in C.C. and Terri were getting along well enough to agree they had to switch seats with Charlie and Amanda. They couldn't hear half of what was going on in the movie, too much distracting breathing and giggling from up front. They traded front for back and yep, back there Charlie and Amanda got to about cloud nine.

C.C. and Terri watched hard. The flick was okay, some interesting bits as far as C.C. was concerned but Terri sorta didn't get it, kinda tried to talk about it but somehow missed it. C.C. knew Julie'd understand what he was thinking and he figured Julie'd make some boss comments about it. Though how he figured this he had no idea since he'd never been to a flick with Julie, maybe once or twice talked to her about some flick or other but that was all. From far away he heard Bobbie say, "Set the context." Okay, C.C. would be nice to Terri, they'd watch the next flick, fifteen minutes till it started, hour and a half for the flick, in a couple of hours Charlie'd drop him at his place, drop Terri maybe, head out with Amanda. Just get through the next flick. Enjoy it.

"Hey, you guys want hot dogs?" Amanda said yes, Terri agreed. "C'mon C.C., let's go get some dogs."

They went off between the rows of cars, hundreds of cars and station wagons and pickups. "Also," said Charlie, "I gotta pee. So. You like her?"

"Terri? She's okay."

"Yeah. Sorry, man."

"I liked the flick." He grinned at Charlie. "Whatcha think?"

"Yeah. Pretty damn good." He laughed.

Lots of couples, whole bunch of kids from school. Past a pickup with the window closed, a quick glance and he'd have sworn he'd seen Julie, but when he looked again nobody behind the glass. After peeing they headed over to the concession stand, lined up, got their dogs, heavy on the ketchup and dripping with relish, cokes and dogs for Charlie and Amanda on a tray, a couple of dogs in hand for C.C. and Terri. Could it have been Julie? In the truck? They headed back, C.C. leading. Dogs that Gramma would have a cow over, the meat wasn't from cows. But the thought didn't make him grin.

"Hey," said Charlie, "this way."

C.C. plowed on, checking for the pickup he'd spotted before, a Ford. There, ahead. He stepped up to the passenger side, looked in the window. On the long front seat Julie's head, her hair a mess, a head buried in her neck, pain in her wide open eyes. C.C. switched his right hand dog into his left, grabbed the door handle— Locked! Around the hood, between the Ford and an Olds sedan, fingers around the truck handle, and he pulled it open. Four legs, two in jeans and two bare, the jeans pair in boots, one foot in a small black shoe, the other bare, little toes he knew. He grabbed one of the boots and yanked, all his weight behind the pull, and the man came sliding out, plopped on the ground. "Julie! Get out!" The furious force of a man on the ground, on one knee— Behind him C.C. might have heard Charlie, maybe not, before the guy on the ground was up, belt open, fly down. "Get out!" C.C., one dog per hand now, slammed the guy on both sides of the face with the dogs, ketchup and relish in his ears and eyes. Julie, searching for her shoe— "Julie! Go!" She slid forward along the seat, grabbed a purse, pulled the button up, reached for the handle. The guy was near to standing, relish coming out of his nose. The guy was maybe a little shorter than C.C. but a lot broader. The guy was truly pissed. The guy—Stanley, C.C. figured, howdy-doo, Stanley—Stanley came at C.C., left hand holding pants, right fist back and lunging at C.C.'s head. Except suddenly Stanley was behind C.C., having flown there over C.C.'s left shoulder, a head-bounce off the sedan's tire. Total silence till he heard Charlie whisper, "Holy shit." A groggy Stanley pulled himself to his feet, C.C. staring at him, Stanley throwing his whole weight at C.C. but C.C. stepped to the side, foot out, C.C.'s shoulder low catching the tripping Stanley left on his chest and now Stanley slid under his Ford and lay still. Twenty seconds in all, maybe twenty-five. Charlie was holding on to Julie, terrified, in tears, breathing hard, to keep her from falling. Charlie said to C.C., "Come on, man. Let's take her home."

C.C. reached for Julie's upper arm, touched her gently. "You okay?"

She was crying but she nodded yes.

"You want to go home?"

She nodded again.

Charlie said, "C'mon, let's get out of here."

They supported Julie one on each side and walked her to the Chevy. Amanda and Terri were standing talking next to the car. Charlie glanced at C.C., who gestured with his head, Get in. Charlie nodded, opened the front door, said to Amanda, "You first. Then Terri." Amanda did, Terri followed. He closed the door, walked around to the driver's side, and sat behind the wheel.

C.C. said, "You want to get yourself straightened up before going home?"

She looked at him carefully, as if studying his face. "Yes. Please."

He opened the back door, she slid in, he followed. "Charlie, let's go to my place."

"Sure thing, man."

No one spoke the whole way. Charlie said he'd take Terri and Amanda home, then come back for Julie and C.C.

At the house Gramma was asleep, Bobbie out for the evening. C.C. and Julie stood in the living room. "Want to take a shower?"

"I want to explain—"

"At least put some water on your face. You'll feel better." How did he know that? He showed her the bathroom, got her a washcloth and towel.

Ten minutes and she came back to the living room. She looked fine. A small smile on her lips. "Thank you. I left the towel and everything there."

C.C. nodded. "Want some tea? A coke? Beer? Coffee?"

"A glass of water would be good."

He brought her a glass of water. A beer for himself. He figured he deserved it.

She sat on the couch. He took a chair.

"I have to tell you—"

"You don't have to say—"

"I do. It was maybe—maybe my fault."

"No way. I saw your face."

"We watched the movie. We—made out. It didn't feel, well, it felt kind of wrong, but not like bad wrong. Like it didn't matter."

C.C. nodded.

"And then when the movie ended, he said— He told me he'd just gotten his draft notice. On Wednesday. He—he has to report next Friday."

Some horrible heaviness C.C. hadn't realized was there lifted from his shoulders, his arms, the back of his head. "Hunhh," was all he could say.

"And he said, before he went, he had to—he had to have me. It was like, I didn't twig. You know? Like he just wanted to be close for a while. I didn't want to, I mean we'd been making out and it hadn't been really good but it wasn't so bad either and I figured he wanted to do it some more and he was practically shipped out so I said, 'Okay.'"

"Jeeze, Julie."

"I didn't know he meant what he meant, I really didn't. And he started, and I saw you walk by, and I think he saw you too. He doesn't know you but he saw me looking at you just for that second and he stopped, and said, 'That's him, right?' and I said, 'Who?' and he said the guy you were dancing with, and I had to say yes. So he didn't do or say anything for a while, like maybe a couple of minutes, he just stared ahead, I tried to talk to him but he didn't answer. And then he reached out his hand to me, sorta gently, and I took it, and something must've hit him 'cause that's when it all started, all of a sudden he was undoing his pants and making me reach for him and—" Her head shook. "He wasn't being mean or anything but even when I told him no, no, don't, it was like he couldn't hear me, he was on top of me, heavy, and I couldn't do anything—"

Her head seemed to shake all on its own. He stared at her face, her small pretty face, hair combed back now, a ponytail, no makeup far as he could tell. He stared at the ground. "You were able to look scared. That was plenty."

"Yeah."

"You scared me."

She squinted at him, as if trying to see his face. "C.C.—you sure didn't seem scared. You were amazing."

He shook his head. He sipped his beer.

The front door opened. Bobbie came in. "Julie Robertson, Bobbie Feyerlicht." A little instant laughter between the women. C.C. suddenly saw Bobbie through Julie's eyes, a strong woman of middle height in a black turtleneck, black miniskirt, good legs, black lace-ups, black hair cut short, a face that allowed no nonsense. Was Bobbie attractive to men? He figured Julie would think so. He guessed a woman could still be attractive at thirty-two.

Charlie came back, he took Julie home, C.C. along for the ride. A gentle kiss at the door. Next weekend they would do something together. She had to talk to Stanley this week.

But during the week Stanley didn't want to talk to Julie, and Friday he was gone.

Julie and C.C. dated quietly for a couple of months, they got to know each other. They gave up their virginity to each other on New Year's Eve. For the next year and a half they were inseparable. Each made the other a stronger person, a finer person. Then graduation, almost invisible when they met, suddenly loomed as the moment of divide. C.C. had been lured to Columbia College and the big city. He made Julie apply to Barnard where she didn't want to go, not really. Her choice was Middlebury, small town, the hills of Vermont. He couldn't see himself being at college in the middle of all that snow, those trees; Median was small enough. But he said he'd apply. And then he didn't. Columbia wanted C.C., Barnard College didn't have a place for Julie. He told her Middlebury had turned him down, a lie it hurt to speak.

The day before the evening of their graduation dance, Bobbie insisted C.C. bring Julie by the house. C.C. filling his dinner jacket in the chest and upper arms, Julie in her off-one-shoulder long white gown transformed from pretty girl to gorgeous young woman, they were lovely together. Once again Bobbie was moved by them, knowing they'd soon leave each other behind.

It wasn't so bad, they figured. They'd have the summer, then despite being miles apart there'd be long weekends in New York and Vermont together in October and November, and Thanksgiving in Median, soon it'd be Christmas vacation. And they'd always have the telephone, and mail. Their love was too great to let mere distance keep them apart.

September was filled with letters and phone calls. Fewer letters in October and she couldn't come to New York for the long weekend, a major exam the following Wednesday and she had to study. He insisted on driving up to Middlebury at the beginning of November, she begging him not to, they'd see each other soon, Thanksgiving was just a couple of weeks away. He agreed, but agonized. Had she fallen out of love with him? Worse, had she met someone else? How could she have? They knew they loved each other.

Over Thanksgiving she told him yes, she was dating Gary, a nice guy.

"But why? We know we love each other, don't we?"

"I loved you, I really did," she told him.

"Then why? Why? Why? Don't you want to be together, like we'd planned?"

"Listen to me, C.C. I wanted to be together, you didn't. Right?"

"Julie? Of course I do, how can you—?"

"You didn't want to be with me, C.C."

"How can you say that?"

"We could've been together at Middlebury."

"Julie, we couldn't, they didn't accept me—"

"You didn't give them the chance, did you? Did you?"

"Oh god, Julie—"

Julie had wondered why they had turned him down. If he was accepted at Columbia with their standards, surely he could get into Middlebury. She had to find out. In October she drew up her courage and went to the Admissions Office. No, the student in question had never applied. "You didn't want to be with me, C.C. Deep down you didn't want that."

He argued, he ached from loving her, nothing had changed, he'd transfer.

"Too late, C.C."

○

Lola stared down over the edge, silent for a while. She shook her head. "Kinda sad."

I glanced at her. She'd spoken the words with inflections pretty close to what I'd heard in Julie's voice.

"But he really loved her."

I shrugged.

"Is that how the young were, in the sixties?"

"Lots of freedom. Of all sorts. But I don't really know, not first-hand. I wasn't around, remember? I died years earlier."

"I wonder what I was like at their age . . ."

"You must have been very beautiful."

"Not what I mean. Did they get back together?"

"I don't know yet."

"How can you just break off like that—"

"Lola. You need to know about other things that were happening."

"Exciting stuff?"

"You'll see."

○

2. (1968)

The bond between Johnnie's mother and father had been a feeble thing for years. Even when he was a child the lack of respect they showed each other had hurt him hard. He remembered a morning, a breakfast table, his father staring at his cup. "The coffee's cold."

"You want me to warm it up?" She reached for it—

"Leave it!" He pulled it toward him, too quickly, and coffee splashed onto his trousers. "Damn it, Beth, you're impossible."

Johnnie thought, He spilled that coffee, not she. And a good thing it wasn't hot anymore.

She brought his father a towel.

"No no no, I have to get these pants off. I don't know what it is with you, too damn smart for your own good, can't even serve me hot coffee."

"I think— It was hot when I brought it."

"You think. Like in your lab? Those idiot experiments? God, Beth." He left the room.

What, Johnnie wondered, did his mother's lab have to do with the coffee?

A very few years more and she stopped responding to his father. Johnnie remembered another morning, he sitting on a stair, reading before school. His mother, bulging briefcase in hand, about to leave the house. His father, stopping her at the door, "You're not driving."

She pushed him away. He caught her by the arm.

"Beth, you will not drive that car. Not in your condition."

"What condition? What goddamn condition!"

He let go of her, grabbed her briefcase, unclasped it, reached in, pulled out a bottle that looked nearly full. "This condition."

She snatched it back. "It's none of your business." She shoved it into the case again. "And I'm driving." She glared at him.

"Okay," he said. "Drive. Kill yourself. Just don't take anybody with you."

She slammed the door.

Johnnie wished, so much, she wouldn't do this. Had she been drinking since she woke up? His father called it her bottled escape.

Soon after, in the middle of the academic year, Johnnie was sent to boarding school.

Even in those days Beth still insisted that her work came first, second, third. She fought for her time. And she drank to leave Johnnie's father behind, as he had left her. When she came to visit Johnnie at school, at those times she wouldn't be drinking. Or only a little. One day, as they walked along the stream at the edge of the campus grounds, he forced himself to ask, "Why are you and Father so angry with each other?"

"Oh dear," she said.

He waited. They walked.

"How can I say this, Johnnie?" She stopped, and leaned against a tree.

He folded his arms and watched her. Her face had many hard lines now. On her cheeks and by her eyes, on her temples.

"I think, in a shared life you've got to be able to have—if not love, at least respect."

"You and Father don't respect each other, do you?"

She shook her head. "Respect when it's regularly denied can't ever be reclaimed."

The absolute sense of *not ever* seared into Johnnie's brain. Everything she said he found complicated, painfully so. Others saw his father as an important man, a wise man, a man who dined at the White House with the president, who received national and international awards, who owned a sixty-four-foot yacht he rarely sailed and had taken Johnnie on only once.

He was told years later that the happiest day in his mother's life had come not on winning the Philipis Prize at age twenty-three nor the Marcus Attenborough Award for Achievement in Biology, the most yearned-for accolade by scientists under thirty-five, but at being told her husband's mistress had overdosed and was dead.

Only twice during his boarding school time did his father visit. The first time, the annual and compulsory meeting with parents, Joe Cochan substituting for Beth, unavailable, her first hospitalization. Joe and John spoke little. The second, in John's last year of school, on a sunny spring afternoon, they drove to a pond north of the school, to walk, for some warm air, perhaps to talk. There was little conversation. Even when John asked, "Will Mother ever get better?"

Joe shook his head, as much a statement of not knowing as a no.

"Father? What really is wrong with her? I mean, why does she drink?"

Again that shake of Joe's head. "I can only say, her work. Her failure in her work."

When John was younger he'd assumed the cell-transforming compounds she'd long experimented with had attacked her mind. In a recurring nightmare the chemicals appeared as thin brimstone fumes breathed out by giant spiders, fumes that befouled the atmosphere in his mother's laboratory. In another the chemicals were tiny lines of gasses carried by bright red earwigs hiding in his mother's hair while she worked, and as she slept in her bed they crawled into her ear and excreted their gasses directly into his mother's brain. Often he woke screaming.

○

"I'm glad I don't remember things," said Lola. "I'm glad my brain isn't full of memories."

I nodded. "But not everything back then is horrible."

"Yeah, I know. And you're going to prove it to me."

Her voice had taken on a new irked tone. And I thought Gods were supposed to bask in ongoing pleasure. Ha! I figured I'd better say something about that. "If you want, I can quit. It's your story. You can tell me to stop."

She looked at me, her forehead furrowed. "Stop? Why?"

"I think maybe I'm upsetting you."

"No. Don't stop."

"You sure?"

She slid over closer to me. "Course I'm sure. If you don't go on, I'll never find out what happened, what's gonna happen to them all." She lay her hand on my arm. "Please."

A god with a paradoxical nature. I decided I was liking it a lot more than finding it off-putting. I stared down over the edge of cloud and searched. This looking back business, trying to find their memories, wasn't that simple. Snatches of memories, wisps. But no story. I shook my head. I made myself come closer in time. Okay: there, and maybe there.

"What?"

"I can't find any memories of note till six years later. 1974."

She smiled, an eager glance now taking her face. "Good. Who?"

○

3. (1974)

C.C. had nowhere he could call home. His apartment wasn't a home. Now with Thea gone, it could never become one.

He tossed the gym bag onto the back seat of the old Dodge, got in behind the wheel, and willed the car to start. He turned the key, a wheeze, couple of grunts, and the motor did turn over. He stared absently through the windshield, sort of at the hood, sort of at the occasional flakes of snow dropping heavily onto it. Parts of the engine down under the hood were as rusted out as the bottom of the driver-side door but the old girl did run. Advantage of keeping a heap like this in the city, nobody's tempted to steal it. Its hubcaps had disappeared a long time ago.

He gave the engine a minute to warm up. In the side mirror he saw blue smoke belching out the tailpipe. Hey, this was New York, that's what cars did in New York. The clock on the dash said 8:19. Late. Thea's early morning announcement had kept him up from half past three on, no way now to beat the rush hour traffic. True, he'd be heading out of the city. Except in the city there's traffic everywhere, always, no escape.

Goddamn Thea. Goddamn snow. More than two hundred goddamn miles to Boston. With a speedy car, dry roads, no problem. But since his presence there would be a surprise, if he didn't make it, Bobbie would never know he tried. But damn, the whole event was a big deal for Bobbie. Even if she scoffed at it. Ricardo had told C.C. she was downplaying it but both of them—the three of them—knew: a top-notch achievement.

He'd had enough coffee, he wouldn't fall asleep. How could Thea have blasted him like that? In the middle of the night? Oh, he knew how, and why. Because Thea was a bitch, a manipulator. And very sexy. Could be any of those, separately or in various combos, at will.

By getting out of the dorms in the fall, taking the apartment on 115th Street, he thought he'd set himself up a home of a kind. The royalties from his father's books even now covered the rent. In that sense it was his home. Then Thea moved in. Okay, he'd invited her, did she want to share his apartment, his life, and of course she said nothing would please her more and then went about not sharing but bending the place into her shape, her style, her mood. Thea was impressive, he admitted this. But to have dumped all her shit on him five hours ago just before he had to leave— Except that was pure Thea.

He'd sold the house in Median, he and Bobbie, early in the summer after his first year at Columbia. He helped fix it up to raise the asking price. Bobbie handled the sale. Gramma had died blessedly quickly, as her friends repeated, after the liver cancer diagnosis the winter before, seven weeks from finding out to the funeral. It could have been there for years, her doctor said, no one knew, no pain until close to the end. Then the morphine, and the second day of C.C. home for spring break she slid away. At least he'd had the chance to see her that one more time. C.C. and Bobbie had mourned with each other, Bobbie actually going to the synagogue because she knew her mother would have been pleased, or at least relieved. Rabbi Grossman delivered a fine eulogy for Barbara Feyerlicht. Even C.C. thought so.

Julie, also home, had come by the house to offer condolences. She was more beautiful than he'd ever seen her but she stayed only a few minutes, talking mainly with Bobbie. At the funeral she sat with Bobbie and him. She'd never been to a synagogue before. He appreciated her deciding to be at his side. First step in coming together again? After the service he asked her if he could visit her at her parents' house, they could talk, figure where each of them— No, she interrupted him, not a good idea, they each had become different people, let's leave it at that. He tried to argue, to explain, to apologize. No, no reprieve. She left. He watched her go. It hurt too much to look away.

Bobbie had tried to make her apartment in Somerville into a home for C.C. He appreciated this. But it could never become more than a base, a resting place at best. She gave him a room where he could leave his things—books, memory bits and pieces from Gramma's house, seasonal clothes—but it remained for him an abstract place.

The summer after his first year he found a Parks and Playgrounds job in Cambridge, and a pizza delivery job in Boston, and slept in the Somerville apartment; usually, anyway. Most of his non-work time was given over to the anti-Vietnam War movement, to participating in the battle against Nixon's version of American madness. His second summer his friend, friend only, Julie suggested they go west together, plant trees in British Columbia, good money in that. And maybe, maybe, out there in the wilderness— In the end Julie didn't go, though C.C. had committed himself. It was an inordinately dry summer. Instead of planting trees he ended up saving trees, fighting forest fires, reducing disasters, sweating soot off face and arms. The spring of his third year he decided to cancel school for a while. He gave his time in the struggle to defeat Nixon, whatever that took. For fifteen months he worked with a series of organizations devoted to the cause. Met some decent conservatives, and some smart radicals. Including Thea.

He stepped on the clutch, slipped into first gear, engaged, turned the wheel hard, pulled around the car in front, and headed west, then north. Checked out the Drive entry. Decided no, it looked crowded as usual. He'd stay on city streets a while longer. He wasn't a New Yorker yet, figured he'd likely never be, but he had learned some of the traffic patterns. Which was all he needed, only this last semester to finish, double major in geography and government, then he was gone. To where, he didn't know. Not likely a city. The time he'd enjoyed most was the summer out west, living in a tent colony for the short time he planted firs and cedar, then just sleeping on the ground, little spurts of rest in lulls as the forest burned.

No, Bobbie's apartment wasn't a home for him. But it had become Bobbie's home. And increasingly Ricardo's. Ricardo was good for Bobbie. The second best thing that ever happened to her, she said. The first? Getting to be big sister to C.C. Who hoped she stressed it the other way around to Ricardo; C.C. liked Ricardo, a lot. In truth, Bobbie made it clear, the apartment was her first real home. She'd lived with Gramma in the Median house where she'd grown up but after her nine months in San Francisco—a rented room, kitchenette, tiny bathroom—her mother's home never became a home for her, couldn't have.

Why did she live in her mother's house? When C.C. had first

asked her she'd said, "Because it's free. I can do whatever I want here in Median. I don't have to worry about a roof over my head. A part-time job and I can pay more than my share of food and heat and help Gramma with insurance and taxes. And I can write my poetry."

Later when he asked she said, "So I can raise you in a small town, keep you out of trouble. Spend time with you. Watch you grow up. And that's kinda neat."

Around the time he began dating Julie he discovered a third reason, saw it in the past over his shoulder, and was relieved he'd not recognized it back then. When he was eleven-twelve-thirteen, more often than he'd liked, she'd go away, overnight, a weekend, sometimes a week or two. Gramma looked after him then. Sometimes spoiled him. But Gramma wasn't Bobbie. Bobbie took complete interest in whatever he thought, needed, did. Which was great then, a bit embarrassing now. Because he never took the same complete interest in Bobbie, what she wanted, what happened in her life beyond him, beyond the house. She went away. He might have asked her a few times where she'd gone but had no real interest in any details, just glad she'd come back. Only much later did he understand she had to have a real piece of life to herself. And as far as he knew Gramma had never asked Bobbie where she'd been, what she'd done. That seemed okay between the two of them. So there'd never been a reason for him to ask.

He eased onto the Drive north of George Washington Bridge. Three-quarters of the cars, buses, and trucks from Jersey turned south toward midtown so traffic northward flowed smoothly. The snow had thickened. Worse than the grayish-white stuff coming down was the splashed-up sludge from tires in front of him, next to him. At least he'd replaced the wipers back in December and filled the windshield spray reservoir last week. With his fingers he searched the radio for some listenable music and found the Beatles singing "Eleanor Rigby." The song ended and the DJ reminded his listeners how lucky they were to be tuned in, it'd be an all-Beatles show till noon. Okay, C.C. could handle that. Though he'd lose the station well before then.

Ricardo was the greatest Beatles fan in the world; anyway, that's how he described himself. Long ago, in Santiago, he'd learned his English from pop songs. He'd cut his syntax teeth on Elvis, got his grammar toilet trained by the Stones, and conjugated his virginity with John, George, Paul, and Ringo. From them he got all the language background he needed, he liked to say, to come up to the US, get a brilliant doctorate in biology with expertise in freshwater invertebrates, go back home and become full professor of biology by thirty-four. Not enough genius, his wife, Natalia, had taunted him, to keep him down under the water staring at fishes with his mouth shut. What kind of honored scientist shoots his mouth off daily at campus rallies and civic forums in support of Allende and those Communists? At last, with Allende elected democratically and popularly, Ricardo figured he could take a one-year leave from Valparaiso and accept the long-offered professorship at Boston University. Natalia would not join him, their sons were still at the lyceum, the city, in fact the whole country, was becoming increasingly dangerous with that Communist in power, how could Ricardo even think of going to the US right now? Ricardo had wanted the boys to spend a couple of semesters in an American school, let them see how Chile was viewed from outside the country, improve their English. Natalia said no no no. Ricardo left anyway, his main reason Natalia herself. This much Bobbie, then Ricardo himself, had told C.C.

C.C. crossed over into Connecticut halfway through the White Album. Just before Stamford the station crackled apart under the weight of static. The snow seemed thinner now, the traffic lighter, but for some reason C.C. found it hard to maintain even fifty-five miles per hour.

○

"Noted with a father's concern." Lola's eyes teased, but with delight.

"Not as if I can do much about it," I said.

○

After the Beatles, only Mozart was worth listening to. C.C. flicked over to tape, slid a cassette in, and let Pablo Casals's cello glide him into the calmness of mind he needed before allowing Thea back in there. He was playing his own cello less and less, his courses demanding too much time. He'd thought about moving over to the music department, studying cello again. But knew he wasn't very good, not compared with others his age who'd given their lives to the instrument. He'd keep his cello for private pleasure. Except over the past few months he'd found his pleasure mostly in the sack with Thea. He did little these days except

85

study and screw. Sometimes he ate a little, too. But with her he had found new versions of his old Moments, the embrace, near to literal, of a piece of time separated from all larger time, a Moment of sheer joyous self-certainty.

For a while the Beatles had kept Thea at bay. He'd needed that kind of psychic timespan at least till he'd put a few miles of highway between himself and last night. Possibly he'd now seen the last of her, which would be both a relief and a sadness. Her arguments had challenged him in his politics as neither books nor speeches could. She almost always spoke as the revolutionary she claimed to be: if one agreed with her first principles, rooted in an absolute faith in the total corruption of all structures of American power and its debasing influence on the minds of many, then the logic of her revolutionary stance was beyond response. But C.C. couldn't buy her starting point—nothing is absolute, he argued, context is everything. He had learned this well and deep from Bobbie, and he believed it. For him Thea's value other than for their shared bed pleasure had been her ability to sharpen his own thinking, to deepen the solidity of the ground he stood on. Though unable ever to agree with him politically, Thea had respected C.C. for this.

Respected him enough to arrive back in the apartment at three in the morning and lay out what she'd just done? She and two others in her cell had firebombed the downtown draft center. It was also possible their cell had now been subverted. It was certainly possible she herself might have been seen. No, nobody injured, hurting some low-level foot soldier moved no revolution forward. Now she had to go deep underground. She told him this because she trusted him. But he had to understand why she was disappearing from his life. He'd argued with her, don't just vanish. Give yourself up, you can pay for this one-time small crime, live a normal life again. No, she said, the crime wasn't hers, the crime belonged to a government that sent its young men to die for no purpose. What she'd done was fully intended, and carefully planned. For over three hours he had tried to convince her to rethink her future. And failed. Long before he left the apartment she was gone.

Casals would not have approved of bombing a draft center. Neither did C.C. He was deeply opposed to the draft, had himself fought against American involvement in the war, had personally lucked into an ultra-low number, had not so long ago picketed outside that self-same draft center. He hadn't reported her act or told anyone she was running because his trust in law enforcement institutions was low? Yes, when it came to the sites of the corruption Thea railed against, New York's finest and the fibbies were luminaries. If they questioned him he'd tell only the truth—she arrived while he slept and was gone in a blink.

By Hartford the snow had fizzled out. Halfway, making good time. In two and half hours in the banquet room of Spregham's, the luncheon would finish. As dessert and coffee awaited, the honcho editor of *The Patriot* would call Roberta Feyerlicht to the podium and present her with the 1974 Samuel Adams Award for Poetry, the highest honor offered by, jointly, the New England Poetry Association and the magazine, the most respected annual prize in the country for a single poem. Bobbie's poem was called "Allende in Socialist America." She had written it for Ricardo.

C.C. crossed into Massachusetts. A few miles farther, just past the Sturbridge exit, the traffic slowed. Suddenly he was creeping through a construction zone. The oncoming lanes seemed even worse. On both the east and westbound sides the state of Massachusetts was widening the highway. 11:20. If the construction ended quickly he'd be okay. On his left a huge semi crowded him, they barely fit alongside each other.

C.C. felt for Ricardo, whose sons could not leave Chile. He feared they would publicly oppose Pinochet, be arrested, get disappeared. Well, Tomás possibly not, he was a mild kid. But Fernando, at sixteen and younger than his brother but as tall, broader, a charmer with no fear in him, could easily get into trouble. Fernando had accompanied Ricardo to rallies, and campaign battles for Allende, with increasing fervour.

Ricardo had had letters from them only twice in the last seven months. They hadn't mentioned his weekly letters to them. Perhaps they could not write more; certainly their phone calls would be monitored, they were after all their father's sons. Perhaps, because they were also their mother's sons, they would be safe— Natalia's father was closely allied to Pinochet. Would the son of a bitch protect them? He had heard nothing from Natalia since halfway through his first year at

Boston University, when she had told him she wanted a divorce. He begged her to wait till he returned . . .

But then Allende was assassinated and Ricardo could not return to Chile. He knew what would happen, stories from friends who after the putsch had managed to escape were clear: interrogation, torture, and at last, with luck, death. Or while alive a fall from a plane into the sea. So he accepted a full-time position at the university. They were delighted to have such a distinguished marine researcher and scholar as a member of the faculty. He missed his sons dearly. In Boston he met the poet Roberta Feyerlicht.

C.C. wanted to get out of the car, get a sense of what lay ahead. But the traffic never came to a full stop. Slim chance of making it now. Another few hundred yards, a hundred more. Did they seem to be speeding up? Then steady. He looked over to the oncoming side again which gave him a clear view of a semi lurching off the edge, first the rear trailer then the front and finally the cab, dropped with elegance, grace even, off the roadway and glided onto its side, a full ninety-degree downslide in a second or two. Stupidity, laying down a new lane on an overcrowded highway. Impossible to stop here, to help the poor bastard in the downed truck. And yes, the speed on their side had picked up. He reached the Mass Pike at 12:20. No hope of arriving in time.

One advantage of snow, heavy traffic and the occasional eighteen-wheeler flipping sideways, Thea had for a moment departed from his brain, gone as much from the present as from his apartment. He pressed the accelerator hard, the roadway dry now, space opening in front of him. Thea returned. Would her absence turn the apartment into a home? Nope. Poor dumb Thea, never again able to have a room, a house, an apartment to call home. Just like C.C. himself, right? For now, anyway. Some day he'd have a real home. Like Bobbie. Was her home becoming Ricardo's? Because, C.C. suddenly understood, Ricardo had no home either.

He passed cars and sped ahead, seventy, seventy-five. His car shook and rattled. The ring road now, on toward Boston. The Cambridge exit, onto Memorial Drive.

The miracle of the day, a parking space on Mass Ave directly in front of Spregham's. And over forty minutes left on the meter. He rushed to the front door. Inside a waiter pointed to the banquet room. C.C. slid in past seated diners. Behind a podium on the head table stood Bobbie. She wore a wide-brimmed shiny black leather hat and a denim jacket. She was reading.

C.C. had read the Allende poem several times. It wasn't his all-time favorite Bobbie poem, but she'd written it at the right moment, the staccato pattern of the words set against her political-scientific imagery set a tone that compelled her audiences' political attention. She'd sold it to *The Patriot* for four hundred dollars. The Samuel Adams Prize was worth five thousand. A lot of money for a poem, Ricardo declared when he'd called C.C. secretly, to tell him of the ceremony. On the q.t. because Bobbie was playing down all this foofaraw, accepting the prize only to make Americans aware that the US had participated in, possibly perpetrated, the murder of Allende and the legitimization of Pinochet.

Roberta Feyerlicht, his Bobbie, neared the end of the poem. It reminded him of Thea. But no, her rants might have used similar words but their meanings differed widely. Or did they? He had Thea to thank for his ability to think clearly. For Thea the need was control: to control the world and make it right, and good, and decent. Bobbie would see how some pieces of the world might fit together, shape them according to their possibilities—

The banquet room erupted into applause, men and women on their feet, an immense ovation. For a poem. C.C. smiled. He worked his way through the crowd to embrace Bobbie.

o

Lola stared down, sat arms folded. She said nothing.

I said, "You okay?"

She took a few seconds before speaking, her words directed at the piece of cloud. "Did our country really murder this Allende?"

I phrased my response carefully. "Many believe so."

She looked over at me. "Do you?"

I nodded.

She sighed. "I know I have no memory. But I have a sense of things. How could we have killed the president of another country?"

Ten years between Lola's death, and Allende's. Now forty years since Lola's death. Lola, with no memory of the years she'd lived. Memories only of what I was telling her. "I don't know," I said.

Now she nodded. "Tell me about Theresa."

"Theresa?"

"She gets angry. I don't understand anger. And besides, I need to change the subject. You're depressing me."

I know I shouldn't be surprised at a God being depressed by my tale. All unusual. Take her somewhere else, she was asking. I searched for a Theresa memory.

o

4. (1974)

After thirty-one hours of pushing, what little remained of Theresa's brain knew she had to find a different strategy. Crazy to bear children after thirty. No, not fair, the twins had come out easily enough. Just two years ago. But this one! He was in there, either him or a balloon filled with sawdust and cement, and it had to be male, she'd not felt such tenacity before. Sarah's obstinacy had shown itself only after her first scream. This one she'd have to cheat out. Or die trying. Oh stop the theatrics, Theresa. Find your tactics.

How about an enema up into the womb, flush him out? The little clinker. She'd battled enough clinkers on the piste, dozens of tournaments with her foil finding its target. Where in heaven is that nurse!

How about that, turning the birth canal into a strip. The fetus had her dead-ended. But not for long. Better be soon. A fencing strip with zones in place. So little strength left—

Far away she heard someone—Milton? Yes—whispering, Keep pushing, Tessa . . . Thank you, Milton. How could I live without you, Milton—

Push. Thrust. Dangerous back in here, no room to maneuver, like fighting your way out of the bottom of a sock. She, the one with her back to the end of the piste, deep in her own zone three, bad place to be for so long, hours and hours.

Doesn't this place have a midwife?!

In competition, matched with a woman of her own class, she had never lost, not once. Damned if she'd lose today. Though that first time Milton had seen her, in Lyon, she'd come close. Nervous because Milton was watching from the stands. He had hitchhiked from Freiburg to see her fence, arrived the morning of the bout. They'd only had half an hour together before she needed to make ready. She'd caught a glimpse of him in the stands, corner of her eye, just for a moment, yet it proved enough distraction to give her opponent the blink of an advantage. Concentration flashed back but it took her near the full four minutes allotted to score her five touchés.

Theresa and Milton were together every other weekend over their European summer. That fall back in the US, Cambridge, they married, three days before her first philosophy class. They'd found a small apartment and moved in. Neither city life nor abstract thought appealed to Milton. But they were for the moment a large part of Theresa's daily existence and he wanted little more, for himself, than to be another large part of Theresa's life. Milton spent some of the autumn with his father at the Grange up in northern Vermont, harvesting, closing the fields down for winter. He'd return there in the spring, help with the planting.

Theresa, on those weekends they spent at the Grange and later the summers when she could study all day in their large room, became entranced by the place. And she adored Milton's father, Jerry, something of a moral philosopher himself. His arguments were fully formed, and clear. Over the years her own jargon fell away. The precision of her thinking increased accordingly. Thanks to Jerry. Jerry was Milton's gift to her. One more thing to thank Milton for.

Jerry had reinforced for her what she instinctly knew: when your tactics aren't working, reassess your strategy. She sensed his lesson with great clarity right now, pressing, thrusting, succeeding! working the little clinker out into zone two.

Winter of that first year had been hard on Milton, a man who needed to be doing specific, immediate things. Sitting in their tiny living room watching her read, make notes, get her papers written, lucid ideas where there'd been only blank space; right for Theresa, impossible for Milton. Insufficient too was keeping house in their tiny space. Though it did mean Theresa didn't have to, she could get on with her work.

Should he be studying too? Improve his German to continue the work he'd started in Freiburg? Didn't feel right. How about getting a job? But they were eking their way through on Theresa's handsome scholarship. Studying what? "Think it through, Milton. What do you care most about?"

"You."

She nuzzled his cheek. "You can't study me."

"I could. I will, all my life."

How could he have known this, already then? Ha! Another thrust and she had the little clinker out to her zone one, footwork easier here, didn't have to watch her back. Now! Accelerate and hit! There, a fast riposte— Yeah, got him back to his zone one! His parry, not enough, and she knew the strategy was working. She felt her forehead being wiped. Sweating that much? Bad form to sweat with foil in hand. Was the clinker studying her? No, that was Milton.

"What else, Milton? What means the most to you?"

"Probably," he said, "the Grange."

"You can't study the Grange. What about the Grange?"

"You know, making sure it works okay. Better than okay. As perfectly as possible."

"Works? Makes money?"

"Enough to support those who work it."

"You need to firm up your plans to study agriculture. Simple as that."

His brow furrowed. "All agriculture?"

"Some. What you do or what you could do at the Grange. To make enough out of it to make sure it lives on." Yes! There on the clinker's face, the same furrow. His father's son.

"Something like agricultural economics?"

"Something like that."

He researched agricultural schools across New England and chose the University of New Hampshire. Was accepted, a two-year diploma at the Ag School, microeconomic analysis his area of specialization. He borrowed money from his father and from the government.

They left Cambridge: Milton degree in hand, Theresa with a thesis yet to write, a lectureship till she defended her thesis, then an assistant professorship. They spent the summer at the Grange, Milton applying his lessons, Theresa writing morning to night, then revising morning to night, handing in the tome before leaving for Princeton. A degree in philosophy from Harvard in thirty-six months? Not possible. But she'd done it. Victory!

A lunge and she had the clinker on the run, into his own zone two. Triumph at hand! Again she felt the cloth on her forehead and from the distance . . . push, push . . . what the hell did they think she was doing? Course she was pushing, pushing till he was out, out back-end of his own zone three. Thrust! Cut! Push! Nurse! Nurse . . .

Like she'd tried to thrust at Princeton, against the reactionary faculty, the reactionary national government, the Johnson massacres, Nixon's crimes, the desecration they were bringing to southeast Asia, 1966 to 1969, bad years. And Milton, concerned for her, not loving southern New Jersey, the bad office jobs he found where he couldn't bring his degree to bear. What Milton needed were the fields and woods of the Grange.

"Why not," said Theresa, and wrote to a colleague-friend who taught at the University of Vermont, "If we're going to live rural, might as well be in a place we both adore."

Milton shook his head. "You'd give up Princeton University for a small state school?"

"Moral philosophy is needed everywhere," said Theresa.

Even here in the birthing canal, here too. One moral push. One physical thrust. Again— Okay, clinker, nowhere else to hide. One last thrust, yes, she had him: touché, and out. Victory!

Karl Magnussen. Nine pounds, three ounces. The recalcitrant son.

o

"A big kid," said Lola.

"Still is," I said.

"And she's one tough dame. How'd she get to be so—so in control of herself?"

"I don't know more than what I've told you."

"I wonder," she said.

"What?"

She shook her head.

Three
COMING OF AGE

1. (1976)

At Cochan Pharmaceuticals, Joe Cochan's realm of medications and sedatives, it was a given that pain and sadness could be ameliorated with a prescription for capsules or syrups or tablets, creams or drips or suppositories. Joe was a chemist, son of Nicolas Cochan, the Montreal founder of CochPharm Inc., which had more than survived the Depression, expanded, and provided jobs in the worst of times. In 1939 when young Joe graduated from Harvard, he started CochPharm US down in a converted Cambridge warehouse. The times were right for quick growth, Canada in a grand war and the US sure to follow. Wars use up drugs like fires burn logs. The war came, profits soared; the war ended, profits rose higher.

Nicolas Cochan died in 1960, and by 1971 Joe Cochan loomed tall at the helm of his life's work, CochPharm now North America's fourth largest pharmaceutical company. On both sides of the border he commanded imaginative speculation, success-driven research, nimble testing, saturation publicity, brisk sales. Life had given him wealth, influence, and power; a stunning and shrewd new mistress; and Johnnie, the cleverest of sons, image of his father except for black ponytail hair and a curly-wire beard. The only fly in this aspic was Beth, alcoholic wife beyond despair. Unable to live with the booze. Or without it.

In 1976, on Johnnie's twenty-first birthday, two days after the young man's graduation from Harvard College, a Rhodes Scholarship in his pocket, acceptance at MIT on his return from England, Johnnie stared at the symbolic keys to the Alfa awaiting his arrival in London, breathed deeply, and handed the key-ring back to Joe. "No, thanks."

"No?"

Johnnie shook his head.

"What do you mean, no?"

Johnnie chortled. "My vats."

"Vats?" Joe, feigning ignorance, knew John's vats well. Elm Spender, his security chief, had discovered why for certain nights John was not to be found. In a small rented warehouse beyond the ring road, often from dusk to dawn, John blended, baked, dehydrated, encapsuled: John Cochan provided paths to an alternative world, elixirs and acids, winding roadways all, leading to pure hallucinogenic understanding.

"Come on, we both know Elm's not holding out on you. Vats."

Joe began quietly. "Opiates, John."

Johnnie repeated a pun he liked: "Solutions, Pop."

"I will not allow it."

"You could stop me. You won't."

True. Because Johnnie would come back. Buy the boy off? But what didn't Johnnie already have? He'd hoped the scholarship and departure for England would close down the vats. Joe felt the rise of his bile and a new ache in his heart. "Why something this—this—this illegal? Not to mention wicked." Johnnie must not continue down Beth's path.

Johnnie shook his head, weary of his father's corporate rigidity, furious with a father who had destroyed his mother—she'd been committed for the final time just weeks after he started college. "To open people's minds is why." He sighed. "To scrape the rust and rancor from human imagination."

"With poison! With—"

"With a communal acid-soaked wafer, Pop. With love, and trust. Without anxiety."

"Dropping away—"

"Out. The expression is dropping out."

For twenty months Johnnie, with lovely Carmen from Wellesley at his side, provided his contemporaries with the means for confronting their fathers' world: aim high, shoot it down, watch it bleed gorgeous color. Over that time the son and his father spoke twice. The first time Johnnie cursed the man up and through, Mom's brain rotten with booze and the man not helping her, each year a new whore! Despite his occasional fear of Beth, his despair for her, Johnnie adored his mother but in the last years she didn't know what she was thinking, saying, doing; didn't know the good of her life, nor the bad. Johnnie Cochan believed he brewed hallucinogens in honor of his mother's grief. He needed to understand why she so hated his father, loved her son, why she'd taken herself into a realm hidden so deep in the dark. He would explore that place stoned, a geography peopled with perverse friends who played with him for hours, days, just as when he was a laughing boy. But in his land of narcotic relief he could locate his dear mother nowhere, nor rescue her.

○

Lola looked unhappy, or maybe just aggrieved. I stopped. "Something wrong?"

She shook her head a little, as if her concerns were of no importance. "Come on. Tell me." Nothing more from her. "Okay. Should I go on?"

She turned to face me, and narrowed her eyes. "She loved her son? His dear mother? What is this? I thought she tortured him, I thought he hated her."

I considered this. "Yes, I think that's true."

"Which?"

"Both."

"Ted—"

"I'd guess— He hated her, yes, but she was his mother so he loved her. He hated her, and she began disappearing on him, fading out of his life, so maybe he had to love her. And he had to save her, so she'd know he loved her."

Lola thought about that. "Are you making him think like that just for me?"

"For you?" I didn't understand. "What?"

"I said I didn't like him much. You're making him sound—well, weird."

In a way I was flattered but also saddened that she thought I could modify John Cochan just for her. "No. What I'm telling you is history, as true as I can see it. Over those years Cochan began to develop a complex style, in fact an altogether more complicated way of thinking. Though then he could still switch it off and on. Like when he wrote his thesis."

"So how you described him, that was really John Cochan."

"As far as I can get it." I glanced again at the down below, as if to underline my words.

"Okay," she said. "Thank you."

Then and there I decided to abbreviate. Well, a little.

○

The second time Johnnie and his father spoke it was in person, a year after their last meeting. Joe again begged Johnnie to leave the vats behind. Johnnie told the man to fuck off and continued to brew and sell the best of stuff, all the while filtering it through his own complex brain as well.

Carmen used it too, acid to acid, trip to trope. At every waking, down into the twirling colors; each evening, way out to the far-off fire. All the mornings through the silvery shades, at every dusk aching for warm, warm. Each dawn riding toward a grayless sun, all the night long frozen to silence. Until one March day, grim high noon, halfway across a bridge over the Charles, she let go, dropped down, and the river took her. Down there maybe—and Johnnie craved this for her from the huge tight center of his grief—she was sunned by glowing water and cooled by the sand.

A week later, early in the night, he stood on the same bridge, his eyes following ice chips on their seaward flow. They'd buried Carmen's body but he could nearly see her just under the surface. He straddled the stone banister. He could join her, real easy. He hadn't used his powders, not tonight, not for the last six nights. The night twinkled slowly, half a dozen smogged stars and a mild moon. He pulled his feet up on both sides and lay flat on the narrow ledge. He rolled toward the sidewalk. Toward the river water. Toward the dry side. He lay still. Then he dropped to the sidewalk, walked to the Business School shore, found his old Pontiac, drove home.

In the morning he called his father and invited him for lunch tomorrow. Joe, uncomprehending, refused. John said, "It's okay, Pop, you can pay for the meal."

Joe, still uncertain, didn't recognize Johnnie. At a table by the window a young man stood up and signalled: clean-shaven, black hair parted in the middle, tweed jacket, no tie. Displays of emotion were foreign to Joe but that day the man came as close as ever to embracing the boy.

They talked. Joe slid between joy and doubt. Yes, it seemed Johnnie was serious: no more truck with drugs. "And what will you do, John?"

Go back to school, get the degree. Even better, at Joe's alma mater. Joe was ecstatic.

There along the Charles River John Cochan began a plan to bring his mother back to sanity: sell CochPharm because it, the board, his father, had forbidden her the life she'd yearned for. Jump ahead to the far side of the sale, and there she'd stand, tall and straight, fully human once again.

But it wasn't to be. She had long before drunk those three, five, sixty, two thousand last bottles. She might die with the company still unsold.

But in ridding the family of pharmaceutical contamination he would acquit himself to the sainted Beth Cochan. He built a strategy, one day to become the bedrock of Intraterra's multiple projects, and wrote out its theoretical foundations. It was possessed, unlike John's later style, of an easy elegance: ever more human beings alive in the world, four billion as the chapters poured onto paper, five a decade hence, by the new millennium well over six. Among the self-invented, caste-select wealthy, a great demand for elegant places to live, work, think, and play. Population increase is growth, growth generates wealth, wealth must play and be domiciled, playground and residential construction yields yet greater wealth. Those of negligible means, fiscal or intellectual, were of no concern to John.

Who to provide these environs but the men of development? And, what with John Cochan an incipient equal opportunity developer and feminist-to-be, the women of development too, of whatever race or color: clever ethnicity and astute gender, proudly at the forefront of progress. In three months of writing, a dissertation was wrought to excite the hearts of bankers and builders, the sons of Nobel and the daughters of Deere, stone masons, carpenters and welders, yuppies and dinks. It was a thesis honored with a Summa Cum Laude, a degree showered with offers of starting salaries near to six figures, a graduate whose future, however forged, would be gilded with success.

The great sadness of those years: during Johnnie's third semester his mother did die. A strong woman, difficult at times but, all in all, he'd loved her deeply. So ironic, had she just been allowed those experiments, expanded her research into marijuana the pain-reducer, she'd never have turned to her vodka bottle, gin bottle, whisky bottle; so indiscriminate, his mother.

On the day of John's graduation Joe Cochan's joy was grand. Now John would come into the business—

Now John wanted to build.

But now John had to make CochPharm number one in—

No!

But why not?

Johnnie told him. "I hate it, Pop, I hate your drugs and salves and implants. I did and I still do. The shit they cause, it's way worse than anything I ever brewed. CochPharm is deadly."

"Johnnie—"

"Sell it all. Start clean."

"Never!"

○

"And that's where you're leaving them?"

"Well, it'll go on like that for a while. I could let you hear about more of the same, but"—I gave her my best puckish smile—"Carney's still around, and just about now . . ." I let the words trail away. "Shall we go there?"

She sat on a piece of cloud, tucked the loose skirt of her robe across her legs, and smiled up at me so seductively. Making fun of me for shifting my story.

She said, "Sweep me away."

○

2. (1978)

What C.C.—or Carney as he had by then turned into—told his new love, Marcie, about the day he met Red Adair, firefighter extraordinaire:

Adair said, "I like what you write, young fella. But it's wrong."

"If it's wrong, why do you like it?"

"I love all kinds of wrong things. My cigars. My whisky. You can have a strong thirst for a thing and know it's not gonna work for you."

"And what doesn't work for you in what I wrote?"

"It's wrong when you say prevention is just as important as solution. See those pictures?" Adair sat back in his chair and waved his right hand. C.C., on the far side of the big red-painted iron desk, glanced around. The office walls were posted with images, photos mostly, some sketches and cartoons, of Adair and his crew fighting oil fires, on land and sea. "That one over there, that was 1959, the CATCO offshore fire. And that one? Louisiana, Marchand Bay, nearly ten years ago. Man, did that baby burn. And there, that's the North Sea in April, talk about cold. But over here's a real wild one, that's the Sahara Desert we were in the middle of, early sixties, that one got called the Devil's Cigarette Lighter, shot up 450 feet, a pillar of flame out of the depths of hell."

C.C. stared, and nodded.

"You know, land, sea, they're all of them the same in what you got to do about it, all of them different in where they come from. Each one's a creature unto itself."

"That I understand." C.C. had watched fire twist and turn, as if manipulating an imagination of its own, to defy the enemy, the fire-fighter, C.C. himself.

"See, I've done made a deal with the devil. He said if I go to his place he's going to give me an air-conditioned apartment down there, so I won't put all the fires out."

C.C. laughed, as he guessed everyone who heard the line laughed. He'd long known that Adair was an original, from his now graying red hair to the red overalls and red boots he wore—when the heat got overpowering he stripped down to his red longjohns—to the red cranes and red bulldozers that, when they reached the scene, told the fire and the ogling TV cameras that Red Adair had arrived. "So what about these fires makes what I wrote wrong?"

"What's wrong is you're talking about prevention. Sure, the fires could all have been prevented if people'd been smart. But people aren't smart. You can't have prevention holding hands with stupidity. And that's what caused these fires, stupid people." He shook his head. "But when somebody's got a fire they got a problem, and then there's us, we solve that problem. The Red Adair Company puts out fires, that's all we do, that simple."

C.C. adjusted himself in the chair. Too bad, no job in the works here. He liked Adair, had admired him since he was eleven after seeing *Hellfighters*. Well, not Adair, just a John Wayne version of him, all guts and smarts. The ultimate firefighter, knowing what a fire would do. C.C. too could read a fire, its idiom and intent, because he could read the lay of the trees the fire intended to attack. And he loved beating the fire down, loved winning. C.C. figured he could learn one shitload from Adair. Not counting his summer in British Columbia, C.C. had started fighting land fires the year after he graduated Columbia—what else do you do with a degree in geography and government?—then again the year just gone by, for the Forestry Service. Between those two bouts he'd taken an MA, on a forestry scholarship, at the University of New Mexico. An abbreviated version of his thesis was what Adair had read. But obviously he'd left in too much of the prevention part. "So if you disagree with me so much why'd you invite me in?"

"'Cause I'd like you around. I know some of these guys you've worked for. They say you're good. I figure I can use you."

C.C. wasn't so sure. "Somebody to argue with?"

"Not about prevention. Waste of both of our time. But you had some other pretty good ideas there. Let's see what we can figure out."

Not the way C.C. wanted to go. "Look. I have ideas. But I don't want to work in an office. If that's the job—"

"Young fella, nobody at the Red Adair Company works in offices. Hell, not even my accountants if I can help it. You work for me, you work in the field, you figure out what to do by being there to do it. Now, what do they call you?"

"What, my name? C.C."

"Yeah, I heard that too. Nope, won't do."

"Look, it's—"

"Yeah but it sounds like sissy. Can't have that here. What's it stand for?"

C.C. paused. His name was information he didn't let out. Even at New Mexico he'd given only C.C. as his name, he'd made them accept that, and his MA was awarded to C.C. Nobody'd ever thought it sounded like sissy. "I'd rather not say."

"The initials of the name you were born with?"

C.C. shrugged.

"You don't like your father's name?"

"It's fine."

"You don't like the name you were given?"

"Nope." Spoken in imitation of Adair.

Adair raised his eyebrows. "Gonna tell me what it was?"

"Nope."

"What about your father's name?"

"Carney."

"Okay, if you work for me, that's who you'll be. Carney. One name. How everybody's gonna know you."

C.C. thought about this. Carney was what Bobbie sometimes called him. Sure, why not.

Carney had first learned to enjoy morning sex from Marcie. Evenings and the night, she believed, were meant for talking, drinking, celebrating, hugging, fearing, sleeping. Waking, refreshed and infinitely more sensitive to touch and tone, outside, inside, all around the town, this was when love got made best.

They had met while skiing, Waterville Valley in Vermont, both alone, each escaping the burdens of overwork. It began by chance, early afternoon, sitting beside each other on the chairlift. An accident of fate. She reached him a mitted hand. "Marcie Appleby."

He took it. "Carney."

"Carney what?"

"That's it."

"Just one name?"

"All I've got."

They talked. They would meet for a drink at the end of the day, below, at the pub.

Her face, the only part of her he could see, had drawn him in: small flow of black hair over her forehead, gray-blue eyes, slender nose, full lips, strong supporting chin. No ears visible, he'd check them out over their drink. They skied their own trails for a couple of hours, arrived at the pub within minutes of each other, found the other immediately, both ordered the same beer, Rolling Rock—"My favorite." "Mine too."—both telling the truth. They agreed to have dinner together. Marcie first wanted to change out of her skiwear.

A shot of a thought: if she left she might not come back. Come on, they were getting along perfectly well. He recognized his fear, of course: the possibility of loss. But what did he have here that might disappear? A drink, an ephemeral drink. No, a palpable drink, a corporeal meeting, a lovely woman, a smart quick woman. Lots of lovely smart quick women in the world, Carney. Oh? How come I can't hold on to one. Yes, from the chairlift ride on he had known Marcie might be special. "I can drive you to wherever you're staying."

"Thanks, I have my car here."

"Okay, I'll pick you up. Where?"

"The Edelweiss, just down the road."

The fear of potential loss instantly swooped back to earth and transformed itself into the pleasure of control. "That's funny. So am I." Fate, again intervening.

"Well," she laughed, "that simplifies it. See you in the lobby at"— she checked her watch—"seven. They say the restaurant there's good. I didn't try it yesterday. Interested?"

A relief—why?—to be dining at their own restaurant.

Over dinner they talked of themselves. He had been working with the Red Adair Company for just over a year, his own role in three major projects, all oil blowouts, Oklahoma, Nigeria, Saudi Arabia. Three months, two and a half months, seven weeks.

"And you enjoy the work?"

He told her of the pressure, the imagination demanded, the possibility of inventing new processes for defeating this cauldron and that one. He didn't tell her, it was too early, of giving himself over to details of each venture so purely that they often became a new kind of Moment for him, so at one with the battle he knew he could do no wrong, he knew the fire from its core to its wisps. When within a Moment the fire was his twin brother, it was himself.

After each undertaking, there'd be enforced time away from fire. Wind-out time, a furlough. Just back from Saudi twenty-two days ago. His next? Never can tell what's going to blow next.

Marcie worked on projects also—much less exhausting or imposing than his but in their own way rewarding. She was a freelance rural health specialist, consulting since her degree five years ago for the budding telehealth industry on the both sides of the US/Canada border, private here, public in Ontario and Quebec. She had reached the point of being able to choose projects that she believed in. Plenty of work, respectable pay, and no one owned her.

"What kinds of projects?" He sipped his wine.

Projects where a community tries to keep sickness from breaking out. She held wellness clinics, she and her physician partner, Lillian, meeting with mothers, teachers, nurses, occasionally with doctors, in the never-ending battle to prevent illness. Much more health-effective. Not to mention, for the community in the long run, way cheaper. "People are, you know, happier when they're well."

Which was when he told her about meeting Red Adair, the prevention argument.

"You doing any prevention work now?"

"Sadly, no. Not for the company. But it's there, back of my mind. I'm learning a lot."

"Keep it going." She sipped her wine.

They talked, they laughed, they got serious. He told her about his parents' death, about being raised by Bobbie. She told him about her mother dying while giving birth to Marcie's younger sister, about her father the doctor. Twice they discovered they were saying nothing, eyes catching eyes, her drumming heart, his pounding pulse. The evaluations, the questions, the wondering.

"And where are you based?"

Could be anywhere, but right now she favored Montreal when she worked up north, Boston when down here.

Too remarkable. Carney lived in Somerville, just outside Boston. Up on Prospect Hill, near the park. A house built in the 1880s, now in cosmetic decay but with good bones. His self-imposed duty while home was returning it to its late-Victorian elegance.

"I'd love to see it."

"You will." They ordered coffee.

He watched as she went to the washroom. A petite woman, short black no-nonsense hair, slim in a creamy silk blouse and long black skirt. Where was this going? She returned, her lips repainted a soft red gloss. Her ears turned finely down to tiny lobes, the red stones in her earrings glimmering, sharing color with her mouth. The coffee came, they sipped, they finished their meal. "A cognac?" Why not.

So it was after ten when they walked to her door. They stood facing each other, she making no move to enter. He took her hand. They again saw only each other. She brought her face to his, her mouth to his, and their lips touched. He touched her cheek. All quietly, neither rushing. She pulled back. "Tomorrow," she said.

"Tomorrow will be good. Shall we ski together?"

"I'd like that."

"And a drink after?"

"And dinner after that."

"Tomorrow, then."

She'd be leaving in a couple of days, but not till the afternoon. Carney had booked for another four days. In the morning they had breakfast together, skied all day. She invited him to her room for the drink before dinner.

He arrived. She poured Glenmorangie. They drank to each other. She wore a tight red jersey and tight black slacks, high-heeled sandals, he a blue dress shirt open at the neck, blue blazer, gray slacks, loafers. She said, "I enjoy being with you, Carney of the single name."

"It's been a while since I've been able to say the same to a woman, a long while." Since Thea, in fact. "But I am enjoying being with you a great deal."

"I would kiss you. Except then I'd have to redo my lipstick before we went for dinner."

"I can think of two responses to that."

"The first?"

"Do you have more lipstick?"

"Yes. The second?"

"We don't have to go out for dinner."

She beamed at him. "Except I'm hungry." She stepped close to him, brought her drinkless hand around to the back of his head, and drew his mouth to hers. Her kiss too told him she was hungry. She drew back, set her glass down. He, with exaggerated mimicry, set his down as well. They stepped into each other, kissed and held each other, held the other for the pleasure of embracing a person suddenly significant, suddenly inflaming, suddenly unique to the other. They pulled their faces back. "Well," she said.

"Very well." He drew away from her and picked up his glass. "Very well indeed." He sipped.

She raised her glass, held it over her head, other hand on hip, her eyes on his, slowly turned half circle, swung her head around so her eyes instantly caught his again, finished the circle, lowered her glass, and sipped.

He laughed. "Yes?"

"I like to see a situation from all sides."

"Ah." He finished his Scotch and set down his glass. "We could eat here again. Then we wouldn't need coats"—he glanced at her sandals—"or winter boots." If she wanted to eat, then eat they would. Sooner being better.

"Good. The food was lovely."

Carney honestly couldn't remember.

"Since we aren't going far, we're not in a rush."

"That's true."

"I have to fix my lipstick. But there's no rush."

He glanced at her lips. Virtually no smear. "No, no rush."

"Two for the price of one."

He laughed. "Or three. Four, six."

"An even dozen." Their mouths met again, again, their lips admitting to appetite growing from what they fed upon.

After a time that seemed no time at all, Carney said, "I think we better go to eat. Or forget that idea altogether."

She smiled, mock-demure, dropped her eyes, and said, "I'll be a very few minutes. Take yourself another drink." Again he watched her walk away. A lusty woman. He felt his own thick lust rising yet higher. He took another small Scotch. He needed it.

At their table, glancing at the menu, they discovered a loss of appetite. Bowl of soup, fruit and cheese, done. She said, "Will you sleep with me tonight?"

"If you will sleep with me."

"All this can be arranged."

He grinned. "Or we can ride the chairlift again . . ."

Under the table the front of the sole of her sandal caught him deftly on the right shin. "Listen to me. I want to tell you something I believe in." It was then she told him her theory of sex in the morning, the best kind of sex, when the whole of the body was refreshed. "So tonight we should just sleep together."

"Oh dear. I don't know if I can do that."

"Shall we try?"

"Right now?"

"In a few minutes, dummy."

"It may prove impossible."

Carney paid for the meal. Marcie bought a bottle of St. Auguste-Dauphin. They walked to the elevator hand in hand. He had to hold her hand, he was again afraid of losing her, he had gone beyond lust. His head was so very clear.

In the room, double bed, dresser with mirror, two stuffed chairs, Marcie turned on a radio, soft music, excused herself, the bathroom again. Carney dropped his blazer onto a chair, turned off all but one light. Marcie reappeared, glowing in the dim light. He poured, handed her a glass, and they sipped, a lavish liquid. They kissed, lightly. He came back, she brought both hands around to the back of his head, brought his face to hers with soft finger pressure, held him to her as he brought his arms around her waist. Their bodies held together tight as skin. They swayed together slowly, to the music.

For ten minutes, fifteen. He said, "I find this very—hard."

She whispered in his ear, "I know." And then, "Shall we go to bed now?"

"And leave all this good wine undrunk?"

"You want more wine?"

"It may be the only thing that can help me."

"Help you?"

"Live by your theory." He could. He would. Until he knew she'd be part of his life long enough to find out if they wanted to be part of each other's lives.

She put a finger to his lips. "Theories grow from practice. You know that. Your friend Adair tells you the same thing. How much practice have we had?"

107

He laughed. He picked her up, kissed her. Lay her on the bed, leaned over, kissed her again. They undressed each other, discovered more of each other. And yet more.

Afterward they drank a little wine. And made further discoveries. Slept, woke early, continued their expedition. In the afternoon they skied for an hour. Back to her room. The night was theirs, and tomorrow till noon. Carney canceled the last two days of his booking, pointless staying in Waterville Valley without Marcie. She would be returning to her Boston apartment this time. They drove south in tandem. They'd stop at his home in Somerville, he'd pick up a few items, stay a few days at her place, all non-working time given over to sharing.

Except at the Somerville house—he'd show her around the next time, place was a mess—a phone message from the Red Adair Company: report immediately at Laguna Mecoacan in the state of Tabasco, the huge IXTOC #1 well was spewing way out beyond the lagoon into the Bay of Campeche. An offshore drilling rig had been demolished by the blast of an oil eruption, thousands of tons already, every available man and woman desperately needed.

He'd be back soon, Carney promised. She'd be here when he returned, she promised. The IXTOC #1 fire held nearly all his attention eighteen hours a day, exhausting but heady work, little time for sleep. Marcie stayed at the back of his mind mostly, sometimes she came to the fore. Once as she was whispering to him Julie appeared, saying nothing, watching only. Carney squeezed his eyes tight to make Julie go away.

He returned to Boston three months later, max time for any project, worn and weary but unharmed. Adair claimed he'd never lost a firefighter on the job. Carney had three weeks, they needed him back at the well, still bleeding oil. Marcie and Carney spent many of their days together and all their nights, six of them in Montreal. He introduced her to Bobbie. The two women got along well. Three days before he left, Marcie asked him to marry her. The proposal took him by surprise, he admitted it. He'd never really thought about being married, his work with Adair didn't exactly leave much organized time for domestic life. Neither did her work, she noted; they were two of a kind. Okay, they'd talk about marriage when he got back.

IXTOC #1 kept him in the Bay of Campeche for an additional seventy-three days. They spoke when they could, too rarely, on the phone. For the first nine weeks they didn't discuss getting married.

Marriage? What would that mean? First, that he and Marcie would be joined together, he'd never lose her. Well, way less chance. Wasn't losing her what he feared? How would she deal with him off fighting oil fires around the world for two-thirds of the year? Still, once he'd been given the date of his next furlough, he began speaking of marriage on the phone. They both found those conversations too brief, the discussions too complicated, best to wait till they were together. On the plane home instead of watching the movie Carney closed his eyes and found, waiting for him on the screen at the back of his eyelids, Julie. Julie said, quite simply, If Marcie can handle his being away, then no problem, right? Because, basically, he loved Marcie. Right?

Which, not mentioning Julie, is what he said to Marcie as they sat facing each other at dinner his first evening back. They filed for a marriage license but held off the wedding until Carney's next return because Marcie wanted her sister and father present. Fine by Carney because it looked like they were finally closing the fire down and he could invite Red and a few of his firefighting comrades.

Carney left, Carney returned. Carney and Marcie were wed. Marcie's father the doctor gave her to Carney, Bobbie gave Carney to Marcie and wrote an occasional poem, filled with wit and tease. Ricardo glowed when he danced with Bobbie, and Carney wondered if they too might one day marry. Actually, from what Carney could see, Bobbie and Ricardo were as close as married now.

The next three years were, as predicted, difficult departures and joyous re-meetings. Carney loved her mightily, her mind and her body twin homes for her quirkiness. He felt blessed with his double life, at home with this exceptional woman, at work with singular colleagues. He experimented with new methods for confronting fire, he invented new substances for damping fire. Along the way he kept notes on where and how prevention had failed. Back home he experimented, too, and so did Marcie. He even made time for his cello.

He enjoyed the balance. She increasingly did not. Their work agreement, once a high-level compromise, became more and more of a burden for her. She'd quit her work in Quebec and Ontario, decided two consultancies in two countries were one too many if she ever wanted intense time with her husband when he came home. But she discovered she also wanted, even needed, continuity. Very hard to create with Carney away more than half her life. They'd spoken of this a couple of times before he'd last left. Those conversations, unended, left the situation unresolved.

Carney returned from five weeks battling a small but vexing fire in Kuwait. She picked him up at the airport. The first few days were as ever, relating the incidents of their lives while apart, those not talked about on the phone or talked of then but elaborated on now. And their sexual rediscoveries. The third evening, dinner at a little Sumatran restaurant Marcie had discovered, she said, "We have been avoiding something."

He reached across the table and took her hand. "Maybe you have. I haven't."

"In the larger than the you-or-me sense. In the we sense."

"Okay. What have we been avoiding?"

"We're getting older."

"Not me. And I swear"—he studied her hair, face, neck, and nodded—"neither are you."

"Inside me."

Now his head shook. "Not true. I've been there. I know."

"Carney, listen to me. I want to have a baby. Maybe even two."

"Hmm," he said. They'd spoken of this before, but only in the hypothetical: what would it be like if? So this wasn't a surprise, not totally. And he could almost see himself as a father . . .

"I'd like to have a baby soon, Carney."

Her eyes, beautiful eyes, covered his face. Her children would be exquisite. He found himself nodding. "Okay. Good."

"But I can't do it myself."

"I hope the hell not."

"I want to have the baby with you."

"Damn well better be me."

"I don't think you're understanding me. I want the baby to be yours too."

Something suddenly unclear fell between them. "What are you telling me?"

"I want us to raise this child together."

"Of course we would—"

"With both of us in the same place. All the time. Most of the time, anyway."

"Oh.".

"I don't care where that one place is. Anywhere you want. But just one place, not three or four different places every year."

"You want me to quit working with Red."

"Maybe you could work for him in one place."

"That's not the pattern for disasters."

"Do you have to be dealing with disasters?"

"What else?"

"You used to worry about prevention."

"I still do—"

"Couldn't you worry about prevention from one place, one home? Our home?"

"Marcie, you're asking a whole lot."

"Can we think about it?"

"Sure, we can think about it." He hadn't meant to put that much emphasis on *think*.

o

"Ted, can I interrupt you?"

I held back from saying she already had. Often it's easy enough to come back to seeing and hearing someone's memory, but I'd recently discovered that sometimes it could disappear—fade, or break away, as if the person it belonged to had closed a window or relocked a box—and the thread would be lost. She wanted the story, but occasionally her disregard for my craft got to me. Yet I only said, "Of course."

"Why is Carney like that?"

"Like what?"

"So much in love with Marcie. He needs her, and she gives him what he needs. And at the same time he doesn't, well, give her very much. Why not?"

I didn't like hearing about Carney's inadequacies but had to admit she saw them clearly enough. "I don't know."

"Ted? Are lots of men just like that?"

Her question shook me. "I—I don't know that either."

"Were you?"

"I don't think so." I remembered my wonderful Annette. Would I have been like that with her, treating her like Carney dealt with Marcie? I couldn't remember. Strange. I said this to Lola, adding, "But we do know one man who doesn't treat his wife like that. Milton Magnussen, right?"

She considered this, and nodded. "But what about John Cochan? I don't think he's very kind about Priscilla."

I conceded she was likely correct. But I could feel Carney's memories of his time with Marcie receding. "I should go on with the story, you know. Before it disappears."

"Oh. Yes. I'm sorry, Ted."

○

Their talk about having a baby lay dormant for a couple of days. Marcie had a contract in western Massachusetts, a clinic in the Berkshires. She'd been dealing with them electronically, now she had to be on-site for a full day. No sense Carney coming along, she'd be on from nine to nine, drive home after. Wouldn't she want company for the two-hour ride back? He could find something to do there for the day. No, she'd be fine and she'd—they both could—sleep in in the morning. Or anything else they wanted. She kissed him goodbye at six-thirty.

Bobbie called to invite him to dinner. "This evening. Around seven."

"Marcie won't be home till late."

"I know. She told me. So let me feed you."

"I can—"

"I know you can. But I haven't seen you alone for ages."

When he arrived Ricardo too was there. He'd joined Bobbie in cooking the meal. Toward the end of a fine coq au vin and rice pilaf, after a chat that had gone in a dozen directions, she said, "Marcie tells me she wants to have a baby."

Aha. The women's conspiracy. Except Ricardo was here. Two men against one woman. Almost equal odds. "Yep. We've been talking about it."

So it seemed had Bobbie and Marcie.

"She wants me to quit working for Adair."

"She mentioned that."

"And you don't want to."

"Bobbie." He looked at her directly for perhaps the first time that evening. Her hair had begun to gray at the temples. Five years ago she'd given up on the tight short cut she'd sported since Carney had known her, let it grow down to her shoulders. Maybe for Ricardo. It made her more attractive, Carney had decided. Mid-forties lines taking hold at the corners of her eyes. Large dangling earrings these days, but her clothes still ran to black. She looked good. He admired her. He said, "I don't think I'm ready to give that up."

"Not even for Marcie?"

"I don't know why I have to." He took a bite of chicken.

Ricardo said, "You don't have to. You only have to want to."

Carney shook his head. "That's a big one, Ricardo."

"Sometimes the big one is necessary for bigger rewards."

Sure didn't sound as if Ricardo was on Carney's side. "Okay I do want to be a father. With Marcie. Some day. Maybe even around now. But quitting work that gives meaning to my life—"

"One sometimes has to."

"You had to, Ricardo." Carney scraped up the last of his rice. "But not by your decision."

"At the beginning, yes, my decision. I had no choice. I still have no choice."

"You miss your sons a lot."

"I gained a great deal from having children in my life." Suddenly the Chilean Latino in his accent took a sharp edge. "But I knew them well before I left."

"And unless I have one or two, and live with them, I won't know my kids."

"Something like that."

Bobbie said, "She cares for you a great deal. And she's a grand and lovely woman."

"Did you and she hatch this scheme, having me to dinner?"

Bobbie grinned. "Entirely my own idea."

"But you know everything."

"Very little."

"Then you have no context for this, Bobbie."

"Maybe enough. I know the two of you."

"Look, if you had to suddenly give up your poetry, your whole life in that realm, what would that do to you?"

She glared at him sternly. "I once did give up that life. And my poetry, as it was then."

"You mean San Francisco."

"They took me seriously. I was a member of something new and very important, the beat movement. I was part of that community. But I left it behind."

Carney blew a sigh out of the side of his mouth. "To take care of me."

Bobbie stared at Carney in silence.

Ricardo said, "She left it behind. And she found—no, she built—a new community. A larger world than what she had been part of."

Carney pushed his plate away. "I don't know if I can do it."

Bobbie figured further conversation was useless. For now. "But you will think seriously about this. I order you to."

Carney nodded, half a dozen times. "Any more wine?"

○

I stopped.

"Why'd you stop? Is something new happening down there?"

"Lola, it's not even three weeks since I started this story."

"Oh," Lola said. "Then you stopped because—?"

"It's all I can see. Right now." A small lie. I did see more of that evening but it went nowhere. And I didn't want to bore Lola, let alone bring back her depressed mood from before. All I asked was to keep her here with me, and happy.

"Oh," she said. "Well then, I guess I'd better get going. I've been away for quite a while."

Damn! Should I chance boring her? I glanced around. "No, don't go yet." I located a sheet in my notebook. "Look, here's more of what Bobbie's writing these days. Want to read it?"

Her forehead crinkled. Then she nodded. "Sure." She reached for it.

SCAR

Veins in living rock, yellow, cold.
Gelid lava, still for millennia.
Far from the sun frozen blood flows, green blue orange
    gold.
Metamorphic rock, radiating bare.
Schist. Layer upon strained layer.

In decades past, small twinges, black, rare.
Now sheets of shale quiver.

New stings and shocks, coarse in stiff rain
As the rock's own burden measures out its fear.
In the hollows poison water drifts, and here's the pain.

A new torment, a wound in granite,
Quarried anguish, drilling into vein.
From above, rupture. Deep below, fire.
They scream in vain.

Roberta Feyerlicht
(February 3–5/o3)

Lola sat silent, even more pensive than she's been in the last couple of days. She handed the poem back. "Why'd you want me to read that?" Almost angry.

I scrambled to respond. "You don't like it?"

She squinted a glare at me. "How'd you get it?"

I didn't understand. "What?"

"The poem. You steal it?"

"Lola!" I laughed, I had to. "If their memories show me their scowls and grins, and I hear their words, why can't I look over Bobbie's shoulder while she's writing?"

"I suppose." She turned from me and stared into some middle distance.

"Aren't you interested?"

She shrugged. "I guess."

I sat beside her. "Come on. Bask in self-pleasure, like you're supposed to."

She glanced at me sharply. "That's what the great God Edsel told me. Except with him, he got his own self-pleasure, saying those words." She smiled suddenly. "You look worried."

"Nope, not at all. What else did Edsel say?"

She shook her head.

"Don't remember?"

She turned away. "He said he knew why I didn't look like I was in self-pleasure."

"And that is?"

"Because I was spending too much time with Immortals." A cool flatness to her words.

"And not enough with Gods." A worry took me. "Or not with him?"

She looked my way again. I imagined a dampness in her eyes. "He took pleasure in upbraiding me. His phrases were harsh and well-fashioned. He enjoyed speaking them at me."

"Edsel's an ass." I didn't know him well, I've seen him at the Near Nimbus holding forth, all pink and pompous. No idea how he got to be a God. But death isn't fair. "Just ignore him."

She let herself smile, and her eyes shone dry.

I looked into the far distance. "Oh," I said. "There's a little more."

○

Marcie came home as late as she expected and they did sleep in, and in each other's arms, till after ten. The next days, full of work for Marcie, slipped by. Carney studied her. In his eyes she had changed, less light and quirkiness, caprice and whimsy muted. In their lovemaking, too. So quick to change? A day later he thought, maybe not so quickly. Could she have changed while I was away? This hope for a baby, was that the culprit? They made love, a dryer more distant kind of love. He was right, she had changed, shifted. He asked her if this was so.

"What do you mean?"

"You know. You remember. That lovely eccentricity about you, your jokes and teases—"

"What are you talking about?"

But she knew, he could see she knew. "I bet it's all still there, all that wonderful unpredictability. I bet somewhere inside of you it's hiding, it wants to come out—"

"Carney, just grow up." A hiss.

Her words cut him sharper than a slap.

And days later she said, "I think you're the one who's changed. A lot."

He went away again, a messy fire in the Alberta oil patch. He came home. They talked again. She said, "If I can't have a child with you, I'll get pregnant with someone else."

"Who?" He couldn't remember when he'd been so angry. "Who the hell is it?"

"No one. I wouldn't ever be unfaithful to you, Carney. But I want a baby, so very much."

"We can have a baby. I said I wanted to."

"And be here to share raising him? Her?"

He said nothing. At the back of his brain he heard again, again, Just grow up.

Did he grow up? Did he grow down? From deep in his brain Julie tried to call out, to advise him: You can keep this from happening, C.C. But he blocked her away. Six months later he and Marcie agreed to divorce. To leave each other behind. Marcie, he learned later from Bobbie, was devastated. To have lost Carney not to a woman but to the dark tease of burning oil. He, and it saddened him for her sake, felt they should have saved the love they'd had in the beginning. But he was only a bit ravaged by losing her. She had changed too much.

o

Lola said, "I wonder—"

"What?"

"Did men ever treat me like that?"

I waited a moment before saying, "I don't know, Lola." And that was mostly true. Yet I thought I saw, so strange, a glimmer of Lola's own memory; then it was gone. No, couldn't have been anything there. "Shall I go on?"

"Now I really had better leave."

I nodded.

"Tomorrow?"

I nodded again. "Tomorrow, back to John Cochan."

○

3. (1978)

For three weeks after John's graduation he and his father had argued, wrangled, and fought. Joe impugned his son's perspective, his industrial acumen, in a moment of dirt the young man's masculinity. John stood his ground: CochPharm's pharmacopoeia contaminated thousands, yea hundreds of thousands of people who took ongoing toxic doses of its products into their bodies.

Adrenalin spewed, blood burbled and boiled. John's sinews and arteries withstood the turbulence. Joe's couldn't. On a hot Sunday afternoon in late June, the elder Cochan crumbled to the floor, his heart ruptured.

Johnnie sat in a small armchair beside Joe's hospital bed, far back enough to keep from contact with the tubes, leads, and monitors that controlled and measured his father's inner workings, close enough to declare the honesty of his intentions. "Pop, I'm sorry. I'm sorry for what I've done to you, I'm sorry about the arguing."

Joe spoke slowly, his bleached lips blurring his words. "I argued— too." He wheezed. "You see where—argument gets you."

"Well, I'm here to say I was wrong. I want to do whatever you want for CochPharm."

Joe's eyes batted hard, a dozen-fifteen times.

"And I think we should go further. I think we should buy back from the stockholders all outstanding shares of CochPharm."

A small nod from Joe. He held himself back from wondering what had changed the boy's mind. He didn't dare ask. "Good," he said. "Good."

The two, father and son, were reconciled. Attuned and, over the following months, far more: Joe's poor heart warmed and mended at watching the boy so involved with, yes, engrossed by, each aspect of the company's affairs, from long-term planning to personal relations. Joe rested proud, and grew easier in his convalescence.

Within a year CochPharm had gone private; no external force could now interfere. But Joe never again stood tall at the prow of his life's work, he spoke less than a full mind to heads of divisions, he shared little of his wisdom in controlling committees. His son, John, laid new bases, and Joe learned to be content.

On a cold May morning in 1979 the three CochPharm lab chiefs, Thomson, Petrucci, and Lee, entered the young boss's office. Cochan guessed the tightness of their faces grew both from what they knew about their labs and what they didn't know about his possible reaction.

"Please, gentlemen, sit."

They did.

"I've read your reports. I take it there's no coincidence the three arrived together on my desk on Friday afternoon. Right?"

Lee smiled carefully as he said, "We figured you'd better learn it all at the same time."

"In unity there is strength?"

"And," Thomson said, nodding, "in unity there's clarity."

"I can see that," said Cochan. "And you're fully convinced it's this bad."

"Not everything is bad, John," said Petrucci. "There are important exceptions. But lots of problems too."

"Put them all on the table." He noted Lee glance at the others, who nodded. Well rehearsed, thought Cochan.

"As the reports suggest, we've got several deep short-range doubts regarding certain of our patents," said Lee, "and can hypothesize a number of long-range disasters rising from their effects. We've been led to believe that there are at least four citizens' groups looming out there, ready with class-action suits, still collecting evidence, waiting for their moment."

"Go on."

Thomson said, "Rhenathon seems to have brought on adrenal hemorrhaging in thirty-seven percent of adults of Nordic heritage."

"Our Eubulemisumena-2," said Petrucci, "it's caused urinary blockage in seventeen percent of patients forty and older and jaundice in some women as young as twenty."

"The maximum dosage of—"

The specifics went on for another twenty minutes. Then Lee leaned toward him. "Look, John. Your father's genius put in place a system that cared a hell of a lot for the brevity of clinical trials, for adjustments to Food and Drug Administration requirements, but barely a rat's fart about the ongoing impact of so many of our products."

"Anything else?" Cochan caught their eyes, bloodshot in Petrucci's face, cold gray in Thomson's, narrower than usual in Lee's.

Thomson spoke softly. "Our attorneys have elaborated a fine-tuned audacity to interpret legislation and precedent as no one before them has ever dared to try. How long can they keep that up?"

John Cochan had been aware since well before he joined with his father of the experiments behind the laboratories' secure doors, tubs of amalgam stranger than any drug he'd ever brewed, the somex-treated mice in their covered cages, the tiny white spiders, the roach plantations, the loathsome *Phoebis sennae eubule* butterflies, the little spit-beetles. The reports provided John with dangerous but valuable specifics as to precisely where the dangers lay. "Thank you, gentlemen."

They thanked him as well, and left.

John mulled. A fool's sorry game to chance suit, his father that fool. John Cochon must not continue to play. Reduce the supply of the most dangerous patents, then quietly withdraw them. Beyond that, little but to wait for a hatchet to fall, which might not happen. Slow down those still in development, more tests, make sure unapproved drugs were safe before pushing them onto the country. He'd handle the lawyers.

So for a time, CochPharm prospered as never before. Careful release of new drugs, devolution of those with noxious potential. Because of non-public status, financial reports remained unpublished. The company reinvested heavily over those years, 1981, 1982.

The early call from Massachusetts General woke Johnnie. His father had been brought to Emergency, then Intensive Care. When he arrived, the old man was unconscious, pale, dull as pewter, again the tubes and monitors. Johnnie took his cool hand. No response. Johnnie stayed for an hour. Joe Cochan died that afternoon.

That evening he called a meeting, the senior partners of CochPharm's law firm, his chief financial officer. "I am making some changes, gentlemen. CochPharm is for sale. Prepare the necessary documentation." The attorneys appeared horrified. The CFO nodded sagely: fabulous move.

But the plan to sell, to the others a bold step—dangerous? certainly audacious—had ruled John Cochan's actions from the first. He mourned his father's genius and buried from sight his father's body just as he turned his back on the monuments, brick and cement, biological and chemical, of his father's life. The old man and all he had created were gone for good.

John Cochan had learned that a base in two countries has immeasurable value. CochPharm, its patents, and its research were sold to others. But the sites of operation remained, and Intraterra was born. In Sherbrooke, Quebec, Intraterra Canada Limited. And in Lexington, Massachusetts, Intraterra US, the head office, moved from Cambridge

So came the test of theory grown to necessity. More, to belief. He began slowly, small housing compounds, medium malls. But soon, with the accelerating speed of vision, a range of projects long imagined attained design, tracts of land were bought and construction began, the length of the continent then around the globe: shopping centers, residential complexes horizontal and vertical, underground malls, amusement worlds, covered stadia. In all, two dozen major colonies since 1984. Each project refined its predecessor, each achievement ever closer to perfecting his vision.

Four
GROWING UP

Lola didn't come back for a couple of days. Just as well. I had to check in on Carney, get into his memories again, see where he'd been in the mid-eighties. And shape the narrative for Lola.

When she returned something seemed amiss: Her step less light? Her lovely eyes narrowed? I couldn't tell. She asked me to continue.

○

1. (1985)

In the end, at the age of thirty-four in the summer of 1985, Carney did leave the Adair Company. He received Adair's blessing and founded Carney and Co. Its mandate, to combat disasters around the world, excluded oil-well fires; that market was cornered by Adair. Carney ran the company at first from his house in Somerville. He had bought out Marcie's share; part of an amicable divorce. Three years later he sold the house and bought a farm in central Vermont, another rehabilitation project to be worked on between disasters.

For the company, Carney had built a team of first-rate people: a couple of ex-colleagues who wanted new responsibilities, half a dozen of the eager young, and his old high school buddy Charlie Dart, who'd been knocking about for years in jobs requiring multiple skills. For the headquarters in Vermont he brought in a centralizing force, Mrs. Madeline Staunton, grandmotherly in appearance but steely and tenacious. From her multiply-wired office in the barn sixty yards from the farmhouse, she controlled the business, a spider at the web's center. By a simple phone line modem she could tap into her office from her home, fifteen minutes away.

Around the world preventable crises exploded into full disasters and Carney and Co. grew, tripling its manpower in four years. Then a tire fire nearby thrust Carney into local heroic visibility. Middle of a blizzard, middle of the night, middle of a dream about Jenn whom he'd met eight months before, the most full-time woman since Marcie. Eight months, but already the Marcie pattern, wanting commitment. The harsh buzz-toll of the telephone beside his bed sounded.

Mrs. Staunton said, "There's a mess in a place called Derbyville, central Massachusetts, a tire dump and it's on fire. Been burning thirty-four hours."

"Asses."

"Yep. And the storm's making it worse. They need you. Can you go?"

"Sure." Two teams were out, both hip deep in devastation and anyway too far away to haul in. But he could pull together at least a preliminary team before the night was out. "Where the hell is Derbyville?"

"Fourteen miles north of Worcester." She gave him directions, name of the mayor, the assistant mayor, and promised him faxes of background data in fifteen minutes.

The air was black and angry, the snow sharp sandgrains on his face. In the garage he patted the Jaguar's hood. Not much desire to subject it to the storm, yet he was glad to be out. He crossed the Connecticut River into New Hampshire, picked up Charlie Dart, and told him what little he knew about the mess.

They drove south. They knew each other's silences. But Charlie looked uncomfortable.

"You okay?"

"Mmm. You figure your Arizona trip's off?"

"Damn. Glad you said that." He tapped out a number, the Arizona friend, on his cell phone, apologies for calling in the middle of the night, maybe he could come in January. The friend was sorry, he'd been looking forward to meeting Jennifer. Carney broke the connection.

Charlie said, "And how's Jenn doing?"

"Okay."

Fifteen miles later: "And you and Jenn?"

"What?"

"How're the two of you doing?"

"Okay."

"Look, Carney, it's none of my business so I'm making it my business. If you want to talk, I'm here."

"Okay."

"We can go fishing, some nice warm place. Or I'll take you on a toot."

"Okay."

"Or both."

Twenty minutes down the road, Carney said, "She wants to get married. Have kids."

Dart nodded. "With who?"

Carney shook his head.

"Okay. When we've got this blaze out we'll go on a toot. After New Year's."

"Whenever." Charlie's toots, a couple of days of booze, music, and the expensive delights of a crawl through some of the world's finest pleasure centers, tended to clear Carney's head for inventive solutions to ever new disaster puzzles.

Drifts of snow on the road slowed the drive. It took over three hours to reach the fire site. The gale had lapsed to gusts, the cloud ceiling had risen to nine hundred feet. Thick brown smoke boiled in the buffeted air, widening upward till it reached the dying storm. Up there it was driven eastward, had been for over a day, an innovative smog. One hundred and ten families had so far been evacuated.

In the Derbyville tire dump, next to a railroad siding and across from storage sheds, flame roared from two-thirds of the surface. Internal temperature had reached 1980 degrees Celsius, Mrs. Staunton's fax reported. For over thirty hours the ground had melted. Derbyville's mayor and Carney marched through mud. Both wore white heat-protection suits and masks. Over Carney's right shoulder hung a small backpack. He stood five inches taller than the mayor. They stopped, they stared up at the black smoke.

"Son of a bitch bastard," said the mayor.

Eighty feet away, ebony-red flame drawn from red-orange flame rose from solid yellow flame bright as a sun. Underneath, hidden in flame, the tires. The fire chief suspected arson.

At the airport in Worcester a weather team monitored the fire. From Logan Airport in Boston they learned that storm-borne benzene and toluene had spread funnel-shaped, low down, over Leominster and Lowell, and from the Boston hub up over Durham and Portsmouth. Logan's computer-generated prediction showed a new wind pattern approaching from the west, a mid-afternoon front off Lake Ontario. It would disperse the clouds and bring a rise in temperature.

Bulldozers pared away a line of tires, denying the flames their edge of fuel. Firefighters trained to deal with buildings sprayed aimless chemical foam into the blaze, their all-terrain vehicles bringing them as close as heat allowed. One monster excavator lay sprawled on its side among tire debris, its steel charred and twisted by an explosion that had hospitalized three firefighters with second-degree burns.

At an emergency session, the mayor and his aldermen had conceded their firefighting team couldn't handle it. Now the mayor turned to Carney. "Okay, you've seen it."

"Yep."

"And how much?"

So goddamn predictable. No concern for the disaster they'd provoked. "It's a standard project. My costs, plus twenty-five percent."

"And that would be . . . ?"

"I'd figure $6 million. Maybe more."

"Plus your share?"

"Carney and Co. gets paid first. It'll be in the contract."

"Look, we can't afford to . . ."

"You can't afford not to, now." Carney looked at the man's fat little face. You could pulverize it, Carney. Just knuckles, or the flat of your hands. He used his grimmest smile to stop himself. "Because it'll get a lot worse. Not to mention embarrassing. And much more expensive. Send your best man to the State House and your next best to the EPA, tell them to start begging right away. You left it too late. That was stupid."

"Listen, I don't have to—to listen to this."

Carney glared at him. "Go find yourself a quiet place to sit for the next couple of days."

The mayor's eye caught, fifty feet away, a blast of smoke smothering an ATV and its two firefighters. They drove out, choking despite their masks. The mayor smeared gray sweat across his forehead. He started to walk away.

Carney grabbed him by an elbow and levered him forward. "Hold on. First come see what you've let happen." He recognized the fear in the mayor's eyes.

Around the perimeter, firefighters had dug a two-foot trench through sandy soil to the clay below. Oil oozing out of the tire heap had caught here. From the ditch, plastic tubing fed the goo to a retaining pool. There bilge pumps chugged it into truck-drawn tanks. Carney clucked his tongue at the corner of his jaw. His contempt built. Cool off, Carney. "See those tires in there?"

"Yeah."

"They're wire-mesh lined. Even piled high, air circulates. Without the mesh they'd collapse and the rubber could choke the flames. With all that air and space it's burning bright, and the storm's made it worse. The oil's draining into the ground under the tires."

"The fire people say—"

"How much oil have they picked up?"

"Over sixty thousand gallons." The mayor smiled.

"Given the size of the heap"—Carney's tongue clicked twice—"by now a tenth of your tires are burned. The ground under them, it's long melted. Figure a million and a half gallons of oil per million tires. You've got troubles, buddy. A lot of the oil's already reached the clay."

"What makes you— You sure?"

"That's why you called me."

"But can you—?"

"The clay and sand, it's killing you, it's guiding the oil down to underground water. But we can use it, make it work for us." He wiped his forehead.

"Oh. Okay." The mayor had no idea what he'd agreed to.

Carney inspected the railroad siding and its access. He took a drill from his case and bored out shallow sand and clay samplings. "Is water accessible at the storage sheds?"

"No, don't use water." The mayor knew these things, it'd been explained to him by the fire chief: no water. Water just lowers the fire temperature, it's doing it right now in the storm, lowering it maybe a thousand degrees, then the tires only melt, melting makes the fire spread more and the oil drains into the ground quicker. The mayor had shaken his head in despair. Now he told Carney, "Water on the fire, hell that's the fastest way to pollute the water tables."

Carney scowled. "Mud." He took a cassette recorder from a hook on his belt and spoke into it for a couple of minutes. He took the cellular phone from his satchel, jacked the tape on, punched numbers, played it out. Then he talked directly: "And two derricks to thirty-nine meters. And some thirty-cc pipes and the nozzles, the eighteeners."

The mayor's head shook. "It'll burn to the ground."

Carney said, "After it's out we'll drill down and feed in a system of weeping drains."

The mayor was ready to weep himself. For three years the Derbyville alderman had urged him to bring in the bond issue for tire shredders and pulverizers.

But $1.2 million was too much.

They'd get half of it back by selling the stuff for recycled heating oil.

Only after four years.

Now the bill would be who could say how many times as high.

Not near as much as letting the fire burn on. And however stupid the mayor and his governor were, they'd grasp that. Because Carney had long ago proven he could put out such fires and with the least collateral damage. Cheaper too for a town or corporation to pay his fee than for them to fight him with a lawsuit. In the last five years he'd gone into litigation three times, won three times.

The mayor asked, "What're you going to do?"

Carney squinted at him. "Go away, Mr. Mayor."

Half past noon his team arrived at Worcester airport, nine men and four women. He was proud of his female colleagues. Women are rarely allowed into the world of disaster fighting, and if they make it they get harassed and put down.

At seven in the evening the train arrived, the railway siding transformed into a delivery port for their equipment. Now Charlie took charge. Flatcars bore flexible piping, derricks, two Rolls-Royce jet engines, compressed air canisters, three gas turbines, fuel cars, Carney tank tractors with built-out rear ramps. Ten rail cars, each carrying three immense basins with lids.

Soot-covered, impressed, puzzled, the mayor watched. His brain burned: so much equipment. Despite the heat he shivered, watching tax dollars by the hundred thousand drain the municipal balance red. "What're those things, those round hoppers?"

"Mixing bowls."

"Oh."

For combining sand, clay, foam, and water. The mixing bowls stayed on the flatcars, back from the fire. Against the intense heat all team members wore heavy protective suits.

The derricks, each with a parallel jet engine, were set up at the fire's edges.

Next to the bowls sat a huge blender. The bulldozers dug sand and thin clay, and dumped it into the basins.

Two hoses attached to the storage depot hydrants flushed water in.

The blender blades descended, spun, and whipped up a creamy mud. At the blender's side an extension arm emptied a foam canister into the soup. More blending. A lid lowered and was snapped shut. A compressed air capsule slid into its moulding.

The forklift raised the readied bowl from the flatcar and eased it onto the back of a tractor. The tractor treaded its way to the fire's north edge. Beside the derrick Carole and Jude lodged the bowl in the depressed module at the jet engine's side.

The derrick was rigged with plastic piping, lashed tight with steel hoops the length of the thirty-nine-meter crane. At the top a supporting curve formed a hundred-and-thirty-degree blast angle.

Carney watched from the derrick cab as piping was plugged into the hopper. Hand raised, forearm cocked: all in place. The moving parts and his concentration interlocked. No longer the embrace of a Moment, but viable.

He swung the crane above the nearest flames and aimed. The jet roared to life. The canister valve flicked open, air forced a rush of muck up the tubing. He could feel the weight as the crane bent. The cab strained forward. Foamy mud surged from the nozzle, gray-brown in the smoking light. The ooze splattered into a couple of square meters of yellow base flame, the flame fizzed, steamed, disappeared under the baking clay. The canister emptied. The cab settled back in its anchors. A tenth of one percent of the fire was dead.

Another canister sat in place. Aim, release. Shoot, replace. Again.

The other team, Charlie in charge, had raised the second derrick. They worked the south edge of the fire. By sunrise eight percent of the tire surface was encased in hot clay.

The nozzle of the first derrick blew off at two in the afternoon.

They lost an hour lowering the crane arm and replacing it. Toward midnight a length of pipe ruptured and had to be replaced; nearly three hours lost.

They slept, four-hour shifts, in two of the box cars. By the third morning the foam-mud had the fire ringed. Still bleeding oil, hundreds of barrels-worth, but down by sixty percent.

For the fire's central section they had to increase the blast power and thin the spray; the tires were stacked too high for machinery to approach. A thaw was coming on, a day or so away, maybe rain too. The last thing they needed.

Carney was working the second derrick when, three meters below the tip, the pipe separated from its lashing. It hung, precarious and heavy, in danger of breaking off. He muttered, "Shit." Below, Dave raised his arm, then angled it down from the elbow. Carney nodded. He lowered the crane arm a degree, two, five. There it jammed.

The culprit proved to be a crack in the base cog. They'd have to drop the arm by releasing the cab's anchor millimeter by millimeter. The cab would upend as the arm came down. Then they could prop the cab in place, remove the crane arm, relax the cab down, replace the gear, relash the piping, reraise the arm. A tricky job. And long, ten hours easy.

Or they could relash the pipe in place and fix the base cog later. Charlie had done this twice. But he was asleep, he'd been on, despite regulations, for twenty-two hours straight.

Carney said, "I'll go up."

"I'll do it," Diane said. "You haven't climbed in, what, six months?"

How clear their memory. "And you never have. Get me a sling and belts."

Carney climbed, his face masked and his hands gloved. Wish yourself into a Moment, Carney. Inside a Moment he could do no wrong. Trouble with Moments, they happen. Or, increasingly, not. They don't arrive by wishing.

The crane rose at a fifty-five-degree slope. It reached out across charred tires. Carrying the rope sling Carney slithered, belly to steel, doubly belted to the girder arm. At each cross-support he released the first belt, swung it above the support, relashed himself, pulled himself up, released belt two, pulled, relashed. Fifteen, twenty, thirty times.

Dave and Carole unrolled double sheets of air-pocketed asbestos foam up the clay-foam surface, staying beneath Carney's climb.

At first it went fast, one double lash every two and a half minutes. The girders grew hotter. Two-thirds of the way up the heat demanded double mitts and goggles on top of the face mask. Each relashing took four minutes plus. At the loop break, steel temperature hit 195 degrees Celsius.

Below, Dave spread the asbestos quadruple thick.

Carney, twenty-one meters up, lowered the end of his rope. Frank tied on pulley and cable. Carney drew it up, affixed the pulley, sent down the cable end. And felt tight in the throat. Below, baked mud. Smoke. He dragged up replacement coils and binding crimps, reached for the loose piping, hooked it, levered it in place, clipped it. His throat, hard to swallow—

The smoke and heat. Normal up here. He loosed his first belt, shinnied up, snapped himself in. Fought off the throat choke. Loosed the second belt, shinnied—

Maybe the first belt wasn't in place, maybe the heat made the clip slip. Maybe you weren't concentrating, Carney.

Carney hung by his right hand. Through the glove the girder scalded. He kicked his legs and swung out. His left hand touched. It caught. His right glove slid along steel. And off. He lunged, he dove. He squeezed his eyes shut and protected his head. He hit the asbestos, elbow and shoulder, then hip. His breath came in hard gulps, his eyes stayed closed.

Carole, beside him now, her face white, whispered, "Carney—?" Dave called for a stretcher.

Carney whispered, "I kinda like flying." He twisted, lay on his back, opened his eyes, gave Carole a weak smile.

She squeezed his mitted hand. She knew he'd fallen before, from derricks, oil platforms, a range of precipices. Many of them had. Later, mouthy as usual, she'd swear he bounced five times before settling, saying, "Can't keep a good man up." But right there, she shivered.

They walked him down the asbestos to solid ground. The team gathered around. How'd he feel? He looked real graceful on the descent.

He was fine. He'd go right back up.

But one of his few absolutes was precaution: after an accident, a medical check. Which would prove he'd displaced his left shoulder. Which he swore he didn't feel. The elbow was swollen, but no breakage there.

The commotion brought Charlie from the box car. He was rested, he'd climb. He checked Carney's sling and belts, found no apparent deficiency, went for another set anyway.

From the ground, Carney watched. Last time he'd free-flown, more than a year back, it felt like an arm had set itself tight on his throat, dragging him down. This time hurt more. At one point while Carney worked for Adair, Red had said, "The greatest freedom I enjoy is the freedom from life insurance salesmen." Carney too had taken this as his armor.

Except right now the armor felt thin. And falling weakened it further. The failed Moment, its tinny surrogate, tasted sour. So, Carney, concentration going too?

It took four hours to get the blaster working. The rain held off. Thirty-eight hours later the fire was out. The boring of weeping-drain shafts would take the best part of a week.

First the storm, then the wind had spread toxins over hundreds of square miles. Much of it had touched ground as carbon snow, more would drift and rain to earth. Underground, water would carry oil to distant wells and irrigation lines. It would take fifty years to disperse.

A disaster. But without Carney and Co. it could have been far worse. Only thirty percent of the tires had burned. With weeping drains as much as half the oil could be recovered. Cost of the operation would exceed $8 million. Cheap at the price, the media exclaimed, growing the Carney myth.

Adulation gave Carney no pleasure. His bandaged-tight shoulder ached through the painkiller. The elbow stayed tender. Blow up at a mayor who nickel-and-dimed his budget? At a dump owner (who didn't even show!) taking on ever more tires? Jail them all.

Charlie Dart drove him in the Jaguar through a blue frozen morning up to central Vermont. The equipment would go by train back to the depot near White River Junction.

At the farm Dart turned Carney over to the care of Mrs. Staunton.

"You don't look good, Boss."

"You never look good, Mrs. Staunton." Carney scowled. "I'm getting more like you."

"You should be so lucky. You want a drink? The mail? Bath?"

"All of them. In reverse order."

Wet heat eased the elbow and shoulder. He breathed away surface memories of tires. He dried and dressed. In the living room he put a match to the fire Mrs. Staunton had set, poured himself a Scotch, sat behind triple glazing, and stared out. His house, a hundred forty years old, all wiring and plumbing revamped, sat on the rim of a shallow ravine. In warmer seasons a stream flowed down there. Three summers back he'd studied his beavers as they built their dam, the pond they'd formed running to eleven feet, water deep enough for trout to survive the winter.

East across the way, rolling horizon soothed his glance. On his four hundred and thirty acres, snow-smooth fields led to a stand of forest. The earth's shadow glided toward and up his hills. The peace was unwordable, its hold near strong as a Moment.

Damage control was his success. His Moments, his thorough absorption in them, had been part of his means. He was distilling his fame from his clients' greed, growing rich enough. What he needed came his way. Except the pleasure of falling in love again, its uncomplicated joy. Jennifer was a pleasure, lithe of mind and quirky quick when she put her body to it. She was not love.

Later he played his cello. It was clumsy, his shoulder and elbow hurt, but for half an hour thick chords and the light of burning logs drifted up to the beams. Pain retreated, cheer filled his arms and chest, his privacy as fine as that rare thing, the best human contact. He no longer played even okay, but for him the sound was pleasure.

In mid-January a bad chemical fire near Taos took the Co. to the southwest. Three cargo jets flew their equipment down. With Carney's shoulder mending slowly, Charlie took on the job.

Carney had been in pain often. It had never stopped him from heading up a serious job.

○

Lola stared over the edge with unseeing eyes. She turned to me. "But we know he's going to be okay, don't we?"

"Carney?"

"You've already told me about him, how he is now."

"Yes," I said slowly. "Yes of course I did." But for the moment I'd forgotten. I've never before told stories, not consciously anyway, by seeing and hearing old memories.

"Ted?"

"Yes?"

"Is anything new happening with him now? With Carney, I mean?"

I looked down. Carney was playing his cello again. On his desk, piles of file cards, and a dozen notebooks. "Not much," I said.

"With anybody?"

I stared down hard. "Nope, actually. All I can see are a few more memories."

She grinned. "Any spicy ones?"

"Hmm," I said.

2. (1987)

Two years ago, when she was fifteen, Sarah had told her parents she'd had sex with seven different guys. And yes, she liked them all. She loved sex, every bit of it, from the tiny eye-catch to the graceful flirtation, from the first setting down of her silent rules of power over the boy or the man—her oldest partner, Donald, just twenty-six; her youngest Cam, thirteen a year back when she was fourteen—from her power over their higher and lower brains to her incessant demand they teach her new ways, to her laughter on learning from him or him or him, from her dismissal of those who knew nothing original to treat her to.

She loved sex in part because even then, nearly two decades after the great late-sixties love-ins, for the many puritans out there such sexual forays were still dirty, nasty, illicit. She knew Milton and Theresa saw sex as a normal part of life, and that a range of delights were her birthright, gentle Milton urging she give as good as she got, St. Theresa of the Whirlwind referring to the range of cautions she had shared with Sarah age twelve, insisting that you engage in sex for love and pleasure, that you need at least one of those or it's no good.

Sarah knew her mind. She knew Milton and Theresa accepted her daily life, and her convictions. So why did she tremble a little as she imagined their reactions? Because she realized she was about to make them, each in their ways, deeply disappointed in her.

It had to be told. It could not be undone.

She'd already spoken to Milton, alone. She had sat with him in the living room, each in one of the blue easy chairs in front of a large warming fire. Theresa, at a conference in Genoa, would be back in four days. "Milton," Sarah had said, "I have to tell you this. I'm pregnant."

He'd stared at her, for seconds no words. Then a nod. He stood, came over to her, kissed her on the forehead. Suddenly she was standing also, and hugging him, hugging hard, holding on. Slowly they released each other, and Milton returned to his chair. She sat on the ground at his feet. He said, "You've not told Theresa."

"No." She shook her head. "I only had it confirmed this morning."

"And who's the father?"

She stared at the pattern in the carpet. "Does it matter?"

Milton raised his eyebrows. "It could."

"Well," she said, "I don't know."

Milton shook his head, and sighed.

"I've narrowed it down to three possibilities."

"You've been busy, little one."

She smiled a little. "They were each quite good."

He sighed again. "No precautions?"

"Yes," she said. "Always."

"It happens." He'd waited, she stayed silent. "You'll tell Theresa, soon as she gets back."

She looked up at him. "Please, be there when I tell her?"

He saw her face, her pretty gray eyes with that hint of green. For a moment she was his little girl again. "Of course."

Four days later, when Sarah came into the living room, no fire had been lit. Theresa knew only that Sarah wanted to talk. Milton had set up the meeting, Theresa not understanding the formality. "About what?"

"She'll tell you."

Sarah did. "Like I told Milton a few days ago, I got myself pregnant."

Theresa snorted a laugh. "Well, you said it right, we do it to ourselves. Who's the father?"

Sarah shook her head.

"We don't need to have him around if you don't want him. But it's worth knowing."

"I'm not sure, Theresa."

Now Theresa looked concerned. "What kind of comparative study was it?"

Sarah giggled, then laughed outright.

Theresa said, "Well, you can finish school. Then you'll get your BA here, Milton and I'll raise the kid till it goes to kindergarten. You'll be less free but everything'll work out."

Theresa's response had been as Sarah had expected. "Theresa, I got rid of it yesterday."

Milton closed his eyes. His hand rose to cover his mouth. He felt what was coming.

Theresa stared at Sarah. "Aborted."

Sarah, already embarrassed, nodded.

"You killed it."

"It was barely four weeks—"

"In our family, Sarah, you have many rights. Over your body, over your mind. But you don't have the right to kill an other being."

"It wasn't anything yet—"

Theresa eyes blazed, her lips curled forward, she breathed at Sarah: "Who-are-you-to-judge-what-is-and-is-not-a-being?"

Sarah had no answer.

For this one act Theresa has never fully forgiven her daughter.

Sarah stayed away from sex for three years. So many good men around, such a lot of good dope. But, Sarah would say of herself, I am a nun.

○

"Wow!" said Lola. "An all-or-nothing lady."

"Yep." I had no more to report. Lola had no further comments. So I looked ahead. "It seems quiet times followed. For everybody."

"What do you mean?"

"I can't see or hear another memory for quite a while."

"Oh. Then maybe I should go."

"No need. I'll jump ahead."

"To?"

"Let's see. Eight years after Sarah's abortion. A memory from Carney."

"Oh good." She smiled. Likely thinking I enjoyed telling Carney stories most. No, I like telling many kinds of stories. But unnecessary to make an issue of it.

o

3. (1995)

Jenn faded to no one. Later Carney met Lynn. Lynn agreed with Carney, morning sex was best. Today the well-tested and excellent theory had already provided another top-notch morning. He liked the idea of first-rate sex with the Chairwoman of the Montpelier Board of Education.

Their kiss goodbye, as much out of memory as in promise, lasted longer than either expected. He walked toward his Jaguar and figured tonight they'd maybe break the pattern. Wouldn't be the first time.

He started the car. Marcie's theory, right now, made him smile. He had heard from Bobbie that Marcie had married a man more suitable than Carney. Or at least more at home. They'd produced two children. Bobbie had kept in touch. Bobbie would.

o

Lola stood. She paced. She marched to the edge of the cloud. She stared down. She nodded. "I understand. I get what you're doing." She sat beside me again. "With your story."

Puzzled, I looked at her. "Yes? And what's that?"

"I know what it's about." Her face relaxed into self-satisfaction.

"Hmm. You going to tell me?"

"Yep. It's about how families work. Three families. Kinda interest-ing. No families up here."

"Well." I thought about that. "I mean, it's certainly about two families, the Magnussen-Bonneherbes, and then there's the Cochan group."

"One more."

"Yes?" She was getting such pleasure out of whatever she thought her discovery was.

"Yours. Your family. Carney and Bobbie. And Ricardo." The laughter left her face. "And you," she added.

"It's hardly about me. A long time since I've been alive."

"But you're still connected. Even now."

A provocative idea. I'd file it away for later.

"Want to know something?" She embraced herself, rocked a little from side to side. Her certainty increased. "I think I'm going to enjoy this. I mean I already am, but—" She fell silent.

"What?"

"I'm not sure." She stared northward, toward the Laurentians. "Yet." She touched my forearm.

○

From the farm Carney drove over to Montpelier on mostly dirt roads. He didn't much like Montpelier, nice-enough architecture but the men and women the voters sent there confounded him. Josiah Fairfax and Carney had fished two dozen streams together so when Joss said, "Come for lunch, someone I want you to meet," Carney couldn't easily say no. Joss said Carney likely didn't know the man, Si Morris, and Si would tell Carney why the meeting.

Lunch at Stenn's was predictable: dark corners behind posts that provided privacy but slowed service, dead sound that kept the Republican group of three at Table 19 from overhearing what the ski-industry lobbyist-lady was saying to the Democratic Lieutenant Governor and two senators at Table 11 eight feet away. Carney met Joss and Si Morris at the bar. Carney said, "Just ginger ale, thanks," though the vodka martinis in their clear cold V-glasses tempted him. Not for lunch.

They sat, ordered. The talk remained small: some nice low-water rainbows being taken down near Rochester, Carney and Co.'s success back in April with that tar-dump fire in southern Nova Scotia, Joss's first granddaughter. Arriving soup cut the talk. Into the momentary silence, Si said, "We're concerned about the Governor. She's got to be replaced."

"What's wrong with her?"

They related for him her dumb fiscal schemes, they described potential effects of nutty projects, all growing from dogma rather than a solid fiscal base.

Carney listened, impassive. For him, politics was simple. Government existed for two reasons, the little one to set policies that'd maybe keep us all from immense disasters, and the big one to clear away the disasters after they happened. So why was Joss treating him to lunch today?

Joss turned to Si. Si nodded. "Simply stated, Carney, we'd like you as our candidate for Governor next year. We think you could defeat her."

Carney grinned. "Be serious."

Joss said, "We are."

"Come on. Nobody's ever heard of me."

"We can turn you into a winning candidate." Si smiled. "And, you're not unknown."

"In politics, totally."

Si smiled some more. His head shake suggested Carney's naiveté. Why do war heroes and actors become such good candidates? Strong previous reputation, name and image recognition.

What they didn't understand: the notion of Carney as Governor of Vermont was a farce, and the acts of that farce stared Carney full in the face. At each tack from Si, from Joss, Carney only said, "Ridiculous," or, "Get serious." He should just say no, he didn't want to consider this. Why not? Wasn't he tempted? Just a little? But you can't say a bald no to an old friend like Joss.

They parted, all friendly. Si said, "Give it a week, okay? Think about it seriously."

Joss said, "As Governor you could do a hell of a lot for Vermont, locate the disaster areas early, keep them from happening."

Avoiding disaster, the chance to analyze, think ahead, sometimes succeed, this was their only real argument. But as Governor of Vermont what could he do about disasters in New Hampshire, or Arizona? And besides, governing was more than avoiding disaster, it was running things, some really foolish things. Besides, he was totally inexperienced, at forty-six too young to run anything that big. Too cynical to think you can govern properly for the good of the lowly citizen. He drove home on his back roads. A thought came to him, that politics stood about as distant from what he used to call a Moment as he himself was from Julie. What a strange way to think it. Back home he told Lynn about the meeting, and waited for her laughter.

It didn't come. She said, "Right now does Carney and Co. gross more or less than the annual budget of Vermont?"

"Maybe a quarter as much."

"Don't you find that a farce too, young fella like you in charge of a humungous enterprise like that?"

"You think I—"

"But you're in love with it, the excitement of disaster. You're like those reporters sending back dispatches from the front, how horrible the battles are, death and dying all around, but they won't stay away. War junkies."

"Putting the lid on disasters is hardly—"

"Same thing. A new place to solve a new problem, each week or each month. Never the same place twice."

"Hope not. When Carney and Co. solves a problem, it stays cleared up."

"Oh, Carney. You're not listening." So she kissed him deep and long, time enough to start a new tack. She pulled back. "As Governor, you could appoint me Secretary of Education."

He squinted at her. A bemused smile. "You're serious."

She held him to her, and kissed his neck.

He said, confronting the danger of the terrain, knowing she'd know it too since he'd told her most everything he remembered about himself and Marcie. "Time to grow up?"

She drew back from him and didn't mean to let her smile reveal even a little sadness. "Some grown-ups want to be responsible to the community. Along the way they make kids. A family. Kids force you to find ways to be responsible."

But didn't she think his work with Carney and Co. was a real contribution? A life given over to cleaning up other people's devastations? He was as close to her as any man could be to a woman. How could she understand so little about his work? "I told Joss I'd tell them in a week."

A week later he told Joss what he should have said right away: No. He didn't have it in him to be Governor. Could Lynn be right, he was a disaster-junkie? Even if he delegated jobs more than ever? Can you ever grow out of being a junkie? Grow up?

4. (1995)

Leonora dropped Milton at the Burlington Trailways station. She insisted on waiting. He insisted there was no need, he was perfectly capable of getting on the damn bus all by himself. When the bus drove in she let him win the argument and drove away. She had to be in court back in Montreal in the morning.

He kept his overnight bag at hand and climbed aboard. The double seat across from the driver was vacant, which pleased him. He felt like a bit of a kid, riding up front. Better than flying and by the time he got to Sarah just as quick, and he didn't want that much of a drive by himself. Not every day your oldest daughter gets married, he thought, and felt a pang, wishing tomorrow were not that day.

Damn it, Theresa should be attending too. But Theresa was in Athens, an international fencing conference. Two issues Theresa felt passionate about were on the agenda: that women's épée should become an official Olympic sport; and that electronic scoring for foil, sabre, and épée be changed to digital scoring. Theresa, so violently opposed that nothing, not even the wedding of her eldest daughter, could keep her from being there to challenge that nonsense—with all her best rancor.

Fair enough, Sarah had given them little warning of the wedding. Milton and Theresa had met Driscoll two months earlier, when he and Sarah had arrived at the Grange. They'd stayed for an hour, wouldn't accept a meal let alone an overnight bed, and drove away. Sarah hadn't even walked about, although she'd loved the place so, growing up. Still did, Milton knew, but the brevity of that visit bothered him. Theresa was mightily unimpressed by Driscoll's stance and dry-as-powder mind, though his forehead tended to sweat; Theresa remained mainly civil. Milton had wondered, What is a Driscoll? Why had they come?

Five days before Theresa was due to leave for Athens they'd found out. Sarah would be marrying this Driscoll Yeager. Sarah's letter was more an announcement of a wedding than an invitation. "Here"—Theresa slid the paper across the kitchen table—"read this."

Milton did. His chest tightened, he closed his eyes.

Theresa said, "Think she's pregnant again?"

"By Driscoll." His hanging head drooped. "Oh god, let's hope not."

"Well I'm not going. I don't think you should either."

Milton faced her, nodding now. "I have to, Tessa."

She stood, walked around the table, stood beside him, and pulled his head to her hip. She stroked his hair, going white-gray. "I know you do."

He took her hand. "Why this guy? She could have anyone she wants."

Theresa had shrugged, and stepped away. "Maybe she wants him."

The bus pulled out of the terminal. Milton sat back and stared ahead. Sarah his brave foolish impetuous pushing-the-edges dear child. Leasie, Feasie, and Karl had never broken a limb; Sarah at five had smashed her ankle falling from a tree, at eleven had broken two teeth by chewing on marbles, and at sixteen had fractured five ribs in a fight with two older girls who had taunted Leasie and Feasie mercilessly for being so tall and skinny. But by climbing where she shouldn't have she'd found the sweetest blackberries. She'd pushed herself to reach them before the others who were coming around the long way, slid, broke the forearm, stopped her fall, climbed up again, and stuffed herself with most of the berries before the others arrived. For weeks after the fight, she became the hero of her younger sisters. Theresa had approved of Sarah taking on two older larger girls; Milton still cringed thinking of it.

But marrying Driscoll, what kind of sense did that make? Though very few marriages, seen from the outside, made much sense. Who could have thought Tessa would have chosen him? Why he would choose Theresa was obvious: her wit, her beauty, her strength, and the blatant fact that she admired him. Human chemistry. He didn't understand it, never had. So what kind of chemistry was drawing Sarah to Driscoll? Why he should be attracted to her, this anyone could see. Sarah at twenty-four was smart and quick, beautiful as her mother had been—was still, a more mature beauty—a charming young woman when she let herself be.

The thought, I am losing Sarah, flitted through Milton's mind for the ten-dozenth time since getting her letter. A foolish thought: he couldn't be losing her, he'd never owned her. But how could they all sit together at dinner again with Driscoll Yeager at the table sweating through his thin hair? How could Milton imagine a half-Driscoll grandchild from Sarah? How could they celebrate equinoxes or solstices with any joy in the presence of that desiccated young man staring at them, judging them? The bus stopped in Montpelier.

Quickly they were on their way again.

Earlier, they reveled in her visits. Only three times since the abortion incident. The first, 1990, the summer solstice. Milton and Theresa returned from their long hike through the woods, smelly with anti-bug goo, to find Sarah had arrived. Over dinner she announced she'd been accepted to the University of New Hampshire as, at twenty, a mature student. They'd given her a year to see if she could handle it.

"Mature?" Karl, sixteen then, snickered. "You?"

"A special student. Smart, the university giving her a chance," said Milton. "Very clever of my alma mater. She'll show them."

"Hey, Milton," said Karl, between smirks, "if I drop out of high school, can I be mature too?"

"Stop it, Karl. I say we open a bottle of champagne to celebrate. Tessa?"

Theresa had nodded, even gave her daughter a smile.

They didn't see Sarah again, all of them together, until the next summer solstice to celebrate the graduation from kindergarten of Ginette, Ti-Jean's daughter, Feasie's stepdaughter; she doted on the child. No children of her own, they'd have more tests in the fall. Meanwhile she and Ti-Jean were immensely happy together and with Ginette.

Who had survived her first year of schooling. Ginette, wildest little girl Theresa had ever spent time with, capable of turning any utensil into a sword or pistol, any two pieces of furniture into a fort, any moment of calm into pandemonium. Theresa appreciated Ginette. And when Sarah arrived it was love at first confrontation, Sarah captivated by her niece's anima: "Hey, are you Sarah?"

"Yeah. What's it to you?"

"My mum says you can run fast."

"She's right."

"Can you run fast as me?"

"Want to find out?"

"Can you run to the moon?"

"Just show me the path."

"Come on." She grabbed Sarah's hand. "There's two moon paths out there." She dragged Sarah to the door, and out.

Sarah saw little of Theresa that solstice, spending the best part of her time with Ginette. Much appreciated, this, by the others, the little hellion out of their hair. That had been a good visit. Then it took a year and a half before they were all together again.

The bus pulled off the highway into White River. Milton got out to stretch his legs. He'd not seen the least spark of Sarah's energy when she'd introduced them to Driscoll Yeager. Sarah Yeager as she might become. If she changed her name. She didn't have to. Tessa had, for legal purposes, but that was thirty-one years ago. Ah well, the name would be the least of it. He climbed back aboard.

Sarah had visited alone, on the winter solstice, about four months before she would introduce Driscoll Yeager and she hadn't mentioned him then, half a year before her graduation. But over dinner, she told them, yes, graduate she would. She'd long been off probation, since after her first term her grades a perfect 4.0, no longer special, regular now like everyone else. At the dinner table, during a rare pause in the conversation, she'd suddenly said, "I have a favor to ask."

An odd moment. At a family meal people talked, they didn't announce they were about to speak. Milton glanced at Theresa, who gave the tiniest shrug. Milton said, "The floor is yours."

"But not the walls," said Karl. No one paid heed.

"I'd like to build a cabin. Out in back. By the little pond."

Milton looked around the table: Feasie and Leasie's faces blank, Karl's grin still present, unchanging, Theresa's brow in a small furl. He said, "Sounds like a wonderful idea."

Theresa said, "Why?"

Sarah waited a moment, breathed in and out. "Because I like to be there."

Feasie said, "You want to come to the Grange and not be at the Grange? You don't want to be with us?"

"I can do both. I don't know what I'm going to do when I graduate. But I want to think that I can build a cabin for myself out back."

"Fine by me." Milton glanced about again. "Any objections? Tessa?"

"You want to, go ahead."

After a moment Karl said, "Nobody really cares, Sarah. Build your cabin."

Sarah, Milton thought, looked crestfallen. Was it of such importance to her, that they should enjoy the idea of her building a cabin on Grange land? "Build a cabin, Sarah. Build it well, solid, so you can use it winter as well as summer. And now we'll celebrate Sarah's idea, a cabin by the pond. When it's done, we'll celebrate again, a housewarming of Sarah's cabin. I'll get the champagne."

Again the bus pulled off the highway, to the Manchester terminal where Milton had a fifty-minute wait for the Durham bus. He bought a sandwich. In less than two hours Sarah would pick him up. Would Yeager be with her? Would his family be present? Not much of a ceremony, Milton assumed; not much of an invitation. On the Magnussen side only he and Karl would be present, Karl arriving late, up from Swarthmore College. No special student; he'd got early admission on merit.

The drive to Durham increased his sense of estrangement. Was it anger he felt? He didn't know enough about Yeager to allow anger. Jealousy, then? Tessa had left her family for Milton, he had for some years left his family for her, until they'd come to the Grange. Milton decided: he would get to know Driscoll Yeager, come to understand him, perhaps to like him. For Sarah's sake.

He saw her from the window. He waved but she didn't notice. He stepped out, wound his way to her through passengers waiting for their suitcases, and put down his case. "Hello, Sarah."

"Hello, Milton."

He spread his arms wide, she stepped close. He brought his hands around her back and held her. She returned his hug. She'd become his little girl again. It was going to be all right.

o

Lola nodded gently but with what appeared to be sadness. "But we know better, don't we?"

"We have a sense of her, later on. But who's to say she'll stay there?"

"A strange thing. Seeing what was. All the while having a memory of how it is now."

A kind of backward remembering. I decided not to say this. I'd just detected another bit of the past. "Couple of days later, John Cochan was handing out cigars."

"Huh?"

"Priscilla gave birth to a boy. She and John called him Benjamin."

All Lola said was, "Oh."

"And a few years after that—"

○

5. (1998)

Nearly from the start, Intraterra North's President, John Cochan, and his Vice-President Planning, Yakahama Stevenson, had, with the rationality of prophets, projected a huge chamber, hidden deep below the ground. Yak because of turns and curvings in the rock: it made sense. Johnnie because he'd seen the chamber in his mind, formed it from blended memories of summers in the woods, days exploring hills and valleys, probing caves in Quebec, New Hampshire, Vermont. Years ago he'd shared his questions with Yak: Do valley slopes stop at the bottom? What's under the hills? And Johnnie's strange concerns elided with Yak's own: If a mass of granite rests beneath the fields of northern New England, what's beneath the mass of granite? If the continental shelf is truly a shelf, what lies below the shelving? Every schoolchild knew, had been taught from enlightened time eternal: below lay rock, rock, on to more rock, rock solid or molten but rock all the way down.

Maybe. Maybe not.

Five years before, Intraterra had set out an apparently ridiculous but strangely effective front: if oil was to be found off Newfoundland on the continental shelf, why not right here in northern New Hampshire, northern Vermont on the outermost banks of the St. Lawrence River Valley, at the first thickening of the shield?

With Intraterra capital they went drilling. Mineralogists wondered, lithologists doubted, mining engineers chuckled, geophysicists were stupefied. Go for it, gents, waste your money.

Johnnie, Yak, and the team drilled. Primarily along the border, a location essential for the economic thrust of the potential project—that large unemployed Canadian labor pool, those cheap Canadian raw materials, so much low-priced Canadian power and water.

In the beginning, solid granite. Granite to half a mile down, below this no sense drilling, working farther down would prove exorbitant.

More drilling. Again, try again, and after that again; and again. Because the earth's very hollows had to be there.

One day, early June 1998, they were. In Merrimac County, Vermont, on a bore down to eight hundred feet, they found— Space. An abyss. Wonderful remarkable emptiness. The same gap on a bore a hundred-fifty feet away and a quarter mile north. Eleven drills altogether, seven of them plunging slap-bang-sudden into a void. The shelf, seen at last for what it was: massive roof to an immense cavern. Space in which to found a city of steel, of light and joy: Terramac. The ultimate earthbound frontier.

o

"So that's what got Cochan started." Lola stared at the down below. "Pretty big ideas, our John."

"Pretty big," I agreed. "But he's not the only one."

"Oh? Who else?"

For Carney, only the idea of the project was there, so far. But it left me feeling proud, because I could already see the next memory.

o

6. (1999)

These days Carney spent as much time writing and giving his lectures as he did on the road with the teams. He was increasingly in demand: a presentation about real-life disasters from the very man who fought them, who limited their devastation to a point where recovery could be seen as feasible, brought in packed houses wherever he spoke.

He had six lectures he could give, according to what the audience was looking for. The oil-spills-in-oceans lecture wouldn't work in Pennsylvania, there he'd remind them of the coal-mine fire that had been burning under Centralia since 1961. Deep-shaft mine fires would be wrong for San Diego, they needed to hear about depleted uranium. And for Portland, Oregon, tell them about the dying sturgeon of the Columbia.

In Cambridge ten days ago, after his lecture, he'd been approached by an editor from Carlson Logan. "The name's Terence Gold, Mr. Carney. You got somewhere to go right now or can I buy you a beer?"

Carney was in fact busy. Gold suggested a meeting at Carney's convenience. "And what's all this about?"

"Your lectures. This is the third time I've heard you. I think you've got a book there, Mr. Carney. A real important book."

They met. A book would need about a dozen lectures of the length and quality Terence Gold had heard from Carney. "I'll think about it, Terence. I'll call you."

Carney didn't have to think much further. Even as Gold made his suggestion, he had decided. He even knew the title.

A week or so later Julie appeared in the middle of a warm night in June. She didn't exactly arrive so much as materialize where moments before nothing had been. She'd changed very little—still the long dark-blond hair and the soft blue eyes, as small-breasted and slim-waisted as ever, still those pretty round toes. Carney knew he was asleep but it didn't matter. He'd take her on any terms she chose. Hi, he said.

Hello, C.C.

He smiled. They don't call me that any more.

I do.

He nodded. Haven't seen you for a long time.

I know.

You've been—okay?

I'm not sure.

Where—where are you now?

Here and there.

Oh. He stared at her. The same little nose, the same lovely smile. It's wonderful to see you. He considered what he'd said. Wonderful.

You look tired.

In a way, I guess I am.

Is that something new?

I've been keeping up facades.

She laughed, a light curl of lifting sound. Of burning buildings?

That too.

And your own.

Yes, and that.

Hard work?

Very hard.

Then let it go.

I can't.

Why?

Why. Carney knew. He could tell no one. He could tell Julie. I'm less and less certain about things. Every day. I used to know a lot. I used to take control without thinking, and it worked. No more. But I can't let my teams know this. I've got to look certain. Appear in control.

She nodded. I understand.

You do?

That's why I came to visit.

Oh Julie. He reached a hand to where she was but she wasn't there. Why did I lie?

She shook her head. Long ago.

Long ago, he repeated.

I've brought you someone.

Carney looked about. No one. Who?

Mot.

Who's Mot?

Mot is my friend. He'll be your friend.

But who?

Mot, that's for Tom backwards. Mot isn't Tom.

So?

Tom doubts, like you.

Huh?

If Doubting Tom doubts, Mot is not to be doubted.

Julie?

Trust him. When he comes to you, trust him.

How'll I know?

You'll recognize him.

Carney laughed a little. He'd have to be tall.

Good. And?

Dark hair. Widow's peak. Thin face.

Good. We can stop there.

Okay.

C.C., meet Mot. Behind her a man, dark hair, widow's peak, thin face. Mot, this is C.C.

Mot nodded Carney's way.

Hello, said Carney. He heard a bell ringing.

I have to leave now, said Julie. And added, with a twinkle, But then, I was never here.

Julie, don't, please don't—

The bell. She stepped close to his side, set her hand on his shoulder, kissed his lips. He tasted her breath, and her lipstick. The bell rang. He squeezed his eyelids close together. She mustn't go. No longer any pressure from her kiss, and the scent of her had vanished.

He opened his eyes. No Julie, no Mot. Only early morning light. And the ringing phone. He threw off the sheet and blanket. He grabbed the phone. "Hello."

"Carney. Please. I need you."

"Bobbie, what's going on? Are you okay?"

"No. It's Ricardo. He was hit by a car. He's dead."

"Oh Bobbie, oh god—"

Jogging along the roadway just after sunrise with Rumples their dog. A drunk driver swerved, smashed into Ricardo from behind, and his life ended. Carney got up, pulled on his pants, his shirt. Slowly. As in a dream.

Five

FATHER AND SON

1.

RAPT, the Richmond Alliance to Preserve Tomorrow, invited John Cochan to address them, 8:00 PM, September 13, 2000, the Community Hall, open to the public, to explain Terramac. Among RAPT's members, Theresa and Milton Magnussen.

At home, all Theresa's comments about Terramac were variants of: What's at stake here is nothing less than a total change in how life gets lived in Merrimac County. Hell, all northern Vermont and a chunk of Quebec for icing!

To which Milton would respond with some version of: Let's hear Cochan out.

So among eight dozen others Theresa and Milton filed through the hall's lower doorway into the Games Room. They sat on wooden folding chairs borrowed from the Bridge Club. Up front, on risers a couple of feet high, the lawyer Dalton Zikorsky chatted with John Cochan. Six minutes after eight, above the murmur of chat and gossip, Milton said, "Dalton. Can we get this thing started?"

Dalton grinned. "Waiting for the stragglers, Milton. There's some not so prompt as you."

"Because you're letting them get away with it, Dalt. We wait at this end, we get kept here longer at the other."

Dalton shrugged, stood, held his hand up for quiet, and introduced the evening's guest. "John Cochan. Our new neighbor." Mild applause.

For twenty minutes John Cochan spoke of the future of northern Vermont, Terramac his context. He would be building, from the ground up, the community of tomorrow—homes, recreation quarters, centers for production and development of information and communication systems, in short, a small electronic city. Elegant shopping neighborhoods, planned in every detail according to exhaustively researched standards for preserving, in fact enhancing, the environment the project would stand at the center of. It'd be a great improvement on the present. Terramac wasn't being built on virgin land, no old- or even second-growth forest around here. In fact, the site of this new city, the one-time Fortier Farm, had been despoiled long ago, over-grazing, over-logging, the standing water unsafe for drinking, over-fertilization, high fecal coliform count. "But change is going on all around. See how Burlington's grown in the last twenty years, a bustling healthy little city. And why? Because its people planned right."

Dalton Zikorsky spoke for the Alliance's largest faction: "You see, Mr. Cochan, we're opposed in principle to this kind of development, condos and so on. We're coping with the old pollution, we're keeping it from spreading. But with a dozen new kinds of pollution, well, the impact on a community can be murder."

"I'd never let that happen." John shook his head. "You'll have the chance to examine the safeguards and securities that'll be in place for Terramac, every detail of them."

"But, see, these kinds of projects get to be environmentally degrading in and of themselves."

John Cochan smiled. "Tell me, what is it you want for Terramac?"

Ira Allen broke in. "What Dalt says is right. We've been here a long time, our families and all. We like it like it is."

"But, my friend, tomorrow will never be like yesterday. Change happens, it's coming all the time. Why not plan for it?"

"Okay, just listen," said Theresa. "Keeping things how they've been, that's our plan. It isn't true that change has to happen everywhere."

Cochan shook his head. "You can't stop growth. But you can organize and so control your future. I'll help with that. Terramac will be central to your growth. We'll work together."

"No!" Theresa's whisper cut the air. "Don't you get it, Cochan? The Terramacs of the world, they pollute what we love. Our land, and our bodies too. We know that, too well."

"If you'll just listen a minute . . ."

"No, you listen, that's not the half of it. These Terramacs, they destroy the soul. As they'll do here, the souls of my friends here in Merrimac County. My soul. Yours."

"Our souls, Dr. Magnussen?" Cochan laughed lightly. "Let me just explain to you why this is different from any—"

"Different? Your Terramac shops filled to bursting, their hawkers screeching, Buy! Buy!"

"Dr. Magnussen. There's never been a Terramac before."

"And there ain't gonna be one here now."

A chorus of "No," and "Right," and a generous shaking of heads.

John Cochan practised restraint. Long ago he might have insisted, or threatened. He smiled at that image of himself. No, one day soon the Alliance's people too would bask in the successful splendor of Terramac.

The meeting ended, nothing resolved. In the weeks that followed, RAPT learned little more about this Intraterra North organization, a private company, family owned, its website as public as it ever got. But what to make of it, this resort? apartment co-op? multi-mall? high-tech industrial park? And why build it here? And who might live in it? And how would it be designed, and organized? And keep it out.

○

"She's real angry, that Theresa."

"Many down there are," I said.

"Not like her. She's something special. I wonder what it feels like, to get so angry."

I said nothing, letting Lola follow her thought.

"You suppose she gets any pleasure, being angry?"

I considered that. "I don't think so. But I can't see very deep into her . . ." I shrugged.

"I bet she does," said Lola.

○

On a Friday in July of the fateful year 2001, late morning as usual, Theresa Bonneherbe Magnussen arrived at the nursing station. Patty the duty nurse greeted her with her normal flighty, "Hi, Theresa. The girl ready for action?" Here Theresa's doctorate was irrelevant.

She chuckled. "Sure. Got anybody old I can take advantage of?"

Patty grinned, checked the list, next step in their ritual. She'd already figured where Theresa's time would best be spent. "There's Mr. Knowles. Operated on two days ago."

"Who's his surgeon."

"Stubbs."

Theresa nodded. "Didn't get it all?"

Patty shook her head. "Bits and pieces all over the place."

"He knows, then."

A sad laugh. "They're dripping him. His wife's been by. He's handling it better'n her."

A sheet covered most of Mr. Knowles, a drawn face ageless in the range of the middle years, eyes closed, skinny arm, plastic tubing attached. Theresa said, "Morning, Mr. Knowles."

Mr. Knowles lay still.

Theresa introduced herself. "May I join you?"

The man said, "Uhhm—"

Theresa pulled a chair to the bed, sat, remained silent.

The man opened one eye to a squint. He said, "D'I know . . . ?"

Theresa shook her head. "No."

"You—a preese?"

Theresa smiled. "No, no. I'm a woman with time to share. Like to share a bit with me?"

The man snorted. With a tad more strength it might have been a brash laugh. "Guess I—need a—a li'l, huh."

Theresa laughed, in turn. "We all do, Mr. Knowles." Then she talked or sat silent for an hour. Leaving, she told Patty she couldn't be in for the afternoon, had to be at a meeting.

Patty watched Theresa go. For nearly seven years she'd been sitting at the bedside of the dying. No one had ever asked why. This was not how Richmond thought of Theresa Magnussen.

Only once had Milton said, "Now you believe in helping people one at a time?"

She'd said, "I'm not healing them, not a bit. They're all dying. I'm just soothing them."

Milton had not argued.

o

"Huh," said Lola. "I didn't know she could be like that."

"I didn't either. Till now."

o

In Richmond, county seat for Merrimac, the town hall was the hearing room. By Monday all would know, in principle and perhaps more, the future for the old Fortier Farm. The adversaries: the

153

Richmond Alliance to Preserve Tomorrow at one end of the long table, Theresa up front, Milton slouching at her side. At the other end, Intraterra North.

Despite the heat John Cochan wore a white shirt and a scarlet tie. His black eyes studied the faces, shiny, bearded, tanned, down near Dr. Magnussen. His mind weighed their possible positions this afternoon, the effect of them. No, he wasn't worried. Nine months since he'd brought up Terramac with them, months filled with the hard work of a first-class team.

At mid-table and separating the groups hovered County Commissioner Charlie Seed, broad, tall, amiable, called Chick. And three Associate Commissioners.

John Cochan smiled a greeting at Chick. Chick nodded in return. Johnnie and Chick had spent a lot of time over the winter and spring in projection, conversation and the pleasure of each others' dinner tables. Their wives got along too. The decision was pretty much in place, and Cochan had no fears. Well, almost none.

Perched on a stool at his right, the place of honor as designated by Johnnie, sat Benjie Cochan, nearly seven years old. Johnnie whispered to the boy, "Later on I'll give you some papers to hand to the lawyer." Benjie nodded. He felt proud when his father asked him to do things like this. Seeing the two, some of the hundred-plus onlookers seated along the wall and in rows from table to door smiled, a father and a son, good friends.

On John's left sat Terence Connaught, lawyer for Intraterra North, brought in from Burlington, more or less a local man. Beside Connaught, the two Intraterra vice-presidents assigned to Terramac, Yakahama Stevenson, VP Planning, wiry, clear-eyed, and Aristide Boce, VP Financial, stout, a broad and bristly mustache.

Among the spectators, flame-haired Priscilla Cochan, filled to bursting with the future Melissa. The ladies of Richmond liked Priscilla. She was available for teas and bridge, for driving the old people to the supermarket, to dental appointments. Her new baby would be a real child of Richmond. Priscilla paved many pathways for Johnnie, clear little lanes toward Terramac.

Theresa, loose white mane flowing down her back, listened as

Dalton Zikorsky, Chair of RAPT, whispered at her ear, Dalt confident that the future Cochan was striving to cast them all into would never come about. She wished she felt Dalt's certainty. RAPT dealt in details and legalisms; Terramac was fueled by obsession and zeal, what Cochan called Herculean vision. More a Medusa's glare, thought Theresa.

The overflow crowd, involved observers all, represented a gamut of often informed opinion: on the one hand, hope-filled desire that Terramac would bring abundance, new employment prospects, a solid tax base for the town and farms around, better schools, a new ambulance; on the other, leave the county as it is, low-density rural and small-town living, clean air, no malls, condos, or resort hotels near Richmond. Why d'you think we stay here, moved here in the first place?

Lawyer Connaught presented the Terramac proposal, clarified Terramac's place among the many contributions John Cochan had made elsewhere. Cochan would bring to northern Vermont a small but resplendent community for the third millennium.

More than once Theresa hissed with anger. Leonora squeezed her shoulder, Milton her hand.

RAPT responded to Connaught and Cochan with tactics designed to show so many problems, make so many environmental demands that Terramac would be shelved. County services were unprepared to handle the influx. New pollution from cars, garbage disposal for thousands of new homes and offices? And Terramac's golf course would bleed herbicides and pesticides into Fortier Creek and the Sabrevois River, this was in the nature of golf courses.

Zikorsky argued on: Excavation at the edge of the Laurentian Shield, a major fault line, would destabilize the geology, multiplying the danger of earthquakes. The old striated rock, blasted into a jumble at Terramac, could become a conduit to shock waves shuddering through Merrimac County.

Theresa, all attention, shuddered also. Half the hall shuddered with her.

Excavation would alter the underground river systems, destroy the water table. Little Lake Stevens, fed by springs, could disappear, and the impact on Lake Champlain was unknown. Here in Zikorsky's hand a geological survey showing how the tunnelling of construction could cause major drainage. The flooding of low-lying parts of Merrimac County was too likely.

Beside Benjie, his father smiled. Benjie knew why. Johnnie had told Benjie water was very important for Terramac, clean water, crucial. Water would make Terramac possible. He glanced up again to show he knew this. But his father was making notes on a piece of paper.

Benjie, on his own sheet of paper, drew a picture of a stream, and trees. Next he'd do a waterfall. And a picture of the big spider in the corner of the window, lots of flies stuck in the web up there. And after that— His mind wandered. He wished he were by the stream.

As the RAPT lawyer made his accusations, John Cochan's well-being diminished. Yes, Terramac would win the day, the month, the decade, because Cochan and his team had proven and would show Intraterra's commitment to ecological progress, distant and deep. But it bothered him profoundly that the Alliance just didn't grasp his contribution, his Econovism. He'd not got through to them.

Benjie finished the picture of the stream, and its waterfall. He passed it to his father.

The picture cheered Johnny. The boy was his posterity, a vindicating lineage. To build for his son a more liveable world would atone for his own father's desecration.

Lawyer Zikorsky concluded: "You have our response to your project. We have so few particulars from you we can barely guess the parameters of destruction. We just can't risk it."

Benjie drew the picture of the spider to look like the face of the lawyer; spider-lawyer said bad things about his father. The spider was a big fat fellow, not like the lawyer but the lawyer did sound fat. He passed the picture to Johnnie.

"Thank you, Mr. Zikorsky." Chick Seed smiled. It wasn't often he addressed Dalton Zikorsky formally. Dalt, Chick, and three friends played poker twice a month. Their names for each other tended to the friendly-crude.

Johnnie Cochan stared at the picture. His hand quivered. The paper slipped to the floor.

"Mr. Connaught? Your final statement?"

"Thank you." Connaught rose, and stepped back from the table. "We've heard with interest, Mr. Commissioner, Mr. Zikorsky's last few words. We agree—"

Benjie felt his father's distress without a word being said. What had he done wrong?

"—he cannot know the range of details of the Terramac project. Because of the magnitude of Terramac, once we have county approval in principle, the details will evolve as our—we hope and expect— joint venture progresses. Joint in promise, joint in planning, joint in responsibility." He recognized the fears of the Alliance as zones of honest concern.

Why would Benjie have drawn such a thing? John Cochan stared at Zikorsky, and Dr. Magnussen. Zikorsky's skin, tight on his face, showed no response to Connaught. Theresa Magnussen, her cheeks gray, eyes squinting, remained impenetrable. Leonora Magnussen sat silent. A spider, for cripesake!

Connaught nodded. John pulled himself together. From a manila envelope he took a sheaf of paper bound in plastic. He turned, his mouth twitched, he handed the folder to Benjie.

Benjie took the folder and dropped from his stool. Maybe doing this for his father would make it all better. Walking slowly, looking ahead only, he carried his package to the far end of the table, to the spider-lawyer beside the white-haired woman.

Connaught said, "Thank you, my boy."

Benjie turned, smiled at his father, and walked slowly back to him.

Half the onlookers, Priscilla Cochan first among them, smiled warmly.

Benjie, pleased he'd done his job well, knew he'd never be Mr. Connaught's boy.

Connaught spoke quietly. "In Benjamin Cochan's package the Alliance will find in detail what I shall explain to you now."

Cochan tested the glance Zikorsky shot Theresa Magnussen. Her head shook once.

"Terramac is prepared to work in consort with Merrimac County, with its own hopes and projections. We therefore commit ourselves to, and request, the following: in exchange for the right to build select dwellings and an infrastructure for human progress on the land known as the Fortier Farm, Terramac Intraterra North commits itself—"

His glance swept the spectators. For fifteen minutes he spoke, and his stratagem undermined their concerns. As if knowing in advance each of RAPT's objections, the supporting documents dissolved these one by one. Intraterra agreed to build to no higher than four stories, use only natural herbicides and pesticides, import decontaminated landfill and clean hydroelectric power. The contract with the Quebec Hydro Company awaited Intraterra signature just as Intraterra waited for Richmond's agreement and license. Intraterra would itself provide Terramac's drinking water, purified from the Sabrevois River. Would construct a sewage treatment and recycling plant on the Svenska Lavowasser model. Had months ago submitted these proposals to Vermont's Environmental Impact Commission, had worked closely with them at emendation, last week had received their approval. More, their commendation. And seismological reports to brush aside all fear of earthquake, and aquifer reports extolling the proposed excavation at Terramac. Actually, Terramac would stabilize the water table. To this end Terramac had also acquired all underground and mineral rights, to twenty-five hundred feet down.

A little smile came to Leonora Magnussen's lips: her mother's fears and RAPT's, made known, dealt with, had allowed this compromise. The smile, for herself only, hid a small shiver.

In exchange there must be no further intercessions by RAPT or anyone associated with RAPT and its members. If complaints or intercessions arose, Intraterra was in a position to sue each plaintiff for such damages, material and defamatory, as might result out of delay or libel. The courts had established this principle as due and just in *Pelegrini versus Squaw Valley*.

Commissioner Seed called the hearing to a close. "We'll take into account all you've told us, gentlemen. We reconvene Monday at ten-thirty."

The RAPT executive met at Magnussen Grange. From Dalt Zikorsky, thin laughter. "Well, it'll be a clean Terramac. We drove them to their knees."

"Their knees?" Theresa Magnussen whispered her rage. "Don't be so effing daft!" Her voice cracked. "They've beaten you at your own game." Milton put his hand on his wife's wrist—

"Sure, it'll cost 'em a dab more." Theresa pulled away and pushed herself up. "But they've got their goddamn Terramac! They knew every argument and conceded it and ran around it." Her face flushed maroon, her eyes scanned the room, she hissed: "They knew!"

○

Lola grabbed my arm. "What's that maroon business?"

Fear? Improbable. But fear from a God is what I felt. "Blood pressure, I'd guess."

"Is this—where she gets her stroke?"

"Just wait and see, okay?"

She nodded, slowly.

○

"Theresa." Milton took his wife's arm, drew her down to the chair, stroked her back. "Calm."

Precisely what Leonora had hoped to avoid. Theresa always, always, went overboard. These extreme dramatics, why'd she have to do this?

The John Muir Society representative, the fellow from the World Wildlife Fund, Stu Blaine the chemist, the two women from the senior center who'd each volunteered fifteen hours a week for RAPT, Ira who owned Allen's diner, the two university students up from Burlington, Danny who ran the Gulf station, Dalt Zikorsky, a dozen others, each felt doubts about the offer. But with certain modifications . . . ?

Zikorsky shook his head: "Theresa, for godsake, we've worked months for this, will you read the document? It's pretty good, close to okay—"

"No! By definition, Terramac destroys."

"It's as near to what we wanted—"

"You won your maneuvers. You lost the battle. If Chick signs, we've lost for all time."

The Muir Society woman added, "Remember, we didn't want any Terramac at all here."

Theresa's head shook, little vibrations. "Once the county agrees,

Cochan's got you gagged. You mutter, he shoves a lawsuit down your throat." She paused. "My throat."

Ira Allen said, "That's what worries me the most, that lawsuit."

"He's right about Squaw Valley," said Milton. "We can't afford a court case. Intraterra can."

Dalt Zikorsky said, "It wouldn't come to that."

Sunday morning John Cochan drove Priscilla's Dodge to Green Mountain Cement, an Intraterra subsidiary south of town. He was alone.

Leonora Magnussen, around the side of the building, slouched in her car. Terramac would have come about anyway. With her help it'd be a better safer place. Over the months she'd come to believe in Terramac. She saw herself as a clear-headed woman. But right now she felt edgy, wished the thing were settled, her part done and distant. She spotted Cochan, got out, and followed him into the office.

"So. What's happening?"

"The full Alliance meets today at noon." She spoke quickly. "Dalton believes Intraterra and Merrimac County can live in harmony." She smiled, sad. "I'm afraid my mother doesn't."

John Cochan nodded but couldn't smile. He longed to prove Dr. Magnussen wrong.

The Alliance met. And cracked apart.

The executive set Intraterra's package before their constituency. Questions, discussion, discomforts; a clearing of the air. Amendments. They voted. Sixty-two percent in favor. Compromise, yes. Still, a victory. Among the minority, bitterness ran deep.

Milton feared Theresa was all too right: Terramac would be a thoroughgoing disaster. Leonora knew her mother was wrong. A painful transition, yes; cities as they grow do alter nature. But better to build a desirable community than let blight sprawl over the land.

On Monday RAPT and Intraterra returned to stand before the commission.

Benjie wondered, Did everybody like his father? They all shook his hand, patted him on the shoulder, laughed with him. Johnnie held

Benjie by the nape and Benjie tightened a little. He made himself look up. He gave his father a smile because he knew his father wanted that.

Dalton Zikorsky asked for a series of modifications to the Terramac document. Terence Connaught, after consulting with John Cochan, agreed.

Theresa, among the onlookers, shook her head. A great sadness took her.

"Well"—a satisfied Chick Seed nodded—"looks like consensus here. These Intraterra concessions are sound. And RAPT agrees to consult, won't bring procedural complaints—"

"No!" Theresa Bonneherbe Magnussen marched to the table. "Never." Her voice breathed as it had not for years, every word a challenge. "Never in my life will I promise never in the future to commit an action which that future screams for. Never can a piece of paper leave me prisoner in a past grown evil with illegitimacy! No aware human being can sign this."

Dalton hissed, "Theresa, please!"

She leaned across the Commissioners' table and growled, "Cochan's got you by the conkers, Chick. Next year and in ten years you'll still be tied back to today."

"Theresa, it's only a contract, an agreement. Take it easy."

She turned to John Cochan. "You got 'em, Handy Johnnie. Smart."

Benjie Cochan drew in close to his father. Johnnie put his arm around the boy. "All our best interests lie in Terramac," Cochan said gently.

"It won't happen, Cochan." She supported herself on the table and bent her face down to his. "It's not over."

"For me it's not." Cochan spoke softly. "I'm building the future. But your fight against me, Dr. Magnussen, yes, that's over. You've been a worthy antagonist. I haven't convinced you. And for that, I'm truly sorry."

She turned, strode from the room, slammed the door hard. Milton stared at the door. Leonora leapt up and ran after her. Milton followed.

Chick Seed consulted with his associates. All was well? Nods of agreement. "Then Richmond, the Alliance, and Intraterra are united on Terramac."

Applause and congratulations. The twitching of a few worried heads.

Chick said to Johnnie, "Well, congrats." He chuckled. "And maybe when you excavate, you'll find gold down there." He laughed heartily. "Start a Vermont-style gold rush!"

Johnnie smiled back. "Terramac will be our city of gold, Chick." With Benjie at his side, he watched the room empty. Cochan and Connaught shook hands, spoke a few words. The lawyer left. Johnnie took Benjie by the hand, walked to the door, knelt to Benjie's height, squeezed the boy's ribs with both hands. "We did it!"

The boy smiled. "Is it okay?"

"It'll be all okay when it's done, Benjie. Every project is a risk. But if you reduce the odds, you can take the risk. Take the risk by the neck, and it's yours."

The boy nodded. His father had done it, all of it.

"We each make the future, Benjie. Terramac is the pinnacle, it's our place in history." He sat Benjie on a chair and crouched in front of him. "Mine and yours."

Benjie nodded again. "Take the risk."

"Terramac, the grandest place on earth, soon to be the most perfect little city in the world. We're building the future, Benjie, we're setting ourselves at the acme of history."

Benjie didn't understand. But he nodded.

Johnnie picked the boy up by the armpits, he held him high in the air. "We got ourselves here, Benjie. And now we go on."

Benjie felt light-headed. And a little scared.

The destruction of the World Trade Center in New York held back the Terramac ground-breaking ceremony by only three weeks. Four months after the Commissioners had reached their decision the digging began, and the blasting. Even at Magnussen Grange the earth trembled.

Theresa felt the ravages as her own. Terramac was a vampire, a starved leviathan, she raged, a scourge, all the vermin of the world. Few listened because Terramac was decided.

The thing, in its way almost as bad as Terramac, was RAPT's inside betrayal. This proximity of treason hacked at her trust, it ate holes in her spirit. Who!? A question Theresa shared only with Milton. But he had no answer. Her shoulders drooped in silence. She cursed Cochan's heart, for stealing trust.

Three weeks into November she complained of head congestion. An hour later her brain roared and her vision blotched. She held herself upright until Milton got her to Emergency. There she crumbled.

Aristide Boce, Vice-President Financial for Terramac, reported Theresa's infirmity to John Cochan. "Old women should stay out of what doesn't concern them, hmm?"

But Cochan took no satisfaction from Dr. Magnussen's ill health. Challenges and crises were rarely brought on by the solitary individual. Mainly he wanted to explain to her why she was wrong, so wrong.

○

"He doesn't care who he hurts. And at what cost." Lola's lovely lips pressed together tight, grim.

I glanced down and a little farther ahead. "Well," I said, "maybe even he can get hurt."

"Poor Theresa," Lola whispered. She glanced at me, her face filled with a knowledge of the future contaminated by doubt. "But she gets better, we know that, you've told me. Right?"

I nodded. "Shall I go on?"

"Please."

○

2.

Benjie Cochan's guidelines were set by his father. If the boy said exactly where he'd be going—around the side of the hill, to the pool below the waterfall—he could roam the fields and woods with his friends Barney and Tick. Three feral puppies, they found rabbit holes and raccoon burrows, bees swarming, mica sheets with shiny jagged blades thrusting out from granite. They explored the twists and backwaters of the stream. They dared each other to climb higher trees.

Their antics unnerved Johnnie. Benjie, just short of eight, could be reckless and bold. He supplied the boy with alternatives: his own big room, a microscope, the newest electronic games, a Yamaha keyboard, an electric train set, baseball mitts. But Johnnie could only contain the extremes: not so late, not like that, less far.

More complex was his son's desire to see Terramac, the invisible part. "Soon," Johnnie'd say. "Right now there's nothing there, just darkness and bugs. You'd hate it. I want you to love it." Because when Benjie did come to love what Johnnie had brought into being, found it the grandest place ever built, then he'd have succeeded. Less would be failure.

The last of the snow in the hills had melted, the water in the river flowed clear again, open spaces in the woods smelled wet and green. On a warm Saturday in early May, the afternoon before Deirdre's birthday, Benjie said to his dad, "Tomorrow, can I take Dee with us, into the woods? Just to the pool, okay?" He wanted her to catch a trout.

"No. She's still too little."

"I'll look out for her."

"Did you hear me?"

"We'll be careful, we'll—"

"I said no."

His father rarely shouted, not even quietly. "You said if I said where I'm going—"

Priscilla arrived with Melissa, already toddling. "What's going on?" They talked, Priscilla, John, Benjie. They were reasonable people.

After a bit his father conceded. "You take special care of her."

"No problem!" He hated it when his father made the asking so difficult. Before they moved into to the farmhouse, his dad had always been so easy with him. Now they didn't play much. Which was one of the reasons he wanted to take Deirdre fishing, to have somebody to fish with. He found Dee. "Tomorrow, want to come exploring with us?"

Deirdre nodded with care, to keep her hope from building too high. "Is it all right?"

"Sure. Why?"

"I mean, with Barney and Tick?"

"They don't get to say. You're old enough." He grew up a little right then, telling her like that. It felt good to be in charge.

Tomorrow she'd be six. She smiled at the pleasure to come, a real birthday present, best thing ever if Benjie made them take her along.

Barney and Tick arrived on their bikes at the Cochan farmhouse. Deirdre sat on the porch steps. Benjie, arms getting spring-brown, his ruddy hair uncombed, spoke with authority. "Dee's coming with us." It was his land they were reconnoitring.

"She's too slow," Barney grumped. He and Benjie were the real friends. Tick was slow too, sometimes.

Deirdre listened. She stared down, she didn't dare watch.

"She can keep up," Benjie said. "Okay, Dee? You'll keep up?"

She nodded, her eyes following a snail's progress on the grass.

Barney sneered, "Look how short her legs are."

Tick said, "Aw, she'll be okay."

She looked at Tick.

He was grinning her way. "Come on, let's go."

She bent down to pick up the snail. The boys grabbed their fishing rods and started off. The snail pulled back into its shell. She set it down at the edge of the bushes and ran to follow.

Out of sight of the house, Benjie said they had to climb the slope where they'd sledded down in winter.

"It's not on the way," Barney grumbled. He knew it'd come to detours.

Up the hill Benjie showed Deirdre a depression between some rocks. "This is where the ladyslippers came from." Last year he'd picked three for her birthday. Their mother, calm yet irked, had explained that ladyslippers when they're cut don't grow again next year. It was true, he saw no ladyslippers coming up there now.

In the woods Deirdre tripped on a root, landed on her elbow, skinned it. Benjie glared: Don't you dare cry.

Barney said after all the side trips the sun was too high for fishing. Benjie said they'd give it an hour. He turned rocks over and made Deirdre pick up the worms. They left a glow of slime. She carried them to the stream in some wet dead leaves and wiped her hands on her jeans. Benjie told her to get up on the big boulder that stuck out five feet into the pool, casting was easier from there. "Look. Here's how you thread the worm on. Hold the hook like this."

She nodded.

"Next time you do it yourself."

When Barney wasn't looking Tick gave her some dates from his lunch. Barney wanted to search for caves. "There aren't any here,"

Benjie said. "They're all way underground. Way down, in my dad's city." His dad told him everything, all his plans; used to anyway. Just one place Benjie couldn't go, the most important, down to Terramac. The entrance to Terramac was on the far side of the land, too far to walk to. But sometimes when he was alone in bed or by himself he heard Terramac call, Come see me, come see me, Bennn, come see me . . . That scared and thrilled him.

Deirdre caught one small trout. They were back at the farmhouse by three, as promised. Her party started at four. She insisted on eating the trout. Her mother fried it and deboned it before the other kids came, two tiny filets. "Where'd you catch it?"

"In the pool by the waterfall."

Priscilla nodded. "The rocks by the water are slippery."

"My boulder isn't. It's beautiful."

"You'll be careful."

"Sure."

Deirdre came to be included in the gang. After Barney and Tick, the next nearest kids lived more than seven miles away, Benjie's dad's land was so big. Pastures, orchards, forests. His dad had torn out the walls of the old farmhouse there and built it over, straight and clean.

Benjie, Deirdre, Barney, and Tick explored and discovered. They fished at half a dozen spots in the stream. The dark pool below the waterfall was Dee's favorite, thirty feet wide and very deep. They could shout and wouldn't scare the fish because the falling water, a curtain of diamonds from the precipice thirty-five feet above, shattered into foam with a whirling roar. At the end of the pool the stream widened and got shallow where it flowed away over small rocks.

"Some of the water runs into the ground near here," Benjie told Deirdre. "Barney's uncle told him that." Barney's uncle was a plumber.

Benjie would see the underground Terramac soon, he told Deirdre, their dad had promised him. When it's finished and beautiful. "Now it's all caves and hollows," he said, "but we'll transform them, now they're wet slimy stones. You wouldn't like it." Benjie heard in his dad's voice two wonderful things. Terramac was the most important thing ever. And Terramac had called to his father, too.

"I bet there's no water in those caves down there," Deirdre said.

Benjie smirked. "Sure there is."

Benjie knew the trout in the pool were growing, feeding on bugs and grubs that got washed down over the waterfall. They'd been stocked, little fellows, in the fall by a couple of Johnnie's assistants for Benjie and his friends. Benjie didn't know that his father was trying to keep the kids in one or two safe places. Or that touching a live fish made his father cringe.

In late May Barney and Tick went to France for three weeks with their parents. Nobody for Benjie to play with, just Deirdre. Benjie worked up a plan. "Daddy? Let's go camping for a night, you and me."

"Now? With all those blackflies?"

"We'll use anti-bug goo. Please? Please?"

"Benjie—" But Benjie wore him down, and Johnnie agreed.

Benjie chose the place: by the pool. Planning details filled him with tingles of possibility. Enough propane for the little stove? Maybe cook only with wood. Get the big tent, or maybe just the pup tent but with insect netting. Maybe Terramac would call to him, right there. Maybe he'd hear it call to his father. Had it called to his father recently? His father seemed changed.

Camping in blackfly season? The worst. Gnats, mosquitoes, ticks crept across Johnnie's eyeballs, under his skin, into his brain. But Benjie wanted this camping thing. Such intensity from the boy. Okay, Johnnie could do it. For one night.

Should they build twig mattresses or carry in inflatables? Eat only fish? Hamburgers too?

Two days before the trip a crisis hit. In a rifle shop in east-central Florida's Mangrove Mall, built six years ago by Intraterra, a man was told he'd have to wait five days for his hunting rifle. He went berserk, killed the shop's owner and two customers, was now in hiding somewhere in the mall's maze of subterranean passageways. John Cochan knew those basements. He had to go, the police needed him. He came into Benjie's room. "I'm sorry, it's necessary."

"But why?"

"It's my job." He didn't tell Benjie about the crazy killer. "You can understand that."

No, Benjie couldn't. He held back a sob. "Sure, okay, yeah."

Others knew the guts of that mall as well as John Cochan. He could have delegated the problem away. But it was better to go, he and Benjie would replan their camping for later. After the bugs were gone. Maybe by then Benjie would have given up on the idea.

His father left for his mall. Benjie told his mother he was going camping by himself.

"I don't think that's a good idea."

"Come on. I'll be okay."

"Your father will be angry."

Benjie would risk his father's anger. "He doesn't like flies and things. He'd let me go."

"Aren't you afraid?"

How'd she know? "Of what?"

"Being all alone?"

"Course not."

She stayed quiet for a few seconds, then asked, "Why don't I come with you?"

No. He wanted his dad there. Or even by himself alone, there he might find out why his dad was different these days. Something had happened to his dad in Terramac. What? He loved his dad too much, please don't let anything bad happen to him. "Okay. But not the girls."

The girls stayed with Diana the nanny. Benjie and Priscilla unrolled their sleeping bags a few feet back from the pool. They put on more insect repellent. They made a fire. This was good but Benjie sensed something more, a distant excitement. They ate trail-mix, and cooked burgers. They slapped at blackflies and mosquitoes. Priscilla hugged Ben. "Goodnight." They lay down in the tent behind the screening but with the fly open and heard rustles in the woods, tree branches swaying slowly, thin whines in the air. Benjie watched the embers go black. He heard his mother's breathing slow into sleep. He listened to water splash in the pool and heard it flow down, it breathed at him, . . . nnn . . . nnn . . . ennn, like a little song. Go look? He didn't want to. He had to. He found the flashlight. He pulled himself out of the sleeping bag. His mother rolled over. He froze. No, she hadn't wakened. He crept up on the big boulder by the edge. He turned off the light. . . . ennn . . . ennn. He saw stars floating in the water, light broken by ripples. He stared down. Black. He heard the water's breath, he felt something, down there, below the water. He flicked on his flash. A face! Quivering. His own face but not quite, his and part his father's. Why there on the surface? He turned around fast, flashed his light up. Nothing. He looked again. A face far below. Out of Terramac? He shuddered. Go? He'd have to risk it; one day. He crept back to his sleeping bag. He stared at the sky, black as water. He slapped and scratched. At last he slept. They woke, packed up, returned home.

"So. Enjoy it?"

He made light of it: okay, just too many insects, his father was right.

Priscilla never told Johnnie that she and Benjie had gone camping overnight.

School ended. Benjie took to sleeping late, head under the sheet. Outside the house lay the strong draw of Terramac.

Before Terramac, Benjie would throw the ball and his dad would run for it, or in the house they'd play Go Fish and things like that. That didn't happen any more. Or was he just a spoiled selfish kid, did he want to be down in Terramac really for himself, hear its stream from up close? He turned in bed, he listened for a whisper of song. Nothing. Too far away? He had to be there, down inside. But also he had to save his dad. Before Terramac— Before it sucked out from inside his dad the thing that made him his dad.

Deirdre teased Benjie for not getting out of bed, a lazy fweep. He snapped at her. "Fweep! Fweep!" she cried, giggling. He nearly jumped up to hit her, but then held back. Without Tick and Barney, Benjie and she had to be each other's best friend.

They marched together through the woods. The trees and rocks felt like something had—what? Changed too? He sensed an explanation. Just beyond his reach. He hated the change.

Deirdre loved fishing more than any other thing. She'd say, enjoying her mature joke, "The excitement of my first trout hooked me forever." But it irritated him, her sitting alone on the big rock high above the water like she owned it. Below, foam flecked by on the black surface. "Aw come on, Dee, let's at least try another place."

"I like it here."

"Pretty soon there won't be any fish left."

"Daddy'll put more in."

His father stayed in Florida for five days. He returned late in the evening but Benjie had permission to stay up. "I want to go into the Terramac caves."

"Benjie, I'm tired."

"I want to see it down there."

"You should be asleep."

"I really want to—to go down there. With you."

"We've talked about this." He took Benjie hard by the hand. "Way past bedtime."

Benjie had to be dragged. He yelled, "No! Stop!" It hurt in his arm sockets. His father ignored him. "I could help you!"

Johnnie stopped. "Help?"

"Aren't you—aren't you afraid?"

"Of what?"

"A little bit afraid?"

Johnnie knelt to eye level with Benjie. "What are you talking about?"

"You know."

"Benjie, you should be sleeping."

"Of Terramac!"

"Terramac?"

"It's taking you. Away." There. Spoken.

Johnnie looked hard at Benjie. Something the boy had heard someone say? Priscilla? He drew Benjie to him and held him tight against his chest. He shook his head hard so the boy could feel the insistent negative movement. "Don't worry, I'm here. Always."

A lie. Less and less here. That his father spoke so easily was the proof he hadn't wanted to hear. He'd guessed right.

John Cochan picked the boy up and carried him to the bed in the big safe room filled with games and toys. Where did Benjie get these notions? A couple of times recently Priscilla had complained to Johnnie he was away a lot. Had the boy overheard? Or had she said that to Benjie specially?

Benjie knew his dad wouldn't let him go into Terramac because his dad wanted to protect Benjie from Terramac. He admired his dad, loved him for this. His dad hated flies and bugs and spiders, all those crawly things. Terramac's caves were full of bugs. His dad went down into Terramac. Many times. Why? Because Terramac—Terramac had control over him?

In the morning Benjie refused breakfast. "I feel sick."

He didn't look sick. Priscilla said, "What's the matter?"

"My head feels big. And puffy."

She felt his forehead. A bit warm. "Shall I bring you to the doctor?"

"I'll just stay in bed."

"Let's not take chances. Get dressed."

Once last year at 2:00 AM, Benjie had had a headache so bad his mother took him to Emergency. Across the waiting room a teenage girl couldn't stop dry-retching, down the hall an old man screamed about bedbugs crawling up his nose. Benjie's headache went away.

At the breakfast table he drank his milk. His face went white, his stomach pounded, panicky tears filled his eyes

Priscilla hugged him. "Benjie—"

He pulled back. "Don't."

Deirdre said, "You can hug me, Mummy."

Priscilla stroked her shoulder. Benjie ran, made it to the toilet just in time. He cried half the morning. Priscilla took him to his pediatrician. Nothing obvious wrong. They'd do tests.

He stayed in bed. Barney and Tick came home from France and Deirdre went exploring with them. They told her about all they'd seen, and had souvenirs from Paris, a tiny Arch of Triumph for Benjie, an Eiffel Tower for Deirdre. They'd gone to the top of the real one, they saw everything. Deirdre couldn't understand a lot but it didn't matter, it sounded wonderful.

Later Benjie found them far downstream, around the curve with the high granite walls. A dangerous place, he thought. Hawkweed everywhere, and daisies. A thin flow of water here, moving fast. His repellent kept the blackflies off but they buzzed around his head. Above the watery rush he thought he could hear the roar of Terramac machines. "Hey, Dee!"

"Here comes the lazy fweep!" Barney laughed.

Benjie stayed cool. "What're you doing."

"Watching ants carry a dead bug," Tick said.

"What're you doing, Dee?"

"I'm watching ants too."

"Well, come back. Mummy wants us."

"What for?"

"She said to come."

"Right now?"

"Yes, Deirdre."

"O-*kay*!"

They all got up.

"You guys don't have to come. My mother doesn't want you."

Tick stared at Benjie. "Our bikes are there."

"Get 'em later." Benjie grabbed Deirdre's wrist. "Come on."

"Hey, Benjie!" Barney shouted.

"What?"

"Fuck you!"

"Well, fuck you too!"

Deirdre followed Benjie, resisting his pull. When they were out of the brothers' sightline he let go. "I'm going to tell you something, Dee."

"What?"

"Don't go with them if I'm not with you."

"Why not?" She stood still.

His hand squeezed into a fist. "Because I said so!" He stepped closer, she pulled back. He spun around and marched toward the house. After a dozen steps, he turned. "Come on." He watched her start, a step, another. He strode off. He turned. She'd stopped again. "Come on!"

"What does Mummy want anyway?"

"She'll tell you."

When they got back their mother and Melissa weren't home. Deirdre went to her room, grabbed her stuffed koala bear and her worn lamb, lay on her bed, and cried into her animals.

His mother mustn't think Dee crying was his fault. Comfort her? He didn't.

○

Lola interrupted me. "I once had a stuffed snow tiger. All silver and white."

Without thinking I said, "So did my son."

She nodded, absently.

I glanced at her. Her eyes sent misty light my way. Stranger and stranger. Lola, remembering bits of her past. Something weird was happening here, as if Lola were evolving into a new kind of being.

○

A couple of days later, a gray morning, Benjie told Diana they were going fishing and took Deirdre to the boulder. He had to go now, he was leaving for camp next week. His dad was away again so this was the time. He left a note for his mother: *We're going to the stream.* Afterward, when Priscilla read the note, she tore it up. Johnnie never saw it.

Benjie and Dee tramped through the high grass and the daisy fields to the brush, grown thick now. The vines grabbed at their ankles, last year's blackberry brambles scraped their arms. They'd smeared enough repellent on so the swarming blackflies weren't too bad. Where low branches cut across his way he broke them and left them dangling which made him feel good. When they reached the waterfall he took off his tennis shoes and socks and sat on the boulder. Deirdre said she wanted to fish from up there, it was her place. Benjie dangled his feet and stared at his toes and at the water below. It reflected the lead sky and trees on the far side. If he waded at the wide end where the pool emptied he could stand in water to his waist. Half of him above water, half below. The lower half near invisible in the tickling stream. Close to the waterfall was way deeper.

No wading today, today was for serious. He stepped back and jumped to the bank. Deirdre clambered onto the boulder. He walked away from her in bare feet, and around, lower along the stream, lots of brush. After a couple of minutes he could hear the waterfall as a thin tickle. Slowly everything became clear. Find the way down, then bring his dad and they'd go there together.

With no path the scrambling was hard, branches blocked him, pointed stones stabbed his feet. He put his shoes back on. Away from the water he pushed downstream through bushes and stunted trees. The skin on his bare arms poured sweat, on his face too. Mosquitoes and blackflies swarmed. He got back to the stream at an open space below a curving run with high wet stone walls, daisies, some wild strawberry blooms, tall grass. Not much water coming down. The flies settled on him where sweat had washed the repellent off. Low to the ground he worked his way back, uphill through thick brush to the top of the run where the wet walls started. He broke out onto a muddy bank.

He'd never been here before. Wide, very shallow water. Then he saw why: the stream divided. In front of him, broad slow water. On the far side, a cut in the rock and an opening into the hill. Half the water disappeared over there. He took his shoes off again. He waded to the other side. A kind of cave, half the water flowed into it. He sat on a rocky ledge at the opening. The right side looked wider.

He followed the ledge, slow, a few feet. His eyes got used to the dark, lots of light from behind, dim shapes ahead. The water flowed in near silence. The ledge petered out at a curve in the flow. He stepped into the water, sometimes you have to take the risk. Plenty of light. The bottom was a bit slimy. He slipped, and sat, didn't matter, his shorts were soaking anyway. Far ahead he heard a thin roar. On his hands and buttocks he inched his way forward. Suddenly a dip in the rock, like a slide at a playground. He grabbed out, much darker now, he slid slowly.

Stop! His own throat's whisper, soft as blackfly murmur. Stop! Back out!

The water ran in silence, the rock slimy-smooth. No!

No! Echo of his dad's voice, Grab out! The granite!

Benjie jerked his arm out, his fingers scratched at rock—

Graaaaaab!

In hard water he coasted across smooth flat slippery stone, nothing left for grabbing at, and the clutching surge of water slid him on.

"Daddy!"

Grab! Hold!

He rode the dark slide, on, nowhere to scramble. Spilling water brought him to the lip, over the lip, down, he rode the water down, all the while screaming, "Daddy! Daddy!! Daddy—"

No one heard.

o

Lola's eyes brimmed over. Their greens and purples swam together, their underwater sparkle speared into my heart. "I shouldn't have—been so explicit."

"I had to know." Her head shook. "Is there more?"

"There will be—" Suddenly nothing made sense. A God, in tears? And with feeling? How much I had taken for granted about the Gods? Or maybe just about Lola? "Should I—go on?"

"Of course!" Her smile seemed forced. "You have to."

Now in her eyes, the brilliant sparkle back in place. Had I really seen tears? "I'll try."

Six

CONNECTING UP

1.

John Cochan trusted few men. He trusted Yakahama Stevenson most, Terramac's vp Planning, Yak his closest friend. He trusted Aristide Boce, vp Financial, much of the time.

Johnnie spoke with Yak about everything, or nearly. Even about Priscilla, how she got down into his skin with her smart dreadful sanity about Benjie. Or how sometimes she went far away, as she never did before Benjie— How, she demanded, could Johnnie blame himself that Benjie was gone, or blame her? Often Yak had to talk Johnnie down.

Half a year back, in early summer on that worst of days, after Dee returned to say Benjie left the stream and hadn't come back, after Priscilla couldn't find Benjie anywhere, after she phoned Johnnie in Lexington, after he spoke to her in shell-control calm, Call the Sheriff, Get-him-now, after Johnnie arrived back and after the search party with the dogs found the sneakers and then the drowned body down in the little cavern fifteen feet below the lip, Yak sat with Johnnie in the farmhouse, drank bottomless gin with Johnnie all the black hours through, listened as Johnnie moaned, shrieked, held Johnnie while he gasped for air, while he vomited, huge heaves, his heart crashing against his ribs. Twice Yak slapped Johnnie's face to keep him from self-injury. The whole time he sat by Johnnie, two men floating in half sleep.

Priscilla too had wept, in her privacy, with her daughters.

All work at Terramac halted. Yak pleaded with Johnnie, Begin again. Pragmatic arguments: We've invested in the community, we've promised Merrimac County. Arguments from finance: We've borrowed too much, Johnnie, we have to produce. Arguments about dreams: Johnnie, this is the city of tomorrow, your city of marvels.

Priscilla cried softly. She too held Johnnie. No one held her.

In the end, Johnnie emerged from his anguish. Yes, they would go on. Terramac, Ben's shrine. Johnnie told Yak, You brought me through.

They began again, blasting and clearing and flattening, elevating, broadening. The tunnelling too began now. Here Terramac would soon rise, and later descend. At last, one perfect human habitat. Once again John Cochan had returned.

o

"Maybe," said Lola.

Best just to go on.

o

2.

The picture on the postcard showed a snow-covered mountain, pristine against a flat blue sky. Carney turned it over and reread the whole message:

> *A Ton of Cure* is a wonderful book, C.C. You should be
> pleased and proud. I thought it was finely insightful,
> and scary enough to maybe make people stop and think
> a little before acting and destroying. Congratulations.

The signature said Julie. No return address. Not even the mountain had a name, only Coastal Range, British Columbia.

How could he find her? What for? Just—to see her? Just to apologize yet again for lying about the application? Just to talk to her again. No, it had to be more than that. He'd loved her once, his first real love.

He returned to the office, sat on his large captain's chair, and Googled for Julie Robertson. He found her as vice-president of Action Entertainment in London, as manager of secretarial systems for T. Hutch and Company in Houston, as an occupational therapist in Raleigh. A hundred Julie Robertsons. He narrowed his search: Julie Robertson British Columbia. No Julie Robertson to be found there.

He put on a jacket against the February wind, and loped over to Madeline Staunton's barn office. "I need help."

"You usually do. What now?"

"I need you to find someone."

"Who?"

"Her name's Julie Robertson and I don't have any idea where she is."

"You know her?"

"I did."

"When? Where?"

"A long time ago." He thought. "Just over thirty years ago."

Madeline Staunton sniffed. "Old girlfriend?"

Carney grinned. "About as old as me." He explained about the postcard and handed it to Mrs. Staunton. "I'd like to know what she's done for the last thirty years."

"Where'd you last see her?"

"Where we lived. Median, over in New Hampshire."

"What do you know about her?"

Carney told Mrs. Staunton everything he could remember.

"I'll see what I can do."

Back in his office Carney sat on a stool and played his cello. More and more cello playing these days, less and less time resolving disasters. In the last couple of years he'd been on the road lecturing, then publicizing his book. He'd had letters about the book, two dozen or so, mostly from fans, a couple from the crazies. Where had Julie found the book? Strange, writing a book and making a reconnection after three decades. Madeline Staunton would track Julie down.

But two weeks later Mrs. Staunton conceded failure. Median had led her nowhere, Julie's parents long dead, no trace of their daughter there either. Middlebury College too had lost track of her, last known address a small town in South Dakota but she was gone from there as well. Still Mrs. Staunton had written to all the Julie Robertsons she had located on the Internet. None who answered admitted to being Carney's, Median's, Middlebury's Julie. Possibly her name was no longer Robertson. In which case, end of the line. Disappeared. Except for a single postcard.

Over a beer with Charlie Dart, Carney said, "Remember Julie? Julie Robertson?"

"Julie. You saved her from that guy. On the skinny side. You and her were some item."

"She wrote me. About the book."

Charlie grinned. "Yeah?"

"I want to find out about her."

"Write her back."

Carney explained; the card, the search. "I want to see her again. I think I need to see her."

"All these years, you still think about her?"

After a couple of seconds, he said, "Yeah."

"So?"

"Charlie, when you worked for that insurance company, you tracked people down."

"Sometimes."

"Think you could find her?"

"Might take a while."

"Would you try?"

o

"Will he? Find her?"

"We'll have to wait and see."

"Okay." Lola lay back on a cloud. "Ted? Anything new happening yet? Down there?"

I had the sense of rustlings in Richmond, at Terramac. But nothing cohesive yet. "All pretty quiet still."

Slowly I said, "You bored with the past?"

"Nope." She closed her eyes and waited for me to continue.

u

3.

Priscilla Cochan returned aglow from Burlington. A soft day in early spring, the late afternoon of a fine fine day, her world spinning right. She loved Johnnie as of old, she loved the baby, Melissa, and her older daughter, Deirdre, and she loved the new growing tiny being inside her. She had ached with love for her lost boy, Benjamin, an ache blessedly weakened with the passing months, an ache she knew would never disappear.

She'd married Johnnie young and Benjie had come soon. Johnnie's genius and his hope had excited her. It taught her that vision, once dreamed, could become a solid thing, tactile, working in the world. Johnnie would build consequential pieces of the future, and she'd walk by his side. She left her life in Boston, family and friends, shops, libraries, museums, to come to Merrimac County at the top of Vermont, Johnnie's adopted community. To build a city! No foundation-financed experiment here, not like that Biosphere Two place out in Arizona. This would be a city for human beings to live in. Johnnie's kind of people. Her heart was large enough for two, for four, for much much love. Would she tell Johnnie now, immediately? Or wait for the perfect moment.

When Johnnie came home she was lying in their big deep tub near-covered with bubbles, soaking away the day's sweat and smell. "Hi," she called. Tell him from the bath?

He opened the door and stared at her. "Hi."

She saw him frown. "You all right?"

"Sure. 'Cept I've got another meeting. Why?"

She smiled, careful. "Well, you're early and—"

"I'm fine. What's up?"

"I don't know. You seem— Nothing, I guess." She felt a chill down her back whisper, sink deeper. "I thought maybe, because you're already home—"

"No, just a lot of little things."

"Good." The foamy soap hid most of her body. Except for her head, the red hair soaked flat. A hint of brown where her nipples showed through dying bubbles. Her crimson toenails down by the faucets. The idea came to her, she was hiding herself. He couldn't see her belly, not even a hint of new bleep curve rising above the water. "Nothing serious then."

"Nothing that can't be dealt with."

She smiled up at him.

"I'll be back late, probably."

"Bye." He disappeared beyond the bathroom door. She raised herself on an elbow, her shoulder in the air. She waited, heard the front door slam. She reached for a plastic bottle, poured in some green cream, ran hot water over it. More bubbles. All of her covered now.

Priscilla Ayer Cochan, after her examination, felt prickly still from Johnnie's glance. Today, this morning and afternoon, she had had several gynecological explorations, one medical, the other two consummately more pleasant.

She'd driven over to Burlington in air-conditioned calm to her doctor, Rachel Ryan, who'd taken her first thing in the morning.

180

Congrats, Pris, you're pregnant again. A few tests, routine, come in next Wednesday? Which left her the rest of the day. For visiting her friend Tina; like she did every Wednesday, right? But Tina was in England. Well, for herself then. She drove to his house, where he'd be waiting as he did each Wednesday.

"Priscilla, you look beautiful."

"I feel beautiful." She smiled, for herself and for him.

They excited each other merely by looking, eyes meeting, holding, drawing closer. The power of his first touch, gentle as breath, shocked her again. A contact of lips and no return. They usually made love first so they could make love again later.

They'd met a few months ago at a crowded restaurant, chance, waiting to be seated. Priscilla's friend Tina wasn't available. Priscilla would treat herself to lunch. Only a table for two explained the hostess, nothing for half an hour, if they wanted they could share it?

Go ahead, Priscilla, she heard her fancy say. Share with him.

Okay, she'd share.

She told him she sometimes came to Burlington for the day, her husband was very busy, the nanny stayed with their children. He told her he liked eating by himself. No, he'd never been married. She said she grew up near Copley Square, she missed Boston, her husband's business kept them up here. He said he liked big cities but felt at home in small towns too, and he liked Burlington. They talked into the middle of the afternoon. The restaurant was empty. The hostess hoped they'd not minded being thrown together so. They asked for separate checks. He walked her to her car, he said, "Would you like—?" just as she said, "Do you think—?"

They did. It went from there. She conceded to herself at their second lunch, the pull was magnetic. The fourth lunch, he invited her to his home. They stood by the window high on a hillside overlooking Lake Champlain. She had known what would happen, craved it. When he slid his arm around her, so easy, a friend's gesture, first physical contact— how careful they'd been not to touch, not even when he helped her with her coat—they knew they had only to turn to each other.

It proved exquisite, this love grown from happenstance, a gentleness she hadn't known since before Benjie's birth. For him a return to hope in the present. He'd not meant to fall in love with her, not with anyone. But it happened.

Her love for Johnnie changed, became an older, more solid thing, a sense of happiness achieved. It decreased not at all in loving this other man. She had long been dazzled by Johnnie, his power and his ease. She had come to love his passion for Terramac, his devotion, loved him now with a fully fitting love. This new plenitude of love, in Burlington and in week-long memory, went on, wondrous. She loved them both.

Her baby, who the father? She didn't know. And, allowing the question, saw she didn't care. Ben had been born dark-haired, Melissa still blond, Deirdre red. Would he, this gentle luncheon partner, Wednesday partner, insist on rights to the baby, should it look like him?

"I have to tell you something," she said.

"Anything you like," he said.

"I'm pregnant."

He smiled, a moment of delight, then caught himself. "And—you want to be?"

She nodded. "Very much."

He embraced her. "Now, do you know—"

"No. And I don't want to." She held him tight. "Do you?"

He laughed. If she needed help for the child, he'd be there, whoever the father. He had no problems about paternity. A good woman, then another, had wanted his contribution to conceive a child. Two had come into the world by him, two girl babies. He cared for them deeply. They liked him too, often spent hours or days with him. Lots of ways to care for people without owning them, and he planned to be close to the girls over the years. As the children and their mothers wanted.

Priscilla loved Melissa and Dee mightily and wanted this baby wherever it came from. She'd had asked him should they take precautions. If she wanted to. No. Good.

Inside her the new one floated, grew, multiplied in its cells, under layers of womb and sinew, under bubbles. What had Johnnie seen beneath the bubbles, inside the stretching skin?

o

"Well," said Lola. "You going to tell me?"

"What?"

She sat beside me on my pillow of cloud. "Who's the lover?"

"Guess."

"I can't." She leaned toward me. So languid, she brushed aside my pages of notes. "You'll tell me right now."

I said, "Karl Magnussen."

"Sarah and Leonora's brother?"

"Him."

"Wowee!" She reached out, she touched her naked finger to my mouth, my nose. With her palm, bare and warm, she grazed my cheek.

I couldn't help myself. I kissed her fingertips.

A tiny smile.

My heart, such as it is, pounded. "Lola. Listen. We aren't supposed to feel."

"Yes, the rules. Who wrote them down? You ever read the rule-books? Do they exist?"

"Lola. The passions die, and so on. It isn't possible."

"I didn't think so either."

"And now?" I felt a stirring as I'd not since my last days on earth.

She grinned. "I'm feeling kinda—alive."

"Yeah." I laughed.

"Their dreams," she said. "The secrets they're hiding. I want to know. All of it. It's almost like—like my heart was pumping my blood around again." She stood, she smoothed her loose gown. Such noble curves at shoulder, bosom, waist, and bum, such graceful legs! "I need to hear everything you know." She settled by my side.

"From right now on," I whispered, "I'm never telling any story, except for you."

She waited, then asked, "What happens next?"

○

4.

The Terramac report Carney had given Theresa Magnussen had so displeased her, in the end he too was dissatisfied with it. So he'd needed all effort this afternoon even to open the cello case. The telephone rang, his line, not the one buffered by Mrs. Staunton; he'd told her to hold off all calls. He let it ring. The machine cut in.

Charlie Dart. Last week Carney had spent two days with Charlie, the debriefing on the K'wan Seah mess. Charlie was supposed to be off on a toot.

Charlie was saying, "Come on, I know you're there. I've got some Julie info for you."

Carney stared at the phone.

"Okay, never mind. I'm coming over. Do not leave. You hear me?"

Carney reached for the phone but the line had gone dead.

No chance getting his mind around to the cello. Charlie lived an hour away. Carney poured a Scotch and added a lot of water. He started a fire. By the time Charlie arrived the blaze had warmed the room to friendly.

"Scotch? Sure." They sat by the fire.

Carney said, "So?"

"So you don't like to pick up your telephone?"

"You cut off too soon. What about Julie?"

"A guy I know, he tracked her down. He called me, told me. So I came back. I had to check her out before telling you anything."

"Okay. Tell me now."

"Well, it took a while. He started out in British Columbia and South Dakota. Nothing."

"We knew that."

"So he went back to the starting point. New Hampshire. Median."

"Mrs. Staunton tried there. Nothing."

"No, but maybe nearby? Concord, Nashua, Manchester. And there she was. Is."

Carney leaned toward Charlie. "You saw her? You met her?"

Charlie nodded. "We talked about old times."

"Is she okay? Is she married? Kids?" He considered, and frowned. "A grandmother?"

"She was married, it didn't last. Three years. South Dakota was a teaching job. She quit after eleven years. She came back to the east."

"Kept her name? Her ex-husband's?"

"Hers."

"Well how's she look? Sound?"

"Carney, don't get weird. It's been more than thirty years, right?"

"Okay. You tell me."

"Two things. She's older, we all are. Still wears her hair long. Like you liked it."

"Like she liked it, mainly."

"And her health's not good. Rheumatoid arthritis. Lots of it. All over."

"Oh god, poor Julie. What's her phone number? Her address—"

Charlie's head was shaking. "She doesn't want to see you. The only way she'd see me was if I promised not to tell you how to reach her."

"Okay, keep your promise. If she's in Manchester I can find her."

"Maybe you can. My guy did. It wasn't easy. But Carney? Don't try."

"But I want to talk to her."

"You'll have to find her yourself."

"Goddammit, Charlie! I was the one who got you to find her. For me!"

"And I made a promise to her. No phone. No address."

Carney downed the last of his watery Scotch. He got up, poured a large one, no water, swallowed half of it. He sat and glared at Charlie. "Where's your sense of loyalty?"

"All over the place, as you can see. You going to offer me more Scotch?"

"Get it yourself."

Charlie did.

Carney leaned toward the fire, staring into the flames. "Okay, keep your promises. You have her address, right?"

"Yep."

"Did you promise you wouldn't write her?"

"No. But why would I write her?"

"Not you, stupid. Me. I write her, I give you the letter, you mail it for me. No broken promises. You tell her the truth, that I don't know her address."

Charlie shrugged. "I can do that."

From eight till eleven Carney wrote Julie, numerous versions.

Dear Julie, I want to see you again, talk to you. I've thought about you so often since we were together so many years ago, and I—

Wrong. Why would she care? More Scotch.

Dear Julie, I've done a lot of foolish things in my life but the stupidest ever was lying to you about—

He'd told her that decades ago. More Scotch.

Dear Julie, I loved you once, you know. And maybe I still do. I've been with three major women in my life, a few others too, and each seemed right for a while, and—

He pulled himself away from the computer, sat on his bed, lay down and fell asleep. In the late morning he wrote:

Dear Julie, I would like to see you again. I know you told Charlie you didn't want to see me, but in all fairness you are not the only one who has to make that decision. Please, Julie. Just one meeting. C.C.

He drove to Charlie's and gave him the letter. "Special Delivery, okay?" He waited a couple of days, four days. On the fifth day a letter to Charlie: No, Charlie. Tell him to stop.

Okay, she wouldn't see him. Damn her. He didn't need to see her either.

PROTECTIVE COLORATION

Movement. Silence.
Taste shape size.

a.)
Wings orange-brown, cross-hatched in black.
Look! It's golden as it flies
to milkweed by the bank.
A monarch. She drops her eggs.

The eggs mature, hatch—
Watch. A thousand rubber legs.
Caterpillars glide across
the milkweed's latex blood.

They drink it in: digitalis.
Poison for the human heart, a flood
of death. Not for the caterpillars.
Each weaves itself to pupa-size,
a chrysalis. Wait. Soon again, a monarch.

For finches, swallows, jays,
it's fine to feast on butterflies.
But not the monarch, right? Monarchs
bring on spasm, retching, cramps.

b.)
The viceroy's wings are orange, black and gold.
Its caterpillar never samples milkweed.
Oh wonderful disguise unbeaten:
the viceroy flits away uneaten.

RF (February 6/03)

5.

At five-fifteen Deirdre Cochan in her jeans and three-bears T-shirt arrived at Intraterra North. She ran along the central passage to her father's office at the end and burst through his door. "Time to come home, Daddy!"

He looked at her, abstracted. Was it that warm out, she didn't need a jacket? She had Benjie's nose. But not his hair, she had her mother's hair, that flaming red. Her chin wasn't Benjie's either, his had been broad, hers rounded away. "Just a few minutes, Dee."

"Can I use Steed's computer?"

"You know how to turn it on?"

She glanced at her father as if he didn't understand anything at all. "Sure." Steed himself had shown her. She strode into Steed's office, the twin of Johnnie's on the other side of the chancel, Deirdre proprietorial here as if the office were her own.

He packed two files into his case. His fingers felt puffy. She'd want to take his hand when they walked home. He joined her at Steed's computer.

She was playing with a program that made colored patterns. "Daddy! Watch this." The supermouse sent blues, greens, blacks, reds slashing into each other, a chaos of design

"Very nice, Dee." But—not wonderful. Not like Benjie's sketches.

They walked in the cool air the three blocks home, not holding hands.

In the living room Priscilla poured him a martini. He sipped. "Good."

"Daddy, we bought marbles today. Swirlies. Want to see 'em?" Deirdre pulled his elbow.

"Careful, my drink." He stroked her hair with his free hand.

"Deirdre sorted them out." Priscilla smiled at her. "Into bags."

"All by myself. Even while Mummy was away."

"By yourself? Wasn't Diana here?"

"Yes, Mr. Cochan, I—"

"I mean with Diana, Daddy. Diana's always here."

"Good. Good." He glanced at Priscilla, and looked away.

"Come on, let's have supper." Priscilla took his hand and Deirdre's, and led them to the dining room. Diana followed, fussing with Melissa, who was a year or two off from staying the course of a meal. Still the table was set, linen and silver, for five.

Diana put Melissa to bed before dessert, Deirdre after.

Deirdre, after her bath, after being read to, after the goodnight kisses, lay awake for a long time. It didn't feel good here. Her chest of drawers was in the wrong place. Her doll house wasn't in her bedroom but in the playroom two doors down the hall. She'd not had a playroom at the farmhouse, she and Benjie played in her room, or his. Benjie's new room here was between hers and the playroom. Mummy said not to go in Benjie's room. Just his things were in it. Mummy said Benjie had gone away, they had to forget Benjie. Benjie hadn't gone away. She knew where Benjie had gone. If Benjie had gone away he might come back. But Benjie wouldn't ever come back. Except, sometimes, when she was asleep. Tonight she would not go to sleep.

She drifted, drifted. She groaned and turned over.

Diana in the room across the hall pulled her curtains tight against the clear starry sky. Melissa's wheezy snoring sifted through a thin door to the connecting nursery. So tiny, such loud snoring. Diana rarely heard Deirdre groan. Sometimes Deirdre whimpered in her sleep. Diana didn't hear this either. She had preferred the farmhouse. This new place was too big.

After dinner, willing the minutes to pass till he could go back to Terramac, Johnnie had sat with Priscilla on the couch. He told Priscilla the Luciflex report was in, and good. Usually she enjoyed these details. Today she seemed distant. He supposed he might be seen that way too, by her. They sat silent for a while.

She lay her head against his arm. "I have some news too."

"Hmmm?"

"We're having a baby again."

For a long time he said nothing. Then he turned, and kissed her temple. "Good." He raised his arm, put it across her shoulder. He stared at the dead fireplace. "When's it due?"

"Early January." She drew into his side and touched her stomach. "This afternoon, for a second or two, I think I felt him."

"It's still too early." He spoke to the room, into shadows. "It's too small."

"The place where he is." She took his hand. "Want to feel it?"

"What?"

"The space." She took his hand, guided it to her lap.

He let it lie there. It angered him, yes, anger, this baroque calm she released. It spun a web of silver cool about her, a flimsy mood. Was she like this inside herself? What kind of fetus would grow in the space she provided?

This new reticence of Johnnie's. Long ago when his hand lay on her skin she felt her heart spin wildly, precarious on its axis. But since he'd started building Terramac again, it was his unreachable balance that crept into her flesh. Long ago she'd learned to locate the quiet sites within her. But these days the little withdrawals from him were a relief. Why ease closer when nearness brought so little contact?

After they'd found Ben and brought him to the funeral home there'd been arguments, even then: what kind of coffin, what part of the cemetery. Or maybe cremation, she couldn't bear the thought of Benjie's skin and little nose and ears and mouth in the ground, the ground squeezing into him. And Johnnie's days of anguish, his drinking. The bottomless nightmares. She held hers in, listened to his dreadful black howls and the sobbing, tried to comfort. Enough. A time gone by. She'd done all she could. For Johnnie and for Benjie too. Now inside her the new one floated, grew, multiplied its cells; under layers of flesh and womb.

o

I raised my head. Lola, watching me. A nod, that I should continue.

o

6.

Bobbie glanced across her desk and down from her bedroom window. Carney's car had not appeared in her drive. She adored her nephew but this was inconsiderate of him. Since Ricardo's death she'd felt alone too much of the time. Her bones ached. Getting tired at five in the afternoon. Getting old. Go to bed early, read a little.

Downstairs a door opened, and then slammed shut. Carney called her name. She pulled the shawl around her shoulders and headed to the stairs. "How'd you get here?" Then she saw the sneakers he was taking off.

He grinned up. "Jogged over."

Nine miles. That boy had too much energy. Oughta have a woman. Needed to find one and stay with her. That Lynn, Bobbie had liked her a lot. Marcie too. Bobbie walked down the stairs, her right hip tight today. "What's your need? Coffee? A drink."

He nodded. "I will have, like you, a whisky. Then I'm taking you to supper at The Bosworth Inn. You're driving."

"What're we celebrating?"

He considered that. "The fact that lots of people are more screwed up than we are."

"In that case I'm ordering a really good wine." She felt a dozen years drop from her back.

They sat in her living room in front of the fire. The sun slid behind the black trees on the hill across the way, backlighting bare branches already tinged running-sap red. Sipping Bobbie's smoky Laphroig, Carney told her about going out to Terramac field headquarters, then reporting to Theresa Magnussen. "She's mighty disappointed in me. And ready to bring in the howitzers."

"How bad is this Terramac?"

"For starters, it was covered in snow. On paper and under its white blanket, not godawful. As developments go. Cochan seems to know what he's doing and that's way up on most."

"He the one built that Hudson Valley complex down south of Albany? That Terra-something group?"

"Intraterra. I think so, yeah."

"And what's so special about this place?"

"Mostly that it's going to be all enclosed. I had a talk with a fellow named Boce, one of Cochan's vice-presidents. Cochan wasn't around. Terramac City is Intraterra in Merrimac County, right? And the place where people will live he calls Summerclime. That's because it's like summer year-round."

"Here? Northern Vermont?"

"Yep. The whole thing'll be covered with clear connected domes, triple-glazed and polarized. Complete with micron-thin heating wire to melt snow, and troughs for water to run off into huge cisterns, with overflow into the stream."

"What do you mean, domes?"

"Just that. From what I understood, some as big as a quarter mile in diameter, over public spaces like the golf course and the central square."

"A covered golf course?"

"That's what he's planning. Covered houses and apartments. And domed public spaces where flowers and even palms can grow all year round. Domes over restaurants and walkways."

"Why?"

Carney shrugged. "They've done their market research. Enough people with real money want to live there."

Bobbie shook her head. "Imagine that. Little Johnnie Cochan."

"What?"

"Your Cochan." She sniffed a laugh. "I knew his mother."

"Oh?" Carney wasn't surprised. She knew lots people. And for those she didn't know she knew someone who knew them. Even more people knew Bobbie. Over forty years her poetry hadn't made her much money but it won prizes and got her around. "When was that?"

"Back in college. Mount Holyoke. We were roommates for a year."

"Friends?"

"The way one is. She was smart. I mean, really smart." Bobbie shrugged. "Badly balanced. She died young. Booze, lots of booze." A small shiver. "She had no real friends."

"Well, she has herself one powerful son."

Bobbie nodded. "She married his powerful father."

"That helps."

"She worked for the corporation his father owned, pharmaceuticals. Elizabeth Shapiro. A scientist when few women went into science, not into the kind of science where you make it big. Libby, she called herself." Bobbie pictured the pretty face. "Then at Cochan's lab she changed it to Beth. The sort of woman who envies other women's successes. Libby Shapiro, Beth Cochan."

"What was she, a chemist? Biologist?"

"Biochemist." Bobbie sipped her whisky. Libby, a woman fully committed to her work. The work killed her. Does full commitment kill you? Hadn't killed Bobbie. Not yet. "Didn't see her for ten years, then we ran into each other again. In Montreal. She drove down to see me once. Her work then was early gene stuff, mutating life-forms."

Carney swirled the liquid in his glass. "Heavy duty."

"Experiments like few women before her could dream of doing. And to get the kind of lab space she'd need she set out to seduce Joe Cochan, the boss. She was clever. Joe thought he was the luckiest man alive, in love with, then married to, wonderful Beth. A non-stop spurt of love, she told me he described it as. When John was born, Libby figured what with the baby she was bound to Joe forever, and Joe to her work, and the work to her near-certain fame."

"A fun arrangement."

"Like most marriages." Only a touch of irony.

"Sure." He sipped. "But you and Ricardo, that worked."

His name spoken aloud still warmed her. "We weren't married."

"More married than many." Carney chuckled.

"Yeah," she said. "More."

Carney let her silence, her glance out the window, be his signal. "Come on. Let's go eat."

In the car he said, "I heard from Julie."

Bobbie turned to him. No sense of his face. "Julie? From when you were in high school?"

"That Julie."

"And?"

Carney told her about the postcard, trying to track her down, Julie's refusal of contact.

"And you still want to see her."

"I did. I don't now."

"Because?"

"I'm not going to beg."

Bobbie nodded silently. Carney had talked of Julie occasionally. Bobbie hadn't taken the talk seriously: a vague sense of a long-time-ago girlfriend. Everybody has little stings of memory. Except maybe Carney's of Julie played a bigger role in his life than she'd imagined.

Julie as context for his broken relationships with women? Maybe. "I think you should see her."

"I don't even know how to find her."

"You'll figure it out."

"Anyway, why? Why bother?"

Bobbie considered the question. "Because she wrote you. Our of nowhere. She wanted you to know she was still out there."

"Then why won't she tell me where she is?"

Because she's afraid to see you? Because she's afraid of you seeing her? Because her life has gone in one direction and she doesn't want even a glimpse of how it might have been otherwise? "I don't know," said Bobbie, "but you should try to find out."

"Again, why?"

"Because if you don't, you'll spend the rest of your life wondering about her."

"Something wrong with that?"

"I'll leave that for you to answer."

Arriving at the Inn ended the conversation. Over dinner Carney showed her the full-color brochure, *Terramac, City of Tomorrow.* She read aloud the smarmiest phrases: "An apotheosis of the world-wide quest for utopia as domicile." "An available human frontier, still affordable at pre-completion prices." "Peerless planning today for your many tomorrows." She chuckled. "Look, I can apply through select realtors in Los Angeles, Chicago, New York, Toronto. Or by visiting the website, like any mote in the rabble."

"And you get a chance to spend from $3.2 to $10.5 million," said Carney. "The former for a bachelor pad, the latter for a five-bedroom unit."

"I'll take one of each."

"Domes cost, I guess. But not all that pricey when compared with Hong Kong or London."

"Northern Vermont as Hong Kong." She read, and checked out the photos. "The amenities of Terramac, it says here." Sixteen pages of gloss. She read aloud, "'Indoor/outdoor living 365 days a year, lavish malls in neighborhoods of delightful professionals, synoptics of the excellent life: total security for enjoying the best in human company, spacious abodes, fine foods, wines, films, music.'" She sipped her St.-Julien. "'With Intraterra's own electronic delivery system via France's Septum II satellite, full penetration of world commerce, instant communication with family and friends. Twenty-second-century happiness available here and now.'" She glanced across the table. "Just for you, Carney."

"Built from the top down, not my kind of thing. But I do admit the man has imagination."

"Sounds like that place in Arizona."

"Actually the fellow I was talking with, Boce, he mentioned that. Don't confuse Terramac with that failed Biosphere project, he said. Terramac isn't going to be hermetically sealed, not tight in the way that place was. They're not growing their own food or trees or keeping animals, that was all nonsense he said. Their vegetation'll be like those high oxygen-producing flowering vines, those did prove successful in Arizona. No experiments with different ecosystems either. All the advantages, orderly and sanitary, electronically controlled and with easy transport to the lesser world outside. That was his phrase, the lesser world."

"For us lesser folk."

"Yeah, I know. But I will say, I've seen some pretty screwy places. And some damn destructive ones. From what I can tell, this Terramac isn't the worst, by far not."

"He impressed you."

"That's too strong." Carney smiled. "Said he knew my work. Which meant he'd heard of but not read *A Ton*. Actually there wasn't much to see, with all the snow. Streets are in place, some frames going up. The big push comes this summer."

"In what used to be forest land, I read."

Carney shrugged. "He's not exactly clear-cutting. Mostly it was logged over long ago. Scrub. Look"—as Bobbie's right eyebrow rose— "I'd prefer he left it like it was. But they've done their impact studies and they're probably on solid ground."

"How solid?"

Carney considered this, again now. Leaving the Terramac site he realized nothing of Mot, his friendly seventh sense. Friend Mot, since the dream about Julie, had been helpful: something wrong here, something dangerous and unjust about to happen there. He usually had come to heed Mot. Sometimes he felt Mot tapping away in the belly, or behind the eyes. Should peril or villainy lie around the corner, Mot cries: Avoid! But while speaking with Boce about Terramac, Mot hadn't insinuated himself. "Adequately solid."

"And you said all this to your client."

Carney laughed. "Not the report Theresa Magnussen wanted, bet on it. But I can't see a way of stopping Terramac." He shook his head. "I disappointed her. She didn't like me saying there's lots of way worse places around."

Bobbie poured them the last of the Burgundy. "Hope she paid you well."

He shook his head. "I didn't charge her. It was a kind of relief, for once being able to say a project didn't look like a disaster in the making."

Bobbie realized she felt content being here with Carney, not at home reading her book. He'd smothered her loneliness. For now. "And the freebie appeased Dr. Magnussen?"

"Nope. She blasted a hellfire sermon at me. I was an ecological Benedict Arnold. Did Cochan buy me off with so much I could refuse her money? Ten minutes' worth. I asked if she had any proof of something truly evil or destructive going on out there. If she did I'd come back and re-evaluate. Evil's her way of thinking, she even used the word. She was still furious when I left." Despite all that, Carney realized, he'd enjoyed Dr. Magnussen's sense of her place in the world.

"So that's over and done, is it?"

"Yep." Except, he admitted, an itch back in his mind. Should've spoken with Cochan personally, Carney.

○

"Hey!" Lola jumped up, all vigor and verve. "What're you doing!"

She's glorious when animated. "I beg your pardon?"

"Carney. You prompting him?"

"I? Never." A weird accusation. "He does what he wants."

"I heard you." She sat beside me. "You're steering him."

"He's just looking at what's out there. Exploring, right?"

"You're making him think—think in other ways." She knelt at my feet. "Maybe that's okay." She thought. "Is it?"

"Hardly, Lola."

After a moment she shifted. "I like Bobbie."

"Good."

"And she's your sister-in-law."

I rarely think of her that way. She's my wife's younger sister and, more important, the woman who raised my son. My gratitude to her is eternal. But I never knew her well. She'd always seemed distant, or maybe just shy, when we were together. "Yes," I said.

She slanted her head. "Did you approve of Ricardo?"

"She took up with him long after I AAed."

"You didn't watch her?"

She was teasing me, I knew. But making me edgy. "I don't spy. Not even Carney. Haven't for years. I only know what I know because you wanted me to find a story for you."

Lola smiled, soft as a dream. "But when you watch, you steer." She lay her forearm on my thigh and set her chin on it. She looked up at me, so serious. "Can I learn to do that?"

"What?" Such splendid lips—

"Steer."

I brought my face to hers. I touched her hair. I let myself speak dangerous words. "It may look as if I play a tiny role, but I never would. If in the down below there's one prepared to hear, he might come to understand things better."

"Yeah?"

"He could, say, find new insight, or ask a question. What gets done with it—" I shrugged.

"Insight." She considered this. "Like perspective?"

"Mortal hubris calls it wisdom."

"And we're the ones can make this happen?"

Careful not to sound paternal, I smiled. "They do it to themselves, Lola. Some have the talent. It's often long and keenly honed. For a man or a woman to be pierced with insight from so far away— I once could do that in the down below." I paused. "It may be how I got here."

"Yeah? And me?"

Again that question. "Lola. You touched their lives. With your beauty, and how you made them laugh. As well, you let them see you vulnerable."

"Vulnerable?" She chuckled. "You mean, exposed? Like my bazoomas?"

I took her hand. "In lots of ways, Lola. You were one with them. They loved you. You gave them hope."

"And that's all over now."

"Lola, you're a God." I shook my head. I stroked her hair. Perfection. "We're separated off from there."

"But you're still toying with them."

"Lola. Listen to me. I watch, describe, I tell you stories. But steering, as you call it, that's impossible, and against all rules. And if it were possible it'd be extremely dangerous. A little steering from up here— I can't imagine the consequences." I let my words hang.

She raised her eyes and searched my face, as mortals might. Her head shook, a delicate sway, silent.

I leaned to her, let my fingers lie against her cheek.

She bent, held my head, brought her radiant face to mine. She kissed my lips.

I shivered deep inside, like the luckiest of living men. How could this happen? The rules we each accept without a thought are clear enough: up here the flesh and all its foolishness is gone. But what do I know of rules? Or for that matter, of what Immortals can and cannot feel?

From far off, a call: "Lola! Sweet Lola!"

I pulled away.

She said, "It's Edsel."

I scampered up to re-aright my mind. I grabbed the top sheet in my Roberta Feyerlicht file—"Water"—and handed it to Lola. "Here. One of Bobbie's new poems. Make like I've been telling you about them for the last hour. Read fast."

In the near distance we saw the God Edsel, glowing so brightly he looked like he'd been super-simonized. Lola read quickly:

WATER

Water into rock. Deep channels, narrow.
Cold, cutting, relentless.
Harsh water. New sediment. A strange chemistry.
The stuff of other worlds, their wounds.
Sepsis.

A trickle, a flash, a maelstrom.
Decades, centuries. Why now?

Water.
A lost friend.
Spread. Flood.

Roberta Feyerlicht
(January 21–23/03)

"Hello HELLO!" Edsel boomed. "Darling Lola!"

His retinue followed, Gods more powerful or popular where they'd come from in life than Edsel ever was. But up here they were admirers, the God Helen, the God Ludwig, the God Christopher, the God George. How to understand the delight they took in their present sycophancy? I didn't care. Except for Lola's sake.

"Hello," said Lola.

He beamed his joy at her. "You disappear so frequently, my dear!"

"I've been taking my pleasure in a whole lot of places." Beside him she radiated.

"But not enough of it with us!" How jolly he sounded, how pleased to be telling her how naughty she'd been.

"Oh, enough." The pleasure of not knowing what awaited her trilled from her voice.

"By actual count"—and with elation Edsel drew from his great dazzling deep-green cloak a piece of flattened misty parchment—"in present time and space just under forty-five percent!"

The God Helen took Lola by her right elbow. "We love the pleasure of your company!"

The God Christopher took Lola by her left elbow. "We love the pleasure of your form!"

"Come 'long! Come 'long!" sang Edsel. He didn't mean me. And the retinue swept Lola away. She turned once, and her glance was full of, what? the delight of fear?

PART II

THE PRESENT

2003

Seven
THE GRANGE AND THE STREAM

Damn! Pieces of the story at last coming together and Lola's not here.

○

1.

On a grim bare day in mid-May, Carney and Co.'s Number Three team was in the process of containing an oil storage tank fire in southwestern Oklahoma. Carney, masked and swathed, in charge this time, didn't feel Mot tell him the naphtha tank beside him was about to blow. He was working the five-three cannon, sending extinguishing foam into the conflagration, when the impact of the blast sent him flying. Despite the protective clothing he could feel points of steel stabbing into flesh and skin. He moved himself back from the job. Way back, home to the farmhouse. First time in the field in six weeks, and he'd blown it.

So, after fifty why do you risk the second half of your life by inhaling clouds of filthy oil-smoke? Can't you quit crossing swords with catastrophe? He said aloud, "Grow up, Carney."

From the bench on his rear deck he gazed over the little valley to the hill across, birches tinted thick green with late spring leaves. He watched reeds in wind-choreographed sway, two crows glide along an air-stream, five butterflies flitter down by the lilies. Four brown ants carried a dead honeybee off along a plank. He felt tied by invisible wires to huge and tiny worlds.

Early in the afternoon he played his cello. Clumsy, his bound leg hurting, the bow drew across the strings, and melody drifted up to the beams. Pain retreated. A sense of cheer filled his arms and chest, his privacy as embracing as that rare thing, the best of human contact. Even with mistakes, the melodies satisfied him.

When Bobbie arrived she found Carney staring across the lush field. "I worry about you."

Carney said, "No worry needed."

"You're not out there making a better world, you're not writing another book, you aren't even getting laid."

Carney laughed. Lynn in their time together had been a rarity, lithe of mind and golden-smooth. So too Marcie. And the rest? All games. "You know a woman sweet as my cello?"

"Have you tried to get in contact with Julie?"

Carney glanced at her, smiled, shook his head once, said nothing.

"You're lost," Bobbie said.

No, not lost. No, Carney hadn't actually tried to contact Julie. Yes, he felt pretty sure he'd find her. Soon.

○

Lola hasn't returned. The cloud floss at my side is empty as a well-made bed. Down below, new events, and she'd be intrigued. What if she never comes back?

○

Carney in the Jaguar, top closed this morning against the cool May air, headed onto the Interstate, cruised through Vermont into New Hampshire, then chose a local road down to Manchester. Just after Hooksett he stopped along a wide shoulder. He got out and stretched. He'd spent several days tracing Julie, starting with where Charlie had left off. No driver's license for Julie Robertson, the New Hampshire Department of Motor Vehicles had told him, no phone in or around Manchester listed in her name, no home address either. She had to be in an institution, constant care. No phone in her name, just the place itself, with extension numbers. Through the Internet he found addresses of six significant treatment centers; she might be in a smaller institution, he'd try those after, start with the bigger places. The first three told him they couldn't connect him, he had to call the room directly as all patients had their own phones. So unless she'd designated her number as unlisted, she wasn't there. The fourth had a central phone but no extension for a Julie Robertson. The fifth: "Just a moment, I'll see if I can put you through." Carney broke the connection.

He lowered the Jag's top. Maybe he'd take her for a long drive and they could talk. Or maybe just walk. If she could walk. If she had a wheelchair he'd push her along. He wouldn't apologize. They could share good memories. He'd cheer her up. If she was depressed. Charlie hadn't been clear about much. He didn't need Charlie's context. He'd have his own soon enough.

Into the northern outskirts of Manchester. East, past the Derryfield Country Club, there it was, a two-story converted schoolhouse, Winchester Center. He parked, walked into a lobby. A small woman with graying hair behind a desk glanced up at him. He asked to see Julie Robertson. He identified himself as C. Carney.

"She doesn't usually accept visitors."

"Please. Tell her who I am. It's very important."

She scowled. "I can tell her. But she makes her own decisions." She got up. "Have a seat." She walked down the hall.

Carney sat. Why didn't the woman just call through to Julie? Carney watched as the woman opened a door, stepped inside.

Half a minute later she came out. "I'm sorry, Mr. Carney, she won't see you."

Carney got up. "She said that?"

"She did."

He sat again. "I'm staying until I see her." One thing to say don't call, don't write. But after he'd driven all this way? "Maybe in half an hour she'll change her mind."

Carney waited the half hour, sent the warden in again, again came back with Julie's refusal. He read a magazine, waited an hour, two more magazines, another half hour. He said to the woman, "Do you have a washroom I could use?"

Ms. Wilkoski stared at him for several seconds. "First door on your left down the hall."

"Thank you." He walked slowly. He found the door, opened it, closed it again and moved, silent as possible, toward the far door the woman had opened several times. No name outside. He opened quietly, stepped inside, closed up again. Dim light. A bed dominated the space. Beyond it, a wheelchair by the window. Two small sitting-room chairs. A door to what could have been a bathroom; Carney thought he saw the glint of white porcelain. Lying in, rather than on, the bed was a small figure. Carney said, "Julie?"

The figure remained still.

Carney stepped closer. "Hello, Julie."

". . . no . . ."

"I had to see you again, Julie, I had to."

". . . nothing to see . . ."

"Charlie told me you didn't want visitors but I—"

". . . see me . . . like this . . ."

"It's so dark in here, Julie, I can't see you like anything at all." He had meant to be light but the words hung heavily in the air.

". . . too late . . . you've seen . . . seen me . . ."

He stepped closer to the bed. He did see her, a tiny body under the blanket, above it a face and arms only, shrunken except swollen at her jaw joint, the skin on her arms tight on bones except at the elbow, the wrist, swollen and red-looking, near to no flesh beneath the skin. He said, "Charlie told me. Julie, this is awful, what can I do? Is there anything anybody can do?"

". . . let me . . . die . . ."

"Anything—anything but that."

She gave Carney a desiccated whisper.

"I didn't get—"

". . . you shouldn't . . . be here . . ."

"I had to—"

". . . taken away . . . the last of it . . ."

"I'm sorry?"

". . . you have . . . what I . . . lost . . ."

"Julie? What?"

A rattly cough from her. ". . . had . . . had . . . what I lost . . . gone now . . ."

"Can you tell me?"

". . . no . . ."

A long silence.

". . . yes . . . gone . . ."

Carney waited. How godawful terrible.

". . . gone . . ."

"What's gone, Julie?"

More silence. Finally: ". . . lived in . . . your memory . . . nineteen . . . long ago . . ."

"Yes. You do."

". . . did . . . gone . . . only place . . . only place . . . in world . . ."

"The only place—?"

"...only place...place in world...still nineteen...beautiful...someone thought of...me...beautiful..."

"You were beautiful, so wonderfully beautiful—"

"...gone...now...not possible...now...memory gone..."

"Julie, it's still there, it'll always be there."

"...no...replaced by...me...now..."

"I—I'll always—"

"...selfish...C.C....too late..."

He reached out, took her hand. Cool little sticks between swollen knuckles, but no heat from the swelling. He wanted to warm her fingers with his hand. Slowly her fingers cooled his. Would her toes, her pretty toes, look, feel like this? For a minute, two, he didn't move, or speak. Nor did she.

The door opened. Carney remained still, holding her cool hand.

A man's voice spoke by his ear. "You have to leave, sir."

Carney felt a pressure on his arm, pulling him to the door. He yanked his arm away. "Just another few seconds, please." He leaned over Julie, saw her eyes again for the first time in thirty years. Too dark to truly tell, but he thought he saw the same fine sweet blue. Her eyelids didn't blink, she stared only at the ceiling. He placed a light kiss on her forehead, a cool forehead. He whispered, "Goodbye." He turned and let the man's hand guide him from the room.

He drove home, to the farmhouse. She's right. I am a selfish selfish man.

He had to speak about Julie. To Bobbie? But he said nothing to Bobbie. It took him five days to call Charlie, who sat with him while they wasted themselves with a bottle of bourbon. Carney cried, furious at himself. Charlie had little to say, except that it had hit Julie out of nowhere. Almost exactly four years ago. An auto-immune attack, the body's own defence system assailing the joints, new blood vessels swelling the joints, stiff and crippled joints. Six months from onset to no longer being able to walk. None of the therapies worked. And she'd been deteriorating from then on. She'd tried to starve herself to death, but they fed her intravenously. And she'd made Charlie promise not to tell Carney where she was.

2.

John Cochan strode up the one-time nave at precisely 8:37 near the end of June, just as he did on most mornings when in Richmond. Setting Intraterra North's headquarters in the old church made him part of the community, an insider. No room dividers here, every aspect of Terramac connected with the others. Halfway up the walls ran a walkway from which little offices enclosed in plexiglass jutted out, a kind of shelving for desks and their people. The ground floor was an open space, work tables, surfaces cluttered with electronic gear. People conferred, yet the room stayed calm, thanks to sound-deadening walls and a buffered ceiling.

At the far end five steps led up to the old chancel. The stage with plexiglass facade was separated from the hall and divided into two offices, each with a large wooden desk, surveying the technological ground floor. His own office on the right, Aristide Boce's on the left. Boce usually spent two-three days at Intraterra's Montreal headquarters.

At precisely 9:10, as most mornings, the phone rang. Yakahama Stevenson calling from Terramac City. Vice-President for Planning, Stevenson preferred on-site work. A week ago, amidst the thunder of a dozen machines, after months of measurement and a marathon calculation stint at his computer, Yak had insisted that a third of a mile below ground in the darkness under nature's roof, there had to be a truly huge chamber. His reckoning estimated it as much as half a modest mall long and the height of a cathedral. But how did it lie, this space carved out long ago by the roar of mighty water tearing through sandstone, leaving the surrounding granite bare? Two years ago Yak and Johnnie had hypothesized such a river once ran deep under ground, now a remnant of its prehistoric volume, rising to the surface as cool springs, perhaps feeding Lake Champlain or silently seeping into the bed of the Sabrevois River.

So Yak over the last week had taken responsibility from Harry Clark, Chief of Architecture, for setting, late in the evenings, half a dozen small blasts deep below, down where only the most trusted Intraterra employees went, a secret kept from the hundreds of aboveground workers; though rumors did arise. The charges were laid by Clark's first-rate demolitions man, Jake "Bang" Steele. The last two little detonations had established the area, empirically testing Yak's equations. Now on the phone excitement filled Yak's voice: "I think we found it, Handyman."

"How big?"

"Not clear yet. But pretty damn big. We'll know tonight."

"Good." Johnnie smiled. "Go-o-o-o-d. See you tonight." Just where would they blast? Not by the little curving passage, please not there.

○

I just caught a glimpse of Lola, drifting in the eternal infinite realm, our eir. She didn't look my way. Doesn't she care anymore? I keep saying to myself, You're an Immortal, she's a God, how can all this matter so to you?

Anger. Fear of loss. Untenable to feel like this. Damn!

○

3.

With scribbled directions to Magnussen Grange, fly rod, cello, and hard-hat in the trunk, Carney eased his Jaguar toward Burlington, into and out of Richmond, a couple of sharp-curved miles to a covered bridge across a burbling stream, Gambade Brook. East along country roads to a white gate.

He still felt shaken from seeing Julie. That such a beautiful human being had been reduced to deadened skin and swollen joints, this was a great sorrow. For the world. For himself. A tragedy for Julie.

Milton Magnussen's phone call had carried the weight of fear and concern. The Terramac project was daily becoming more visible, more outrageous, helicopters battering the air overhead, busloads of workers down from Quebec, massive deliveries. Theresa on her own had filed for an injunction to keep Cochan from continuing. Intraterra immediately slapped a lawsuit on her, the requested injunction was turned down, the suit stood in place. More worrying, half a month ago Cochan had made an offer to buy the Magnussen land, all of it, for $10 million; if the offer was accepted he would drop the lawsuit as well. Of course they'd refused. Then last week they received a second offer, a sharp formal letter, the price now $9 million. And no mention of the lawsuit.

So. Could C. Carney come out to the Grange? Despite what he might assume, Theresa admired Carney's work. She'd read about the lead decontamination camp he'd set up in Idaho, and seen Red Adair on TV calling Carney the best there was, and heard on the radio about the coal-mine fire in West Virginia. In what sounded like a well-timed afterthought Milton let Carney know that Gambade Brook, where it flowed through Magnussen land, held some first-class trout and these days pretty much nobody fished there.

○

Lola's back! Here at my side! She says nothing of where she's been. Her eyes, though turned my way, seem trance-like. But she's listening again. Her smile, small as it is, propels me. I've caught her up on the down below.

○

Beyond the gate Carney saw a large white-clapboard house, windows trimmed in green, a wrap-around porch, solar roof-panels. He turned in and parked on rough grass beside a brown van. He walked up a ramp to the porch. His shin, still strapped, ached not at all, despite the hot and humid July afternoon. He knocked.

Dr. Theresa Bonneherbe Magnussen unlocked the screen. "Glad you made it, Carney." She set her chair in reverse, pulled the door open, and held it in place with the chair wheel. A solid handshake. A woman about thirty appeared behind the chair. "Feasie, this is Carney. Carney, Feodora. We alone get to call her Feasie."

Feodora stuck out her hand. "Welcome." She stood tall and well-rounded, as by country living and solid eating. "Come in."

The screen door slammed and Carney entered Magnussen Grange. Pleasantly cool inside, out of the midsummer sun. Polite questions about the drive. Years ago, Theresa explained, Milton had moulded the old farmhouse to fit her needs and wishes—colonial furniture, many bookshelves still overflowing, shiny long-plank oak floors. The ramps between rooms on different levels were new and removable. After the stroke they'd moved to a smaller house outside Burlington. But she'd be staying at the Grange tonight. Milton too. Feodora offered cold sweet cider.

"Thanks." Today, Carney noted, Theresa wore her hair in a single long white braid.

"Don't let her get riled, Mr. Carney. These days she blows up at a bird flying the wrong way. I'll be right back." Feodora left.

Carney said, "Impressive library."

"Only the rag-ends here, storage, reference, two more rooms upstairs, a lot already in the new place. This is the realm of my previous life. It's too scattered, can't ever find things I need. Last week I tried to track down what Augustine used for contraception, took me two days." She nodded, chuckling at her reference, whatever it was. "Sit down, sit down—no, not there, here!"

"Theresa. Some calm, please." Feodora set a tray with a jug and three glasses on a little table. "You know better."

"I am calm, dammit." She nodded at Carney. "Though sometimes I need to get mad."

Feodora poured. "Avoid that, Theresa." She handed her mother, then Carney, a glass.

Carney sipped. "Delicious."

"Last year's." Theresa gestured to the back window. "Great trees. Season's late this year, apples're scrawny. Perfidious acid rain."

"Ti-Jean says he'll fertilize different this fall." Feodora spoke in serene phrases, as if designing a tone to soothe her mother's vexations.

"He's smart, Ti-Jean." She glanced over to her daughter. "You'll have to forgive Feodora, she's got a one-track mind about my health. Like Milton. He brought me back. From the stroke. They're both wonderful but they all think I'll live forever."

Carney looked at her. "Milton did a great job."

Feodora smiled and shook her head. "Theresa wasn't about to let go."

"The donkey-doctors gave up on me. Chemicals to send me into gaga-space, turn my brain circuitry soggy."

"Enough." Feodora lay her hand on her mother's arm. "We're here, and it's a quiet day."

Theresa nodded. "Some good trout in the stream. Did Milton say? Wish I could show you. Wonderful place, this Grange."

Carney smiled. "I'd like to try." Something easing about Feodora's care of Theresa.

Feodora said, "You'll catch."

"We rebuilt the place. Ten-twelve years back." Theresa looked around the room. "How long ago, Fease?"

"Theresa and Milton lived here a long time, they're still moving out.

We live here now, Ti-Jean and me." She smiled. "Milton and Theresa're staying a couple of days." She glanced gently at Theresa. "They sleep on the couch down here now, Theresa can't really get up the stairs. They rewired it, replumbed it, insulated it, drywalled it. 1979, 1980."

Carney nodded in sympathy, recalling his own version of gutting and restoring.

"That long ago. Huh! Milton did a lot of it himself. The kids helped, have to give them that. And now we got that monkey-dump Cochan down the road."

Feodora scowled gently, then turned to Carney. "We're pleased you'll take another look at what Cochan's doing. Real lucky Theresa read your book."

"A lucky coincidence."

"Coincidence?" Theresa hunched toward Carney. "You believe in coincidence?"

"Don't you?"

She shook her head. "Over the long haul we create our coincidences. They're not out there waiting for us."

Carney sipped his cider. "Have you been out to the Terramac site?"

"Me? He'd never let me in." She shook her head. "You go. Find a way to stop him. Make that happen. Nothing happens if we don't make it happen." Theresa Magnussen lifted her glass and sipped. "You put yourself in a certain place. Where you want to be, need to be. Wouldn't work for me with Cochan. But I am in the right place sometimes. If once in a while it's also the right time, I've got myself to thank. Not some coincidence."

"So me being here isn't a coincidence."

She snorted. "I read your book, I wrote you. Milton called you. Whatever it takes to lead us, yes and to confine us, we create that for ourselves, we choose it. We call it happenstance. And do we think this is wonderful? Course not. We step away, we say, '*Just* a coincidence.' We take no responsibility. Even for our hopes."

"And if by some chance you hadn't read my book?"

"That'd be impossible. You wrote it for me. Thank you. There's a harmony to the strings of chance, friend Carney."

Carney laughed. "The strings of chance?"

"Most of us, we let the chance slip by, we even push it away. And then it's too late."

And how does her family deal with this woman of the impatient opinions? Carney turned to Feodora. "You were going to tell me about Terramac."

Theresa answered. "Handy Johnnie owns the county." She shook her head. "A slime."

"Theresa. Please!" Feodora spoke sharply. Theresa shrugged, but nodded. Feodora said to Carney, "Some say he's our grand benefactor, others that he's destroying everything here."

"I'll go see what's going on there now. But if he's playing by the rules—"

"He makes his own rules," Theresa growled. "A slug who's oozed his way up from south of the line. Lexington."

"Lexington?"

"You know. Cochan Pharmaceuticals. He sold it off. Remember the lawsuits? Birth defects. The buyer-boys ended up with pill bottles full of dynamite." Though she spoke softly her cheeks had gone mottled. "Deserved it, the bastards."

Feodora crouched beside the chair. "Want one of your soothants?" Theresa nodded.

Feodora said to Carney, "Please, you won't talk to her till I get back?"

"Fease, I'm not unrelaxed, I'm only trying—"

"Mother. Please."

"Yes, Feodora." White blotched her reddened face.

Feodora left. Carney got up, looked around. Beside one bookshelf a wedding picture in black and white caught his eye. A broad man with black hair parted in the middle, heavy forehead, round face, large ears, a three-piece tweed suit, and paisley tie. And a lovely blond woman, bobbed hair an aura round her head, her tiny mouth dark, lips near to a bow, buxom, a slender waist. She wore a knee-length shirtwaist dress, light in color. Both were in their mid-twenties. She was holding his arm, looking up at his face, admiring. The young Theresa, a beauty.

o

"Holy shit," I heard Lola whisper.

I turned to her. She glowed in purple light. Her eyes held mine.

She was here, she was safe, she was listening. "What a way for a God to speak," I scolded. But I did smile.

"She looks like I once did." Lola shuddered a little.

I studied her face. Memory? "Maybe a little," I conceded.

"What would I have come to look like over the years, I wonder."

"Hard to say." Something was seriously wrong here. Gods don't concern themselves with such questions. Had Lola lived she'd have been seventy-six this year. She died at thirty-six, resplendent as I see her now. She overdosed, they said; an accident. Her death turned out to be the second biggest news story of that year, 1963. I'd been up here four years already and had never heard so much commotion. She died in Connecticut, her big house on the Sound. It's at the southernmost edge of my down below, just about as far as I can see.

"Maybe something like Theresa," she murmured. "That'd be good."

I stared at her. Lola and Theresa.

"She's kinda amazing, you know. I would've liked to be amazing."

"You were, Lola." You still are, I said silently.

"All that range of emotions. Way more than pleasure. I don't even have a wisp of a memory of feeling anger and fear and those things." She shook her head, marveling.

○

Theresa's eyes had fallen closed. Her drawn-in cheeks reduced her. Carney sat.

She'd heard him move and looked over. "Married, Carney?"

"You should stay quiet." He waited. "I used to be. Years ago."

Theresa nodded. "One of the ravages."

"Marriage, or its end?"

"Forty years, Carney. Can you imagine that? Forty years of living with the same man. That's a bond. You'll meet him at supper." She did sound calmer. "Children?"

Carney cradled his glass. "Nope." And a relief. "How many do you have?"

Theresa seemed to think about that. "Four?"

Carney grinned. "But you're not sure."

"I'm sure I haven't been their happiness. They came along and each in turn endured me."

"Feodora, and—?"

"One son, three daughters. Sarah was first and left the house first. Later she made a rotten marriage. Anyway that's over. The twins came next, Leonora and Feodora. Leasie and Feasie." She grunted. "We labeled 'em the Noodles 'cause right away they grew tall, skinny too when you compare them with me and Milton. Feasie married Ti-Jean, good for her, widower, eleven years older than Feasie, raising a daughter by himself, great kid. You'll meet Ti-Jean tomorrow. He made Fease get some meat on the bones. Leasie never married, too late now." She shook her head. "They're okay. And Karl, he's the youngest, he turned Catholic, can you believe that? After the blue-ribbon atheist upbringing we gave him. And after following his so-called dream, sowing more oats than's good for any man. And along came a couple of offspring. That he talks of." She nodded to herself. "Two little girls. Nice kids."

○

Lola's fingers found my forearm, as if to draw me back. "Ted—"

"Yes?" A touch from her set my bone-memories atremble.

"I need to interrupt for a minute. I have to ask you something." She spoke softly, as if in fear of being overheard. She found my eyes with hers, so large and green, those shafts of purple.

I would tell her anything. Almost. "Yes?"

"Can Gods dream?"

"I don't know." A scary question. "I doubt it."

"I think I had a dream a little bit ago." She smiled, pleased with herself.

"Oh?" I spoke as lightly as my throat allowed. "About what?"

"Myself. Me and my lover. From long ago. A very wealthy man, I knew that."

"Ah," I said. "And?"

"Nothing. I was with him. His face wasn't clear, nor where we were. Just him and me."

I heard myself say, "Strange."

"Yes, isn't it." She took her fingers from my arm, dropped both her hands down to her lap, sat primly, stared ahead. "Well, I had to ask you that." She smiled to herself.

A memory. A dream. A lover. It took a time, relocating my story.

○

Feodora returned with a small brown bottle. Theresa scowled but took two yellow capsules and swallowed them with cider. Feodora said to Carney, "My daughter, Ginette, and her friend Yves will join us for supper. Like Theresa to show you the garden?"

"Good." He turned to Theresa. "Not too hot for you?"

"Let's go."

Carney reached for the wheelchair—

"No no, I can." She flicked the switch, released a kind of clutch, pushed at a lever, and the contraption jerked forward.

They wheeled out the back door, down a short ramp, and across a broad lawn to a garden warrened with trails rolled flat to smooth the wheelchair's passage. First the orchard, twenty-one apple trees, then a large patch of kitchen vegetables, then a quarter acre of high corn. "Over there," Theresa pointed, "Those are walnut. Unusual this far north. Bred for me by a French friend near Angoulême, in the Cognac region. We'll have the nut oil in the salad at lunch."

Bees hummed and damselflies flitted in the hot still afternoon sunlight. A small squadron of whining mosquitoes located Carney and Theresa; she handed him some bug repellent. In the barn lived a dozen chickens, half of them laying, and three cows. One they kept for milk. Across the stream stretched a large-mesh in-water cage six feet by six feet and about three deep, the trout locker. "They eat whatever bugs and grubs wash through. In low water we supplement the feed. When we want trout for supper like in an hour, they're fresh."

Behind the barn stood a small mill for grinding and pressing the walnuts, and immense grindstones for the corn they'd made their bread from years ago. Beyond the wheel the water dropped maybe a dozen feet, enough to power a little generator. "About all we ever need for electricity," Theresa muttered. "There's batteries in the shed, for storage. The roof panels heat the water. And in winter the water heats the house. We've got three stoves for wood, they boil up the water when the cold turns intense. A backup in case of storms." Theresa shook her head. "People think anarchy means chaos. Nitwits."

Built and kept going by the family? If so, impressive. "All this, but no telephone?"

Instantly Theresa's face told Carney he shouldn't have asked: "Device of the devil! Any fool can barge into your life by sticking his finger into a few holes and turning a dial. Never in my home." She shook her head. "Ti-Jean and Feasie, they've got a cell phone. Turned off when I'm around."

She had whispered, but her face was white; could any conversation turn unhealthy? She rolled toward the cornfield. "We built up most of this, me and Milton. And the children, when they were small. All his life he's been a farmer, Milton has, a farmer and a good man. We used to have a hired couple. These days Ti-Jean does most of the work, plowing, planting, milking, and so on." She thought about him. "Another good man." She nodded. "A man of single syllables, Ti-Jean Seymour." She chuckled. "Those as gets irritated with him pronounce it Say-more, if they like him it's See-more. He'll be back late, his mum's sickly."

Carney nodded. "So the Grange is self-contained. Or nearly."

"Can't be self-contained any more. State bureaucracies, corporate bureaucracies. Nobody lets us be." She rubbed her forehead.

"At least your family owns the land."

"Sure. But we're rare birds. Capitalism, self-ownership, it could've made good lives possible for everybody. But it turned venal, it destroyed real ownership."

Glad she wasn't his enemy. He laughed. "You're supporting the capitalist state?"

"No! Capitalism's a soup of putrefaction that breeds madness and villainy."

"Easy." He liked her rhetoric, felt concern at her anger. "Stay calm."

"Sure." She stared up at Carney. "But how can I? With those soups poured into the cauldron of our brain"—her whisper scratched, her eyes held Carney tight—"soups festering in our psyches for eons, drowning the senses inside-out, drowning us with everything that money buys, money, money, more blessed money. The diseases of individualism, run ay-cursed-mok."

Carney had to say, "But you're an individualist, no?"

"Individualist? This old crone, my friend, is only an anarchist. All the difference in the universe. In the individualist state where you and I live, a few self-select individuals dominate over everybody. But in an anarchist society you create vast space for the development of every human being's individuality." Her eyes, still on Carney, glowed sad.

Her renewed intensity . . . Bad. "Shall we go back?"

She pointed. "That's our well. Couple of years ago we learned the water—a hundred ninety-three feet down, Carney—it had a coliform count 2.1 times beyond safe. A couple of centuries to get the drainage of night soil down there, but now even in water that deep we've got the shit of our lives. Ain't humans wonderful, boiling water brought up from near two hundred feet? And that's before Cochan spreads his blight across the terrain." She wheeled herself along the path, staring straight ahead. "I'll destroy that bastard. If it's the last thing I do."

Carney said, "Easy, Dr. Magnussen."

Theresa nodded, again to herself. "It's Theresa to you."

"Okay, Theresa. Back to the house?"

In her eyes, a new gleam. A twitch came to her lips. "May I tell you something?"

"You have to ask permission?"

"You might think this is a different order of thing. It isn't." She paused. "I've given some thought, lately, to immortality."

Carney cocked his head. "From what I've read, mortality and death, you've wrestled with those a long time."

"No, I said *im*mortality."

"Isn't that the other side of the coin?"

A slow shake of Theresa's head. "Maybe it makes no sense to talk about."

"Tell me."

She squinted at him. She shrugged, she discharged significance from her words. "I have, you see, something new in my life. Starting soon after my stroke." She made a nasal snort, derisive. "A regular visitor."

"Who?"

"Suddenly she's there. As if she'd walked through the wall. She gives me a hard time."

"The anarchist and her ghost?"

"No. How should I know? She seems corporeal. Except of course she can't be."

"You mean you're having conversations in your mind? We all do."

"No no no no no. My embodied morality, my—ethical visitor. She's simply there. External. She sits in a chair. Pretending to be all-knowing. Always judging. A large young woman. She sneezes. She's slim but heavy-breasted, she adjusts her bra. Her hair is short and blond, her mouth is small. We have rambling conversations, if you can believe that."

○

Lola blinked and her forehead went wrinkled. "Is it—one of us?"

"Course not. That's impossible."

She pulled away.

Why was she upset? I leaned over to take her hand.

"Since the stroke, she said. Is it oncoming senility?" Lola half folded her arms, skin aglow in clinging light.

"I don't know. Maybe."

"Yeah? Let's see."

"If it happens, Lola. Then."

She sulked. I put my hand out, touched her wrist. No response. I dared, I bent to kiss her fingers. She winced. "Should I go on?"

She nodded but wouldn't look at me. I stroked her hand. She pulled away, long inches.

A new distance. Come on since Edsel's lordly scolding? She'd returned from romping with the Gods. She sits so close. Feigning cool-ness, or is it real? She stabs my bloodless heart.

What can I give her? A few thousand words, such paltry weapons. Stories of desire, chance, promise, brought from the down below. Against the rules of heaven, what hope is there?

○

Carney considered Theresa's visitor. "I believe Theresa Magnussen could banter with the devil."

"Thank you. I'll take that as a compliment." She squinted at Carney. "You're pretty quick yourself."

Carney accepted, with a nod. "Do you have exchanges with this—incarnation."

"Arguments. Difficult arguments."

"About?"

"Not the question to ask, not right now."

A third-grader, facing a surprise quiz. Then he knew the answer. Or rather, the question. "Anybody else observed this apparition?"

Theresa's head twitched no.

"And you recognize her because she looks like—?"

Theresa's head bobbed up-down two-three-four times. "Yes. Like me. Forty years ago."

"And you're turning her into what? Some kind of household god?" The god word tasted stiff in Carney's mouth.

"Not a god."

"A godlet?"

Theresa shrugged. "Maybe."

"Of judgment."

"And rancor."

"Because you're not the woman you used to be."

"Because I'm not the honest woman I used to be."

"Why should Theresa at twenty be wiser than Theresa today?"

"Along the way"—again she looked tired—"I've seen myself falter."

"And this ethical godlet? If she's an earlier you, she's mortal, right? If you die, so does she. So she can't provide immortality."

"Correct, Carney. Even gods are mortal."

o

Lola started to smile. Then she shuddered instead.

o

Theresa sighed. "We make our gods, we forget them. The 'me' she looks like, that's gone. Literally dead and gone if you talk about cellular matter. But still she visits, she keeps returning. Unbidden. She challenges."

"Challenges how?"

"What I'm thinking."

"Like about Terramac City?"

"Even that. She made me rethink asking you to come back. Your report there in April really pissed me off, you know that?"

Carney laughed. "I do that to people."

She grunted. "There's something going on at that place, Carney. Something vile. We keep getting rumors. No question there'll be a putrid cancer on the skin, but we think in the guts it's something even

220

worse. He's blasting down in the bedrock, I'm sure of it. I tried to enjoin the work till we could figure out what it was. But we signed that cowpiss agreement and now the bastard's suing me."

Carney wondered. "But the agreement gives him underground rights, doesn't it?"

"Yeah, but how far down? Into the bedrock? Below it?"

"You mention that in your injunction request?"

"Of course."

"And?"

She shook her head. "No proof."

We heard a call, "Gramma!"

Theresa said, "It's Ginette." She looked up at Carney. "Feodora's stepdaughter. Please, Carney. It's bad. Find out what's going on. Some proof."

Ginette set her hand on Theresa's shoulder and kissed her cheek. "You okay, Theresa?" Despite the heat Ginette wore a black sport-coat, her miniskirt was black, black tights to her ankles, flat black fourteen-lace Doc Martens. A pretty face, late teens, her hair crew-cut. She introduced Yves. His T-shirt was black, his painter pants baggy and white. A gold ring passed through his left earlobe, a mouse-tail of blond hair dropped down his nape.

"I'm fine, fine. We're having a good talk." She smiled, great affection for Ginette. "Ginette's a cabinet-maker."

Ginette grinned. "Construction and carpentry, Gramma."

They followed Carney and Theresa back to the house. Milton, an older version of the man in the wedding picture, but easily recognizable despite the white hair, had returned while Carney and Theresa were talking. On his cell phone Carney called the Intraterra office in Richmond. No, neither Mr. Cochan nor Mr. Boce were in. Mr. Carney would find Mr. Boce at Terramac, would Mr. Carney like to be connected? Sure. He spoke with Aristide Boce: Of course Mr. Carney could come by tomorrow. Mr. Boce would do all in his power to assure the presence of John Cochan. Because Mr. Cochan so admired Mr. Carney's work, and Mr. Cochan very much wanted to meet Mr. Carney. Early afternoon would be best time. Say two?

Over supper the family each let loose their anger at the Terramac project. So few months; so much new development. It's a quiet evening, said Theresa, and suddenly the earth shakes under your feet like you were fencing on a trampoline. The ground flowing like a boat on hard waves, said Yves who'd had two years in the Coast Guard. Sometimes like a Richter 4.5 earthquake, said Feodora. And Milton: Like a dozen silent jackhammers breaking cement in a circle around you.

Carney listened. Tomorrow he would find out more about what was happening there, this heavy-duty construction begun since his earlier visit. Clearly the Magnussens were deeply distressed. Well, he might be too if he lived here day by day. They spoke of Terramac in different terms, but with a single voice. Strange thing, a family.

IMMUNE

Then the earth was alert, bones braced,
thymus of rock ready,
lymphic streams ready.

Virus Radiation Bacteria Cancer.
Number uncountable,
power nigh infinite,
through sores and lacerations
the antigens invade the earth.
Attack, maim, rot, kill.
Fungi Chemicals Parasites.

Where are the rivers of monocytes,
where the macrophages of liberation,
where the cleansing filtering sands?

R.F. June 1–4/03

4.

After supper Carney drove off to fish Gambade Brook. "Work your way upstream from the covered bridge," Milton had told him. "Too much activity 'round the Grange." Carney liked Milton, gruff but gentle. Especially compared with Theresa.

At the bridge he pulled off the road. Tomorrow he'd check out Terramac, meet Cochan. Despite all the invective, nothing said about the place sounded damning, and blasting was an inevitable precursor to construction. He felt irritated, letting Milton rope him in. The fishing better be good.

No wind. He worked his way upstream. After a hundred yards sweat had drenched his shirt, but the ache in his leg seemed gone. Now every might-be mama mosquito within fifty feet needed Carney blood. An oozing film of repellent coated his hands and face, his neck to chest and shoulder blades. He was the essence of repulsion but still the mosquitoes whined blood blood blood!

Fly rod in hand, tackle bag over his shoulder, he searched for deeper pools in the low water. He was a believer in solunar tables, charts of times when fish and animals are most active in their foraging, and by the book a period of major activity began twenty minutes ago. The mosquitoes were proof positive. And a mayfly hatch was in progress— he saw the swirls of an occasional trout feeding where the surface lay quiet. Over half an hour he had eight solid strikes, took and released three good fish, two browns and a rainbow. He called it a first-class brook if the little ones stayed away till their elders finished eating.

He followed the bone-dry shoreline over rocks and silt, stepping into the flow mainly to cool his feet. He waved mosquitos away from his eyes. On the stream's ledges hairy moss had dehydrated to gray. He reached a run draining a long pool beside a field of grass and flowers. Across, an angled maple overhung half the stream. A dark, pretty place.

Still the mosquito monsters swarmed, inches from his face; a stand-off. He examined the pool. The mosquitoes gathered tighter, hovering by his eyelids where the repellent lay thinnest, ready to attack his eyeballs if he stopped blinking.

He felt a buzz in his chest: Mot, his seventh sense, foreboding activated. But years of fishing pleasure spoke louder: go on, there's a couple of good fish down in there.

Half a dozen dragonflies darted over, gorging themselves on mosquitoes. He waited, one distraction at a time for these trout. The bushes lay far enough back to make careful casting possible. He set his bag down and whipped the fly, a just-hatching mayfly larva imitation, to the head of the run. But he set it down badly; Mot's buzz must be throwing his timing off. He twitched the fly downstream, some underwater spurts. Nothing. A better cast, a third. Enough. The water was too delicate. Let it rest.

He drew back from the stream, smeared on more repellent, cast under the shadow of the maple branches, worked the fly along. Nothing. On the second try, a strike. The trout—felt like the largest so far—ran hard toward the head the pool, whirring line from the reel. He held his rod high and followed on land, keeping to the daisies and grass. The trout went deep, Carney could feel it searching out a hole or a root system to snag the line in. He strained the leader nearly to its limit. The fish made a diagonal rush up and swirled; he saw its green-black back and felt a sweet shiver take his spine. It did that when a hidden thing first came to view. He went fishing for the shiver.

The fish dove again, again the rod tip up—

A slam on his casting arm at the elbow, then a sting of pain. The rod dropped, he grabbed his forearm— Beside his ear a whine of speed and a ping off a boulder eight feet away. He fell to his knees and wriggled to the only cover, tall grass on the bank. He felt a sadness that he'd never land this trout. He wondered if he'd get his rod back. At last, he thought, somebody was shooting! At him? No sound. A silencer? Get out of here—

He glanced downstream. Grass and field-flowers shielded any view beyond a body-length away. He couldn't see; could he be seen? He lay flat. The earth trembled. His whole body, quivering? With buzz-effects. The incessant mosquitoes. He turned and peeked upstream. Along the riverbank hawkweed reached up two feet and more. Mixed in, white and yellow daisies, black-eyed Susans. He'd never seen hawkweed from underneath, evening petals folding for the night—

"Get up."

He rolled over.

The visor of a baseball cap low on a forehead, bib overalls, plaid shirt. The sun by the right hip. And a steel slingshot, poised, a pebble in its pocket.

"C'mon, stand up." A female voice, impatient.

With his casting hand he pushed himself around. His elbow gave, pain jagged through his upper arm. A broken bone? He touched the elbow. No blood. Powerful weapon, that slingshot.

She kicked the toe of his wader. "I said stand."

"Okay, okay." He rolled, left arm supporting, and curled himself to his feet. Now in his leg, the older ache again. "For godsake why'd you shoot at me?"

"I don't like killers."

"Hey, you did the shooting."

She gestured to the pool with her head. "You kill trout."

He looked. His rod lay by the edge of the water, submerged tip to ferrule, the reel on shore and full of sand. "I *take* trout with it. When I'm lucky."

"That one you had on—"

"I'd have released it. Like three others today."

"Your hands scrape off their scales, they die anyway."

"Look, what is this?"

"You're on my land."

He shook his head. "It belongs to the Magnussens. I've got permission to fish it."

She stared at him. "Shit."

"Theresa Magnussen gave me her map." He glanced around for his tackle bag.

"She's a killer too."

"Lady, she hasn't fished this stream in years."

"I know, I know."

· "Look. Here's how I fish." He walked to the water, reached for the rod, rinsed off the reel, took in line. The fish was gone but the current had kept the hook from snagging. If the fly was on— Yes. He grabbed the end of the leader, held it toward her.

She backed off and drew lightly on the slingshot's elastic.

"Go on, examine the fly."

"Reach it over with the rod."

He raised the rod tip her way, line dangling. She looked at the wool-feather-thread-steel mayfly larva. The fly bobbed. She grasped the leader a foot above the hook, wrapped it around her hand, glanced from the fly to him.

He felt the tug, watched the rod arch, and examined her. Mid-thirties, overalls and heavy-soled boots, brown-blond hair in a clumpy tail poking out the back of her cap. Middlish height. From one shoulder hung a small red backpack.

She let go and the line went slack. "Okay."

"Thank you." Carney had clipped the barb off his hook. To release his catch he only had to turn the hook without lifting the fish from the water. He lost a lot of fish and it'd be a dumb way to fill a larder but most streams needed fish more than he did.

"Even barbless hooks torture fish. You still exhaust them."

Carney shook his head and again pain cracked along his forearm. He reached for his elbow, the rod whipped about and lashed her right shoulder. She backed away, grabbed for her slingshot, pebble drawn back—

"Hey, I'm sorry."

"Stay there."

He set his rod down, shoved up his sleeve, ignored her. Swelling had started, a red glow at the crazy-bone. He looked at her. Rubbing her shoulder she seemed less in control. "You okay?"

She nodded. "You?"

"No big deal." Except his bare forearm was prickling. He glanced down. The mosquitoes, thousands of them, a dozen anyway, syphoning away. He slapped at them.

"Why the hell don't you use repellent?"

"I do. The sleeve covered me there."

She found a small clear bottle in her pocket and lobbed it to him. "Smear it on."

He slathered the liquid, even more vile-smelling than his, on his arm, checked his elbow and pulled the sleeve down.

She said, "You need ice on that. Let's go."

"Where?"

"Can you walk okay?"

"Just don't knee-cap me." No response. "It's all right, I'll head back to the Grange."

"Staying there?"

"Yeah."

"They must like you." She glanced at him. "That your Jaguar, up at the bridge?"

He nodded. "Where it says POSTED, NO FISHING."

"That's over a mile."

Working the water, it hadn't felt that far.

"Come on."

"What did you mean, your land?"

"My father's. And my cabin."

"You're Sarah Magnussen?"

"Magnussen-Yaeger." She pointed upstream. "Cross-country's easier. About half a mile."

"Well—"

"I'll drive you to your car."

"What d'you have, one of those all-terrain vehicles?"

"Let's go."

○

I enjoy watching Carney. I even flinched a little when the pebble from Sarah's slingshot got him on the elbow. I don't think Lola noticed.

○

5.

For the last hours a mean uncertainty had eaten away at John Cochan's agenda. His distress had brought back his sense of irreplaceable loss. Would Yak's suspected cavern call for a detonation on the southeast line, where the thick wall there might close down that narrow passageway? To a connected moment when Johnnie had felt Benjie's presence? Just ask Yak where the blast would be. He picked up his phone, pushed two.

"Terramac City," said the voice.

"Is Yak there?"

"Sorry, Mr. Cochan. He's below."

"What about Steed?"

"Sorry, sir. Haven't seen him all day."

"What about Harry?"

"No, he's not around either."

"Well, track them down for me!"

"Yes, Mr. Cochan. Oh, and Mr. Cochan, Mr. Boce left a note, to remind you about your meeting here, with Mr. Carney, at two tomorrow."

"Yes, yes." Damn. Boce did say Carney could be useful. Choosing to live in Terramac? But more important matters plagued Cochan. Steed would have reasons for being away. Still.

Steed, Aristide Boce, son of Alexandre Boce the banker, pure-wool Quebec money, and a nephew of two bishops, Steed knew—as Yak was fond of saying—the value of a retreat. He could disappear to many profitable places just as he might turn up near anywhere. He was as much at home in Montreal's Societé St. Anselme as at Washington's Dubbin Club. His breadth of fiscal awareness was as substantial as his girth, as smooth as his lustrous gray mustache. Educated at the École Polytechnique and the London School of Economics, he entered the private sector and became, at twenty-nine, Chief Executive Officer of Québois Fina, the presswood revolutionizing the construction industry. His shares had made him a wealthy man. Québois Fina's success trickled down a long way, Boce made that clear to many an audience. It brought hundreds of unproductive souls off welfare, scores of the younger ones for the first time in their lives. A recognized leader, Boce was drafted to membership in the team that in the late seventies oversaw the rural revitalization and economic growth of south-eastern Quebec. From there he went to the provincial cabinet, Finance portfolio, and three years ago to Intraterra.

For the Terramac project, so few miles south of the international border, the bridges to Quebec were essential: cheap building materials, hydroelectric power, lower wage scales, a cheap dollar. No neater way for John Cochan to tie the bond than by borrowing from Quebec banks, implicating Quebec money. And no better man to smooth these relations with the sometime recalcitrant NAFTA neighbor to the north than Aristide Boce. Especially valuable in reducing the many border-crossing hassles, after the disastrous consequences of September 11 nearly two years ago.

The week before, Yak had guided Johnnie through the cavern past Bobcats and electric shovels to the area that hid the possible chamber. A space like most of the others, large but undistinguished, granite and sandstone, needing massive transformation. Johnnie had left Harry and Yak deep in logarithmic speculation. Small passages everywhere that he knew from blueprints. Suddenly a narrow space on the south side seemed to beckon. It led round one dark corner after another. The machinery faded to a hum. Then, in the gleam of his lamp, something had moved toward him. In doubt he pulled back; what to expect in this nether world but the stony remains of ice-age rumblings long settled to eternal peace? Again the movement, a figure, drawn yet flexible; a head but its angle askew and arms akimbo. Johnnie stepped closer. "Hello? Is anyone—?" He knew, or felt he did; yet it couldn't be. He played the lamp to one side, slow. At its beam edge he caught the figure again. It reached to him. He stopped himself then, stood still, breathed silence. He couldn't move his legs, forgot how to try. His arm shifted, he sent the beam to the side. The figure, a small body, three-quarter face, arms toward him, beseeching.

"Benjie . . . ?" No sound, no answer. "Do you want—should I—come closer?" Tiny echoes of his words died. The figure stood still, they both stood still. He didn't dare move. Except as he slid the beam a degree, three, four, farther away, the figure glided in his direction, a foot, two, yet another. Slow, sweating, Johnnie arced his beam from the figure, watching it as it leaned, posture unchanging, closer and closer, closer . . . closer. The darkness between them near complete, the figure a yard, a foot, inches away. How could he be sure, a touch on his arm, gentle, the least pressure, was it really there? Or not— Without lips, in his mind, he breathed, Benjie . . . how can I help you? He waited, long, longer, couldn't tell, how to tell? The sense of touch remained. With infinite slowness he began the beam's arc back. Would the figure withdraw? He'd give all Terramac, the whole of his place in history, if the figure were—alive. The penumbra of the gleam touched the old dark. Nothing. The darkness pushed aside, and in it, nothing. He flicked the light out, a pleading gesture, and heard, and saw, nothing. He waited. Waited. Nothing at all. Benjie would not take his help.

Would he ever sense Benjie again?

In the black air the buzz, far distant, had been like silence in Johnnie's ears. Till from its midst came a voice too familiar, a friend's voice: "Johnnie? Hey, Handyman! You there?"

○

"Poor man," said Lola.

I wondered at her sympathy.

○

6.

For fifteen minutes Carney let himself be led along a dim trail, through brambles, ferns, blueberry thickets, over a rise, along a ridge. Only the low sun gave him a sense of direction. His leg ached, his elbow throbbed. Felt like she'd chipped the bone. Ice?

She said, "So who are you?"

"Carney."

"Carney what?"

"That's enough."

Her brow wrinkled. She turned and walked on.

They arrived at a clearing. A small pond lay dark, mute, opaque. A cottage sat back from the water on a grassy spread, dark green, dappled with more hawkweed and daisies. Beyond, trees and brush sloped upward to a sheen of high crag. Minutes earlier the hillside would have been washed with the dipping sun; now only the upper granite glowed. Under thick branches where cleared land met the pond stood a second structure, a tiny log cabin, no windows visible. Thin gurgles of water, close by, heightened the stillness.

The peace spread with the shadows. "Beautiful," said Carney. But she knew this. Likely the trees and rocks themselves knew.

She nodded and again led the way.

Ice? He searched overhead. No electric lines. Just the dim sparkle of a small spring. He glanced at Sarah. A blink of fancy, and the woman's poised face became a deception. In her cottage she'd turn into the witch, she'd stuff him into the oven.

They reached the stairs. "Step into my parlor."

A sense of humor? "You do have ice?"

She gave him a weary glance and walked up the steps.

He joined her on four square feet of stoop in front of a porch. The big screens would transform to storm windows at a slide of glass plate.

"In, quick."

He slipped through the doorway. She followed. The porch was a jumble of chairs, wicker tables, boxes, a half-dozen nets hanging from nails, yellow, green, various sizes, small mesh. For butterflies? A saggy brown couch. A table. Shelving that held seven kerosene lamps. On the wall, four watercolors of insects. Through a front door, the house. Carney wasn't invited farther.

She tossed her slingshot and pack onto the couch, lit a couple of lamps, hooked one by the door, one on the wall. "Sit there. I'll get the ice. A beer?"

"That'd be great."

She disappeared inside. Did she patrol the hills daily, sling in hand, looking for so-called killers? And when she found one, invite him home?

A darker silence. The screening filtered the water's lilt. Carney, no air moving about him, stuck to his sweaty clothes. A porch that gets evening light holds the day's heat. He pulled at the heel of his wader— His elbow screamed. He waited. For the other wader he used his left hand, for the socks, his feet.

He heard a back door slam. A moment later he saw her march toward the little log house. A generator? She disappeared inside. He stared across the pond. His elbow pounded down his forearm in time with his heart. He closed his eyes and tried to think the pain away.

"You grimace well." She stood next to him, in one hand a towel and an eight-inch wedge of ice traced with sawdust, in the other two frosted bottles. "Roll up your sleeve. Sit over there."

He shifted to the armchair. An ice house. In the twenty-first century. On the broad wicker arm she set the wrapped ice. He touched his elbow to the ice, the towel cool and damp. "Thanks."

She opened the beers. Without looking at him she said, "Santé."

The beer washed smooth across his tongue and down his throat. She observed him.

"You shoot stones at everybody on Milton's land?"

"When I drove in I saw your car at the bridge. I thought you were with the development."

"You shoot development people?"

"Somebody was trespassing and I went looking. You were fishing so maybe you weren't Terramac. But you were killing fish."

No he wasn't. He waited. She wasn't pushing it. "What do you do here?"

"I live here."

"And?"

"Isn't that enough?"

Carney shrugged.

"Sometimes I think here." She took off the baseball cap. Her hair lay scrambled down her back and sweat blackened her shirt but she looked cool as the bottle she touched to her cheek.

"What do you think about?"

"You know me well enough to ask that?"

He took a swallow of beer. "You drink with people, you ask questions."

A puff of a laugh. "I think about my trees, my pond." She stared out at the fading light.

"Does the ice keep all summer?"

"Pretty near."

He adjusted the cold to the other side of his elbow. "How much d'you take out?"

"Couple of tons."

"Hard work."

"Yep."

They lapsed to silence, thick as the air, till Carney said, "You work for pay too?"

"I work in a lab."

"Around here?"

She took some time to answer. "At the County Hospital."

Saying nothing was difficult. "Interesting work?"

"It can be."

The ice helped. And the alcohol, beer to blood to brain, had softened his irritation. He should go. He sat, eyes half closed. The earth vibrated lightly.

"Bastards."

Not a rush of movement, more like the trembling he'd felt after her second shot with his head lying flat on the ground. The tremor passed. "What was that?"

"Goddamn Cochan. That Terramac development."

A known type. What Carney in his book had called an environmental paladin on a previous generation's estate. He didn't oppose development out of hand. All kinds of people buy themselves some peaceful country air, Carney included. Can't do that without going where other people, country people, live. "What? This land is mine, go build your retreat someplace else?"

She shook her head. "There's one huge reason for this Terramac thing, just one. To make lots of money for Handy Johnnie Cochan. Don't nimby me."

"Look, people have to live somewhere."

"Wait till you feel it."

"What?"

"It may happen. Wait."

Carney tested his elbow. The ice was working.

"Another beer?"

He should leave. He shrugged. "Great."

She went out, by the front door this time, into the dim light. His glance followed her to the ice house. Pleasant to watch, the unknown woman's walk: good stride or pretty amble or inadvertent shift of hips. The overalls gave Sarah Magnussen-Yaeger the sensuality of a grizzly. But no, anyone getting him another beer has to be appreciated.

His sweat had dried. He looked around as if an accuser stood behind him. He waited.

Sarah came back. As she closed the door a mosquito flew in, a tiny shape against the lamplight. Carney felt sudden relief, unconscious till then, at their recent absence. She opened the beers. He watched the pest's flight. In his direction. A whine past his ear and he jerked away. It hovered, lowered its flight pattern, made an approach toward his repellent-thin elbow. He cupped his hand. It arced, his fingers stalked—

"Don't." She flicked at his fingers with the rim of a net.

Like getting his knuckles rapped.

A flit in mid-air caught the mosquito in the skein. She drew a string.

Webbing closed over the net top. She stepped outside, closed the door, loosened the cover, released it. Came back, picked up his beer, handed it to him. "Around here, killing isn't on."

"House rules?"

"My rules."

"Ah." He raised the bottle in salute.

Her right eyebrow curved up. "You know it."

This Magnussen daughter, thought Carney, is weird.

o

"Damn right," said Lola.

"You judge quickly," I said.

"She used to be kinda terrific. What got into her?"

In truth, I wasn't sure yet. "Hang on, hang on."

o

Sarah took down another lamp, lit it, trimmed the wick, set it on a low table. She looked at Carney's face, shoulders, arms, in open appraisal.

He drank down half his beer. Her stare felt full of questions.

"You met Feasie and Ti-Jean at the Grange."

"And your parents. Ti-Jean was away." Carney finished his warming beer. "Ms. Magnussen-Yaeger, thanks for the hospitality. Now could you take me to my car?" He stood.

"Magnussen-Yaeger sounds strange, here in the woods. Look. A favor?"

"What?"

"Stay a bit longer."

"Why?" The wicked witch flitted past.

"I'll take you now if you want. But if you don't mind, an hour would do."

"Well—"

"I'll bribe you. Another beer. Or Scotch? I don't have soda. You hungry?"

Too hot for appetite. Beer had turned ache to weak sociability. "Scotch would be nice. And water, just a little."

She examined his face again and said nothing.

"My elbow and I make such good company?"

"Not very." She smiled but to herself. "I didn't mean it like that." Her gaze returned. "You'll see soon, maybe."

"A puzzle?"

"Kind of."

And what could an hour of puzzling hurt? Spent with insects'-rights Sarah. She left. Trying to seduce him? Too late. Parties with new people, bar pick-ups, it'd been years since any of that attracted him, even before Lynn. The presence of others, women and men, had become off-putting, Except for Bobbie. More and more he enjoyed his own company. Carney wasn't uninteresting, and who knew him better than himself.

o

"You, possibly?"

"Glimpses, Lola." I try to search out memories of, and then be omnipresent for, important events of the story. All-knowing, all the moments all the time, is impossible. "Glimpses."

o

Sarah returned with a tray and set it on the table. Scotch, two glasses, a bowl with ice, a jug. "It's cold. It comes from a hundred seventy-seven feet down." She poured Scotch.

"Thanks. Enough." He picked up the jug and poured a little water. "Cheers." He sipped. And what was its coliform count?

"Now we wait."

For a few minutes they sat. Silence is hard with somebody else. Way easier when you're alone. Carney asked, "You live here all the time?"

"Where else?"

A minute later: "Always have?"

For a while it seemed she wouldn't answer. "I've been away. But I grew up around here, at the Grange."

"Where I'm staying."

"There."

He sipped thin Scotch. From the corner of his eye, he watched. She held her Scotch in one hand, the other grasped the arm of the chair. Her face was in profile, a bit of upturned nose, brow half covered with mussed hair. A woman wanting the silence of Carney's company. Original. "And this cabin, did you build it?"

"Yes."

"You carted all this in, and a construction crew?"

"Walls are pre-fab. A helicopter landed it on the lake seven winters ago. I put it together."

"By yourself?"

"You have trouble believing that."

"It looks like a big job."

"Took me three summers." She resumed staring out, and sipped Scotch.

They sat for ten minutes, fifteen. He bet himself he could avoid looking at his watch. He won. Though invited to her parlor he hadn't left the porch. A bathroom would be nice, too much beer to sweat out. "There a toilet in there?"

"On the right. To pee, anywhere outside."

"I'll use the night."

"Put on some repellent."

To hell with it, he'd go in. But that felt like defeat. He spread the goo on his arms and face. "What is this vile stuff?"

"Garlic, chili peppers, onions, corn oil."

"No vinegar?"

She handed him the flashlight. "Don't take your time."

Careful to let no creature in he stepped outside, gingerly in bare feet. He peed, paused, turned off the lamp, stared up. Heat haze hid all but a few big stars. He returned. A moth got in.

She chose a net with a four-inch diameter rim, stalked the animal, snapped it up beside the lamp, outside, release, back in quick. "That was an ilia underwing."

"I can even see not killing moths but, be serious, mosquitoes?"

"You talk a lot, don't you?"

"Just curious."

"Is it necessary to kill anything?"

"Mosquitoes bite me."

"They want a bit of blood. Call it symbiosis."

"And the whirring that keeps me awake? And the itch after they've got me? Come on."

"What, a nice man like you buying the old eye-for-eye philosophies? Kill or be killed?"

The woman was a nut, yes. And his only way back to the Grange. He glanced at the couch. Comfortable enough for a night's sleep? Anyway, no mosquitoes.

"You a carnivore?"

He laughed. "I'm not a vegetarian, no." From somewhere a shred of memory: that roses, when cut, scream. "And you, you kill plants? You don't hear the tiny cry for help just as you let the sweet little string bean fall into boiling water?"

"I cause as little pain as possible."

"So? What do you eat?"

She shrugged. "Vegetables. Grains and seeds, they drop in the normal way of things."

"And the future life of seeds? What about baby plants?"

Her stare through the screen looked weary, with the conversation, with Carney. "Like your own seeds. You don't make babies each time you expel semen."

He laughed. "Then beer's good. And Scotch. All that barley, those hops."

She drank her glass empty. "It's good." A long accusatory silence. "Look, I fly in planes, they spew down contamination. They do if I'm in them or down here. I drive a Jeep and poison pours out. But the idea is, maximize life for the living and minimize pain. Okay?"

Some of Theresa's lessons, Carney figured, were planted deep. "You atoning for something? What'd you do"—a thin darkness rose in her cheeks as he went on—"pour kerosene into anthills when you were fifteen and set them on fire?" Carney had.

She stared straight ahead. After a while she said, "I've taken a vow."

Vows were private and Carney let it go. "You still want me to wait?"

"You like to talk. You don't like to argue."

"Look—"

"A few more minutes. Whatever happens. Or not. Then I'll drive you back."

"Okay." Not another word.

They sat. Her breathing grew audible, a rhythm set in. Carney felt himself go sleepy. Don't drift away—

He barely felt the beginning but the middle rumbled him to his feet. Except standing was unnatural. Not whisky. The ground itself, a heave, a roll, another, rattling, and vibrations, less, quivers, a tremble, tiny, then still.

Her eyes were misty. A release of breath, a hiss: "Bastards."

Eight
TERRAMAC

1.

The explosion smithereened away a wall. With it went the small passageway. Necessary, Yak had explained. Johnnie had let it go, couldn't admit to Yak that Benjie might be in there. He stood behind the screen and felt the echo-waves of the blast die away. No Benjie in that passage now.

Dust settled. They stared through it. "Damn!" From Yak.

"What?"

"You can see. Over there. Why it didn't work."

Johnnie saw. Bang Steele rarely erred, but this time two-thirds of the rock face remained. A fissure, visible now between the crumple of dynamited stone and the still-standing granite, had dampened the shock. No, no sonar probing would ever have computed a fissure to be back there.

"Okay," Yak allowed, "tomorrow we'll refigure, in the evening we get through."

The plans for Terramac had been drawn up by the architect Harold Middleston Clark of Pretoria. Winner of the Wright Prize, the International Association of Architects Medal and the Linden Prize. Designer of the two-mile long Anabaptist Mall; of Chikoree Fair, plexiglass englobed, the world's biggest amusement park, open for business every day and all night whatever the season; of Adirondack Stadium the convertible race track, football and baseball complex with module seating and retractable roof; and of a two-page list of shopping centers from São Paola to Helsinki.

On first meeting, John Cochan said to the architect, "Do you believe, Mr. Clark, that unspoiled nature, a hundred or a thousand years ago, was kind? I don't. Plague, famine, drought ran rampant. Yes we've overcome some of it, but wherever we've created cities we've brought in filth and degradation, we've introduced new miseries. Now wouldn't it be fine to breathe city air and drink urban water without worry? A city without stink, grass without bugs crawling up your legs? No bugs, no poverty, no hooligans. Never too hot nor too cold. A cleansed space for human beings to live. Consider it, Harold. We'll make it happen."

Harold Clark understood. He himself had once proposed a dome-enclosed golf course and been near to smirked out of the Association. He told this to John Cochan.

Cochan smiled. "Harold, design it. The domes, the playgrounds, parks, and condos. The utilities, the transportation, the lakes and streams, the shops, the viewpoints, the power. The golf course too. All part of a whole."

A handshake. Followed by legions of lawyers and reams of contracts. Clark brought in three dozen of his people, the brightest of tomorrow's designers, for the city of marvels. A conscious choice not to go after Pei, Safdie, or Graves. Among many, Clark hired Bang Steele, New Zealand demolitions expert extraordinary.

First came satellite, aerial, and on-site ground inspection. From exhaustive research into and simulations of the past century's climatic conditions, they calculated weather projections up to 2050, including forty-seven *el niño/la niña* anomalies. With sketches, print-outs, designs, models, and multidimensional imaging, Clark rendered tactile the details of Cochan's surface vision, and his own. Simultaneously, following clandestine rock bores to reveal extensions and levels of the hollow space, he planned the entrenchment of Terramac's great secret: a third of a mile below, a man-made yet natural realm, resplendent caverns of light where wise and healthy human beings, Jane and Jim, could laugh, love, hope, plan, conceive, and build: Underland. A neo-ecological urban workplace and pleasure ground, insect-free, element-safe, fully connected to yet withdrawn from the upper world, its beauty greater even than that of Summerclime.

Clark and Cochan had consulted daily. Variant projects grew on inspiration, inspiration multiplied on discovery. John and Harry felt themselves, if not gods, certainly titans. Only occasionally did they disagree.

For Clark, a single nuclear generator, small, perfectly clean, could power all Terramac.

But John mistrusted the nuclear factor.

"If it's built right," the architect claimed, "not cutting corners so public service councillors grow wealthy on tax-payer money, nuclear power's safe."

About nuclear power Cochan had read a great deal and feared yet more. Still, Clark was the expert here. A team of thirty conducted the study, six weeks of undivided research digitally assimilated. All information received, assumed, even speculated, was given its value, fed in, chewed up, analyzed. How to ensure forever that the core wouldn't Three-Mile-Island Terramac into glowing radioactivity? They explored new systems, the about to be tried, the hypothetical. Vitrify the waste. Mix the garbage with molten glass, let it cool, bury it solid. Chill it with helium rather than water. Send it to Nunavut.

No, there'd always be waste, radioactive garbage already produced would take three ice ages to deactivate. Clark retreated: nuclear power and human safety, antagonists unto eternity.

They approached the premier of Quebec. Yes, sir, up north in the province a dam three times the height of Niagara Falls, producing five thousand megawatts of power, that's five billion watts produced, monsieur, every second. A hundred times the power your Terramac needs, a thousand times. And if you expand, then for your Terramac our Quebec will build another dam, we're projecting one this very minute, gargantuan, to power all New England, New York, it'll dwarf that Hercules the James Bay project, soon we'll have dams all over the place.

A shaking of hands. More lawyers, more contracts.

The world of potential buyers knew only this: that Terramac is Summerclime. Harry's domes rising high above the whole of Summerclime were projected onto the public imagination, a natural yet pristine environment for homes of perfection. A countryside community built from the foundation up. Vegetable gardens and flowering trees, fruit trees pollinated by hand. A lake for swimming and fishing, wave machines to produce perfect surf, and water slides. A stream with trout breeding in balanced pH. The golf course beneath twenty-three interconnected bubbles. Woods for strolling amidst a multitude of genera each a consummate specimen to delight the mind, the eye and the nose in a temperate climate free of acid rain and snow. All beneath giant domes, and human-scale domes.

An econovum, 99.9999 percent insect-free. Cochan knew bugs were his phobia. He lived with and accepted this. So for Terramac, no mosquitoes, blackflies, ants at picnics, no slugs or beetles. No gnats, dragonflies, caddis-flies, blackflies. Bug-free fruit and vegetables. No drones, hornets, bumblebees, yellow-jackets. No springtails, no cockroaches. The occasional blue or yellow butterfly, imported, rendered sterile, no way to reproduce crawling things. No night moths. No locusts, grasshoppers, crickets, cicadas, termites, earwigs, spiders, maggots, mites, fleas, lice, or nits. No wasps.

But condominiums, shops, schools, a hospital. Airy work places, wired and Wi-Fied, cabled, digitally sustained. A small, well-paid, friendly police force. And soon, soon, within four years, the world would learn more: Terramac's most closely guarded secret would be, literally, unearthed: Underland. For Jim and Jane of Summerclime, ease of transport to Underland, the urban miracle beneath the shelf, both a pleasure ground and a self-sufficient dwelling place, there to meet up with Homer and Helen, together delighting in their lives and controlling their destinies amidst the finest of eateries, the best in entertainment, the fascination of one another's company.

Cochan knew too that Harry, Yak, and the others sometimes found his bug mania a bit extreme. But that's how Terramac would be.

2.

Carney slept badly. Before sunrise he set out to catch a couple of breakfast trout. His elbow ached mightily. Humidity gummed his brain. And last night's explosion? No warning, not from Sarah Magnussen-Yeager, not from his friend Mot. Road construction, blasting through granite, produced a fraction of yesterday's force; demolition was a series of simultaneous much smaller bursts. Carney had razed enough buildings damaged by fire or quake to know how those detonations felt. "Well, what was it?" he'd asked Sarah.

"I don't know," she'd said. "An explosion."

"How'd you know it was coming?"

"Most nights this last week. About this time." Her head shook.

"Way the biggest so far." She got up. "I'll drive you to your car."

That was all she could tell him. When he arrived back the house was asleep, no one to talk to about the blast. Surely they'd felt it? Now, early morning, once more only he was awake.

The water of Gambade Brook had gone a range of ruddy yellows, from bile to brick. The level had risen four or five inches. Not even the hungriest rainbow could see beyond its snout. He'd met with roiling water often, this kind of surge usually following a flash mountain rainfall. But there'd been no rain nearby for over a week. And the flow smelled murkily chemical.

Last night's mosquitoes were back. Ten more minutes and he gave up. He'd have kept casting if his elbow hurt less. A damn slingshot pebble.

He returned to the Grange and showered. From the window he saw, in the yard below, a tall skinny man in jeans and red T-shirt, splitting wood. Carney dressed, went down and out. The curving upswing of the tall man's axe was smooth as a breeze, the slash a clean flow of steel from shoulder to blade. When the axe pulled him straight he stood an easy six-six.

He stopped his work, noted Carney, nodded. "You're Carney."

"Right. You're Feodora's husband?"

The tall man nodded. "Ti-Jean." He went back to splitting. After a couple of minutes he stopped to wipe his forehead.

Carney said, "I tried for some trout this morning but the water's gone muddy."

Ti-Jean nodded again.

"It stank, too."

Ti-Jean went back to splitting. After two logs he glanced Carney's way. "Sulphur."

"Where's it come from?"

"Hell."

Carney laughed.

"Terramac." Ti-Jean's lips tightened. "The blast."

"Last night? That brought on the sulphur?"

"Maybe." Ti-Jean's measured way of speaking should have left Carney time to think, but it didn't. He met Carney's eye without blinking. "Or our demons."

"Demons?"

His glance had gone elsewhere. With the axe-head he rolled a log close to.

Carney said, "I met your sister-in-law. While fishing."

"Yep. She's out there."

"She made me wait for the blast."

"She would." Stooped, early forties, gangling till he swung the axe, Ti-Jean seemed to guard thoughts Carney might never fathom.

Or maybe Ti-Jean just wasn't very bright. Except Theresa had praised him. "Why?"

Ti-Jean glanced toward the house. "Feodora's about. She'll get you breakfast."

Dismissed. "Thanks." He found Feodora in the kitchen.

"Morning, Carney. Ham and eggs to give you strength to take on Cochan."

"Great."

"Since you're not seeing Cochan till this afternoon you better stay till tomorrow, have supper with us. My father enjoyed talking to you, hopes you'll stay another day."

Yes, Carney could do that. "I liked talking with him too."

"It's Milton mainly that holds us all together. He's there, he's quiet. Our glue."

"I guess families need a little glue." Very little from Carney. Just enough for Bobbie.

Feodora nodded. "It's not simple for him." She smiled. "Theresa's not an easy woman." She cracked an egg into a frying pan. "She wants you to kill this Terramac thing."

Carney sat. "Milton wants that too?"

"In his way." Feodora glanced at him, and cracked another egg. "They're different. Always have been, I guess. Milton was going to Europe to study when they met. A shipboard romance. They were twenty-three. She'd come for a fencing tournament. She was from Barre. You know, just fifty miles from here. Needed a boat to Europe for them to meet." She shook her head, looking pleased with her explanation. "They been together ever since. They married young, and they've spent their conscious lives together. Nearly two-thirds of their lives."

Carney saw Theresa, self-certain, provocative. "She calls herself an anarchist. Is she like that, dealing with your father?"

"Ha!" In another pan Feodora melted some butter. "Drives Milton crazy. It isn't anarchy, she just makes up her life as she goes along. Ooop—now here's her defender."

Ti-Jean had come in. His head shook back and forth, determined as a pendulum. "Sure she's an anarchist."

"Yeah?" Carney turned his way.

"Keeps trying to find out. Don't care for how she does it, myself. But it's like Feasie says and not the other way."

"What?"

"She makes her life."

"Instead of?"

"Taking on other people's failures."

"Sorry?"

"Ti-Jean means she tries to make things anew, instead of trying to fix the old stuff."

"Ah." Carney glanced about. "She's still asleep, and Milton?"

"Takes them a while to get started, these days," said Feodora. She turned a ham steak in the second pan. "You see, Theresa thinks all of us are pretty much failures. Sarah started it. She disappointed Theresa hard so she came to expect disappointment from us. Except I'm not completely a failure." She laughed, and flipped the eggs. "'Cause I married Ti-Jean and brought him into the family. There's a special rapport between him and Theresa. Who'd have guessed it?"

Ti-Jean shook his head and poured them all coffee.

"My sister Leasie's a failure. Her being a lawyer, for Theresa that's near as low as it gets, lawyers grow rich out of trash law only a charlatan tries to interpret. And law's almost as bad as selling life insurance or psychotherapy, and since my brother, Karl, did the first and now does the second, he's the biggest failure." She slid eggs, then ham, onto a plate and handed it to Carney. "And he near to destroyed Theresa by converting to Catholicism, they didn't talk for a year. Theresa wasn't that speechless again till her stroke. Oh, and Sarah's a failure because she married the Skull, he's dead but she's still a failure."

"And your father, does he think of any of you as failures?"

Feodora looked Carney full in the face, measuring his curiosity. Okay, she told herself, feed him some details, see how he does, see if Theresa's right. "That's not Milton's test. He has a happiness quotient. Leasie's medium happy, she's got good work but no husband." She poured three cups of coffee. "I'm mostly happy. Sarah's deep-down glum. Karl, he doesn't understand."

"Why not?"

"Well I sort of agree, how can he be happy, how can any intelligent man become a psychotherapist these days?"

Ti-Jean nodded. "Dumb."

Feodora asked, "Eggs?" Ti-Jean nodded some more. "For Milton, worse than dumb." She broke a couple of eggs into the pan, put the ham on. "See, for years before he converted, Karl had his affairs. He was plain randy, taking on most anything in a skirt. Then he turned Catholic, my guess being he wanted to shock Theresa. But mainly he ended up hurting Milton."

"Why?"

"The Catholicism, for Milton that's the worst. Absolute belief. The Pope knows all."

"Shits." Disgust in Ti-Jean's voice.

"We don't know how they got to Karl. Even angels fear to tread before they leap." Feodora laughed.

○

"What? What'd she say?"

"Ah." I explained: "Feodora, early on, invented mixed clichés. Now she can't help it."

"Oh." Lola thought about that. "How do you know?"

A relief, her no longer just trance-listening. "A few traces of memory from her life before, they're visible up there in her mind. Bright patches."

"Go on with the story," said Lola.

She gives back so little.

○

"I met your sister Sarah along the stream." Carney touched his elbow gently.

246

Feodora poured coffee. "I love Sarah, don't get me wrong. She's taken some bad turns."

"That's it," said Ti-Jean.

"I pointed them out to her." She chortled. "We've had our strained moments."

"Yeah?" Carney sipped coffee.

"Well, Sarah, as they said back then, she dropped out. From everything Theresa thought was valuable. Like, Sarah didn't have to go to any college, she could do battle wherever she wanted. Long as she fought for what she cared for."

"Like Theresa."

"That's it."

"But see, for Sarah, she had to reject everything Theresa loved. Or hated. She was a kind of come-lately flower child and druggie." Feodora thought about it. "To be fair, more flowers than drugs. But she did her share of coke and all that. Lived in an old-fashioned hippie commune three years. She got turned on to farming without chemicals, felt great on the food she grew. She told me her best highs came from corn she threw in boiling water right after picking it or peas wet off the vine or a ripe tomato warm from the sun, she ate them like apples, and juice ran down her chin. She was on to something, already then."

"Yep," said Ti-Jean.

"Then she dropped out of the commune too. Went to the University of Vermont, mature student, didn't have a high school diploma but they took her anyway. Finished when she was just twenty-four. She hadn't talked much to Theresa for years before then, they'd had some kind of falling out, nobody ever talks about it. Her degree was in biology, don't recall what kind."

"Small animals."

"No, not that. But I don't remember. So the day after she graduated she married. Driscoll Yaeger. He'd gone back himself after years away, masters in computer science. Only Karl and Milton went to the wedding. Leasie and me, we'd met Driscoll. We called him De Skull because the skin on his head was stretched tight like there wasn't enough to fit." She laughed. "When he got nervous his scalp sweated, he had short

short hair, then Leasie called him Drip Skull. But we think he and Sarah
got along, at least early on."

Ti-Jean refilled the coffee mugs. "He was a mistake."

"You never met him."

"Never had to."

"Then when Sarah graduated she wanted to live in the country, at
least a village. De Skull got a position as a federal welfare administrator
in the middle of New Hampshire, east of Wolfeboro region, third man
down in a four-man office. They bought a farmhouse and some land.
His job was to bring together data on the eligibles."

Ti-Jean nodded. "Idea was, make sure nobody's eligible for nothin'."

"Right. In a couple of years De Skull headed the office, he was
doing his job so well."

"That's it."

"He proved so competent they promoted him, double-step, to run
the Boston office."

Carney grinned. "Theresa must've loved him."

She shook her head. "Never got to know him. All those years she
saw Sarah only when she came up here, when she was building a cabin
out back there." She jerked her thumb over her shoulder. "De Skull
never came. The fights between him and Sarah, we didn't hear about
them till later. She loved her farm, didn't want to live in a city ever. But
De Skull's job offer was too good so he sold the farm and they moved
right into Boston, apartment on Beacon Hill."

"De Skull hated being in traffic jams."

"Well, it tore Sarah up. I visited them once, only one night, more
of De Skull would've been an overdose. He'd come to think he'd be in
Washington in two-three years? Maybe even an assistant undersecretary
at H.E.W."

Carney tried one of his ruses for telescoping to the end of the
story—"Be right back"—and went off to the bathroom.

Feodora said, "What d'you think?"

Ti-Jean shrugged.

"Doesn't talk much."

Ti-Jean smiled. They waited.

Carney returned. "I think I'll drive around, look for an undisturbed trout stream. I'll grab a bite, then head off for Terramac City."

"Have to finish the coffee." Ti-Jean divided the last of it, three half cups.

"Where was I? Yeah, Boston." She sipped. "Right. Well, Sarah got a couple of office jobs, hated them, didn't last long. She spent days out beyond the ring road, looking for green space. Down to Cape Cod, into Rhode Island, somewhere with trees. One day she found herself in Durham, up in New Hampshire, at the university. For the heck of it she went over to the Ag School, said she was looking for a research job. She filled out forms. They didn't say no, asked her for an interview, and took her. After a couple of years she went over to the Bug Institute."

"Ah. Is that where her bug love started?"

Ti-Jean said, "She gets crazy."

"Girl Friday to begin but pretty soon she was part of a bunch of 'em working on ants, linked up with some professors at Harvard. Since she lived down there she was the contact woman, she commuted. The commuting traffic went the other way, she felt smug about that."

Ti-Jean nodded. "About all she and De Skull had in common."

"And when Theresa had her stroke Sarah flew up. Nobody knew how Theresa'd react to her. The strain was there, but less. Sarah'd stay a few days every two-three months. With De Skull, they were living parallel lives."

"But he died, you said?"

"Right. See, she loved it up here, her cabin out back there. With no De Skull around. Maybe she had a lover in Durham."

"We hoped so." Ti-Jean, nodding.

"Then last winter De Skull was driving on an icy street. A car skidded through a stop sign, smashed into him, he hated seat belts and his head bashed into something. The hospital said light concussion and sent him home. So next morning he called Sarah, he had a headache, he was going back to the hospital. He took a cab, to Emergency. But when the cabby turned around De Skull was unconscious and an hour later he was dead."

"Pretty grim."

Ti-Jean grunted. "For some."

"Now that was March. Sarah quit everything, closed up the apartment, sold everything, retired to her cabin. And she blamed herself. If she'd been home, he wouldn't be dead. So she got herself drunk, stayed drunk for ten days. Then she wouldn't kill bugs. Or eat meat. Even fish."

"Stupid." Ti-Jean shook his head.

"I figure she's still in mourning, her own way. She comes by every week or two."

"Well." Carney made a point of draining his cup. "Thanks."

They gave him directions to Terramac. He drove slowly down rough road. The portrait of Sarah didn't make the woman any less strange. Though being a widow in your early thirties can't be easy. If he met her again he'd just stay out of her way. But he liked Ti-Jean and Feodora.

PIKE

Sit in a boat. Raise the oars.
The river takes you, smooth aimless drift.
Lean over the gunwale,
stare through surface glaze
beyond the reflection.
A shiner.
Wait.

In middle depth at the thermocline,
arm-long, pike stalks the flow.
Something new, a rift.
He glides, waits.

Upstream a dorsal fin, ruddy. Yellow perch waits.
A burst of silver.
Perch snatches shiner across the middle.
Teeth and tongue turn it, headfirst down it goes.
Shiner tail passes perch gills.
Digestion begins.
A moment of calm.

Pike lunges, teeth spike into barred yellow scales, firm flesh.

Perch stares at cartilage inside a pike skull. A gullet
approaches. A jerk, and unexpected grace:
perch slides down,
down.

Water flows past teeth, out gills.
Pike drifts in near balance.
Perch in the gut is bitter.
Sit. Stare. Wait.

Roberta Feyerlicht
June 11/03

251

3.

You know what you want, Johnnie, just head out to Terramac. Not to meet that Carney guy, not to meet anybody. To go down below. Maybe they hacked through the stone this afternoon—

○

"Hey!" Lola grabbed my arm. "There it is. Clear. Putting ideas in his head. Leading him."

"He's just trying to convince himself, Lola."

"Listen! I used to know all about leading a man on."

"I never would."

"I remember my lover saying to me—" She stopped. Her face drained to white. Her mouth opened, a long shudder shook her, "Oh—! Oh oh oh!"

"Lola!" I grabbed her wrist, to steady her. Her arm trembled lightly. "What?"

Color and control bled back. "Oh Ted— I saw his face. My last lover. Very wealthy."

"Ah," I said. Nothing else came to mind. Envy closing down my brain? Of course not. Jealous of a man from decades back? Nonsense. And how can she possibly remember?

"He used to say I led him on, I could lead him anywhere, leading him on turned him on." A smile took her face as years fled from her mind. She covered my hand with hers. "It's a little different, but you're doing it to Johnnie."

"Hardly." This was getting irksome.

"Leading him. In bits of ways."

I shrugged. "I'm telling you how he thinks."

"Nope, you're manipulating." She shivered. She smiled. "I didn't understand."

"Lola, if I could manipulate Cochan, wouldn't I lead him away from Terramac?"

But she wasn't listening. "You're breaking the rules." She stared at me. "I'm pretty sure."

"I'm reinforcing what's there." I couldn't say more, I wouldn't say less.

"Some of it." Her eyes softened. "You surely are." She gave me a different smile. Of wonder? Again she found my eyes, left, right. Her fingers gripped mine hard. Then she chuckled.

I could only go on.

○

John Cochan checked his face in the mirror of his personal Intraterra North bathroom. He smoothed back his hair. He combed his thick mustache. He wet his eyelids to cool them. His cheeks he rubbed to warm away their whiteness. He pulled his black-striped shirt tight into his gray slacks, pinched the Windsor knot in his carmine necktie, buffed his black shoes.

He crossed the vestibule, stepped under the peak of the old church's wooden archway, past massive stripped doors, down marble steps. He walked across flagstones set in gravel, by rows of blazing geraniums, the lawn beside him trimmed as for bowling. Past white-clapboard houses, their green shutters drinking in the sun, past three blocks of semi-detacheds, the general store, the diner, and the gas station, and along the Common, two blocks by two blocks. Roses bloomed, a dog pooped, a couple of frisbees flew. A baseball found the hole between second and short. Ethan Allen, green shoulders pigeon-whitened, stood firm in bronze. On these warm sunny days Johnnie enjoyed returning the greetings of his fellow Richmonders. He noted with pleasure his neighbors' squared-off gardens. Important, being one with the community.

His big house, also white, stood halfway up a gentle slope. He prepared a salami sandwich, the sausage made especially for John from beef organically raised at a test farm fifteen miles from town. He kept the air of his home at a sixty-eight-degree ionized balance; as the atmosphere of Summerclime and Underland would be.

Upstairs he found Deirdre and Melissa playing hide-and-seek with Diana, their nanny. He lifted the older girl to his chest but Dee's wriggling limbs irritated him. Priscilla, in Burlington today for her weekly obstetrics appointment, usually Wednesday but this week Thursday, was due home soon. The excellent County Hospital wasn't good enough for her.

Behind the wheel of the Rolls he gave himself two minutes of quiet transition, started the motor, then headed down the drive. Richmond lay only twenty-five minutes from Terramac. The visionary distance between Terramac and Richmond was that many light years away.

In the distance Terramac beckoned, as clean a magnet as a child's call. Approaching Terramac softened Johnnie's mood. The Rolls straightened curves and smoothed the shoulder. A winged beetle ended its days as yellow cream on the windscreen.

Through the covered bridge, then in a hundred seconds he was on Intraterra land. The old farmhouse stood far on the other side of the property. Terramac began here, two miles inside.

Where they had set the guardhouse, at mile 1.1, a fence ten feet high met the road on both sides. The barrier, chain-link through brush and woods, four miles long on all four sides, was electrified. The boom blocked the road.

This Intraterra project was hardly a secret. In the months after the Commissioners' office had accepted Terramac, Summerclime was written about in popular journals and papers from *The Times* to *The Forum*, had been criticized, debated, analyzed, praised, and discredited by a spectrum of architectural critics, urban planners, and environmental advocates. "The City of the Third Millennium," *U.S. News and World Report* had lauded it. Drake Shane in *The Washington Post* annihilated the dream city sardonically. The *Small Wonders* comic strip parodied it for two weeks, turning Terramacian yuppies into beetles, lizards, and groundhogs. *The New Republic* rejoiced: in Terramac, ultimate environmental control met the grandeur of exceptional human imagination. *The Richmond Patriot* spoke of a need for controlled growth in northern Vermont. In Toronto, *The Globe and Mail* despised it.

John Cochan had ignored it all, praise and chiding, jibes and commendations. They didn't know, literally, the half of it, the grand secret of Underland. His credit rating triple-A, he had turned his liaisons with mid-size banks into massive loans and impressive lines of credit. Intraterra shipped in heavy machinery, tons of cement and Québois Fina presswood, and closed deals, often locally, on materials from engineered beams to nails and bolts. In Richmond residual furore died away.

A guard peered into the Rolls, saluted, raised the boom, and waved Mr. Cochan through. The guards and fences were important. Nothing clandestine about Terramac's Summerclime, yet best to avoid pseudo-environmentalist vandals. They could set Intraterra's schedule back by days.

The new cavern beyond the wall: the place to consecrate Benjie's shrine?

Yak, if he were there, would know Johnnie didn't want to speak with any Carney. Yak knew lots about how Johnnie thought and felt; spooky to Johnnie sometimes how much. True, Yak understood people, because he had fathomed the dimensions of nature. His intimacy with shapes and passageways had begun at birth, his entrance so smooth he might himself have designed the canal of his arrival as he swam from womb to air in twelve minutes. His liaison with corridors in stoneways and airways was nurtured on sand castles, rock collecting, termite-hills, spelunking, the balanced flight of pelicans, his own hang-gliding off the cliffs at Malibu. His knowledge of seam and striation was refined by a Cal Tech doctorate in chemical engineering and by a post-doc in geological physics at the Sorbonne. He had spent four years at Taisei Corp in Japan formulating the early plans for Alice City, an underground development. Japan, with a population half as large as the US living on land the size of New England and New York, needed space to expand. So Tasei had developed designs to cut huge rabbit holes into the earth. No, wrong, Yak had argued. Use the earth's own bones and belly. Follow its lines. But Taisei wouldn't listen. Nine years ago John Cochan hired Yak away from Taisei and put him in charge of Planning for Terramac, the biggest project of both their lives.

Johnnie glided the Rolls past spruce, maple, and birch, all midsummer green as the road curved upward. And now the ridge, the crest. There, spread out before him, his world of majesty and hope: Terramac.

In Johnnie's mind as in the blueprints, the whole was divided into sixteen Segments, four rows of four. The approach road entered at Segment 15. Beyond the Trailer of Planning and the Trailer of Architecture, to the right of the trailer village, the sweet ceaseless interaction of engineers, masons, carpenters, electricians, plumbers, road-layers, bulldozers, excavators, derricks, backhoes, cement trucks, steamrollers, sheet rock, pipe, and cable. A city block of two-by-fours and six-by-sixes and six-by-eights. Powdery cement by the container-load, racks of steel webbing, precast slabs of siding. For roofing and flooring, ten-foot-high stacks of four-by-eight sheets of Québois Fina, the revolutionary presswood imported hundred-thousandfold from Canada at the advantageous rate set by Aristide Boce. And heaps, pyramids, clutters unrecognizable even to John Cochan.

To the far right, on Segments 4 and 8, several dozen buildings three and four stories high were reaching completion. Along right-angled avenues of crushed rock, foundations for more. Construction machinery rumbled, trucks delivered, men in hard hats and overalls dug trenches and holes, laid pipe, erected wall, earned their wage. At Segment 6, directly above which a helicopter now hovered, and Segment 14 stood windowless block-houses four stories high, their segmented entry gates opening to full or half height. Inside ran the elevators, by November to be replaced by the world's first communicator bubble. The entry to Underland.

Johnnie Cochan's spirits soared. To the eye of an imaginative beholder, an eye capable of espying domes agleam high above cleansed earth, able to scan homes and shops and parks that would return grace and meaning to humankind's most daily activities, even to such a beholder Johnnie would not divulge his dream for what couldn't be seen: the subterral lands, deep beneath. Except, possibly, under land he didn't own. Under Magnussen land. Yak's discovery, this new chamber.

Cochan stopped the Rolls beside the Trailer of Planning. No, no meeting, not now. Certainly not with this Carney. He needed to learn how far, how wide— He had to have that land. The trailer door opened, and Yak waved. John squeezed his eyes shut. His mind intoned: Benjie and Terramac lie in the earth, the earth is a wall, the wall separates, step through the wall.

Yakahama Stevenson marched across the trailer's porch and down to the Rolls.

Johnnie got out. The air felt heavy.

"Howdy, Handyman. What's new?"

One of Yak's traits that Johnnie shared: the chance for something new in the world. Change, the stuff of their lives. The result of change was creation. "Sorry, nothing. And here?"

"A shipment of Québois went down this morning. We're half a day ahead of schedule."

Johnnie nodded. "Good." One and a quarter would be better. Though they were, for the year, two weeks up. Schedules got advance-dated every month. "What about the big cavern?"

"Tonight."

He would have preferred now. "Okay. Tonight." He shook his head. "I'm going back."

"Steed said you had a meeting with a Mr. Carney."

"Never cleared it with me. I have to be in Richmond. You handle the meeting with Mr. Carney." He started to walk away.

Yak grinned. "Not my kind of thing, Handyman. Steed can do it."

Johnnie shook his head, but in agreement. "I'll be back around ten."

○

All is well again. Lola sits and listens, asks a few questions, and is satis-fied. She smiles, she takes my hand, at times gives my fingers a little kiss, and I'm content.

○

4.

Carney found a small brook, tried to fish it, no luck. Too many mosquitoes and he'd been spoiled last night by the Magnussen's private stream. He drove back to Richmond for lunch, and headed off on his mission. A couple of miles down he found the sign he remembered, shiny steel letters set on varnished wood:

TERRAMAC CITY
An Intraterra Venture

He turned onto a two-lane highway, neatly groomed, each looming ridge and gentle curve constructed as to prove beyond doubt and forever that country roads need fine curves and ridges. The Jag set a sixty-mile-an-hour pace, as steady as if the road itself had ordered up this speed.

Ahead, a guardhouse. A red lift-pike crossed the macadam. Carney stopped. Beyond, raised spikes angled toward oncoming tires.

A guard, cell phone holstered on his hip, came out of the shelter. Clipboard to chest, tight-lipped: "What's your business?"

"Coming to see John Cochan and Aristide Boce. Name's Carney."

"Have an appointment?"

"Yep."

"I gotta call." He scowled. "You got identification?"

Carney showed him a driver's license.

The guard returned to the hut, drew his phone, spoke, nodded, made a notation on his clipboard. The pike, a five-inch iron pipe, rose till it pointed to a fluffy cloud. The spikes withdrew. The Jag drove on down the smooth road. Ahead, a car that grew larger roared past. Looked like a Rolls-Royce. No doubt many Terramacians would own such cars.

One minute more, a crest, and Terramac lay below. Carney stopped, got out, stared.

Last time snow had hidden all this. Down there lay over a thousand acres of near to flat empty soil, sand, stone. Not so much as a shrub or weed to be seen. Straight streets, at least their curb sites, cut rectangles into the landscape. Scattered about in this strange checkerboard rose the skeletons of maybe forty cement buildings, two, three, and four stories tall. A culvert carved a curved diagonal across the patterned space. Nearby, immense spreads of building materials waited. Carney saw a small army of men in hard hats, forklifts rolling, backhoes piling, dump trucks emptying. The air was heavy with the roar of machinery. Good thing Theresa wasn't here.

He drove toward two trailers separate from the others. From the one on the right a man emerged, stout, round face, smiling, a blue blazer, white shirt, flannels, a cravat. He strode toward the car. Boce again. The only shade lay at the edges of piles of cement blocks, siding, steel beams, lumber. "Mr. Carney! So good to see you again!"

They shook hands. Carney said, "Looks different now."

Boce beamed. "We're moving forward. Ahead of schedule." He scowled, and scolded Mr. Carney, "But why didn't you let us know a few days earlier you were coming back? Mr. Cochan was here but couldn't stay, hmm? When I reached him he had a previous appointment."

Damn. He needed to confront Cochan. "A shame. For both of us."

"True." Boce beamed. "And how can we help you today?"

"I'm coming close to deciding to buy."

Increased sunlight from Boce's face. "We'd be pleased, you living in our midst."

"Two places, actually. One for my home and work, the other for my aunt."

Boce's smile dimmed. "You know, Terramac isn't a retirement community."

Carney's smile grew. "Bobbie's just a few years older than me."

"Ah," said Boce, and invited Mr. Carney to enter the trailer. An air-conditioned living space: two graceful rocking chairs, an elegant oak desk, polished sideboard, dining table set for four. From outside the trailer had seemed longer. At the near end gleamed a little tile and steel kitchen imported from *House & Garden*. Carney appreciated the windows high on three walls; when sitting, he couldn't see the outside devastation. Along the fourth wall, for half its width, descended white plexiglass charts scribbled with marker numbers in black, green, red, and blue.

"You've read our literature now, yes? So you're familiar with the Terramac vision."

"I showed your pamphlet to Bobbie. She wondered about your certain income minimum."

"Oh yes."

"No one in Terramac should embarrass us"—the communality rasped in Carney's throat—"financially, is that it?"

"That's correct. And conversely none should flaunt their wealth. We set income maximum as well, though more flexibly. We expect an annual income, for say a family of two, of between five seventy-five and one-point-nine."

Carney smiled. "A solid upper middle-class utopia."

Boce smiled right back. "At Terramac we believe the well-controlled life of the upper middle-class is as utopic as it gets."

"And if one's income is lower?"

"One couldn't afford to live here."

"And more?"

"Complicated." Boce suddenly seemed shy. "A member signs an agreement, hmm? Should his means increase, either he'll move, most likely he'll want to, to somewhere more exclusive. Or he'll make

259

ongoing donations to the Terramac Senior Trust. It does happen: in their post-retirement years one or another of our residents might find his income dropping. Of course they will have planned with care to keep this from occurring, but if for reasons beyond their control— We wouldn't ask our seniors to leave after living here for decades."

"That would interest Bobbie." A kind of well-heeled socialism? "Yeah, sure."

Boce wondered about this Bobbie; some little plaything of Carney's? "Part of John Cochan's philanthropy, hmm? Economic cares shouldn't disturb life amidst rural beauty."

The words not spoken here, Carney understood, were race and violence. As if, by virtue of the silence surrounding them, these were forever banished from the world. No gangs, muggings, drugs. No robbery because everybody had it all already. Though there might be some people that this wouldn't stop. To ask aloud about security here would sound like a fart between movements of a cello sonata. The most Carney could say was, "It still looks pretty raw out there."

Boce scowled at this ignorance. "Landscaping, of course, comes last. Clean little parks, splendid ponds full of healthy ducks and robust fish. You'll have noticed the stream, hmm?"

"You really will have fishing here?"

The ruddy Boce face lightened. "When Terramac City is complete, pike, pickerel, bass, and perch will be available in the lake, trout in the stream. Nothing finer on any Irish preserve."

"All controlled? No real brooks and lakes?"

"Mr. Carney. All our waters are real. And ever-recycled. No external contaminants. Far more real than what you intimate by real. Not a jot of mercury, or heavy metals, or PCBs. Appealing, hmm? Our fish are bred in pure spring water, our trout hatched in perfect pH balance, they'll have eaten only freshwater shrimp. Surely you prefer the pink flesh of trout fed on shrimp, hmm? Our shrimp-feed is blended for us from essential grains and proteins. Our pike and pickerel reach maturity eating crayfish, frogs, and minnows, which of course have been fed our own minnow- and frog-feed blend. Like in hatcheries, or fishbowls."

"Astounding." Nature as sterile zoo.

"We have here a model, hmm?" The plexiglass wall slid up and back, revealing a maquette of Terramac City, buildings agleam in silver and glass, the surrounding space fully landscaped. The snaking culvert, transformed into the stream, complete with pebble boulders between paint-green banks, bisected Summerclime diagonally. Replacing the trailer park, a large empty space. "In a moment we'll examine a specific unit. First, please glance here, the overview. Here is the first block of homes. Going at cost." He pointed.

"Tough time unloading them?"

Boce's beaming smile. "Terramac's philosophy is to work with those who believe in us. We've rejected a number of potential buyers we have learned would be speculating, hmm? Prices vary according to size. But even at full cost, a square yard of home here is less expensive than its equivalent in, say, Manhattan. Prices go up once we've completed the first stage. Only then does Intraterra realize its profit, here on dwellings in blocks two through six, here, here, and here. Now, if you buy before your unit is complete, during your first five years Terramac covers all maintenance fees. In the next five we phase in the expense at the rate of twenty percent per year."

The fast sell paralleled by an exclusivity shuffle. "And what if I buy and want to resell?"

"At any time. To anyone on the approved waiting list."

"If nobody's on the list?"

His smile grew. "There will be." And spread. "But if not, Intraterra buys you out at fair market price, determined by the sale of a previous unit of equivalent size and condition."

Carney conceded the fairness of this. He pointed to the empty space. "What's this?"

Ongoing smile. "I'll come to that. First let me show you, here." Boce pointed to the maquette and pressed a button. Half a dozen huge and maybe eighty smaller transparent domes descended, enclosing the maquette. "Summerclime, the perfect country environment. Note the museum here, and the concert hall. Above it all, the permanent domes. Never get wet in a rain storm, virtually no vermin. Mr. Cochan is committed to an insect-free environment, hmm? We guarantee a ninety-nine percent reduction of pest life here, as compared to the external world."

"What's bugging him?"

Boce chortled. "We're speaking in utopian terms, Mr. Carney. No ants at the picnic."

Carney let his glance scan it all: low condos, open spaces, broad streets. "Population?"

"In total, we now project twenty-three thousand." Boce pressed another button and the maquette began to turn. A hundred eighty degrees around, Summerclime gone, and a model unit appeared, a two-story apartment, three bedrooms, small garden. "Nice, hmm?"

Carney said, "Very." In truth, an elegant little home.

"Thank you." Boce slid the wall closed. "Well, you asked about this space. A landscaped, cedar-encased parking lot, three cars to a detachment. Travel within Terramac City is by electric mini-trains with rubber wheels and, once you're close to home, rolling ramps you step on to. Local carts for deliveries. Every half hour from the parking lot, snackbar- and electronics-equipped Terramac buses, armchairs only, take you to Burlington or Montreal airports. Terramac vans bring tradespeople in with all due speed. And once inside, no cars to pollute the air."

Sick building syndrome multiplied to city-size? Carney didn't ask.

"Our surveys show the average Terramac citizen, hard-wired to the office, would work at home 3.4 days a week. They'll rarely leave here for longer than three workdays, depending on the distance they have to fly. Far less commuting, all told. Parents spend more time with or near their children, so Terramac strengthens the family. We're engaging master teachers for the schools. And young Quebec women as nannies. You have children, hmm?"

"No."

"A shame. Our playgrounds are fully supervised. Under eighteen, one isn't allowed in the bars, or the nightclubs. The young do have access to clubs where no alcohol is served. We obey Vermont laws but we're a liberal community."

"I see." Time to shift to reality. "Last night I felt a large blast. It came from here?"

"Quite possibly." For a moment Boce said nothing more, then nodded. "In Terramac we honor natural forms. Many are imperfect and have to be modified."

"It was an immense explosion, Mr. Boce."

"We're dealing with a substantial territory, hmm?" Boce's beam dazzled. "Even granite can be shaped to the needs of Terramac City."

I'll bet, thought Carney. But he's not moving on the blast. "Well, I'm interested." What more to learn from Boce? "I think my aunt will be too. But I want to meet John Cochan."

"He'd enjoy that. You could meet him at the Richmond office first, then come out here."

Carney said he'd check with Bobbie. "Thanks." He opened the door. "I'm going to drive around Terramac City, get a sense of the place."

"The site isn't open, it's a hard-hat area. You've seen the maquette, the prospectus—"

"I always keep a hard-hat in the trunk. Anyway I'll stay in the car. I'll call about the appointment. Looking forward to meeting John Cochan." Out of the trailer, to his car, trunk open, hard-hat on, a wave to Boce, and driving along a narrow roadway. To be a minirail line?

Curved angles, three- and four-story condos, blank blocks, the stream's culvert. The only building that didn't match was a four-story place without windows but with a two-story gate, closed. Site for a museum? Concert hall? Half a dozen more blocks. On to the western edge of the site. Nothing but shattered rock. Pulverized. He worked his way to the northern, then the southern peripheries. More evidence of blasting. But nothing here worthy of what he felt last night.

He drove away from Terramac. By the covered bridge he stopped, walked to the stream, a real one, pulled off his shoes and socks, rolled up his pants, squished through a muddy bank, sat on a rock and soaked his feet. He watched as a mosquito landed on his arm, searched out a tender spot, stuck her dagger in. Her saliva diluted a drop of blood. She syphoned the solvent away. Her body bloated ruddy. Mot suddenly appeared, gliding a shiver down Carney's back: Watch your front, rear, sides, said Mot. The mosquito tripped through Carney's forearm hair, stumbled, her wings flapped. She was too full to fly. *Culex pipiens*, he thought, and squished it flat.

○

The image of the overdrunk mosquito delighted Lola. When she left she was in the best of moods. But not when she came back. Her lips crossed her face as a straight line, and her eyes had gone too dark for the day. "What?" I asked.

"Edsel and Helen and Dante," she said.

"What about them?"

"They've officially warned me."

"About coming here?"

"Of course." She glowered in the direction of the Near Nimbus.

"But you've been so careful."

"Damn right! Barely a quarter of my time."

"Didn't you say—"

"Of course. Still complaining." She shook her head hard. "Yeaghghgh!!" She shook her fist toward them. She collapsed onto the cloud-fluff. "What's happening in the down below?"

○

5.

In the late afternoon Carney spent a couple of hours at Richmond's library, reading back issues of *The Patriot*. By the time the place closed he'd gained insight into local views of Terramac City. The newspaper, a supporter of the project, took what he'd learned was Cochan's own line: change in Merrimac County was inevitable but such change could be directed by those it would most affect. Letters offered other opinions. None from Theresa Magnussen.

Back at the Grange for supper, he parked between the van and a Ford sedan. From inside the house, Theresa's voice: "Bastard! Keep off this property!"

The object of abuse, now a few steps from Carney, was a narrow-chested tall man wearing a suit, yellow shirt, and skinny tie. He tapped a manila envelope against his left palm.

Milton's voice: "For heaven sake, Theresa! He's only acting on his orders."

"Not on my porch! Get that poodle-puke outta here!" Her voice remained disembodied. The gray man hid the envelope behind his back. His body swayed as in a breeze.

Then Milton's large form filled the doorway. "You better go to your car. She's gone to get—" He saw Carney. "Sorry, Carney. Jed's just leaving. Come on in."

"It don't make no difference, Milton." Rich Vermont accent. "Not me, somebody else."

A squeal of brakes. "Get off the porch!" A shotgun barrel poked at the screen.

Jed nodded, found the handrail. Watching the doorway, he stepped backward down the ramp, turned, headed for the Ford, got in. And sat there.

Milton screwed the shotgun out of his wife's hands. "He'll get bored."

"Just doing his job," Theresa repeated. "Another of civilization's lesser bastards."

From inside Carney glanced out the window. The sedan stood still. "What's that about?"

"Oh, Cochan," Theresa muttered. "Another threat or offer." She shouted at the sedan, "Keep that thing out of this house!" She glanced out the window. "Some bird-shot over his roof, that'd get him moving." She flicked her wheelchair motor on. "Where'd you put my shotgun?"

"Never mind." Milton, his voice soft. "He'll leave soon." He clicked the chair's motor off.

Carney glanced over to the Ford. "Who is he?"

"Works for Henry Nottingham." Milton's head shook, weariness in his eyes. "Henry's our Sheriff here, got an investigation agency on the side. Jed's his man and Cochan uses the agency."

Theresa said to Carney, "Henry used to be a good man." She slumped back in her chair. "Cochan keeps on harassing us. He'll kill me." She frowned. "Unless I kill him first."

"Enough, Tessa. She enjoyed the stroll through the garden yesterday, Carney. She likes talking with you." Milton smiled. "Feasie and Ti-Jean said to tell you so long, come back any time. They're spending the night at his mother's place, she's feeling poorly."

"Sorry I missed them."

"Take Theresa around again, till dinner's ready. Do her good."

"Don't treat me like a little old woman."

Carney said, "If you promise not to explode I'll tell you about my visit to Terramac City."

Milton said, "Carney—"

"I will be very calm, and so will Theresa. Right?"

Theresa scowled. "Let's go for a ride."

Out to the orchard. Carney told her what he'd seen—the minirail tracks, the domes, the condos. The outlying sites with evidence of recent blasting. "The explosions happen regularly?"

"The little ones, sometimes once a day, usually at night. Sometimes a few days of peace. The big ones, there've been four-five of them over the last month or so."

"Look, I think you're right, I think the blasting is deep underground."

From her stare at him he couldn't tell, was this wonderful news, or terrible news. She only said, "Okay," and thought, and muttered, "Yeah."

"But it's impossible to tell where, or why. Nor explain why he's trying to buy you out."

"Look." Theresa stopped the chair. She pointed.

The Ford was driving away. Milton walked from it, a manila envelope in hand.

"He wouldn't!" She pushed the lever to high and rolled fast as running toward the car.

"Theresa!"

She was shouting: "And so do thund'rous legions cry, embracing hope upon the fields of danger, the ancient gods rejoice—" The whine of her motor drowned the rest of her words.

Carney sprinted across the grass after her. Milton saw them coming, grabbed at the chair as it swept by, set himself against the built-up thrust. It turned sharp, flung Theresa forward. He grabbed her too. He shoved the bar to Stop, pushed her to sitting upright, held her tight.

Carney caught up. He felt strangely winded.

Theresa's white forehead, puffy cheeks, sweat—

o

Lola breathed, "No!"

o

"Theresa?"

"Please—?" Theresa reached her hand over.

266

Carney took it, a heavy thing.

"Carney help—us—?"

6.

John Cochan waited for the dust particles to settle. Trembles of awe twitched at his guts, the exalted joy of discovery. He stood framed in the seven-foot opening in the rock, and stared.

Yak said, "A true stalactitic chamber, Handyman."

As if Johnnie didn't know. Four-hundred-watt beams probed the dim space. In the distances spread a cavern blessed with soaring arches and smooth dripping walls. From the arches, massive and medium and tiny stalactites hung like icicles in dripping reds, greens, purples, some already joined to their basal stalagmites, some still growing into each other with the drippings of millennia. Cone-shaped stalagmites stood in clumps, the beams playing brilliant chaos onto their glistening stone. Johnnie felt the calcareous water seeping from hundreds of pores, thousands, cool water dripping. He saw and heard the water, its plunks and burbles, and smelled rock so rich with carbonate of lime he all but tasted it. Here was an infinity more than living space, commercial space, entertainment space. Here was magic. A fairyland!

Yak said, "Our own little Carlsbad Cavern."

"Not so little," said Johnnie.

"If we redirected some of the water, we could grow our own stalactitic forms."

Why Johnnie loved Yak: these surges of energy, the hope, the vision.

"And, see, it's fantastic! The ground where the stalagmites rise; it's like slate it's that flat. No calcium in the lower rock. What we thought, it's true, it's two separate formations. It's clear here: they never got together. A strata of nothing. We were absolutely right."

"You were right, Yak. You figured it."

"We, Johnnie. Both of us."

Johnnie felt a great contentment. He had located Benjie's ultimate resting place. "Okay." He closed his eyes, his mind reached, further—No, nothing.

"I see the near part as slides and water-chutes, moulded from the

267

same rock. Where it's imperfect Harry can figure a way to blend cement to get the rock texture, make it look like nature herself formed the whole playland for us. Incredible, huh?"

Johnnie smiled. Like a kid, Yakahama. "Incredible." And so much to do now, out of business and love. Figure where precisely to place Benjie, to let him rest eternally. Damned trip next week. "We'll get to planning soon's I get back."

"Back?"

"From Lexington. First National's had to refinance their Guadalajara loan, now the bastards want a full half point more. You know how it is."

"Yeah." Yak shrugged off disappointment. He preferred his life here, in the field it was better every time. If he could protect Johnnie from the handshaking, the lunches, the reports— But John Cochan's strength lay in the power he brought to this personal interchange, the huge authority he took from it. With his amiability he made such moments his own, the finesse leading to Intraterra's extraordinary growth. Though here too lay the soft edge of their projects, areas Yak didn't want to understand, and felt uneasy with. The hallucinatory edges, he'd once joked.

Johnnie had said, "You don't know hallucination, that's bad stuff, stay away."

Yak did; often bringing Johnnie out to real daily things. Like now: "But listen, there's more. Over to the right and across there's some kind of fissure. Where I sent the probe before the blast, it's two hundred feet anyway. And the vibrations suggest water rushing down there."

John Cochan clicked his tongue. "Long as it doesn't get into the system." Full annihilation of bugs might not be possible but water impurities he would control.

"Nope. It can't flow up. Our systems are safe."

"I'll worry it through with you soon as I get back. First thing. Promise."

"Okay." He waited, but had to add, "Listen, Handyman, I'm pretty sure part of the cavern is under the other land. The Magnussen place. As we feared."

Johnnie stared into the distance, and shook his head. "No. Not far enough east."

"I don't know, man."

"Don't concern yourself about it."

"Okay, whatever." But Yak worried. The law was murky, and the way Johnnie played it—

"Anyway it doesn't matter what it's under. We'll get that land too." Johnnie smiled.

"Yeah? They've accepted?"

"I've made another offer. Delivered today. And the lawyer daughter's coming in when I get back. It's a good offer. More than fair. They won't turn it down."

"More than fair." Yak watched Johnnie's head nod. "Great." Light caught the few white hairs at Johnnie's temples. "In fact, fantastic, because—you ready?"

Johnnie couldn't keep from grinning. "What else?"

"Looking mostly ahead, just a bit to your right." Yak played the beam against a far wall.

"Near where the fissure comes in?"

"Not so far right. Come back maybe twenty degrees."

"Okay."

"The sonar says there's another space back there. Huger even than this one. If I'm right, by itself it's maybe a quarter as big as everything we've already found." He stopped. "Except this for sure is under their land."

The perfect smile spread across Johnnie Cochan's face, cheeks, neck even. The pit of his stomach warmed. A voice, sweet, confident, whispered: It's yours, yours.

But it was answered from the sour juices of memory: Yours, Johnnie? Yours like what you dare not lose?

○

"What?" asked Lola.

"I don't know yet," I said.

○

Johnnie shook his head. He leaned toward Yak. The smile was gone. "The land is ours."

LAND

In the roar of a moment, balance leaves
nature and time.
The trout are going, and the beaver.
Moose, hawk, rabbit, moth.
The summer's silent drain.
Wind, pond, trees, sun.
And sour rain.

In the end, will the soil, too, grieve?

R.F., April 11–12/03

Nine

DIVIDED KINGDOMS

1.

They were there, male, female:

Her scent drew him on. His head swam. He understood only one direction, ahead. Where she waited.

She sensed his approach on her legs and on her hair.

They faced each other, reached out, closed the space. Their bodies passed a message, you, me. Electricity sparked through each. And out to the other.

She needed more.

He turned, showed her his back. She approached, closer. His glands were ready, she would be his release. His scent called to her, whispering. She climbed on his back. Just—so. She lay there, licked at his scent, at its juices, its stickiness, the viscous chemical taste. Her sex opened, a wide crescent, ready for him.

He, still beneath, pushed rearwards, his back to her sex. She licked him again, along the back, then higher. She licked and his genitals extended, rose, pushed up toward her, grasped her hook-like, gripped her crescent. They held each other, a tight clasp.

Slowly, to one side, he pulled himself from under, connected to her he turned, turned in, more, clinging, and now they faced away. He held her tighter. New hooks entwined her, full penetration. Slowly the organs slid, strafed, tiny pulsations, the barest pull, push, pull and the discharge began, went on, on, on, on, and on, on. Minutes of orgasm, ten, thirty, longer—

His seed was launched, she its receiver. Both were content. The moment of linkage was their lives' one splendid act. The seed would burst soon into new life.

A thousand times, in millions of households, in as many alleyways and fields, the act was repeated, and repeated.

○

Lola said, "Neat." She stroked the robe on her thigh.

"In the hidden places," I continued, "the coupling of cockroaches."

"Oh." She flicked me a grin, but it fell away. Something was troubling her, a lot. Near as much as Theresa's stroke, it felt like. But she didn't say what.

○

The ones Carney could see:

Out of the corner of his eye, kitchenward, across a chalk line, in the shadow between the stove and the sink cabinet, movement. In the half darkness, four of them, two pairs, huge, back to back, antennae swaying. He got up, eased his way to the kitchen switch, flicked it on. They and he stood frozen. He charged.

Off they scrabbled toward the cabinet; in a second they found the slit under the sink, their private chasm, and down they wiggled. He tore open the lower door. The light hit dozens of them diving for cover. He slammed at them bare-handed and crushed three as they tried to evacuate. From the survivors, was that laughter?

He washed his hands. He stared at the chalk line. No, the roaches hadn't crossed it.

Three hours ago Milton had offered Carney his choice, a couch in the Magnussen living room or an apartment in downtown Burlington. "Sorry, we're not set up for guests. Not like in the Grange days." The apartment belonged to Natalia Bewdley, a colleague of Theresa's, off on a summer-long field trip researching west coast redwing blackbird family structures. Milton watered Natalia's plants. Use the place to bed down any visitor you can't stand having at your place, she'd told Theresa. So Carney chose privacy. Tonight for the first time in years he would, in a manner of speaking, sleep in a woman's bed.

Milton had shown Carney the apartment and told him about the roaches. "Nat and the bugs share the place. They live under the sink. Don't worry, they're trained."

"I can see." Wonderful. Only in Vermont would roaches understand chalk.

"Organized them herself. At night you draw a chalk line, five feet this side of the stove. They stay over there. You stay here."

Not like his New York City roaches. Back in New York, Thea had needed garlic. But those had been tough roaches.

Seven hours ago Milton and Carney had lugged a mattress to the van and slid it in back. They'd lain Theresa flat and covered her with a couple of blankets. Milton sat with her, his hand light on her shoulder. Carney sped them into Burlington. Theresa muttered, "I feel cold, it's—too cold."

Milton covered her with a third blanket. "Better?"

"I'm cold—right through."

The duty nurse wasn't Pat but everybody knew Theresa. Now in a hospital wheelchair, she complained she couldn't reach the stick, couldn't move herself forward.

"It's a different chair, Tessa." Milton stroked her arm. "We'll push you."

"Where?"

"Wherever we need to go," said Carney.

"I can't see where."

"We'll take you," said Milton.

"The light's . . . very bright."

Milton put his hand on her forehead, and let his palm slide over her eyes.

"Harsh. Very . . . cold."

"Close your eyes for a bit, Tessa."

"Where are we?"

An orderly took her off. Carney and Milton waited. Milton stared across the room, down at the floor, out again. Neither spoke. What to say? Again and again Milton took his lower lip tight between his teeth and sucked on it. Sometimes his head shook.

Carney said, "Shouldn't you call Feodora, or one of the others?"

"Yes," said Milton but didn't move.

"You want me to call?"

Milton said nothing.

Carney went out. Milton sat alone. An hour and a half later they were allowed to see her.

How was she? Still difficult to tell. Preliminary tests indicated ischemia, a sudden deficiency in the blood supply to the brain. Definite paralysis on the left side, hard to know about the right. More tests tomorrow.

Carney said, "I'll wait out here."

"If she wants to see you—"

"You two should be alone."

She lay on the bed, eyes wide, face chalky blue, motionless. Two tubes to her left arm, monitors above the bedhead. Milton sat on the mattress, stroked her right forearm, whispered. No sound from her, no quiver on her lips. He held her hand in both his and his head hung down to the three hands together. He cried, a soft rhythmic breath. She didn't look his way but her eyeballs did seem to shift their gaze.

Carney by the door saw her eyes move. He knew little about strokes but took this as a small positive sign. After a minute he went away, walked around, gave them time.

He came back. The heel of Theresa's palm lay at the bridge of Milton's nose, his hands holding her hand in place, his brow bent toward her as if she supported his head. Carney touched Milton's shoulder, squeezed gently, left, waited in the corridor. Twenty minutes later he looked in again. Neither Milton nor Theresa had moved. A new silent world for them.

After a while a nurse separated their hands and led Milton from the bed. Milton dried his cheeks, smiled to Carney, asked to sit alone for a few minutes. Not in the room, in the hall.

Carney went in. He hadn't meant to but his legs took him to the bedside. He bent forward to catch her glance. Her eyes, open, motionless, stared at Carney; not focused on Carney's eyes but—Carney felt it this way—to catch a glimpse of what or who Carney was. What did she see?

Her pupils dilated, slightly. Could Theresa Bonneherbe Magnussen still see anything? But her non-focused gaze seemed to probe space, to ask the skeletal questions. Was there such a category as post-stroke stare? "Goodnight, Theresa." He found Milton in the hall.

Milton smiled weakly. "She'll come out of it again."

Carney nodded. "She will. With your help."

At last Milton called Feodora and Ti-Jean. They'd stop at the Grange, pick up Carney's car. But, keys? No problem, Ti-Jean could start any car. Yes, she'd contact Leonora and Karl.

Milton and Carney sat in the hall. Milton said, "It'll be good for

Theresa to have Feasie here." He continued speaking softly, as if clearing up a mess in his mind. As if hearing his own words could make him more present for Theresa. He talked about his offspring. The twins he found easiest. About Sarah he was mainly sad, her distance from Theresa, from him too. For Karl, his concern was greatest, he felt a fear for him, and more, for his choice of profession. Earlier Milton had worried about Karl's debauchery . . .

Debauchery? "A dated notion, no? Too much drink? Too much sex?"

Milton shook his head. "So many women, a kind of flailing search. He seemed in anguish. He told me once, so few women he was with were really with him. Since his conversion he's become almost a hermit." Milton spoke with increasing weariness. "He's our only son."

It still sounded as if Milton was trying out shared words, shared knowledge—could it bring Theresa back? At least keep her, tonight, from falling further away. And what are you doing here, Carney? In the middle of all this?

Feodora and Ti-Jean arrived, Feodora in tears as she hugged Milton. Then Milton had taken Carney to the Burlington apartment and returned to the hospital. When Carney at last found sleep a shifting woman in her thirties haunted his dreams, sometimes in a kitchen he almost remembered, at times a garden, once nearly the woman in the photo over his desk, then a bright-lipped vamp in a tight white fifties dress. All the same woman.

○

"Do you know who she is?"

Yes.

Through the filter of Carney's dream she looked like my Annette. Forty-four earth years since I saw her last, in any manner. When we Achieve Ascension we get to choose our locations. From the down below of 1959 I chose to be over the place Annette and I had enjoyed most.

Annette. To breathe the clarity of life into images of other people had been her great talent. The artist in her painted what lay beneath surfaces. Her gaze penetrated walls, moments, the ground, skin. She saw in others what they had done with and to themselves. Her paintings taught many of them to see this too, from a kindness in her stroke and line.

Annette and I were merry lovers and best of friends for twelve years. She read my stories, confirmed what I'd done right, helped me transform what was weak. Her pleasure when I succeeded was greater than my own. Without her *The Lives of Elena* would have been a narrow tale of aborted lust, *Mustache of the Walrus* a cracked melodrama instead of high comedy, *Twelve Lucky Pelicans* a mildly veiled courtroom drama. I assumed we'd be together always.

Annette had a patron, an elderly—and powerful because wealthy and generous—uncle. He convinced the board of the Art Institute of Chicago to offer her a retrospective show. She'd only been painting sixteen years! I went there with her, *Pelicans* had just appeared, for me there'd be interviews and readings. Her uncle sent his private plane. Over central Ohio we ran into a storm, lightning on all sides, massive turbulence. Suddenly we were falling. The pilot shouted out his instruments were jammed, freak electric circuits— The plane plummeted, he tried to pull us out. We had no parachutes. The plane crashed, and we died.

I don't know what happened between hitting the ground and my arrival up here but with enormous surprise I discovered I'd become an Immortal. Of course I never knew such categories existed. Even if I had, I hardly possessed the hubris to think I'd end up here. But I always did suspect that little brings superstar popularity to a writer so much as dying. Here I am, not a God but still a mighty privilege, my books securing for me in death the fame I'd never attained while down below. *Pelicans* received three major prizes, and my estate the revenue from huge posthumous sales, including film rights. I think my son was proud of me. If I'd been able to feel parental emotion I would've missed him terribly. But here I could bask in my glory with Annette.

Except I couldn't find her. I searched everywhere. No, they told me, she hadn't Achieved Ascendence. Impossible! She was way more famous and much more important than me! If such emotions were possible here, I'd have burned with fury. No, she definitely was not around. It turned out that in the down below, apart from the community she worked in, few had even heard of her. I will never quit, I cried, till she too AAs!

But no. We're granted heavenly benefit by virtue of our work on earth. Once dead we're either well remembered or soon forgotten. That's it. In the down below, Annette had already faded from most memories.

I left those clouds behind, the ones we'd loved each other under. I found the space above Mount Washington aloof enough, and soothing. Years later I started telling stories again, for the fun of it. Annette lay faded deep inside my earthly memory. Till times like now, Carney's dream.

"Ted? You there?"

I shook my head. I feared Lola's jealousy—was she capable of jealousy?—jealousy of someone I once loved, just might edge her away from me.

But Lola said, "It's Carney's mother, isn't it?"

"I think— Well, maybe."

She smiled, gentle. She took my hand.

○

2.

"Hank. To rebury the dead, who do I talk with?" John Cochan spoke softly, a midmorning call to Sheriff Nottingham. He heard the silence at the other end. He stared out through the plexiglass. The dim buzz of smart people down there stimulated him. As it should.

The Sheriff said, "In this county, that's under the auspices of the Coroner's Office."

"How does it work?"

"You make a written request. It's got to be approved. And the reason, it has to be solid."

John wished it were not. "It is." He paused. "Does it take long?"

"If the reasons are valid it goes pretty quickly."

"Like?"

"Oh, the same day."

"Great. Do the legal work. When can you meet me at the cemetery?"

"Whose grave?"

"My son's."

Silence.

"Sheriff?"

"May I ask you why, Mr. Cochan?"

"I need to bring him somewhere safe."

"Sir—"

"Hank, he's my son."

"He was, sir." The Sheriff spoke softly.

"Will be forever, Hank. I think you understand. Maybe I can put it like this. Maybe you can just come with me. A favor. Bring a shovel." John paused. "Okay?"

After a moment the Sheriff said, "I assume you want this done as privately as possible."

"Damn right."

A breath. "If I remember right the last patrol drives through around ten-thirty. We can meet, say around eleven."

"Can't be tonight, got a late meeting. Tomorrow night?"

"Weekend's no good, Mr. Cochan. People there till late, and now in the summer they lock up for Saturday and Sunday night, keep the kids from parking there, drinking, getting in trouble."

Kids get in trouble wherever, what difference does it make. Hell! "Well I've got to be away Monday and Tuesday, back Wednesday. Wednesday night. Can you be there at eleven?"

After a moment the Sheriff repeated, "Eleven."

"Thanks, Hank." Cochan set the phone down. Damn having to be down in Lexington, damn credit shifts, damn bankers can't tell bile from blood. He gazed out. The ceiling twenty-five feet up loomed white and heavy-beamed, lofty, cool, as surely it had to worshippers for near its two hundred years. Yes he did understand how the Sheriff maneuvered things. Give the man space, a job gets done. His way, and slow, but done and thorough.

3.

Carney went out for breakfast, returned to the borrowed apartment, looked about. No roaches. Bobbie had told him about roach sex. She knew her insects. He admired her curiosity about parts of life that others never noted. Including Terramac? He phoned her. "Want to see Terramac?"

"I'm working," she said.

Her tone was answer enough but he asked anyway. "Just listen a minute." He told her about wanting to meet Cochan, couldn't Bobbie make herself free for a while?

"I'm busy today."

Irked at being interrupted, was she? Fair enough. What about tomorrow? He knew she liked to keep her Saturdays open till the last minute, in case something intriguing turned up. Okay, she agreed, tomorrow. Carney would make the appointment.

He called Intraterra North. No, Mr. Cochan wasn't here just now, would he speak with Mr. Boce? Sure. Yes, three, tomorrow afternoon, Ms. Feyerlicht and Mr. Carney to meet with John Cochan who, Mr. Boce knew, was certainly eager to meet with them.

Carney put the phone down. It rang. He let it go. The ringing went on, on. He took it.

A male voice said, "Mr. Carney?"

"Yes."

"This is Karl Magnussen." Silence. "Theresa and Milton's son. Glad I caught you."

"Is Theresa worse?"

"Nothing's changed, Milton says." A long sigh from Karl. "He told me how you helped Mother. Thank you. Can you come to lunch? He said you might still be here. He's coming too. He needs to eat too." A shorter sigh. "My twin sisters are coming. Twelve-thirty."

Nothing awaiting Carney home at the farmhouse except peace. It would still be there in the evening. "Thanks. That'd be nice." He liked Milton and Theresa. Feasie, her ease in this company, intrigued him. Sarah, he couldn't figure out. Might as well meet the other two.

Families. Unfathomed groups where individuals played settled roles? For him Bobbie was friend, mother and father, long-time unquestioning love-giver, many potential siblings, and an entire cousinage; all in one. Each of the two women he'd loved and lived with for a time were, maybe not by coincidence, also only children.

He found his Jaguar parked downstairs: Ti-Jean Seymour, benevolent auto thief. Carney drove to the hospital. Milton, leaning forward from the chair beside the bed, glanced up, haggard. "How is she?"

"Well, maybe a little better. I think she recognizes me."

Carney saw a small frail woman lying still, staring up.

"Her doctor said—" His voice caught. He forced himself. "This time the paralysis is permanent." He forced a grin. "He's wrong." His thin lips showed no bravery. Only conviction.

Carney left. Milton would stay there till lunch. Why Karl's invitation? Likely Milton wanted to express thanks. Unnecessary, Carney had told him so twice, simple accident that he, not someone close to the family, had been around yesterday. But Milton must've pushed Karl: Invite the man. Carney grinned a sour little smile. Carney, running from disasters, now dithering in Burlington because an old woman with a stroke feared potential disaster brought on by a nearby techno-urban development?

○

Lola was barely listening. I said, "You want to tell me what you're worrying about?"

She slowly turned to face me. "Earlier, I remembered something."

"What?"

"Over a—a period of time, it all got increasingly silent."

"Where?"

"I think, in the down below."

I squinted at her. Did I really hear what she'd just said? That she remembered? "Increasingly silent? What got silent?"

"Where I was," she said in a small voice. "There."

I sat next to her and lay my hand on hers. "And this was when?"

"I think—" Her voice was now a tiny whisper, hoarse, as if holding tears at precarious bay. "I think, as I was dying."

My fingers covered hers. "Lola. Listen to me. How can you remember this?"

She shook her head, once. "I don't know. It's just there."

I said, I had to, "And—was there anything else?"

She waited a few seconds before saying, "It hurt."

"What did? How?"

Her eyelids closed. "I don't know." She sat still, she breathed deep. "I remember pain."

I put my arm about her, and held her to me.

"And then the pain was gone," she whispered against my chest. She pulled away a little. "Ted? If I ask you something, will you tell me?" Her soft sweet eyes stared past my head.

I can refuse her nothing. "If I know."

"Ted, how did I die?"

I'd been told the story up here but couldn't verify it. "I heard—" The sound of my words left me suddenly unsure. "You overdosed. Heroin. You killed yourself. An accident, I heard."

"How strange," she said.

"What?"

She shook her head again and relaxed against me. "I have no memory of that." After some time she said, "I'm okay." She drew back, her eyes open now.

○

4.

Yak said to Johnnie, "A bad idea, Johnnie."

Johnnie looked honestly surprised. "Hey, I figured you'd think it was right."

Yak shook his head.

"What?"

"First of all, Benjie should just stay in place."

"But Terramac is his."

"But he doesn't have to be there."

"Where else? That cemetery's irrelevant."

"It's where most people go, in the end."

Johnnie could feel anger creeping in. He stared beyond Yak, through the plexiglass, down the nave. "Benjie isn't most people."

Okay, no arguing, not along this line. No flexibility when it came to Benjie. Another direction: "Does Priscilla know what you're thinking about doing?"

"She'll be happy I did it."

"Handyman. You have to tell her. Before. Okay?"

Johnnie nodded slowly. "Sure." His face said, Discussion over. He sat back. "When we consecrate Terramac in Benjie's honor." He was far away. "Benjie wanted to go down, watch the exploration, the building. Now, symbolically, I can give him that chance. A small shrine."

"But with all the activity, the machines—"

Johnnie shook his head. "In the new cavern. Up on the left, the little slope up. He can watch it all from there."

5.

At half past a humid noon, driving to Karl Magnussen's home, Carney felt a Mot-twinge of misgiving. He parked, high on a hillside beside an immense outcrop of boulder, overlooking the lake. He walked up the drive through a desiccated garden to a two-story stone house. The door opened before he reached it. Lying in wait?

Milton brought him in and sat him down in the living room. "No problem getting here?"

"No problem."

"Hot, isn't it? Lemonade? Beer?"

"Lemonade, please."

Bookcases rose to the ceiling on either side of the fireplace: light fiction, science for the layman, popular biographies. No overflow here, not like at the Magnussen farm. Not like Sarah's cabin either, no books there, no magazines, not even in the bathroom, the inside one where he'd peed before leaving, having forgotten he should be peeing outside.

Milton returned with two glasses on a tray. Following him, a man and a woman. "Karl, Leonora, meet Mr. Carney, call him Carney, no known first name. Don't ask me why."

In feature Karl looked a good bit like a younger Milton: black hair instead of the white, eyebrows thick, bifocals, rounded clean-shaven cheeks. The soft Magnussen chin in Karl was merely thin. Same solid breadth of shoulder and chest as Milton, and as tall. Slacks and an open dress shirt. Sandals. And beside him a woman who had to be a Noodle: skinny indeed, around six feet tall. Still, in a disciplined white blouse, wide black belt at her tiny waist and a straight fawn skirt, she suggested slender and expensive elegance. Lean face, strong brows, retiring chin; but the cosmetic crafts, shades of artifice applied by a subtle hand, had softened nature.

She figured she should sit, so he could; make him feel easier. An appealing man, Carney.

No change in Theresa's condition; they'd just come from the

hospital. Professor Bewdley's apartment was satisfactory? Very good. Humidity getting to you? Not bad.

The doorbell rang. Ti-Jean and Feodora. Karl kissed Feodora's cheek, shook hands with Ti-Jean. Ti-Jean kissed both Leonora's cheeks, greeted Milton with a smile, and quickly shook Carney's hand, a shy gesture now. The twin sisters stood equal in height, Feodora's roundness beside Leonora's angularity proof that genes leave room for daily living. They were shockingly alike in face and gesture.

"Ginette sends her apologies."

"Ah," said Karl. "Is she with her young man?"

"In charge at the shop."

Feodora wore a blue shirtwaist dress cut yards from Leonora's boutiqued bearing. Ti-Jean's white T-shirt and blue jeans were clean.

In the kitchen alone with Leonora, Karl said, "Stay after. A small confession."

"Oh?" She decided, and let guilt show. "I have one too."

At the table Carney sat beside Leonora, bowls of jellied consommé before them. All the family except Sarah; hard to reach her in the middle of the woods. Okay, Carney, make yourself amusing. Leonora, the others too, laughed at his wit.

A wide-roaming meal. Nothing and many things were talked about, a time at once both free from and haunted by Theresa. Carney found it engaging, the easy give and take of the Magnussen family. Even Ti-Jean's dour comments were convivial. But if Theresa were sitting down at the end of the table, would they even have come? Milton, his offspring—even Karl—about, seemed happy, energy and stability in a large package. Karl brought cheese and fruit.

Feodora said, "So what's happening at Terramac, Carney?"

It felt like a demand. "I saw the site, I spoke with somebody Boce. I'll go back, meet Cochan, hear him out."

Feodora said, "Theresa hoped you'd write an exposé of Terramac. She thinks your book's really important."

"You read it?"

"Yes."

"Horror stories. People like reading horror stories." He smiled without pleasure. "Easier than actually doing something."

Feodora said, "Terramac's a horror story."

Carney shrugged. "Lots of people live with crime and drugs all about. They think they like the country but they want to avoid the inconveniences of rural living. Maybe they think Cochan's giving them the best of both worlds."

Karl said, "Be serious, Carney—"

The doorbell rang. Karl jumped up to answer.

An attractive woman in a bare-shouldered light-green sundress and glowing light-brown hair, clutching a red backpack, face glowering in disgust, greeted the others. Sarah Bonneherbe Magnussen, transformed. She said nothing, opened the pack, took out a plastic-over-newspaper-wrapped package, set it on the table by Karl's cheese plate, unwound the plastic, pulled away the sopping layer of newsprint. Inside this, a clear soggy foam-filled plastic bag.

Leonora said, "Yeaghgh."

Milton said, "Sarah, for godsake!"

"Come on, get it out of here." Karl pushed his chair far back.

Inside the plastic, from the shape, two large fish. Patches inches in diameter between skin and scales had blistered away, oozing jaundiced bubbles, the flesh a swamp of gray-mauve pustules and foaming abscesses.

Feodora's head shook, a tiny vibration. "What's this about?"

"Washed up. Over by the spring. The water's gone muck-green there. The stuff hovers, twenty feet wide, it doesn't dissolve. And the spring, now it's stopped flowing."

Karl shook his head, his small jaw framing a forced smile. "And the source of the pollution, Carney? Terramac." Deepening the ache in his gut: how could his lovely Priscilla stay with a man who created such havoc?

"Maybe." Carney knew the syndrome. Passing along streams in the rock or rising from pockets of groundwater, some manufactured substance contacts matter stable for millions of years. Matter and substance react, find their own special chemistry, and out flows a toxic soup. Natural mercury gets released that way, flowing into lakes, poisoning fish. "Certainly something's happened to the groundwater. But directly because of that explosion?"

Sarah said, "The groundwater's right under our land."

"Hard to tell." Shooting him with her slingshot, tracking him down, making him sit and wait for an explosion, did Sarah do this on family orders? "You find groundwater in still ponds. And in moving streams."

"Carney." Feodora spoke softly. "What can we do about it?"

"Investigate, definitely—"

"Carney, I was there at the meeting with the county." Milton suddenly looked drained, weary. "Look at those fish. That's proof aplenty that Cochan's not living up to the terms of his agreement with the Commissioners. All that improving-the-water-table stuff, all nonsense now."

"You're right. Except legally proving cause or source is often doomed beforehand. Not to mention tedious and expensive. Still it has to be tried."

Feasie muttered, "Give Cochan an inch, he'll get the worm."

"Maybe we've lost perspective." Milton leaned toward Carney. "You're outside this. Realistically, what can we do?"

Karl gazed at Carney, impassive. Milton, Feasie, and Ti-Jean wore hopeful smiles. Leonora looked embarrassed.

"Begin the investigation. I'll try to learn whatever I can. Then bring legal action."

They glanced toward Sarah. She paused before saying, "I'll do what I can."

○

I saw Lola in the distance, coming toward me. She'd want to hear about the fish. But when she arrived, there was defiance in her eyes. Uh-oh. "Okay," I said. "What happened?"

"Ha!" She grabbed me, and hugged me tight.

I, naturally, hugged her back. "Yes?"

"I gave them great pleasure. Just a little while ago." She looked smug. "They delighted in surrounding me, a dozen of my brother and sister Gods, Edsel and Frank and Victoria, a whole bunch. Loved every minute of it, not letting me out of the circle. They were overjoyed when I asked what it was all about. And, guess what, their greatest enchantment came from not answering, not speaking a word, not a breath, just dancing slowly around me."

The Gods, shunning. "How charming."

"But guess what else, the very best." She paused for effect. "I didn't like any of it."

"Whoops." Something serious here.

"And it's more than that. I'm not getting much pleasure at all out of being a God. That rule about everything giving pleasure—"

"Because of my story?"

"No idea."

"Lola? Do you care?"

She thought for a moment. "I—don't think so." She thought some more. She glanced over the edge. "Anything new down there?"

○

6.

Damn Aristide Boce, he'd lost all sense of proportion. To meet Carney tomorrow afternoon was not appropriate, no matter how famous the man might be. He had to spend more time with Dee and Melissa. And Priscilla, pregnant, so she needed him around more, that was important. Besides, Saturday belonged to the cemetery. Hank understood, lots of people at the cemetery on Saturday. Clever guy, Hank.

But not clever Steed. A message forwarded on voice mail, for Petesake! He tried Boce's line again. Same damn message. Had he gone to the Montreal office? Not his day to be in Montreal. Go home for lunch? Too much to do, stupid trip to Lexington. Anyway Priscilla or Diana had fed the girls by now, she was likely lying down. The new one inside her: she kept saying he. She went and got herself tested? If a boy, like Benjie? Benjie's—replacement? Stop!

Tomorrow at the gravesite he'd apologize to Benjie for this kind of thinking. He'd meet Carney, sure. And the cemetery afterward, no rushing back from there.

7.

Sarah left, then Feasie and Ti-Jean. Carney went home, Milton to the hospital. Leonora stayed to help Karl clean up. The loaded dishwasher sloshed quietly. Karl sat on the couch. "You first."

"What I've done," Leonora dropped down beside him, "I don't think you'll like it."

Karl shrugged. "Tell me."

"I love the Grange. But it's going to be hard to make a case against Terramac. I hated those fish and what they might represent. But I'm not convinced that Terramac's the cause. And besides, Shaughnessy, Vitelli, Goldman, and St.-Just has invested in a dozen Terramac condos."

Karl cocked his head. "They wouldn't listen to your advice?"

"I recommended buying."

"Why?"

"Makes sense. We're suggesting it to several of our clients, both Canadian and US. A first-rate base for our free-trade people in the Toronto, Montreal, Boston, New York circle."

He stared at her. "But—John Cochan's Terramac?"

"It meets the needs."

"What needs?" He felt his anger burble.

She took a breath, and released it. "In the last eight months the firm has lost two new partners, bright people. They don't want to live in a city. Even Montreal. They've moved. Eastern Townships, small towns. So their kids don't grow up on urban streets. They want out." She smiled, ironic. "But where they've gone or could go to, they'd miss the urban advantages, right?"

"But Terramac, for godsake!"

"Look, they can live there and still work with us. Come in to the office twice a week. Do what they need from home. Fax and Internet take them into data banks and image banks wired into every possible research system going. Full city advantages, and country living." Preaching like a brochure. "Whatever we think of Cochan, Terramac's a winner."

"It's shit. Polluted water, polluted fish, polluted land, polluted people."

"Look, all sorts of institutions are buying in. Magnabank took five places for their people, Alton Life four, and an option on six more. Sapei Corp has nine, Allgemeine Werkstätte about as many. It'll be an international town."

"I can't believe you're saying this."

"It makes sense, Karl. A computer-artist friend, he lives on the Plateau, his thirteen-year-old got raped, knife at her throat, in her school cafeteria. Nine-fifteen in the morning, for chrissake. He wants to live safer, okay? His private software plugs into Terramac's delivery systems, his work bounces off their satellite connection and arrives anywhere in the world. Instantly just like from his Montreal office but this way he gets time with his kids."

"Your partners are really buying in?"

"And get to live next to all kinds of intriguing and smart people. Not rapists."

Karl's head shook as it drooped.

A week ago she'd called on John Cochan, furious at his offers to buy the Grange's acreage. He'd spoken with sincerity and enthusiasm, he'd never build on the land, it would become parkland for Terramac, fenced, a preserve for birds and deer, a place for woodland walks for those who needed something less than the perfection of Terramac City. He handed her an envelope. The deed to a two-bedroom unit in Terramac, valued just over $1.7 million, legally in her name. She could use it, rent it, sell it, give it to away, but even if she threw the deed in the trash the place was hers. She'd tell Karl about it maybe next month, next year. "Look, Karl. I'm sorry I upset you." About her deal with Cochan two years back she'd wait longer than forever to speak. "Okay, I don't like it so close to the Grange. But Terramac's there to stay."

Karl's head shook in ongoing disbelief. "And you recommended it."

"Yep. And better me telling you than you just hearing."

"Oh, great. Thanks."

She leaned toward him. "And I'd just as soon the others don't find out. Not right now."

He smiled, grim. "Embarrassed, are we?"

She sat straight. "Avoiding unnecessary grief."

"Except the little bit for me." He sniffed a laugh.

She smiled, and spoke brightly. "How about your confession?"

"Not important."

"Yes it is."

He twitched a shrug. "Doesn't matter."

"Come on."

He looked at her for a couple of seconds. "I'm in love with someone."

"Oh?" She felt a pang and gave him a smile.

288

"She's wonderful."

"Someone I know?" A big bright smile.

He waited, as if thinking. "No," he said finally. "No, I'm sure you don't."

"Well? Who is she?"

Karl shook his head again. "Tell you some other time. Got an appointment." He stood.

She got up too, took his arm, and drew him to her side. "You really won't tell me?"

"Maybe it's good business, Lease. But it makes me feel, I don't know, nauseated."

She pulled away. "It's first-rate business. But he's not going to get Magnussen Grange."

"Well now, that's something."

If she did tell Karl about how she got Intraterra to modify its plans, maybe he would understand. No. That'd be really stupid.

Karl bussed her cheek quickly. They walked out together.

She drove away first. Her thoughts turned to Carney. Maybe she should get to know him better.

8.

Carney, back at his farm, itched with irritation. Terramac City. He saw its blacks in shades of gray, its whites shone first bright with promise, then flashy with dazzle. All too clear, and yet fuzzy. Its parts made a sense he knew, fabricated ease and comfort, mixed neighborhoods of shops and homes, work and domesticity commingled.

But in the last minutes Carney had gone completely partisan. Two dead fish had pulled him in.

Ti-Jean had asked Carney, "What do you think killed them?"

Carney had said, "We could send them to the lab at—"

Sarah had gotten up. "Leave him alone, he's useless." And a moment later added, "Like the rest of us." Then she'd packed up her rotten fish and left.

Too late for prevention at Terramac. Damage control? Of what?

Something was off. Villages, towns, cities grow up because they're located at crossroads, natural ports, fast water to turn spindles. Why choose the Fortier farm to build Terramac? Why buy the Grange? Then he had a thought. And it made sense. He'd only seen part of what Terramac would be. They were blasting underground not to build foundations, not because they were mining. For what? Could it be that part of Terramac would itself be underground?

Leaving Karl's he'd said goodbye to them individually. Feodora, upset. Ti-Jean, unreadable. Leonora, as if hesitant in the face of Terramac. Karl, confused. Milton, quietly angry. No goodbye to Sarah, she was gone, fury in a bare-shouldered sundress.

o

Lola said, "Why don't you just put her hand in his?"
I ignored her.

o

Carney passed a night riddled with dream fragments, hollows in woods and underground spaces and mountaintops. At eight in the morning he remembered only the notion, caves. Was Cochan blasting underground in order to build? The cost of opening up a subterranean space would be prohibitive. Unless he were simply— simply?—improving a space already there. As in, caves.

The phone rang. Karl. "When are you meeting with Cochan?"
"This afternoon."
"Come by here before. I need to talk to you about something. A real disaster."
"What?" Didn't they have anyone else to talk to?
"It's important."

I specialize in disaster, breathed Carney's rational mind. You people don't know what a disaster is! But his thought-free self said, Interesting. And Mot whispered, Watch yourself, fella. But Carney rejected the itch. Mot had been on his case for days now and nothing had happened. Was he losing the insight arising from behind Mot's widow's peak? "Okay, I'll drop by."

"And if you've got a few minutes, will you look in at the hospital? Theresa'd like that."

They were organizing the day for him, and he was assenting. So his "Sure," was as much verbal shrug as agreement. Bobbie would be with him. Well, that'd be Karl's problem.

He spent the morning at home Internet-researching the geography and geology around Merrimac County, from the low-lying south shore of the St. Lawrence River down to Vermont's Granite Hills. The Grange and the Terramac tract lay in the knobby rises where flatland met the foothills. That stretch of terrain, he learned, was doubly drained, southwest into the Missisquoi River and on to Lake Champlain, north via Fortier Creek and Rivière Sabrevois to the Richelieu, on to the St. Lawrence. Fortier Creek rose from springs in Vermont and flowed north into Quebec, the national boundary an afterthought unsponsored by nature.

○

Lola touched my forearm. "He sounds like you."

I nodded. I hid my smile from her.

○

A nineteenth-century system of locks and canals, recently revived, makes it possible to sail from New York Harbor, head up the Hudson and along the old Barge Canal to Lake Champlain, through its hundred-mile length to the Sabrevois and Richelieu Rivers, on to the St. Lawrence and back to the Atlantic. The New England states plus the Gaspé Peninsula of southeastern Quebec, together with New Brunswick: thought of in this way, they become a huge island

The headwaters of the Missisquoi and the Richelieu were rapid little streams, the Sabrevois more peaceful, sluggish even. From where Fortier Creek emptied into the Sabrevois the water dropped seventy-nine feet over forty-one miles to the St. Lawrence and was navigable by pleasure boats its full length.

The phone rang. Charlie Dart. "Checking if you're in. Stay there. I'm coming over."

"Sure, but what's—"

"I'll be there in half an hour."

What was up with Charlie? Carney went back to his research. The fist-bump north containing the Cochan and Magnussen properties was covered with shallow-earth fields. The land around was lightly forested. A granite shelf began just below the surface, now and then erupting into visible crags and low cliffs. The light soil produced patches of corn, and some hay. The roots of such pine, maple, spruce and birch as managed to grow spread broad and shallow.

To the north, over into Quebec, lay rich farming land. Only sixty-five hundred years ago the area had been an immense lake, large as Erie. At its eastern end, on the far side of what was now Quebec City, a massive ridge creating falls to rival Niagara had dammed it in place. But under the force of erosion the St. Lawrence deepened its channel and over centuries of surge and thrust the falls collapsed. The lake emptied forever, revealing new land, a bed that had filled over millions of years with rich soil drained from the plains and prairies via the Great Lakes and the upper St. Lawrence. Now five months a year when the sun warmed the soil the land provided wondrous corn and hay, berries, apples.

He heard Charlie's car arriving. He set his computer on standby.

Was there a pattern to all that information? Nothing about caves, caverns, underground spaces. His head shook a little.

Charlie made himself comfortable in a chair across from Carney. "There's no way to say this easily. Julie died last week. I just found out."

Carney's head dropped, he massaged his forehead, he rubbed his eyebrows. He felt a chill down his back. His nose began to run. He saw her again, a shadow of her young self, on the bed in the semi-dark. No, he would remember her as the young woman she'd been. He sniffed, wiped his nose with his hands. "What happened?"

"She starved herself. She had a living will. They didn't try to keep her alive."

"Oh god, Charlie."

"She wanted to go. You saw her. You know that."

"Yes. I know. Doesn't help, though."

"Want a drink?"

"No." Carney stood. "No, I've got some work to do this afternoon. Is she—is she buried somewhere nearby?"

"Cremated. Ashes thrown into the wind."

Carney nodded. "Into the wind."

9.

The afternoon meeting with Carney swelled into a brain-boil in Cochan's head. He should go to the cemetery now. Be gone when Carney arrived. What difference, one more sale of Terramac property. If not a Carney, someone else.

He stood. He thought, I am not dominated by the demands of others. He walked down the steps, past the silent worktables to the front door. He pushed it open. A warm sunny day. He stepped outside.

Ridiculous. Giving in to urges? Childish.

He could go home, maybe talk now to Priscilla, tell her his plan for Benjie. She would say, What a lovely thing to do. She would say, Then he'd be with us forever. And she'd say, He's coming back to us. And Johnnie would say, Yes.

And she would say, Soon. And, He's a quarter of the way here. And, He's growing again, just like before. And, He's here, feel him, touch my belly, press—

No!

Yes, she'd say, I'm going to rebear Benjie, our Benjie.

No you will not! How could she say such things, there's only one Benjie, that Benjie is away, far away forever.

Johnnie banished her from his mind. Sweat poured from the back of his scalp down his nape. He opened the door again, went back in, headed for the washroom, a little water on his face. He stared at himself in the mirror. His black hair lay stiff and clotted on his head. His mustache was too long, the thin bristles dribbled into his mouth. His eyebrows had gone all but hairless. His ears stuck out too far. But his nose, straight in profile, thin and elegant, united the elements of his face and turned it handsome. He cupped his hands and splashed water.

○

"Ted!"

I stared at her. Her eyes were wide. "What? Lola, what?"

"That's him!"

"Who?"

"His face." She grabbed my arm.

"Lola. Whose face?"

"Him. My final last lover. The very wealthy man." She slammed the heels of her palms over her eyes.

I shook my head. "This is Johnnie Cochan. He couldn't have been more than a boy when you died."

She opened her eyes slowly. "You're right." She shook her head. "But you described him so clearly, the nose of his face—"

293

I shrugged. "Lots of people look like that."

She nodded. But her thoughts were elsewhere.

○

John Cochan returned to his desk. To prepare for Lexington. When Carney has left, go to Benjie.

10.

Carney told Bobbie about Julie's death. They had sat still and silent in the Jaguar, the top down. Finally Bobbie hugged him. Nothing to be said.

Then for an hour while she searched a couple of bookstores for the few good among the many bad new poets, Carney visited with Theresa. And Milton, sitting in silence. Theresa lay flat, her unwavering stare examining a single spot in the ceiling.

What Theresa saw there: a picture, a photo, a young woman, blond bobbed hair a halo round her head, tiny mouth, dark lips pouting, buxom in a tight sweater, slender waist, long legs beneath a long skirt. She brandished a fencing foil. My ethical visitor, Theresa said, and, Where were you when I needed you? The woman in the photo remained silent. Theresa's brain shouted: Get down from there! The woman clung to the ceiling. Theresa couldn't yell louder so she whispered, Please, help me. No response. She breathed, My embodied reality reduced to a picture. I am powerless to help myself.

Carney saw he could do no good here, so left and drove up the hill to Karl's stone house. He would mourn Julie in due time. Not now. Karl opened the door and drew Carney in. "Now what's your greatest need? Scotch? Vodka-tonic?"

"Too early. Just a fruit juice, thanks."

"She likes you a great deal, you know. You charmed her."

"Oh?"

Karl nodded. "She was impressed. First time she met you. Each time after that."

"Wouldn't have guessed it." At her cabin he recalled Sarah as fully uninterested.

"She doesn't take to people, these days. Hasn't for years."

"And why's that?"

"People disappoint her." He stopped, his head angled down to his right shoulder. "The family not least."

"I see." Carney waited.

"She was gorgeous when she was young. You should see pictures of her. Could've won any beauty pageant." Karl dropped ice into two glasses. "Can you imagine? Men fell in love left and right." He shook his head. "She put on a lot of weight. Not good for her."

"Weight?"

"It didn't matter to Theresa. And Milton liked her that way." Karl laughed. "She lost most of the weight after her last stroke."

Ah.

Karl shook his head. "She's never been attracted to any man but him, she had all kinds of appetites but I don't think she ever strayed, not sexually anyway. One man her whole life long, can you imagine?"

Carney, to show he understood, said, "I saw a wedding picture in Theresa's study."

"They were a"—Karl's voice broke, he looked away—"a fine couple."

"They still are."

"Yes. I suppose." He poured Scotch over the ice. "He was an unhandsome young man. Ugly, you could say. Took him years to grow into his face, turn it more complex. Good job, eh?"

Karl the cynic, romanticizing his parents. "You care for them a lot."

"Yes. I do." He was staring through the big window overlooking the lake. "I love them."

Miles from the distant son Theresa had described. In Karl's face, kindness there, but also uncertainty.

"I bother some people. Often that's okay." Karl sipped his Scotch. "Sometimes not."

"You enjoy bothering people?"

"As a rule? There's no rule that's always true. As Theresa might say."

Carney nodded. "I've read some of her essays. And the book on anarchism."

"She's no anarchist. She's herself. She doesn't much like previously used categories, so she's always creating her own to fit the situation."

Carney shrugged. "Could make her a good historian." He sipped.

"Makes it hard to be her son." He sniffed. "Or anyone close to her. Except maybe Milton."

"Maybe he's a good historian too."

Karl's head shook. "He understands her too well. And all of us."

"He doesn't think he understands you."

The drink at his lips stopped so sharply a couple of drops spilled on his hand. "My god, he did take to you. He talk about his peeves? Why I turned R.C., why I was once a Wild Young Man?" He laughed. "Don't believe him. He gets it wrong." He sipped. "Know why?"

"I give up."

"Because he forgets there are many many ways to live."

"Yeah?"

"And if you don't try them when they come around it's a piece of life lost. A shame. People want to be normal, whatever that is, so they live their lives in agony because they never give in to their golden perversities. You know what golden perversity is?"

Carney knew he wasn't being asked for his version of anything perverse. And felt several misgivings at Karl therapizing some poor patient's psyche. "Tell me."

"It's loving where you find love. I don't mean screwing, I mean loving. I don't mean screwing anyone we want in the privacy of our bedrooms, our mothers and brothers and sisters, our kid—"

The doorbell rang.

"What's truly golden perversity is loving more than one person at the same time. They always make us choose, truly loving two women at the same time, a woman loving two men, three—"

The bell again.

"Everybody's multiply-desiring, and multiply-bestowing. So few admit it. If people allowed themselves—"

The bell. Carney gestured with his head. "Better answer the door, no?"

"We'll talk more." He raised his glass, saluted, took a sip. "Later." He opened the door.

Ti-Jean Seymour stooped as if he might scrape his crown on the lintel. He nodded. "Doesn't your doorbell work?"

"Yes, Ti-Jean. It works fine."

Ti-Jean came in and sat on the couch, acknowledging Carney with a nod. Karl offered him a beer. Ti-Jean crossed his legs, raised the bottle as a kind of toast, drank down half, and turned to Carney. "Seen Cochan yet?"

"Made an appointment. Through his front-man, Boce."

Ti-Jean swallowed more beer, stared at Carney, and in his eye a small spark flared.

The spark held Carney. He fought it. He couldn't look away.

Ti-Jean said, "His spirits are corrupted."

"Who, Cochan?"

Ti-Jean's head shook. "Aristide Boce. Handy Johnnie can't be anything except what he is. Boce is a mercenary."

"Wouldn't you say"—Carney's eyelids squeezed and opened, trying to soften Ti-Jean's uncompromising gaze—"both of them are?"

Ti-Jean's eyes never blinked. "No. Somewhere in the shadow Boce sold himself." His glance held level.

Carney broke away then and looked for his glass. "So?"

"Boce kills the life in his ancestors' land. My ancestors' land! We're cousins from far back, Boce and me. He transforms a tree into flooring and siding. I know, I buy it. But Boce does more, he markets the earth's living body and calls it real estate property."

Carney laughed, took a sip. "Ah."

He touched Carney's elbow, and again held Carney's eye. "Literally."

Carney couldn't stop looking back to the glint there. Stuck between amused and chilled.

Karl said, "I agree, Ti-Jean."

In Ti-Jean's eye the glimmer faded, faded, and was gone.

"Karl? Why'd you ask me to stop by?"

Karl reached out and took Carney by the elbow. "Make Cochan leave them alone. He's going to kill them."

"Stop Terramac?"

"Too late for that. Just the harassment, the offers to buy."

"I'll talk to him, that's about all—"

"I couldn't stand it if he killed them." Tears welled in his eyes.

11.

"How good of you to come," said John Cochan. "Please. Sit." Cochan pulled a chair out for Bobbie, and one for Carney. "Easy trip up?"

Yes, they conceded, very easy.

"Good. Now, my colleague Aristide Boce tells me you're interested in Terramac units."

"That's right," said Carney, thinking, Okay, go for it. "Ms. Feyerlicht is more traditional than I am"—Bobbie scowled a little—"so she's considering a two-bedroom surface place. Myself, I'm interested in one of the underground units."

John Cochan said nothing. Suddenly he smiled. "I'm impressed, Mr. Carney. We've not released information on Underland. Is this merely first-rate research, or have you been spying?"

Bull's-eye. Carney chuckled. "Must be hard, concealing all that work down there. But one hears the stories." He smiled gently. "In the industry."

"Of course. Of course." And what really does this Carney know. Damn! "Underland, you see, is far less advanced. And there won't, you see, be any living units down there, just shops, very light industry, communication hubs. And of course, Terramac's Pleasure Ground."

"No homes? I'm disappointed. I was eager to live in Underland."

"And why would that be?" Cochan felt fingers of betrayal squeeze his gut.

"It's an obsession with total security, you see. I need the security of living underground."

This made sense to John Cochan. "Are you suggesting that Summerclime will not be totally secure?" The other one, the so-called aunt, says nothing, what was she about anyway? He smoothed back his mustache.

○

"I know that man," said Lola, nodding.

○

"Not as thoroughly as an underground home would be."

No, John Cochan would not tell Carney there'd be condominiums in the caverns. That wondrous living space would become public, part of a fully constructed information campaign, once the seeds of demand

298

had sprouted. "Summerclime can offer you the security you need," said Cochan. "And, in case of a wide-spread emergency, Underland offers all Terramac's citizens the safety of its depths."

"Safety," Bobbie repeated the one word.

He glanced at her, and smiled.

"From nuclear attack?" A wry smile now curved her lips.

No, Cochan decided, this woman was not a dummy. He laughed lightly. "No, living underground would provide only a little protection against a megaton blast. But, yes, serious protection against chemical warfare, and biological warfare. Not to mention insect-borne diseases, West Nile Virus, and the ever-evolving strains of influenza. Because Terramac's Underland will be a hidden land, designed precisely to keep out all that's undesirable. Many of my colleagues find it strange in me, that I get pleasure in avoiding pests, especially insect pests. Keeping them out, you see, is a metaphor for all I believe in. If you can keep the bugs out, you can keep anything out. But if you have the ability, you're allowed inside. Safety behind the walls and, one day, under the ground. But not as a place to live, no. A shared space, a collective space."

"For those," said Carney, "as Boce explained, who have an upper middle-class income."

"It goes without saying," said John Cochan.

"Your mother was my college roommate," said Bobbie.

Cochan stared at her. Why was this woman here? "What do you mean?"

"Just that. She'd have been fascinated by what you've achieved."

Johnnie fought away a desire to shrivel to boy-size and ask, Do you really think so? "Did you know her well?"

"Well enough. At Mount Holyoke when she was Libby. And I kept up with her later, in her Beth days. Also when she became ill."

"Ill." What had his mother told this ancient hag? Libby? She'd never been Libby. Was she, once? Why was everything out of the past so vulnerable? Let his mother rest in peace.

"I met you, you know, when you were about eleven. I brought you a small birthday present. You didn't want it."

"No?"

"So you remember me?"

"No," he said again.

"I liked her," Bobbie said, "and she was truly smart."

John had not pondered this in a long while. Many many issues I won't consider now, he thought. But something came clear right then. "You didn't come here to buy a unit in Terramac."

"No," said Carney.

"Then why?"

"I want to see your Underland."

"Impossible," said Cochan.

"Nothing's impossible," said Carney. "And I'm deeply impressed with your vision, your skill. I'd like to view this underground world of yours in its infancy."

"I thank you." John laughed, his gut now easy again. "So I'm even more sorry to say it's simply impossible."

"Will you invite me to visit?"

"No," said Cochan.

"Then," said Carney, standing, "there's really no further purpose for us to be here. Coming, Bobbie?"

She stood, and nodded to Cochan. "It would be a good idea for you to show Carney this Underland of yours."

"No, no," said John, "that's just not viable."

"A shame," said Carney. "For both of us."

They climbed back into the Jag. Bobbie said, "Too bad. Waste of a trip."

Carney smiled. "A first-rate trip. He confirmed the underground city."

○

I slowly realized Lola had gone distant, almost absent again. "Is something wrong?"

"Is Theresa going to die?"

"Soon? I don't know, Lola. After a while everyone does, you know."

"I won't stay for the end." She stood. "Thank you." She turned and walked away, her step quickening.

I leapt to my feet, dropped my papers, and ran after her. Her back was to me when she stopped to stretch her arms wide. Her fingers flared, she threw her head back. Her laughter broke the air, a trill, and filled the patch of cirrus where we stood with silver waves. Delight rushed through my belly. And a flash of fear. "You all right?"

She turned. On her lips the grandest smile I've ever seen amidst the clouds. She lay her hands on my shoulders, her eyes settled on my forehead. I'd have sworn she'd grown a foot. She murmured, "Never better." She turned and walked away.

"Stop." I caught up again. "Where're you going?"

"To the edge."

"What for?"

"'Cause that's the closest point to down."

"No!"

"I have to."

"You can't!"

"Of course I can."

"But you're a God!"

"Yeah, and that's the trouble."

"Trouble?"

"It's kinda boring, you know? All I get allowed to feel is pleasure, and that doesn't work any more."

"But you're at the greatest pinnacle—"

"But Theresa's way more interesting. Except I don't understand her. Yet. My mind—heck, Ted, my imagination—can't grasp her from here. So I've got to go down there to find out. And besides, I think she's calling for me."

"For that ethical being on her ceiling!"

"Maybe that's me."

"Lola!" What a crazy thought. "Anyway, Theresa's mostly dead."

"Then I should get there before she's all dead."

"But you can't!"

"Why not?"

"No one ever has."

On the right of her face, a tiny smile. But from the saddest little mouth. "Imagine. You. Saying that."

"You'll never get back up!"

She took my hand. "Walk with me." She stopped. "Or better, come down too. See your son again, up close."

I squeezed her fingers tight. My eyes tried to hold hers. "That's impossible."

"Lots of things are possible."

"Not this."

She nodded slowly. "Maybe." She turned and walked away. I knew I couldn't stop her. But I followed. Three steps ahead, the edge—

She stood. She faced me. "Thank you for your story." Her fingers touched my temples.

I tried to speak. Her lips stayed my words, and my breath. Her kiss was that much sweeter, for in moments she'd be lost to me forever. My cursed story! "What will Edsel say?! The Distant Nimbus crowd?"

She smiled. "Who's Edsel?" She drew away.

I grasped her forearms tight. "I can't let you."

She shook her head. "Yes."

I felt my fingers loosen. I had to speak, to make her change her mind. But no words came.

She smiled, turned, glided to the edge.

I stood with her. A half step back. My heart approached exploding.

She pointed. "Just there?"

I moved her arm. "A bit more to the west." My voice held steady.

"I see." And she stepped off.

Ten

DOWN TO EARTH

Do I go on? I think I have to.

○

1.

Theresa's right arm, punctured with needles attached to tubes, lay on top of the sheet. From under it less dignified piping drooped to a low platform under the bed. "Hello, Theresa." No reaction. "How goes it?" Not a flicker. "Good to see you." How does one talk to someone who may not be there?

Carney sat. Bobbie had asked him why he was going to the hospital again. Carney said it felt like he owed Theresa something. What? He couldn't make this clear. And wouldn't make himself say, I feel drawn by her, and by Milton, even by Feasie. Bobbie would find this silly.

The skin of Theresa's cheeks was pulled smooth as by some force inside sucking at her underskin, temples to chin. Her eyelids, open wide, pupils thrusting through irises, focused on the ceiling as if the meaning of the world were printed up there, no glance away till she'd grappled with it all.

What to talk about with her? Anything but Terramac. What worked best in *A Ton of Cure* were the perversely funny disaster stories. Stories are able to convince people of many things, Carney believed, and the best stories make you laugh—a certain cynic's view of laughter notwithstanding. He'd read how someone had been cured of ankylosing spondylitis, a cell disease, in large part by the act of laughter. No, you don't laugh yourself all the way back from a stroke, not one as huge as Theresa's. But a little bit back?

So Carney, medical experimenter, jumped in where neurologists feared to make waves—Feasie might have said it better—and told Theresa a fishing story. "Want to hear one of my favorite fishing stories?" and chose to think the empty look slipped for an instant from Theresa's eyes. "Okay, this is about the time my friend Charlie swamped me, ready?" He smiled. "Well we'd been out on the water all afternoon, a hot summer day, we'd found a couple of schools of bass, taken and released maybe a dozen apiece, all around two pounds. Charlie was using a Mepps, me an old Wob-L-Rite. Something heavy struck my line. I said to Charlie, 'Hey, this one's bigger, get your line out of the water.'

"He said, 'Nothing here but babies.' Charlie figured I'd located another school and he cast toward my fish. He got a strike right away. 'Hey, maybe you're right, these fellows are bigger.'"

Theresa's mouth, yes, quivered.

"It was tricky keeping our lines from tangling so Charlie led his fish around the bow to take him on the other side. And by now my fish was close but still deep. Then it swam under the boat, pulling still harder. I muttered this to Charlie and heard him say, 'Yeah.'

"I leaned over the side, what the hell was going on? The fish gave such a yank I lost my balance, lunged forward, dropped my rod, hit the water. Lucky it was warm, I grabbed onto the boat and shouted, 'Charlie, for godsake give me a hand!'

"All I heard was, 'Innnn—credible.' I pulled myself up the gunwale and looked. He had the bass netted and was staring at its mouth. And in its lip, his Mepps and my Wob-L-Rite."

Now, was it there or had his imagination set it on her lips? At the far corner, a twitch? He stared. Nothing. Another story? "When I was fifteen I was fishing with my father for pickerel. We had shiners for bait, little ones. We used bobbers, those red and white ones, and hooked the shiners just under the dorsal fin. On maybe my fourth or fifth cast, over by some lily pads, my bobber went under. I waited, let the fish turn my shiner around, and struck. I started to reel in when suddenly the bobber came back to the surface. Damn, I'd lost it. But then the bobber dove and my fish ran with the bait, screaming line from my reel."

Was that a new kind of attention around Theresa's mouth?

"Suddenly from deep in the water the fish took to the air, red gills flashing. A pickerel that would be at least twenty inches if I got it in—where had he come from? I worked the fish away from the weeds, but he had a mind of his own, he had to get away. He tried to jump two more times, the second much more wearily, nose just out of the water, but my rod, bent into a U, was in control. I brought him to the boat and he made another run, shorter, and I knew I had him. Back to the boat and my father passed the net under him and hoisted him into the boat. Five pounds easy, I saw, as he thrashed around. And then I realized: I'd caught not one but two fish. There, in his mouth, my original catch, a perch about seven inches long. With the hook in its mouth. I'd never hooked the pickerel—he'd been so greedy he'd never released the perch."

A new movement from Theresa: her lips flicked, her chest shook, huunhh— hunnhh— Like laughing without muscles. Like tiny dry heaves. A body fighting for the power to laugh. In her right eye, at the temple corner, was that a shine of water?

She lay still now. An excellent large idea came to him. He stood, touched Theresa's shoulder. "I'll be back, Theresa."

2.

Into his case John Cochan slid the three files he'd need for his meetings in Lexington. He left the old church building, walked briskly, greeted neighbors with a wave. Soon Benjie would be in his proper place in Terramac. In minutes Priscilla would mix the martinis again, like she— Like that. It'd be okay.

Okay like in the memories? Of a wife, her beauty fine as fire, who brings to you an essential life? Yes. The memory of a boy, tan arms, long legs? Of course. Yes. But later, later—

He reached his driveway. Deirdre came running, jumped up, arms around his neck, "Daddy! I learned to sew, Diana's teaching me. I'm making clothes for all my dolls!"

"Hey, Dee, terrific." He carried her into the house. Yes it was pretty good. She didn't feel as Benjie had, a different heft here. Which was as it should be.

Priscilla did make him a martini. Two. They all had dinner together. A soft peaceful evening and they spoke of good things. Diana took Lissa to bed, then Dee off for a story. Once it had been, yes, more complicated. Better.

A cognac in the dark on the enclosed rear deck, and stars.

"The alcohol's not bad for the baby?"

"He loves it."

"He?"

"A way of speaking."

He sipped. "It feels okay?"

"Everything's great. Rachel says I'm perfect."

Once, had he thought so too? Then a distance came. Now, better. Though not as it was. Could it be again? "I'm glad." After the baby. "Listen, I was thinking, shouldn't you have a doctor here too? I mean, if something goes wrong."

"Oh no, Rachel's so good and what is it to Burlington, forty minutes? No problem."

"Still, in November, if it arrives during a storm . . ."

Why did he have to keep saying "it"? "If anything happens there's the County Hospital. Rachel would come. She'll deliver."

"The road might be icy."

Priscilla laughed, and hid a shudder. "I couldn't have this baby without Rachel." Not go to Burlington? Burlington wasn't much but Johnnie had taken her away from Boston. From friends, from shops to buy pretty things for the girls. From restaurants, and people. She could never give that up. "I need Rachel."

An answer for everything. The perfect wife, the perfect mother. Well why not, what else for her to think about.

She sat back, felt her belly, that bit of a bulge? She looked forward to Wednesday. Tonight could be okay too. Everything might work. He used to be so gentle. Still was. Less recently. Tonight they'd make love. Maybe it would be good tonight.

The cognac was excellent. He had a second glass. He followed her upstairs, early.

It didn't work. It wasn't good.

○

I've been thinking while recording. Didn't I swear to tell this story only for Lola? Then what am I doing, noting all I see? Do I expect her back? I guess I must. Record for Lola!

○

3.

Carney, delighted with his idea, explained it to Milton. Milton wanted to believe Carney, that Theresa had tried to laugh. He needed to see Theresa laughing. It took them much of Sunday first to find Theresa's doctor, then to convince him. Okay, the doctor acceded, non-orthodox techniques did interest him. So long as the movies didn't interfere with hospital procedure they could try it. But the technician they needed for this wouldn't be in till Monday morning.

Milton shared the doctor's prognosis with Carney: "They talk like they did last time."

Carney nodded. "What do they say, exactly?"

"Paralysis of the left side, face, shoulder, arm. And great weakness on the right, still unclear how much of that'll stay paralyzed."

"What can they do?"

"With therapy, maybe give her some mobility." He scowled. "But she'll get better than that, you'll see. She will laugh." He grimaced. "And another letter from John Cochan."

"Saying?"

"An offer again. But going the other way. Lots more money. It's $12 million now."

Carney raised his eyebrows. A new form of harassment?

Milton spoke as if Carney had always been there. The easy intimacy felt okay to Carney. It seemed like a good time, so Carney told Milton what he and Bobbie learned yesterday. "He's building under the ground. There're caves down there, caverns maybe. Maybe under your land."

Milton's face went tight. "It's true, then." He shuddered. "I didn't want to guess out loud, especially not in front of Tessa." He glanced her way. "Glad she doesn't know."

"What do you want to do?"

"Get legal advice, first off. Can we enjoin Cochan on building? Under his own property? Poking around under Grange land? We signed that damn agreement, but is this included?"

"It's possible."

"Leasie's coming down tonight. I'll hear what she's learned. We'll figure something."

Among Carney's phone messages back at the farm, one from Leonora. Was he free for supper? He told her answering machine he wouldn't be in Burlington till tomorrow. What did she want?

Theresa could tell: Carney had arrived early. He was doing something. Fussing. Too much bustle. She wanted to get angry. But no energy for anger. She had to tear loose. Tubes, chemical malleable—

How, old woman.

Old? Who? Me?

Has the stroke made you crazy?

Looser. Loose. Hey! Look at that! Two of me. Two Theresas.

What?

No. Impossible. Two souls in the body maybe, but no two bodies for one soul.

One Theresa, old woman.

Two Theresas. Me, Theresa old dry skin tired tubed struck—

Not so tired.

And you, Theresa down from the photo. Silver. Lithe. Laughing. Bright. Wondering. Clear. Theresa herself. Firm. Silver glowing. You. Theresa, forty years ago.

○

Lola, tangibly interfering! Talking to Theresa! Don't! But I could see everything, and hear Theresa speaking, silently:

○ .

Do I sleep, an old woman needing her beauty sleep? A joke, two Theresas. Big joke, too funny.

Nope, sorry, Theresa, no joke.

No? Maybe not. Get angry? No general anger. Anger is specific. Anger as category but no such thing as general anger. Do-no-let-this-stroke-blur-your-thinking!

Do you really want to let go, Theresa? To let it all be past?

No! The rot of the heart. How much putrescence and silken mendacity will I tolerate? Before a tiny rebellion can begin.

Why rebellion?

○

She's as clear as if she were up here: Lola, red lips pouting. Merry eyes. In the room. With the technician, the nurse, Carney. Who couldn't see her. "Lola, for heavensake, get out of there!"

She didn't hear. Or pretended not to.

"Lola! You're breaking every rule!"

A wicked grin. I'm sure she hears me. But, and this horrified me, Theresa could see Lola.

○

Her. Theresa. From—long ago. White-gold hair, shining in the dark. Very—beautiful.

Lola grinned. So you can still judge beauty, old woman?

Not the same. Not young Theresa. But—how not? Almost Theresa? Theresa, the white dress. Laughing. Dancing. Used to dance but who can dance beside the rivers of bile. Theresa, how can you— My god-damn voice!

Don't try so hard, Theresa. I hear you.

What—

I hear everything. Lie still.

What else to do.

Lots, lots of wonderful things.

Yeah, except, see, there're complications.

Theresa, I want to be your friend.

Friend. Hell, that's too simple.

And more. You'll see. But first, friends?

After so many years

It's a long road. Twisting. Want to try it, Theresa? Want to come?

Look. You can tolerate only so much. Beyond, it makes no sense.

Nonsense. I just heard the better you.

You heard what?

Your little rant on tolerance. I agree. Want to come with me?

Where?

To find a joke to laugh about.

Ha!

That's a good start.

With sinew like mine one doesn't go damn anywhere.

Okay. Bye.

You don't have to leave. Please.

That's better. Think about me. Okay?

Sure. Why not. Uh—who are you, anyway?

You can call me Lola. See ya.

Uh, you coming back?

Maybe. After you've thought. You need to think a lot.

About?

A wonderful joke, a huge joke. The best of jokes.

A joke?

A last chance. To bring such healing laughter to the world, why it could prove the physic 'gainst the shocks and traumas of our time.

Who said that?

I did. And maybe so did you.

Me?

Bye, Theresa.

Listen, when— Blast! Where— Sure, go behind the bed. Where I can't see. Coward!

o

My heart surged, my hands shook. My foolish meddling Lola.

o

4.

John Cochan rose early, before the girls woke. Priscilla had coffee ready for him in the kitchen. Yes, she was a good woman. But times like now he'd have preferred the pleasure of the start of day alone. They spoke a few morning words. He kissed her lightly, said he'd be back late Wednesday afternoon. They'd have supper. A small supper, he needed to be at Terramac later in the evening.

A bit of a lie. His appointment with Hank, at the cemetery.

He drove the Saab from Richmond to the Burlington airport. No way would he leave the Rolls in a parking lot for three days.

5.

Milton sat with Theresa. He tried to remember funny stories. Ti-Jean and Feasie arrived. This Monday morning they couldn't come up with a single joke between them.

Carney, carrying a cloth bag, came back with Theresa's nurse and a man.

What's Carney doing now? Milton! No—don't do that!

The nurse held Theresa by her arms and pulled her up to sitting. "Okay, good."

Not sit, no!

The nurse said, "There. How's that?"

The other man, the technician, moved the large TV screen closer to the end of the bed. Theresa stared at it, as if hypnotized. Carney said, "Get used to it slowly, Theresa. The nurse'll put it on a few minutes at a time. They're bringing a DVD player in, we'll put on some movies."

Colors. No! Colors bounce shine jump. Ache. Eyes. Noise, whir, rising— No-o-o!

Carney pulled a half-dozen DVDs from the bag. "Great old comedies."

The screen seemed to overwhelm Theresa. Milton found her glasses and set them on her face. The DVD player arrived. They watched a Keaton two-reeler. From Theresa, no visible reaction. But during the early Chaplin, a twitch at Theresa's lip edge! Milton took Theresa's hand. It was cool, not cold. His eyelids were batting hard.

Out in the hall Ti-Jean and Feasie questioned Carney again. Cochan had conceded part of Terramac was, yes, being built under the ground.

Ti-Jean said, "Like to come up to the Grange for the evening, spend the night? The water in the creek's running clear again. Just as low. Maybe lower."

What else to do? "Sure."

Mid-afternoon Sarah came to sit with Theresa. Ti-Jean, Feasie, Milton, Carney, Theresa, an off-duty nurse, and two hospital volunteers were watching *City Lights*. Sarah said, "Movies?"

Milton said, "Look. She smiles sometimes, and twice she's laughed. It was Carney's idea."

She looked at Carney. "Clever."

Ti-Jean said to her, "Carney's coming to dinner and some fishing. Want to come by?"

"More fishing?"

Carney said, "If you and your slingshot aren't around."

"The fish are dead anyway. No thanks." To Carney she added, "Staying the night?"

"Sure," said Ti-Jean, and to Carney, "She does not enjoy my tourtière."

"Come out to the cabin in the morning. I'll show you what's happened to the pond. It's your kind of thing. Professionally."

In the evening Carney tested Gambade Brook. Three heavy strikes, all missed. He took time to sit statue-still, watching shadows in the water. No sign of small fish. He tried some lowly worms. To a purist this was a base kind of angling, but for Carney the best way to teach kids. Let a six-year-old feel the insistent tug of a perch or blue-gill and fourteen chances out of nineteen the kid will be hooked for life. That statistic came from a study conducted, over many years, by Carney. The study had brought him fourteen first-rate young fishing partners across the continent, best hedge against old age. Over future years they would take him fishing in return, carry outboard motors, handle the boat while he'd sit back and cast. And, he suspected, each would consider it the very least she (five of them) or he (nine) could do for Carney. But it would be the most.

Worms on barbless hooks were the best way to test unknown water. A little one would tap at a worm even if it wasn't hungry, giving away its presence without getting caught. From the nibble Carney could get an initial sense of fish activity in the water.

Or so theory had it. Tonight his worms produced nothing. While not conclusive about the lack of small trout, it was an indicator. He took a water sample to drop off at a Burlington lab.

The tourtière—ground beef, veal, and pork, onions, garlic, and spices Carney didn't recognize—tasted delicious. "Feasie's never learned to cook our way," Ti-Jean said. When Ti-Jean wanted to eat the dishes of his first twenty-five years, he did his own cooking.

They ate and Ti-Jean talked, his say-more side. Family history, they'd married when Feasie was eighteen, she fell in love with him because he was the only man she'd ever met who made her feel, well, dainty. "Oh, for other reasons too." Feodora giggled.

They sipped wine. They'd lived here only a few months. Before then their home was Chiptree, where Ti-Jean ran the garage. Now he did fix-up construction. Four months back when Ginette turned eighteen they'd made her full partner in the business, signing power and all; she had a real head for it, and the hands too. Another part-time carpenter worked for them. Ti-Jean got to take days off, he loved the Grange as much as Feasie did. "When the girl hits twenty-one we'll let her buy us out. She wants to." He grinned. "We'll grow more vegetables here, get some more cows, a lot of chickens. If Cochan's underground city doesn't suck us all into the pit."

Ginette too had been one of twins, Feasie told Carney. The other, a boy, didn't come out right; he strangled when the doctor reached in to turn him. A disappointment to Ti-Jean, he'd been one of eight. He'd grown up here just south of the border, after his first wife died went back to school, UVM, met Feasie.

"I figured you for English with a name like Seymour."

"French on both sides, three generations back. Before that I don't know, has to be English or Scots somewhere, lots of French Seymours, all those Catholics intermarrying, French O'Donells and Flynns and MacDuffs."

Carney nodded.

"Mother's mother was Mi'kmaq from Restigouche up near the New Brunswick border."

Carney listened to stories about birds, and farming, and fishing. And the garage. It turned out Ti-Jean was afraid of motors. He had to drive a truck but he wouldn't work on its motor.

"How small?"

"Largest size a motor should be, five horses."

"Uh!" Carney's own sense was ten, especially for an outboard, the extra power safer for a good-size lake. Bigger caused water displacement and undermined the shoreline. "Why five?"

Ti-Jean looked to Feasie. Her smile seemed to say, Whatever you want. Without looking Carney's way he said, "Biggest demon I can handle."

"Demon?"

"That's it."

Feasie tore at a cuticle. Carney shook his head. "I don't understand."

"Demon. You know. Like a monster. A devil."

"A motor's a demon?"

"Not the motor itself. Inside it."

"Like, in the gas tank? In the cylinders?"

"No. In the motor. In the steel, all the parts. What gets it to work?"

"But in steel?" Ti-Jean Seymour, animist in an age of machines. Why not, for this one evening? Wine helps you see clearly. Carney nodded. "I like that."

Ti-Jean looked over to Carney. In his right eye, the glint. "There's demons in all machines. I've worked with machines my whole life."

A common-sense man, Ti-Jean? "These demons, they're, uh, dangerous?"

"Yes."

They sat, and thought about the dangers.

"Has one, a demon, ever tried hurt you?"

He spoke slowly. "At a gas station I had. Small garage. With another guy. He got killed."

Carney waited.

Feasie said, "His little brother, Jacques."

"Was this on the job?"

"In the garage. A Buick, it started up. He was under."

"Somebody started it and didn't know he was there?"

Feasie said, "It started itself."

"Is that possible?"

"A demon." Ti-Jean nodded, six-seven-eight times.

"A demon starting a car?"

"Jacques believed in them. He told me about them. I didn't believe him."

Carney thought, the man isn't arguing. For him this is fact.

Feasie said, "Four times it's happened to Ti-Jean."

"What?"

"Some—demon tried to, well, at least harm him."

"How?"

"First time, he walked away for a wrench. Engine turned over, the car ran forward."

"I looked at the ignition. The key was there, I leave it there. But always on lock."

"No one else there, Carney." She sipped her wine. "And once he was leaning over a motor and it started up. His hand was against the fly-wheel, the belt came down and around, must've gone around dozens of times before he got his hand away."

"That's it. I was holding the wheel with them, a bolt in the others." Ti-Jean grinned, held up his left hand. "Could've been the whole hand."

On the pinky and ring finger, two missing knuckles. Carney had never noticed.

"Once a chainsaw cut the toe off his shoe. The flesh down to the bone. Started by itself?"

"The last time it wasn't the motor but the hood."

"He was bent over the motor sideways and the hood crashed down on him. Front end slammed into his hip bone, lucky he has long legs." She put her hand on his. "His shoulder must've taken some of the weight, lots of bruises. Lucky. He couldn't sit for a week." Feasie giggled. "Never work with big machines again. Wouldn't touch one with a plugged nickel."

"Construction's better, more outdoors work."

"I do the books and I make deliveries too. Anyway Ginette takes over soon." She scowled. "She's no intellectual but she's smart."

"That's it."

Demons. In-lawed to Theresa Bonneherbe Magnussen, philosopher of rationalism abiding. People find lots of ways of making pieces of their realities fit together. He sipped his wine. A private mythology, a way of forging life. From a successful garage, to a construction company they'd soon be opting out of, to the Grange. Progress of a sort.

6.

Priscilla Ayer Cochan, heading south, accelerated her Dodge across a flat stretch, seventy, eighty, eighty-five. Johnnie would be home this evening, she'd be back early, have pepper-pocket steaks ready, he liked that, and he would tell her about his success with the bank. Johnnie always succeeded. Except in the one thing, and he blamed himself so. But it wasn't Johnnie's fault, none of it, none! Damn it, she too loved Benjie, nursed him, how many thousands of hugs? Played with him just as much as Johnnie did. More. But she had let go of the pain. Not the grief. Had she loved Benjie less? If Benjie were alive would she be living this other life? Yes, yes. Was she still mourning? Of course. But not this lamentation.

She rolled the window down, breathed in hot road air, leaned her head over to dry her face. The dreadful night before he left, nothing worked, not her gentlest, her most sensuous. True, he had tried. But there'd been no connection, between his mind and her desire an unsounded chasm. And his terrible whisper, too late, too late. What is, Johnnie? He'd breathed it again, Too late— He crept away from the bed, lay in the guest room, not even Benjie's room.

She'd knelt beside that bed, by Johnnie, for who knew how long. To his slow breath, she talked: Too late for some things, Johnnie, not for others, we can try, Johnnie, we can. From him the one phrase, nothing other, Too late.

She went to her own bed, their bed. Hours she'd lain awake, scared by no longer feeling pain like his. The old ache, that was there, and she knew it would never leave her, a part of her as Benjie had been part, still was in that way. As the new one was, would be.

She'd stared at stars through the skylight. She'd not felt a heartache like the anguish in his words, this iron stretch of his guilt, since the weeks after the accident. He'd said, "From here we'll make our history, and the world's." She wanted this too. She wanted to rebuild the farmhouse right there, that spot. Now she could think as he used to say, If only we'd put it up farther from the stream. She'd shushed him. Or if they'd still lived in Boston, or moved into Richmond sooner, what then? Car crashes, maiming them all. Some maniac murdering them in their beds as they lay. Yes, the chance was tiny. Like that of a boy slipping down a water chute. She squeezed her eyes shut to make the image go away. A child long months dead—

She heard wheels on gravel, opened her eyes, yank-swung the wheel, the car lurched left, right, foot off gas, the brake and an uphill slope slowed her. Her heart slammed at her ribs. Not good for the unborn one. She accelerated, at the top of the rise slowed, pulled to the shoulder. The gravel now gave a calming crunch. She stopped and turned off the engine.

The time since the accident. His occasional impotence, when did it begin? After the accident. Of course after, she unable to make love too, who could want to? Later he'd been all right sometimes, in the winter, the spring. Soon it'd be a year, couple of weeks— Was that it? The anniversary!

She'd be late for her appointment. She started the car. After the accident. Days, weeks of haze. Before? Unlikely. What was before, early last June?

Think hard, Priscilla. Remember.

○

It's true: their stories go on without Lola beside me. I have to go on. It's as if I'm shouting it all down to her. Except I don't see her, haven't since her visit to Theresa. I don't want to see her down there. I don't want her to be down there.

○

7.

Mid-morning. John Cochan picked up the Saab at the Burlington airport and headed into town; he needed more coffee. Getting back early was good. He'd go first to the cemetery, sit a while with Benjie, tell him what would happen in the evening.

Already too hot. Johnnie would spend half an hour at that little restaurant by the lakeshore, cooler, loosen his tie, take off his jacket, stare at the water. Plenty of time.

Thinking all this, he saw what was surely Priscilla's Dodge pull out of a driveway. A happy coincidence. Her doctor's office, old green frame house, he recognized it from when they'd gone there together. He had approved of Dr. Rachel Ryan, smart woman, no nonsense. Glad Priscilla found her. Who told her about this doctor? Right, that friend what was her name the one she always had lunch with. The woman had two kids. Ryan was her doctor too.

He'd catch up, apologize for Sunday night. He needed to grab hold of his moods. Damn, she was through the yellow light. He concentrated: don't lose her. Caught at a light ahead, good. Green, and he took off. But he was plugged up now, two old ladies ahead, one per lane. He saw the Dodge turn west, toward the lake. She'd get stuck behind something slow somewhere. They'd talk. At the corner, turning, way ahead, there she was. A hundred yards before the two lanes became one he accelerated, across the center line, and back in. Not an old woman, an old man. He couldn't catch the Dodge. She was speeding along too. A Toyota pulled out of a drive between him and the Dodge. Just keep her in sight. Looked like she was heading out of town. Did her friend— Tina, that was it—live out this way?

He started to pass. A huge grill barreled toward him, back in quick scarily near to impact, goddamn truck! He wouldn't interrupt her morning, a couple of minutes. A curve and, far ahead beyond a pickup now, the Dodge. Faster. He pulled around the Toyota and gave an angry blast. Two minutes later he passed the pickup too.

But her car had disappeared. Turned off? Not to the right, just cottages there, and the lake. He slowed. Now the pickup was dead on his tail, ten feet back, damned if he'd pull over. Or go faster, he had to scan the right and watch for a road to the left. A horn blast from behind. Bastard. For an instant he glimpsed, left, a road up the hill, blind entry. He sped ahead, pulled off right, turned, headed back. At the roadway he swung uphill. No Dodge. He took the right. Now the land lay flatter, a plateau. New houses. On the right they overlooked the lake. Again the road forked, he took the left. Homes, no Dodge. A four-corners. He took a right. He drove a quarter mile, not many houses now, ahead it looked like only woods. He stopped, got out—

Ridiculous. His place this morning was at the cemetery, he'd worked half the night to leave Boston early. He turned around and headed back. The road forked. He turned right, drove a few hundred yards. Houses again, a road to the left, he'd catch the other fork. Except it ran uphill. Strange, he thought he'd reached the bluff. An open space now. Far below, the lake reflected hot dead gray-blue. Burlington lay ahead, easy to wend a way down. He and Priscilla could talk this evening. Maybe he'd take her out to dinner. Slowed at a curve, started down— Slammed on his brakes.

On the up side of the hill, protected by a low ridge of stone, a driveway. Down along it stood their Dodge, and beyond it a gray Volvo, Tina's probably. He glanced at his watch. He backed into the drive.

The two-story stone house had a large wooden door. He rang the doorbell. Voices? And rang again. Silence. She had to be here, the car was here, had they gone for a walk? He stood back, looked in the window, a living room but no one in there.

The door opened. A man stood there. In a bathrobe. "Yes?"

A dozen lightning details converged— Cochan lunged at him and knocked him down, smashed by him. He tore open the door on the left, a study, on the floor a man's pants, shirt, a woman's shoes; no one.

He ran to the back of the house, a kitchen, no one, a bathroom, no one, a cellar, no. The fatface man the Magnussen son, same goddamn cheeks and eyes— Back to the staircase, up, a door, a bedroom, no one, another door another bedroom— There. Naked, white, a bedsheet like a web around her, waiting in the middle, waiting.

"Hello, Johnnie."

"No."

"Let me tell you, Johnnie, please?"

"No!"

"I want to. You have to let me—"

"You let him—let that fucking—that shitprick—into you!"

"Johnnie! No!"

He was on top of her, holding her down by the neck, bashing her shoulders, breasts, his knee in her belly, again, again—

"No-o-o-o!"

Karl slammed him on the head with a lamp. It shattered.

FISH

In springs and ponds, in the mill race:
micro-organism, phytoplankton, water-beetle, dace.
Rainbows, smallmouth, musky
wait. Red gills close, open, dusky.

The sun and moon, ready.
The season waiting, sore.
The hour dark, unsteady.
No mercy more.

The world bursts.

Lighter than a firefly hatch,
richer than a flashing storm,
A roar of plenteous grandeur. A mighty feast.

R.F., July 6, 2003

7.

"Your brother-in-law hates machines." Carney sipped beer from the bottle.

Sarah said, "He even hates driving."

"He thinks some cars are possessed. By demons."

"He tries to be good to demons. He says some he can never deal with." They reached the edge of the pond. "I tell him, if there are demons, you can't buy them off, big or small."

"Sure, that's consistent."

"I think he's crazy."

Carney glanced at her, she turned to him, and they burst out laughing.

Her smile fell away. "You do get all kinds of people to trust you."

"You trust me?"

A moment—"No"—and she turned away.

A breeze made tiny waves, splashed at the bank.

"I'm not saying he's completely wrong."

"Ti-Jean?"

"There's a revenge building up. Draughts and earthquakes, demons, plagues of locusts,"

"You sound like Theresa."

She shrugged. "Who knows. Something's pending." A moment later she added, "Milton told me you learned Cochan's building in caverns extending under our land."

"He could be."

Her smile was private. "You hedge all your bets, don't you."

They let a silence hang. Today Sarah had on a plaid blouse, slim jeans, white sneakers. Carney wore a blue shirt, chinos, and hiking shoes. His elbow ache was mostly gone.

They reached the far end of the pond. Where the spring had burbled the stones were dry, the water below stagnant. A splotch of green emulsion hung invader-like between surface and depth. Did it rise from below, or wash in? At the far end no water spilled out downstream.

She touched his wrist, he turned, she pointed: a dragonfly, its shaft black, wings banded silver-blue, iridescent. "A male," she whispered. "He's mosquito hunting."

"Good for him."

"Look."

He landed on a swampgrass stem. He twisted his tail under, and forward, tip to thorax.

"That's his abdominal pouch down there."

"What's he doing?"

"See on his thorax? That's where his penis is. But his sperm develop down in the tail tip. He's loading up. Look at him! He's sticking his tail tip into the pouch there, it's the pouch that hides his penis. Now he's dribbling the semen in drop by drop." She suddenly stared up. "Look!"

Carney followed her gaze. Another dragonfly.

"He'll have spotted her before. He's got immense eyes, they see in every direction. He's been following her flight. She's up there in his territory."

The male rose, swept across the water, and up. The sun caught his wings, a blue sheen. Above her now, he followed her lead.

She darted, and fed. Then he was behind her, over her. His legs grabbed her long body and, still flying, held on.

Sarah chuckled. "It's an embrace. Watch."

They flew together, paired. Then he was carrying her. He looped his abdomen again.

"For her this time. He's got tail-tip hooks to clasp her, they fit in pits behind her head."

His tail at her neck completed the coupling. Then his legs released. The two swooped, one presence. They found a shoot of sunny swampgrass and settled there. She looped herself forward, tail half circled to his abdomen.

"See? She's stroking the sperm sac open. If we were close enough we'd see his penis grasping her and then intruding."

She was under him, bent round, affixed.

"They'll stay like that for maybe an hour. Know the technical term for that position?"

"What?"

"The wheel. He's filling her with sperm."

They walked slowly to the cabin.

"Then what happens?"

"Oh, they'll fly off. Apart, but together. They'll find sticks, maybe some rotting grass. She'll land, make a hollow, away from wind and light. He'll hover and flit about. She'll squeeze the fertilized eggs into the mud."

"And when they hatch, the next generation's there?"

She laughed. "It's way more complex than that, but basically, yes."

Inside the porch a couple of flies buzzed, and a moth. At the corners, active spider webs. "You want to catch that moth, put him outside?"

"He's not bothering me." It whirred past her head. "You?"

"Not at all."

She waited. "Did you understand at all, that evening?"

"Two possibilities. One, you were looney-tunes bats. You took a vow, you deep-ended. Or deep-ended and took a vow."

"Deep-ended." She shrugged. "Maybe I have." She thought about it. "The second?"

"You don't like flies and you leave them to the spiders. It makes no difference, one mosquito more or less. You got rid of it because you didn't want it to bite you. You didn't kill it because you drew that line. Your vow."

She sat back. "Not bad."

Felt like she'd given him a grade of 75 when he deserved 98.

"The pond's a mess." She spoke quietly. "Something's blocked, down there." She shook her head. "Hard to say what it'll take to open it."

He laughed. "How about a Roto-Rooter."

She ignored him. "We're due."

"They say that about California, Vancouver—"

"Lots of little tremors out there. We don't get many. There the loose shale absorbs shock waves. Here it's older rock, long striations. Easy for a tremor to travel horizontally, build by increments."

"Not likely." It felt like she wanted this, the land to take some sort of revenge.

"Possible." She turned to him. "I went to Intraterra. To confront Handy Johnnie."

"Yeah?"

She had driven, armed, onto Terramac land. An iron bar and

road-spikes stopped her. A little man with a dumb grin, on his hip a portable phone, leered at her. No entry.

She wasn't defeated. She spun the Jeep around and headed to Richmond, to Intraterra headquarters. She stepped into the one-time Anglican Church. "Ex-shrine of a voided sectarian heaven become a temple for terrestrial venturism, as Theresa once said."

Carney laughed lightly.

The red pack had been heavy on her shoulder. She set it down and stared. No inner walls. Blocking the way sat a receptionist, first impression of Intraterra North, the young woman no antagonist to evolving style. Her gelled black hair spiked, spines on a chestnut. Over the right ear a padded hook held an earphone and mouthpiece, the speaker the size of her pinky nail, a green plate, smallest of ten, the longest an inch and a half extension of emerald lacquer. Rings on her fingers, a dozen easy, and rings in her left ear, seven. Plus two in each nostril. Under her electric-green blouse, shoulders to embarrass a Heisman Trophy winner. The rest, better hidden under a desk, wasn't; beneath a surface of clear plastic, black trousers with tight cuffs, ankle-high two-inch-platformed red canvas shoes. After work, would she play football or basketball?

Carney laughed again.

By comparison with the fingernailed athlete, Sarah, her yellow sundress clean, had felt innocent of the act she was about to commit. "I'd like to speak to John Cochan."

No eye contact. "Got an appointment?"

"Yes."

"No you don't. He doesn't have appointments today."

"I called. His secretary made it." A lie.

"What's your name?"

"Sarah Yaeger."

"He's not here."

"Who isn't?"

"Mr. Cochan."

"Why'd you ask me all that?"

"Policy."

"Look. I want to talk to Cochan."

"Sorry, hon. Can't today." The secretary opened a see-through

324

drawer, took out a package of M&Ms, popped one in her mouth.

Sarah picked up the backpack. It felt heavier than before. "Who's that over there?"

"What's the difference, hon?" The gray-tech eyes, black-lined, looked up for the first time. Curiosity, not interest.

"I'll talk to him." She marched away.

"Hey, you can't go through here!"

Sarah knew she could, she just had. She saw the man on the stage pick up his phone, then glance toward her. She guessed Ms. Fingernails wasn't running the hundred back behind.

The chancel man put the phone down, straightened a sheaf of papers, centered them on his desk, adjusted his tie, walked to his door, pulled it ajar and stood blocking the entry. A solid round figure, all charcoal-gray three-piece suit with long flat ears.

Sarah walked up the steps. "You're Mr. Cochan's associate?"

"That's right."

"I had an appointment with him. I understand he's not here. I'll talk to you."

"About?"

"May I sit down?" Yes, a pin-stripe, near invisible.

"If you could give me an idea?"

"Your explosion last Wednesday night. About ten."

"Ah." He thought for a moment. "Please. Come in."

Sarah and her bag did. She sat in an uncomfortable chair.

"We will be brief. I have a lot of work." He smiled, and shrugged apologies.

From the lilt of an accent she figured him from Quebec. "What's your name?"

"Aristide Boce. And yours?"

"Yaeger, and I live on the piece of the land you were blasting under last Wednesday."

"I'm sorry, that's not possible. I'm not sure what you mean by blasting but I assure you Intraterra doesn't carry out its projects beneath other people's homes, hmm?"

"Yeah well it crashed right up through. And it's made chaos of the water system."

"Now look, young lady, this isn't—"

"Forget the young-lady bullshit. You screwed up the groundwater with your Terramac."

"That's impossible."

"Somehow you've managed it."

"Now listen, the receptionist can make you an appointment with our assistant engineer—"

Sarah had stood up. "No, seeing your baby engineer isn't on. Just give Handy Johnnie this." She reached into her pack and pulled out a plastic bag. She set it on the desk, took it by the bottom and held it upside down. What last week had been the two rainbow trout, now splatted across wood and paper. Viscous glop mushed over the files, heavy juices oozed under the telephone and dribbled onto Aristide Boce's pin-stripe lap. He'd pushed the chair back, leapt up, with bare hands brushed at the liquid, stared at his fingers— Thorough disgust.

"I'd left the fish wrapped up in the ice house," Sarah said to Carney. "I had a weird sense I'd need them. The sunny ride to town did a lot of good." She chortled, spiteful.

Carney smiled but would not laugh. "Those fish needed a good burial."

"Martyrs to the cause."

As well, more evidence—though not yet proof—of possibly connected cavern and water systems under this piece of geography. "Did Milton say anything about his talk with Leonora? What she's learned about the legal implications of the blasting, depending on where it is?"

"She told him she was working on it. She and Dalton Zikorsky—he was the lawyer for RAPT—they need some kind of additional background, and then they'll file a restraining order, make Cochon stop blasting until the precise sites of the explosions can be determined."

Carney nodded. "Can't they just bring in some inspector from the county office?"

"That's what they need the restraining order for," Sarah said.

The RAPT lawyer Zikorsky, from what Carney knew of the man, was not whom he'd have chosen for this role. But Leonora was in charge of the legalities.

At the moment of leaving, Carney realized he was asking Sarah to have dinner with him. Say, tomorrow or Friday evening? Halfway between his farm and Burlington was Twenty Oaks Inn, a favorite, eighteenth century. If she was visiting Theresa he'd pick her up in Burlington. She knew the place, she said. She'd find her own way there. They agreed on Friday.

Fish ooze on Boce's pants. Her little fits of malice intrigued him.

○

The God Joan deigned to speak with me. A casual "Nice day" for starters. Yes, I agreed, it was, and did not ask her if, since AAing, she'd ever had a non-nice day. Then: "What do you do here?" Well now, how curious, this sudden interest by a God. True, Lola had become intrigued with my stories. But over a period of time. Had Joan heard rumors of my narratives? "I find stories to tell." Bafflement took Joan's face from brow to chin. Suddenly she came right to the point. "Have you seen the God Lola?" Aha! So she'd been delegated. She'd done her job and now wanted to get away from me, quick as possible. "No," I said truthfully. I could've added that I had no idea where Lola was, but that would have been true only in the specific. The no alone proved sufficient; instantly Joan wafted away. I guess word of my pleasure in storytelling hasn't reached the Gods, let alone excited them.

○

9.

John drove the Saab. The clock said 11:03. The gate of the Village of Richmond Memorial Park said An Interdenominational Cemetery, which meant all kinds of Protestants lay buried there. Johnnie, a technical Catholic, had followed Priscilla's ways in such things. Benjie's coffin was brought here, a quiet place. Before the accident Johnnie had paid no more than passing attention to the gray headstones, or the green of the grass. Now he drove through the gates guided by the habit of ownership, and swung right along a drive.

It had been the worst of days. At the hospital they said the cut on his head was not deep, no apparent problem, but they kept him six hours just to be sure. He'd walked out, better things to do, important things. He drove himself home, nothing wrong with his head, he knew that even as she'd driven him to the hospital. He'd sat beside her all the way to Richmond. They said nothing. Now up the drive. He stopped the Saab. Charge Fatface for assault? Not worth the time.

She turned to him. "Johnnie—"

"Not a word. Not one word."

Inside the girls ran to her. She hugged them, asked them to go with Diana. She took herself to the guest room. She lay on the bed, and wept.

Johnnie had heard her in there, crying her life away. Well, what did she expect?

Sheriff Henry Nottingham, in T-shirt and jeans, cool in the night heat, leaned against his private car. He stared across the cemetery and the valley over to the eastern hills, a hazy half-moon hanging two of its diameters above the horizon. The years of his job had taken him around the county, he knew it all, its wealth and welfare, its roads and woods, its kitchens, politicians, back rooms, dole. He patrolled the northern border and till recently kept control over the influx of illegal workers from Quebec, limiting it to those from families whose men had for generations crossed over to work in Merrimac County. Since the seventies some women too, but from the old families. His preference had long been to keep the crime rate low and judges' burdens light by working out arrangements between perpetrator and victim: a real estate broker, rumored driving while drunk insensate, might suddenly contribute heavily to the Little League; a kleptomaniac wife, caught in the act, would agree to accept a year's responsibility for the Meals on Wheels program, feeding the aged and bedridden; two teenage boys from good families seen breaking into the Texaco station might pay back the pilfered cash, volunteer to serve as Big Brothers for a couple of unfortunate younger kids, and both the teens' fathers would generously give their time stomping door to door in mid-winter for the County Hospital's drive to enlarge its paramedic service. In much of daily life Sheriff Nottingham helped keep the balances, and enjoyed doing so.

He knew also that unemployment in the county was high, the public purse overspent, and too many families undernourished. So he'd been in favor of Terramac from the start. He'd never personally challenged the Alliance, though, partly because he believed Shapiro and

Magnussen and the rest had the right to oppose Terramac. Still he'd become a member of the Approval Committee.

So these days the Sheriff looked on as two hundred and eighty-five workers came across the border every day, five hundred and forty new jobs all told. Should've been more county residents doing that Terramac work but near-half was way better than nothing. Everything had been dealt with legally between the Commissioners' office, the Governor's office, and the Quebec Premier's office. The Sheriff figured it wasn't his business to clarify whether these international borders were subject to state law, federal law, or whatever. Except he knew the flow had to be approved, controlled, whatever, given all the terrorism in the last few years.

The Saab stopped. Henry Nottingham shone his lamp toward it and walked over. "I had a word with the groundskeeper. Tomorrow he might see the upturned earth. I brought along a little bush, we can plant it by the grave."

"Thanks, Hank. Very good."

"You got the disinterment form?"

"It's in the car."

The Sheriff nodded slowly. They stood facing each other, the air still thick with the day's heat, Nottingham dubious, not liking the way Mr. Cochan clenched his teeth.

John Cochan asked, "You bring a shovel?"

The Sheriff nodded, opened his trunk and took out two. Also two crowbars and a sealed beam lamp. "Go faster this way, we'll get done quicker."

John nodded and wished he'd changed clothes. He loosened his tie and pulled his coat off. He hadn't thought about the actual work of digging. He hadn't thought about much of anything, up at the house. There'd be time to think through what she'd done.

The Sheriff turned his headlamps on, damp yellow light across the gravesite. They dug. Sweat pasted shirts to skin. Mosquitoes bit through cotton. The ground was not packed tight. They went less than five feet down. It took less then fifteen minutes.

How cold the winter must have been, how terrible under the dirt. At least the coffin was snug and tight, no bugs could get in there. In there, Ben, in his suit. It needn't have been a suit. But she'd insisted. No, he'd said, shirt and pants, far more normal for Benjie. Eight years, it wasn't right, she and too many women looking out for Benjie. Priscilla. Her mother too but John had put a stop to that. And Diana, Deirdre, Melissa.

The Sheriff balanced his sealed beam on a neighbor headstone. He pointed the light slanting down.

They worked soil away from the edges of the coffin, a small thing, five feet long. Hardwood, no decay, only in one corner had the cold and damp cracked the lacquer on the top. Inside lay the boy who'd grinned at Johnnie ten thousand times, the arms that hugged—

Henry Nottingham, puffing, stopped, wiped water from his brow and neck.

Wasn't just moving the coffin enough? No. Did he have to look inside the coffin? There was no choice. Henry hoped there'd be no more than the skeleton. He wiped sweat from temples, mustache, chin.

He handed John the flashlight and grabbed the crowbar. The beam searched the hole. The Sheriff reached the other crowbar over to John, they kneeled, reached down, the Sheriff caught a handle with a crowbar hook, and loosened the box. John found the other handle. They pulled the coffin out, set it flat on the ground. Stared at it.

Cochan broke the silence. "I have to see him. Once more."

"Mr. Cochan—" He sighed. "If I can say? I wouldn't."

"I know you wouldn't. And it's good advice, Hank."

"There's no telling what he'll look like. I've seen a few, sir, and, well, they all— None are— You don't want to see them."

John squeezed his eyes shut. Five seconds, fifteen.

The Sheriff wondered if maybe John Cochan was praying.

John knelt, grasped the coffin lid. Yanked. It didn't move.

"Wrong side, Mr. Cochan." His beam played light on the other side.

John nodded, lifted. The lid loosened. With a sharp yank he threw it open. He stared.

Empty.

The Sheriff squatted, searched with his flash, ran his hand along the yellow silk lining. No decomposition. Stained at the foot where water had leaked in. He looked up at John.

John's head was shaking, the tiniest of lateral motions left and right and again, again, a dozen times, twenty. The bugs.

"Mr. Cochan, I've heard of such things. But I've never—"

"No, no." It had to be the bugs. Nothing left. No clothes.

"I'll make a report, we'll find out."

John reached over, lowered the lid, closed the coffin. "Hank, you've done me a big favor. I'm in your debt." Not a trace. "Someone in debt shouldn't ask for more. But I need another favor. Don't make a report. Forget what you've just seen."

"But don't you—"

"Yes. But it has to be something—else. Please." The bugs have taken Benjie.

Sheriff Henry Nottingham considered the request. He nodded. They shook soiled hands. He caught John's eye, then looked away. This was messy, very messy.

Putting the coffin back, covering it again, planting the bush, took forever.

Eleven

GRAVE COMPLICATIONS

1.

Priscilla remained in the guest room, locked in from her side. A silent breakfast for Johnnie. He walked to the office. He had not slept. His gut churned with bile. What does one do with an adulterous wife? Where was Benjie? The world was deeply flawed this morning.

At least he'd set one element in place. Oh, he would aright the others too. Leonora Magnussen was due at nine. A nice irony, his ally of old the one to accept his offer formally.

The morning was again hot, his shirt already moist. And Ms. Magnussen already there when he arrived. Tall, so tall, skinny as a line but spread out by the full white skirt, shoulder pads the caricature of an older fashion, for cripesake, two-inch heels. Women who allow vogue to dictate judgement— Thinks she's real successful, independent, one more who can't tell hope from glory. "My office is at the back, Leonora, old friend. After you." He followed, watched her stride, her shoulders. Boasting her pride by her stance.

She felt his eyes on her spine, his stare of dominance. She walked up the steps. Over two years since she'd first dealt with him, ten days since he'd handed her the deed to a small piece of Terramac. In the office on the left Aristide Boce, stout in a three-piece suit, smiled at her. Did he know what she'd done, years ago, last week? She waited. John Cochan opened the door to the office on the right. She stepped in, and he followed, pointed to a large padded chair and closed the door. She sat.

"Coffee?"

"You plan to use this kind of plexiglass for the domes?"

He took a moment. "No. The material for the domes is much lighter. Far stronger. Our own patent. Would you prefer tea?"

"No, thanks. Shall we talk?"

"I'm delighted to see you again." He smiled. "Your parents have studied our offer."

"My mother's ill. The land belongs to my father."

"Of course. And I was sorry to hear about Theresa."

"Do you truly care one way or the other?"

"Oh, I assure you, yes. I think she's an admirable antagonist, you know that. As I expect her family are responsible negotiators."

"As in selling my father's land?"

"Right."

"I'm sorry, no."

John Cochan drew his lips tight. "You find the offer inadequate?"

"We simply don't want to sell."

"Hmmm." Not good. "You once thought Terramac an important project."

"I still do."

"I assure you, it's a generous offer."

"Perhaps."

"Then why not accept?"

"It's our land. It's been ours for two hundred years."

"And you expect its value will increase as Terramac grows, is that it?"

"It'll be ours for another two hundred."

"For your children?"

"For ourselves. And our children."

"Who? A girl running a third-rate carpentry shop?"

"Old enough for her responsibilities." A dry smile.

"And two bastards?"

"Born out of wedlock? Even bastards are human, Johnnie." So Cochan had done some more snoopy homework. But why expect different. "With legal rights."

"Bastard kids of a man who lives only to eat and fornicate? They're the inheritors?"

"That's none of your business."

"Come on, Leonora, a piece of scrub land? Those kids' lives would be improved immeasurably from the interest alone. Their entire futures." He smiled. "Your own as well."

"Don't concern yourself about my future. We're keeping the Grange and the land."

"For all to enjoy?"

"I've got to get back." She stood.

"Posted? No hunting, fishing, trespassing? No breathing the air? Generous, Ms. Leonora."

"What happens with it, we'll decide."

"You? Or that spy Carney you've hired?"

"Give me a break, John."

"Watch him, he'll ruin you, all of you. You'll lose out on $12 million, account of him."

She waited, then spoke slowly. "We make our own decisions."

A nerve found? "He's got his hold over you, yes?" Leonora Magnussen, smitten by Carney? "You know and I know." She was standing, turning. "You think it'll stay the same? With a center of wonders on your doorstep? Your pathetic little piece of despoiled nature?"

"There can be development and there can be preservation. Side by side."

Cochan folded his arms. "No, Leonora. People, coming and going. Many thousands of people every day. Soon, an airport. You don't own the airspace. You can't hide."

"We'll see."

"Very well, keep the land. I'm still in the market. As of right now my price drops by half. You have seven days to accept. So if you'll excuse me." He stood.

She decided, and sat. She opened her purse, took out a cigarette packet. "May I smoke?"

"Please don't."

She replaced the pack.

"I can still be generous. Back to my first offer of the day."

"I'm not finished." She heard herself sound hard. Inside she trembled. Here came the break—from all she had thought she believed, from the compromise she had hoped to achieve.

Cochan too sat. "Okay, go on. I've got a lot to get done."

"In two days we'll be in court seeking an order to restrain you from developing any lands beneath the Grange acreage."

No! No! Afterward John guessed he wasn't frozen in place for more than a second or two. It felt like that many minutes. "Anything else?"

She stood. "Enough for now." She opened the door and walked out, no nod of acknowledgment to chubby-suit next door.

John stared after her, stick-figure with tiny breasts.

Leonora sat in her car. She shouldn't have told him. Nor met with him. He'd try to stop the restraining order. But he'd have done that anyway, soon as they filed. So? Worth it, seeing him turn to stone. She felt cleaner. She drove through Richmond and north, to the border. Well-versed about the family was Mr. Cochan. Informants everywhere. She shivered.

2.

Friday morning Carney got back the test results on the pH in Gambade Brook. The water was too acidic for trout to breed. All those big rainbows, the last of their kind. He'd have to tell Ti-Jean and Feasie. A fist of sadness held him tight. He'd been looking forward, in a mild way, to his evening with Sarah. Tell her about the creek? He played his cello, a mournful tune.

At five-thirty he shaved and turned on the water for a bath. He heard a car stop in his drive. The doorbell rang. He grabbed for his dressing gown, opened the door a slit. "Just a second." He stepped back to pull his pants on.

Sarah eased the door open. "Don't worry about me, you don't have to be formal." She plopped her red backpack on a chair.

"I thought we'd agreed on meeting at the Inn."

"I was driving around. I wanted to see where you lived."

"How'd you get my address?"

She studied his face again. "Milton, of course."

"I was getting cleaned up."

"Clean away. I'll follow."

In her jeans and plaid shirt she didn't look ready for a dinner date. Carney's long bath became a quick shower. Into slacks, a shirt. Why had she come here?

She grabbed her bag and went into the bathroom. Her ablutions took longer. She came out elegant: green silk dress, hair glowing, a slim necklace gold against tan skin, shawl in hand, heels, bit of makeup, a smile. "Shall we head out?"

"We're"—he checked his watch—"an hour and a half ahead of schedule. The reservation."

"Okay. How hard is it get a drink around here?"

In silence he made a pitcher of Scotch sours. An attractive woman, he conceded. He filled two glasses and set the pitcher on the coffee table. He sat on the couch, she in a chair.

She sipped. "Tell me about Carney."

"In exchange for hearing about Sarah Magnussen Bonneherbe Yaeger."

"I've dropped the Yaeger."

"Oh?"

"Yesterday."

"Why?"

"To travel a bit lighter." Her glance flicked across his face. "Like, Carney?"

"Something like that."

"The name you were born with?"

"I had a first name. Never wanted it."

She raised her glass. "To brevity."

They drank, and talked. He heard versions of stories he'd had from Feasie and Milton, family stories. He got more of a sense about her lab job: blood, urine, and fecal analysis.

"The shit and piss of life," she said.

They talked about Theresa, her strengths and limits. "The twins and I bought her a kitten once. She gave it to a neighbor." She wished her mother well, admired her, after her stroke saw her more often. But didn't know her, wasn't sure if she wanted to, wasn't sentimental about her own childhood. Over fifteen years out of her parents' house. Too much had happened.

He told her about his cleanups. "I've taken some time off, till the end of summer."

"The work isn't—what? Exciting enough?"

"It demands complete commitment."

She raised the right eyebrow. "And yours isn't."

"In the old days I'd start a project and suddenly, ping, I'd be inside it. It would feel like my own long-time neighborhood, I knew it so well."

"Absorbed." She nodded. "At the cabin I can get like that, like there's a bigger context and I'm right in it, inside somebody else's world."

"Yes." He sipped. A long while since he'd talked like this. Scotch loosening the tongue.

"Last week," she said, stopped as if deciding whether to go on, then did, "a couple of barn swallows, they were building a nest, feeding. I watched them. For hours. Till I was late for work. They brought back mud and dry grass, it was like I knew where they'd head next, how long till they came back. I couldn't pull away. As if, if I stopped looking there'd be no more reason for them to build the thing. And then I realized I was part of it, they were part of it, but the mud and grass and the insects they were eating were part of it too?"

He nodded. "I get like that when I'm fishing."

She smiled. "I believe you. Shame."

"It can be the best of times. Like in the middle of fire and smoke. Only prettier."

She nodded. "Those dragonflies we watched, I could have stayed with them till they disappeared."

If he'd not been there, did she mean? "You left."

"We had to go."

His right hand rubbed the other wrist: we had to go. "Sometimes, in my work, there's a strange thing that happens." He found himself telling her about his friend Mot, the warner, the doubt-refuser, who sometimes alerted Carney to instant or impending dangers. He did not tell her whose gift Mot had been. He did say, "Recently Mot's not been around much."

"Ah."

Now why did he tell her about Mot at all? "Instead there's something else."

She waited, watching.

He filled their glasses, sat, leaned back. "Sometimes in a simple action I'd feel clumsy. I mean, in the middle of a cleanup, say. Out of control, right there." And suddenly he felt out of control now. He'd told no one about any of this, except bits to Bobbie. He tried to stop by taking a sip but his mouth had developed a mind of its own. "If I started to tell somebody what to do next, that was easy. But committing some simple act, I was suddenly awkward."

"I don't understand. What?"

"Like, say, trying to speak a language with only a couple of tourist phrases."

"Mmmm."

"But I'll tell you the opposite. Fishing." He shook his head, felt a touch of awe. "When I'm out on the water I'm"—he shrugged, and said with no embarrassment—"graceful. It's an elegant thing, the curve of a fly-line, dropping a tiny bit of hair and feather just where I want it."

"And steel. Don't forget the hook."

"Ah, but without a barb."

She smiled.

"It's beautiful, the line floating for a long moment between heaven and water, it creates its own elegance. Like there's a kind of fluency in my muscles and I'm part of the air. You know?" He felt a witless grin but it didn't bother him.

"Is that what *A Ton of Cure* sounds like?"

"Like what?"

"Like how you're talking now."

Blather brought on by booze. "A little less corny."

"Why'd you go on the lecture circuit?"

He hesitated. What the hell. "It was a kind of cure for a condition I'd developed."

"Yeah? What?"

"It's called cricopharyngial dysphasia."

"I didn't hear right. Better pour me more sour stuff."

He did. And for himself, the last of it.

"Crico-what?"

"I have to go back. About eight years. Something was wrong but I couldn't figure what. I'd be in the middle of a job, everything going right. Suddenly I'd glance up and see myself. It was like I told you before. I looked ridiculous."

"I still don't understand."

"At least strange. Me wearing what looked like a spacesuit in water and muck up to my waist at some river edge, explaining to a dozen people how to scrub oil off a heron's feathers. What the hell could have brought me there?"

"What did?"

"Among other things, twenty years without thinking about why, what for."

"Maybe you wanted the heron to live."

"Sure, but it was a lot more complicated. I'd been with a good woman, Lynn, and we broke up. She was deeply hurt. Recriminations by the ton. We were carving flesh from each other's bones. I was drinking too much and eating too much. And one morning I woke up with, I was sure, a bone stuck in my throat. I figured a fish bone, I'd had swordfish the night before."

Sarah smiled. "Revenge from the deep."

"No, something else. Be quiet if you want me to go on."

"Sorry sorry, go on."

"Well, by the end of the day it was a chicken bone. I could hardly speak and I was worrying about breathing. Alcohol helped." Carney sipped his whisky sour. "Next day, X-rays, nothing there. I went to a throat man. He nodded wisely and gave it a name, cricopharyngial dysphasia. He said my cricoid, that's a kind of ring-shaped cartilage at the lower part of the larynx, from there to the pharynx, was all out of whack. Under stress the cricoid can tighten up. I'd feel like I was choking, something stuck there. Yes, I said, that was it, that he'd described it dead-on. He told me it used to be called globus, a kind of folk name, these days throat people were seeing a lot of it. And the cure? I shouldn't be so tense. Thanks a lot, I said. He prescribed some little pills, take two when the throat tightens and don't use them while driving."

Sarah's right eyebrow went up again. Top half of a question mark.

"I took two and fell asleep for fourteen hours. I cut down to a half and used them as little as possible. Then one evening I had a date, somebody new, second date since my break-up. I liked the woman well enough and told her about my cricoid. It used to be called globus, I said. She burst out laughing, funniest thing she'd heard in a long time. The joke? 'There is some shit you will not eat,' she said to me."

"She sounds wise."

Carney nodded. "Globus, she told me, is short for globus hystericus, well known in the nineteenth century. Common 'specially among middle-class women, the children grow up, leave home, the woman finds herself tense to the gills because there's no more purpose to her life. Except these women did have to swallow whatever was dished out. And here it was in my throat, end of the twentieth century, one big globus of stress and no purpose."

"Stress in macho damage control? I thought stress hit the likes of senior ad men and lady associate directors."

"And me. And the end of the story is, I began to lessen my time with the Co. and went out lecturing about damage control. That was her idea, my friend's. A way of transforming what I knew, making it useful."

"It worked?" She touched her whisky glass to her brow.

"Soon as I made my decision my throat cleared a bit, couple of weeks and it was gone. Telling a crowded hall a horror story about a mess keeps it away. The stories became the book."

"So everything's okay now."

She was watching his face again, her eyes an invasion. Scotch re-enforced. He felt way more naked than when she'd arrived. She stared in, no words. For self-protection he looked back. Into her eyes, one to the other, the tiniest shift. Not a flicker to hers, they were gray, a flash of green, the center black and exacting. He felt hypnotized.

She drew back, still gazing at him. "How long will they hold our reservation?"

They drove in Carney's Jaguar. A fine evening, the air soft. A large truck in front of them exuded gray fumes. She covered her nose.

"I'll drop back." He grinned at her.

"We smother nature to death. We turn it into an anthrosphere."

How quick to shunt away the earlier mood. "What's an anthrosphere?"

"As opposed to biosphere. A world only for humans, not for the rest," she said. "The Old Testament God wins again. 'Be fruitful, multiply and replenish the earth, and subdue it, and have dominion over the fish of the sea and the fowl of the air and over every living thing that moveth on the earth.'"

At the Inn the background music was muted, undemanding. The mood soothed. They ordered, tuna for Carney, a vegetable stir-fry for Sarah, and a bottle of Australian Sauvignon Blanc. She relaxed into silence, let her eyes close. Again a lovely woman sat opposite him.

The food arrived. They probed each other's pasts. No, she'd never wanted children, likely too late now. He was relieved he never had any, considering his divorce, his work. In the fall she'd look for another job.

"Tired of the human functions?"

"Just their output."

"Where'll you look?"

"I don't know. Not in an office or a lab."

"Something outside."

She nodded. "That was smart, making a book out of your lectures."

"You think so?" Right then Carney discovered he wanted Sarah to think the things he had done in his life, and what he believed, were dead-on and smart and important.

"Yeah. Doing something. I should have divorced Driscoll years ago, done something with all that time. We had so little in common. At the end. And in the middle." She dunked a piece of cauliflower in some sauce and popped it in her mouth. She chewed, mulled, and swallowed.

"What kept you together?"

She shook her head. "There's something about divorce. To me it's like an admission of failure. A car accident killed him. I felt guilty. Not that I could've kept it from happening, just I couldn't figure how to mourn. I learned how little I'd respected his life when his death caused me so little sadness."

He asked, "And are you unhappy about the other break?"

She squinted at him. "Which?"

"Between you and your mother."

She thought about this. "Things can change."

"You felt distant from, uh, your husband"—he nearly said De Skull—"for a long time?"

"Oh, since about when we moved to Boston. I mean, I didn't hate him. And I don't think he had affairs. He was married to his job. He gave me everything, time to find what I should do, what I liked doing, freedom to take the job way up in Durham."

"Maybe," Carney said, "these weren't his to give."

She sat still, staring. Slowly, she nodded.

On her face only the gaze, committing more of him to memory.

Mot suddenly said, Pull back. Her eyes held him to her, and—he was struck by this—her search made him shiver.

She lifted her glass. "To you. Thank you." Her eyes never left his face.

He felt himself slide.

She sipped the last of the wine. "Shall we go?"

He paid. They drove. Neither spoke.

Then from her silence she said, "When I was seventeen I had an abortion."

They drove on.

"My mother never forgave me. My father— I told them I was pregnant. I took care of it."

"You were brave."

"Scared. Good and scared." She shook her head. "I explained what I'd done. I'd never seen Theresa so devastated. She'd already said they'd raise the baby, she and Milton. I think they never told Leasie and Feasie, or Karl. I certainly didn't."

They drove, speed unchanging, as on slick ice.

"From fourteen-fifteen on I was pretty wild. Lots of boys. Men." She laughed lightly. "Theresa forgave me the wildness. And the pregnancy. She didn't forgive the abortion."

The wheels of the Jag made no sound.

"Later I didn't forgive myself."

"Why not?"

"I should have respected her stance. I knew what it would be."

"Hmm." But does one really, Carney wondered. "And the baby's father?"

"Who it was? I don't know. Three or four possibilities."

"Hmm."

"After, I stayed away from sex for three years. A real nun."

"It must've been"—how not to sound stupid?—"tough."

"Yep."

Carney turned toward her. "Sarah—"

Her right eyebrow arched up.

"Thanks."

She nodded, and they drove. A new kind of silence. They reached his farm, and went into the living room. It had gotten to be eleven-thirty. Carney asked, strange question, "You driving back to the cabin tonight, or going to Burlington?"

She smiled. "I'm staying here." She gazed at his face, a glance. Then she was kissing him. The gentlest kiss, as if she didn't dare bruise his lips. She drew back. "If you want me to."

He kissed her. An embrace so right and new he might never have held a woman before.

They sipped armagnac, they laughed, for a time were too drunk or too giddy or too wonderstruck for more. Desire increased its demands, the spell of the other a magnet, a sudden sweet greed. They touched, joined. Afterward they held each other for a long time, and fell asleep. In the morning they did even better.

o

Six of them arrived this time, the Gods Helen, Dante, Dmitri, Elizabeth, Weng, and Edsel himself. They stood in a circle about me. Wherever I turned, one or the other would be facing me. So I stopped turning. I'd deal with the big fella himself. "What d'you want, Edsel?" Silence. "Okay," I said. I would walk away. What could they do, close in and not let me pass? Grab me and pummel me? These great Gods who'd AAed? Unlikely. I stepped forward, between Edsel and Helen. And all of them moved with me, the circle remained, striding across the clouds. I shifted direction. So did the circle. Simon says. I stopped, I said to Dante, "You Gods are weird." I sat down. They too sat. Monkey do. I said to Weng, "Having a good time?" Weng said, "Lola." Amazing! They can speak, too. At least one can. "Ah, Lola," I said. I looked around me. No Lola, just six seated Gods. I lifted the hem of my robe, flicked away some imagined dust, and looked under. "Nope. Not here." I checked up my sleeves. "Sorry, not there either." I picked up a piece of fuzzy cloud and looked into the hole I'd made, shrugged, smiled sadly at Weng and shook my head. I pulled the fuzz apart. "No idea, guys." I stopped speaking to them. I had nothing to say. I lay flat, and closed my eyes. Gods to watch over me in my sleep. I think after a while they got up, and closed the circle tight by all standing around me, looking down, waiting for what? Lola, springing suddenly from my forehead. She didn't. When I awoke, they were gone.

Not sure what to think of all this. Could they do me any harm? No known evidence of such an act up here, at least not by me. On the other hand, I'd just stood off six Gods. I'd never heard of such a thing either. But it felt okay.

○

3.

Cochan watched Sheriff Nottingham march up the nave. Merrimac Investigation Services's head agent, bringing his report to the President and Chief Executive Officer of Intraterra.

"How are you, Mr. Cochan?"

"Great, Hank. What's happening?"

Two things were happening. One was easy to talk about. The other the Sheriff and Jeb hadn't investigated far enough. Suspicions. Fears. If they checked out he didn't know if he could talk about it. He took a folded paper from his shirt pocket and spread it open. "Well, Mr. Boce was right in worrying about that Carney. We did a search on him—"

John sat back. "Hank, I don't need to know this. Tell Steed."

Henry Nottingham nodded, a kind of self-encouragement to spend as much time on Carney as possible. "Just the context, Mr. Cochan, and a couple of interesting details. You see, this Carney, he's worth millions."

"So?"

"So I read some of a book he's written, called *A Ton of Cure*. It's not pro the kind of environmentalism Terramac's all about. Not your Econovism, sir."

"Hank, there's only one real environmentalism. Let's not get into that now. What else?"

"Hang on, Mr. Cochan, let me finish. You see—" He glanced at his paper.

Goddamn laconic Vermonters.

"There's another reason why this guy's around. Seems he was brought here by Theresa Magnussen."

"I've already gathered that. And?"

"He's gone to visit the professor at the hospital several times. He's visited the home of the son, Karl. He's stayed at the Magnussen Grange, supposedly to fish Gambade Brook."

"Hank. Spare me his itinerary." What did Carney have to do with the whoring shrink son?

"He met with Leonora Magnussen." The Sheriff looked up. "Couple of times."

"Okay, Hank."

"Took me longer than I hoped but everything's solid. I'll type it up tomorrow."

"That's okay." John smiled. He didn't feel like smiling. "I prefer some reports verbally."

"Whatever you say."

"Good work."

"I'll be going, then."

"Sure, thanks— Wait, wait a minute." John had to ask. The empty coffin. He'd told Hank not to investigate. Still— "Was there anything else?"

"Uh, no sir." There was. But till he got it clearer, he couldn't say anything. He handed Cochan the Magnussen file. "Take care." He left.

John read it through. Full of Hank's good research, way more than he already knew about the family. Photographs. The woman who'd thrown the fish at Steed. The twins. The fatface stud. John would get him good.

4.

Sunday lunch at Karl's with Milton, Leonora, Feodora, Ti-Jean, and Sarah now included Carney. Little awareness of his relationship with Sarah. Milton, his face glowing, announced to the them, "Theresa's coming home, they're releasing her Wednesday. She'll go for physio-therapy every day, I'll stay with her. We could all be at the house when she gets out, it'd give her such pleasure." To Sarah specifically he said, "Can you come? About noon? It'd make her so happy."

"Of course. Her mind's going to keep working till her heart quits." Sarah raised an eyebrow. "I'd take odds on that."

Milton looked at her sadly. But Sarah had meant this as a compliment for a one-time combatant. Carney wondered if Theresa would want such a reunion. Was Milton inventing this pleasure for her sake or his own?

Feasie said, "I think it'd be good for Theresa to spend some time at the Grange. It's close enough to town for the physiotherapy."

Milton wasn't sure. "The ground at the Grange isn't level. I've got her a new chair, it's coming this week. Twelve horsepower."

Ti-Jean muttered, "Too big."

Lunch was a roast capon smothered in tarragon, roast potatoes, asparagus. And a small multigrain casserole for Sarah. They drank Theresa's health. Over coffee, Leonora told them about her meeting with John Cochan. "Dalton Zikorsky filed for the restraining order against the blasting and Cochan's lawyers tried to block it right away. They'll set the hearing date this week. Dalt's feeling positive." They cheered her. Good to be back on the offensive.

All except Karl. In the last week he hadn't called Leonora, although she'd phoned him twice. Worry about Priscilla dominated everything.

"The hearing." Ti-Jean squinted at her. "When could it happen?"

"Likely not till September."

Ti-Jean, still muttering: "Lawyers."

Leonora ignored him and reported on her research. "What's complicated is the trespassing issue. The laws of Vermont and of Merrimac County—and Johnnie Cochan's activities have to be considered under these—these are, regarding our options, contradictory in an important way."

Karl muttered, "Normal." But he did realize Leonora was diving into all this work to wash away her foolishness. Recommending buying into Terramac, for godsake!

"In certain respects the law is all too clear. If he were mining, well he's got the go-ahead for the Terramac project. His underground rights included."

Carney asked, "So what's unclear?"

Leonora turned to him. "Are they really building underneath our land? We don't know."

"We do know he's blasting."

"Specifically under Grange land?"

Feasie said, "But if he's building wherever, we've got him?"

Leonora's head shook. "That's equivocal." She had to make them see how hard she'd worked on the case. To give the Grange land the greatest possible protection. "The law's direct enough on mineral rights, with approval you can mine or quarry your own land or with a lease you can remove ore or rock or fossil fuels from under somebody else's. His agreement with the county lets him mine to five thousand feet. So if he's less deep than that, and if he's not taking anything out of there, if he's building deeper than several sub-basements—" She shrugged. "In Vermont law, no one's ever posed this question."

Ti-Jean liked his wife's twin sister well enough, except when she epitomized the legal profession; like now. He shook his head. "You say property rights extend into the ground?"

"Right. Except no one I've consulted knows how far down. So it's not clear if his five thousand feet is legal. Some states have laws, but not Vermont. If you go down far enough into the earth, everybody's property meets. In that sense."

"The only issue we should be concerned with"—Carney spoke slowly, deliberately—"is if he's under land to which he has no rights. If so, whatever he's doing there is illegal."

"Goddammit," Feasie breathed. "The explosions, they're under the Grange. I can feel it."

Milton looked baffled, discouraged. "Under his own land he can blast what he wants?"

Leonora said, "In one sense, yes."

Carney turned to Milton. "Do you have underground mineral rights at the Grange?"

"I don't know." Milton frowned. "My father never said. We never worried about it."

"You should acquire them. Before someone else does."

"He's got plenty of space of his own."

"This is Handy Johnnie, remember?"

Leonora felt as if she'd been set aside. She leapt in again. "Look, his prospectives for the Fortier farm have been approved by the county, his power and water and waste disposal requirements are satisfied. At least on paper. He's self-contained and we can't do a thing." Leonora smiled, in control again. "But, if he has moved under our land in order to build, we can go beyond restraining orders, and lay charges. It could take years and it'll cost. But we'll beat him. And set important precedent."

"So now what? Wait?" Feasie was furious. "He's already messed up the stream. The well water tastes, I don't know, different."

Milton squinted at her. "You sure?"

"Maybe it's my taste buds. But Ti-Jean thinks it's different. Don't you?"

"That's it."

Carney was nodding. "Like Leonora says, it's a slow way. But it has to be done. Stop him here, you'll stop him in other places too." Long-term prevention. Always a patient process.

"Sure, Carney. Slow, polite, easy." Karl leaned forward, his face flushed. "Step back, let the bastard do what he wants. He destroys whatever's in his way." The land, his wife— Damn! He turned to Leonora. "You think there's a law to deal with the likes of John Cochan? He does what he wants with whoever he wants. He beats and smashes. And by the time you get to him, it's too late. Too fucking late." Tears filled his eyes.

Leonora leaned over his chair, she put her arm around his shoulder. Her neck felt hot. "I've got some vacation time coming. I'll do everything I can." With a grim smile she glanced around the table. She took Karl's hand, he squeezed hers.

Carney said, "It's a shame we can't see where the blasts have taken place, check the site with global positioning. That'd tell us all we need to know."

Lunch broke up. Sarah left with Carney. In full view of all they drove away.

Monday Carney again visited Theresa. She could roll side to side now. Not up and down, she had to be pulled to a sitting position, but, Milton said, with therapy that too might return. Once up she could hold herself straight, her chest and back muscles again hard at work. Her neck had regained some strength and she could turn to face whoever was speaking. If she wanted to.

No trouble with her hearing. But her speech was badly jumbled. Her right hand was steadier from the therapy and the doctor had started her on acupuncture. Her fingers could grasp a spoon. On the left side, no recovery. Two doctors told Milton they'd pretty much given up there.

Milton wouldn't believe it. He'd bring her back.

5.

Yak stared at blue equations on Steed's computer screen, tabulations of around-the-dome Luciflex strength per square meter. He saw only blue lines. Go across to Johnnie's office, let him ruminate, wind him down?

He turned his head halfway, he watched Johnnie, but the Handyman— Well, he was sitting, more broody than in a long time, exuding cool silence. Yak would help Johnnie any way possible, if Johnnie'd let him. He did understand, he'd heard the sad news of the miscarriage. Though not from Johnnie. Wrong for John Cochan to bear this all alone.

No, leave him be. The Handyman didn't want to talk.

John Cochan stared at the plexiglass wall. He turned, let his eye roam the other wall, solid and smooth, the old church wall. A better wall. It led up to the steeple, a pinnacle. His own pinnacle

It stood there. Grand. Up there nothing had changed. Only here, at the bottom. She.

Johnnie gazed up. Way up there, the tower. To rise above the menaces, the falsehoods, the horrors, and alarms the mind constructs. A pinnacle for standing isolate. A tower of peace, above the chaos. Far, far from the fearful bugs. Grand heights, for safety. Apex of his triangle. Only down below lie the bugs. He picked up the phone, pressed two buttons. The ring—

"Hello?" Harold Clark, in the Trailer of Architecture.

On that phone, why did Harry answer Hello? as a question. "It's me, Harry. Who'd you expect, Ethan Allen down from his horse?" Cochan's throat-and-stomach laugh, lips unmoving.

A snicker from Clark. "How're you, John?"

"First rate. Listen, I have a question."

Clark waited. Silence from Cochan. "Yes?"

"It's about when you're blasting."

"Okay." Clark waited. "What about when we're blasting?"

"Bang plants one of his big charges, he sets it off from where you can see it, right?"

"Sure. On remote. Why?"

"And the remote sets it off through a timing device."

"Yeah. A minute delay, couple of minutes. What're you asking?"

"He can put it all together, watch the timer being set, pull back before it blasts."

"Sure. What's this about?"

"Nothing. Just an idea. Thanks, Harry. See you later."

"Yeah, but—"

Johnnie set his phone down. For a moment he felt pleased, and allowed a small smile. His first real smile in days. He stroked his mustache flat.

Benjie wasn't in the coffin. The daily world was twisted. What madness to have thought Benjie was—reachable. Empty coffin, empty womb. Double betrayal. Benjie never had a chance.

All those visits to the cemetery. All those conversations with Benjie, and he wasn't even there!

She. She'd pampered Benjie, treated him like a tiny tot, for cripesake, made him so he couldn't fight the bugs. Beth, Johnnie's own mother, had never treated him like a baby. Now Priscilla, with that fiend of a fatface Magnussen. Had Johnnie loved Priscilla? Ever? Must have, once. Otherwise unbelievable, sleeping beside her all those years, then her defiant silence. Did she chortle inside at her little joke? No more.

But the sweet Priscilla, she wouldn't quit. Every night the weeping, the brazen explanations, her pretense of reason. Where did she find her scurrilous courage, those attempts to comfort Johnnie as if he, he, he were the one who'd committed some act of turpitude, as if he stood in league with fear and chaos?

Since Wednesday, he'd gone over and over their life together. The woman had been his wife. Still was, in that technical way. They had lived in the same house, conceived Benjie together, loved Benjie together, though she could never love with Johnnie's might and heart. They had planned Terramac together—

How, how had he been so duped by her? Over two years this— affair had gone on. She'd admitted it! But much longer was her mind's desire. Or more than mind's desire? The flesh as well? She admitted only to this present one. The whore. And with this one, what did she think, if she fucked him brain-dry, he'd gull his father into selling the land? Ha. The wasp-whore. She would burn for it. But later. Now she would be taught.

How does one who feels no guilt learn the agony of remorse? In an earlier day he might have beat it into her. Today Johnnie couldn't slap around his one-time wife, however low she sank. In such an act, there at the edge of darkness stood the pit. But the pit was her.

She had worn her wifehood as a disguise, had slipped into this camouflage at will. And, out again. In public moments she looked like a wife, mother to his son and daughters. She acted like a wife, in bed, yes, spoke like a wife, smiled like a wife. The hood of wife was her protection, the image of a sweet and natural wife. There, inside the hood, the camouflage, a package of duplicity and lies.

Not sweet. Her breath, her kisses, her sweat, a stale and fusty damp. Smiling, she'd made him inhale the poison. Daily the toxin mingled with the breath in his lungs and lodged there, a bitter virulence that spread to his flesh, belly, heart. In the days after Burlington he'd felt the chills of nausea. How could he have saved himself from this?

Not he. Benjie! From this, from her!

John Cochan would pass beyond this toxicity. And trust no woman again.

Benjie had tried to save him, tell him. What prepares a husband for this? He should never have married. Women devour. No, the fact was he did marry. Kids, a house. All the plans, six-eight kids roaming the house. Benjie the eldest, big brother Benjie. That one time, if the bogus wife had pampered the boy a bit only that one time, held him instead of stealing away to Burlington, back an hour late. One hour!

What was left? Terramac, alone, beneath the ground. He'd known this from the first. Down. One more blast would do it. With the new large chamber, elegant stalactites, Underland's estate would be complete. A frontier beyond frontiers. What they might find there! Lives to build there. Decorum, worry free, to dwell there. A metropolis to quicken the heart.

How he'd atoned for his father's mistakes since he'd sold off CochPharm and built the mighty Intraterra. How he fulfilled Terramac's promise in all spheres: not amelioration but vital creation: control, managed transformation. To be forged by its citizens from within their

Terramac libraries and data banks, comfortable with their systems of knowledge interchange, matrices of imagination and power across the earth. Fear of the new, eternally conquered.

Terramac, City of Creation in memory of Benjie. Twice lost. Nowhere would he not search for Benjie. The bugs had gotten in. Let in by someone Johnnie trusted. He'd scour every cave and cavern, search out the attics and cellars of each house, shop, laboratory, apartment, school. To reclaim Benjie's little body, anything.

6.

Theresa made talk-like noises. To Carney when he walked in she said, "Ghoo . . . thhe . . . zsee . . . oo . . ." meaning, Milton told him, Good to see you.

"How're you feeling?"

"Nherr . . . err'r." Never better.

Carney sat beside the bed. Theresa and Milton were watching *Some Like It Hot* on TV.

Theresa said, "Eesge . . . ay-ki . . . ourr—"

"Make it louder?" Milton asked.

Theresa's eyes blinked hard. "Eesge—"

Concentrate, and the slurs took on meaning.

"Actually, I'll stop it for a bit." He flicked the remote. "While Carney's here."

She's pretending to scowl, Carney thought. A fake scowl.

Milton beamed. "We're getting a big TV like this brought in for when Theresa gets out of here. We've never cared for videocassettes, not on the tiny screen like we have up in the Grange. But with this now, it's just about as big as in those small movie complexes."

Milton and Carney had organized a number of Carney's all-time favorite films for her, various Marx Brothers, more Chaplin, W.C. Field's *The Bank Dick* and *My Little Chickadee*, some Doris Day–Rock Hudson items. And *Red Carpet Treatment*, *Gentlemen Prefer Blondes*, *A Pocketful of Miracles*, Mel Brooks's *Blazing Saddles*— Theresa adored the post-bean-eating flatus scene, she had made Milton back it up to resee it, four times. She also liked *Mustache of the Walrus*; Carney didn't tell her his father had written the book it was based on. Some of

Woody Allen's, especially *Love and Death*, Theresa roared in wheezes at the tiny shovelful of sod, a piece of the homeland. She watched these over and over.

Carney sat through the end of *Some Like it Hot* and all of *The Seven Year Itch* that afternoon with Theresa. Out of the room he said to Milton, "She's insatiable."

"Her real favorites are those Marilyn Monroe comedies, and all of Lola's."

"Dirty old woman."

"It's as if she's trying to catch up with her laughing. The delight she takes, the way her laughter rises. It's wonderful." He laughed, and his eyes teared. "Neither of us had seen a film with Lola before. We were watching *Beyond Venus* and it was like Theresa had been hypnotized. She kept asking for more of Lola's films. She's a new Theresa. And that's because of you."

"No no."

"Yes yes yes. She sees humor in everything these days. You know, yesterday in the afternoon she reached out, her hand works pretty well, maybe the rest will soon again—"

"It will."

"She reached out and touched my hair. Sort of stroked it, and she burst out laughing."

Carney would have sworn Milton blushed. "She enjoys having you there, Milton."

He glanced away but allowed a grin. "I hope it's not her mind weakening."

Hear him, Theresa? You getting soft in the head?

○

By the door down there, her silver shape. Lola. Her whisper warmed me, my face and fingers felt aglow. Lola? Where've you been?

No answer.

I shouted, Lola! Lola!

○

Theresa muttered, I hear an echo of your name.

Lola smiled at her. In your imagination, Theresa.

No, here.

What? Those two outside? I'll go see.

Don't leave— Damn it, Lola.

Theresa fascinated Lola. She stood between Carney and Milton. Had she not died young and beautiful, so tragic and grand, she might have aged like Theresa, quick and jolly.

○

I imagine Lola thinking: Not so bad.

I called again, Lola! It's not too late! Come back!

○

Theresa yelled, Come back here!

Lola reappeared in the doorway.

Come closer!

Orders, Theresa?

Or I'll run you through.

Oh yeah? You and what sword?

My pole.

What pole?

My foilpole! Fishing fencing fighting pole. One hand left to slice with. Take my hand. Good. Two hands, one mortgaged to the finger-tips. Like my own poor mortal soul.

What did you say?

One hand left—

What was that you mortgaged, Theresa?

The fingers? The mortal soul?

What a curious expression.

Don't shake my faith in mortality.

Not me, Theresa. I'm eternal, remember? Will be forever, don't you think?

Haha! That's a sneak question.

Was it funny?

Sort of.

Good. Answer it.

Okay. Gods aren't anything. Gods don't exist.

I exist.

Only in my mind.

Well, Theresa, I like that. You have a mind powerful enough to create a magnificent gorgeous being like me, sweet pouty lips, my crown of chestnut hair, the laughter of these green and purple eyes, my curvin' features sheathed in shiny white from bosom to a graceful turn of heel?

Sure. So long as fantasy remains.

Oh you make us so casually, you humans.

I know how the mind works. You're some conglomeration—

That's pretty funny.

Look. Tomorrow they take me home. My husband, Milton, a kind large man, he'll feed me with a spoon, he'll wipe my nose and my ass, he'll change my drippage and drainage. That's John Milton Magnussen. And I'll be easy in that care. Got it? That's what's left.

And that's okay with Theresa?

That's how it is. A three-bedroom, white-clapboard, green-shuttered house. A deck for sun on the warm days. A garden. No place for you.

Do I take up space?

You're here. I talk to you.

You believe in me, then?

Does it matter?

Absolutely. To both of us.

Okay. I believe in you.

Words.

All I've got.

No, Theresa. You've got your—what did you say?—mortal soul. And some of your body.

Negligible. A neck, an arm. Hey, what're you—do—ing—

Huggin' you. Be quiet.

That—brings back—

Memories?

Yeah.

Good.

How about you? Got any memories?

Course not. I'm eternal. Unlike you.

A vital distinction.

Theresa, punning?

So what?

You know I'm eternal. I killed myself and woke up eternal.

What? Killed yourself?

Overdosed myself.

Not what it says in your biographies.

What? It says what?

You were done in.

Me? Who?

Come on. Your lover's wife did it. You don't know? I thought that's why you're here.

I'm here because you called me, Theresa. Who is my lover's wife?

Was. You know, her. Mom. Handy Johnnie's ma.

I didn't—kill myself?

Why should you?

Beth. Libby. Wife of Joe. Oh my.

That's what the books say. He had her committed. So she couldn't stand trial for murder.

Imagine that. Just imagine that.

You really didn't know. Ha!

Yes. Ha! Theresa. A deal? I'll come with you. You'll come with me?

What's in it for you?

New memories, maybe?

Okay. And maybe I can get to do one more fine, special thing. When do we start?

Tomorrow.

You're leaving again?

I'll come back, Theresa.

By then I'll be—at home. Does she know the address? Damn. Maybe she'll hug your bulgy shoulders again? Haha!

7.

"Oh Sheriff Nottingham! Just thinking about you." John smiled, stood, all grace. He drew up a chair for the Sheriff. "Sit, talk to me. Tell me what you know."

Henry Nottingham sat. "Not all that much, Mr. Cochan." Trouble was, the Sheriff sensed more than he knew and knew more than he said. "Not much at all."

John smiled his most genial. "Now come on, man like you, you know everybody in the county, finger in every pot and scandal." He sat across from the Sheriff.

The Sheriff grinned. "You'd be surprised how little of what I know is real knowledge. Most often just educated guesses."

"It's the educated part I like."

"A feel for the region, Mr. Cochan."

"Now look, Hank, I've told you to call me John for years, haven't I?"

"You have, sir."

"We've been through a lot together, some very personal moments. We're friends, right?"

"I appreciate that. John."

"Good. And I know you have something to tell me."

"Yes, sir."

"But you're reluctant."

"In a way, yes."

"Because of an earlier conversation we had."

"You could say that, John."

"I understand your hesitations. After all it's very delicate. But you see, I need to know."

"I guess you do."

"Let me make it easier. You know what happened to Benjie, don't you."

"Mr. Cochan— John, I don't think—"

"I'm afraid I do, Hank. I have to know."

"Yes sir."

"You investigated, didn't you? After I asked you not to."

"Yes."

"Come on, that's your job. You had to. I understand." John smiled, careful.

"It's good hearing you say that."

"Though I can't imagine where you'd nose around. With a question like this."

"It's delicate, like you said."

"Delicate? More complicated than delicate, I'd bet."

"Yes, sort of."

Suddenly John was afraid. Of what he might hear? "They must be near impossible to track, the—bugs."

"No, sir, no bugs, I didn't have to do that."

"Well you can't exactly talk to them, little conversations over a drink, whatever methods you use." He laughed.

"No, you can't." This conversation was getting too testy for Henry Nottingham. Say what he'd learned and get out.

"Then what'd you do?"

"Well, first I checked all the mortuaries—"

"Why'd you do that?"

"Oh I figured if they'd put the coffin in the ground maybe they took it back out."

"And that proved a false lead—"

"No, a pretty good one. Third place I tried, Henniken Brothers, said yes, it'd been them."

John leaned forward. "I don't understand."

"Well, of course I should've tried the Coroner's Office first, but I didn't need to. Tom Henniken said they'd been asked to, sir. They showed me the disinterment order."

"I can't believe this."

"I'm sorry, John, you said you wanted to know."

"It's impossible."

"Should I go on?"

"On? Yes, go on."

"Well, the body was brought to the mortuary, cremated there." No. Wrong. Over an instant John Cochan had gone pale. Henry Nottingham should've denied he knew. He hoped Yakahama was still in the other office. "I understand the ashes were thrown to the wind."

"The wind."

"On your land, sir. The Fortier Farm."

"No."

"That's what the order said."

"No."

"I imagine you realize who signed the order, sir."

"No."

"I'm afraid, uh, it was Mrs. Cochan."

"No. No."

"I'm sorry, sir, you did say. I mean, that I should—"

John stared at the Sheriff. Face unmoving, eyes blinking sharp jabs, breath shallow, for seconds no breath at all.

"Can I get you something, sir? A glass of water?" He turned around. Yakahama was bent over his work. "Maybe Mr. Stevenson's got a bottle of brandy, want me to go look?"

"No." A hoarse whisper.

"I'm sorry, I should have stayed with my instincts, not said anything. But you're an insistent man, Mr. Cochan." He tried a grin.

The insistent man looked drained, and scared.

"If there's nothing else then, I'll be getting along. You don't mind?"

"No, no. No."

"Well, take care." He stepped out, turned, fingers to brow in salute. He knocked on the other door. He explained he'd had to give Mr. Cochan some complicated news and he hadn't taken it well. The Sheriff was glad not to be asked, What news?

Yak looked through the clear partition at a man he'd known for years. The Handyman sat motionless, his face pale as chalk.

8.

Possible ways of getting below ground at Terramac: Another request to Cochan? Wait till dark of night, break in? Even if he got past the guard gate and any night watchman patrolling the site, where to go? Where was the entrance down? Maybe that building without windows? And once inside? Carney didn't know. He fought visible disasters, he wasn't the break-and-enter type—

A knock. He hadn't heard a car drive up. At the farmhouse door stood Karl Magnussen. "Hi, I was passing, thought I'd drop by and say hello."

Passing? Hardly. Carney offered coffee.

"Sure, why not."

Carney made good coffee only for those who cared. He poured a cupful of warmed-up lunchtime leftover. "You okay?"

"Me? Yeah sure."

"Want a shot of brandy in that?"

Karl grinned then. "Wouldn't hurt."

"So you're not okay." Carney went for the bottle, poured in two glugs.

"Thanks." Karl sipped, nodded. "Good." He seemed to be collecting thoughts, or words, or strength. "Look, can I convince you to go for a walk?"

Sarah would be arriving later, after she was done at the lab. Did he want Karl to know this? Did he care? They went out.

The air felt light on his arms. They walked toward the dip behind the house where the stream, now a trickle, cut a rocky bed between the land he kept cultivated and the wilder upslope beyond. Karl remained silent, wooden. Carney let him be. They followed a small trail uphill.

"Great afternoon," said Carney. "Cooler."

"Yep."

They walked in silence, higher up the dirt path, Karl sweating lightly. Swallows swooped, late-lunching on mosquitoes. Carney would have to break through. "Do you just let go or is it a conscious decision to seduce every woman you see?"

Karl's head snapped around. He stared at Carney. "Who said that?"

"In your way, you did."

Karl snorted a laugh. "My face is my billboard?"

"Well?"

Karl shrugged. "I like sex. A lot."

"It isn't an experiment, then? Trying a theory?"

"Why d'you ask that?"

"From how you talked the other evening."

A wistful smile. "No. No theory. Just—the touch of skin, the smells. The tastes. A woman's body is a beautiful creation."

"Some, anyway."

"Many. The first time, it's an exploration. Learning what's there. Sometimes the discovery goes on. But too often I need only one time to learn everything that's there."

Provoking was one thing, grubbing about in a man's life something else. Trees thickened around them. The trail, still uphill, had grown wider so they could walk side by side.

Then Karl said, "Do you mind if I tell you an unpleasant story?"

Carney suppressed a flip comment. "If you want to."

"It's in the category of a confessional."

"Maybe you should talk to a priest."

"I did. He recommended several forms of spiritual cleansing."

"Unsatisfactory?"

"Not what I need."

A tale of loss of faith? "A therapist, then."

"No, no." No humor in Karl's response. "I'd like your advice."

"Why me?"

"You don't know me. For my cheerless tale I need a pristine ear. You're circumspect."

Carney chuckled. "One of my few virtues. I'm a regular oubliette." The path divided. Carney led them down the trail to the right.

"You see, I'm in the middle, more correctly at the beginning, of a very strong—relationship. Love. With a woman who's quite wonderful."

"The rake backsliding from apostasy?"

"A lot to discover. A lot about love."

"Yeah?"

So he told Carney. It began like many love stories, the meeting a coincidence, then a conscious decision to seduce her according to his patterns, in part because of who she was.

"And who is she?"

"It's not important, it's not what I want to tell you about. You see, I'd been, well, testing myself. Examining my emotional stability."

Save me from shrinks. Carney kept his face blank.

"It was a successful seduction. But then there was a problem. It had all begun as a kind of—I guess I have to call it revenge."

"Against?"

"Her husband, of course."

"And who's he?"

Karl shook his head. "An old enemy."

"Of?"

He stopped walking and looked at Carney, a small ambivalent grin. "Mine." He considered his next words. "The world's."

How unstable was the man? Time to get back. "Go on." He resumed walking, faster now.

"It went beyond revenge. Somewhere inside me this incredible attraction was born, a swell of, well, rich honest desire. In her too. It's led to a remarkable closeness, and to love."

"So what's the problem?"

"To that point, nothing. Not even a couple of weeks back when she told me she was pregnant, by me or by her husband she didn't know which. And it didn't matter to me. Or her."

"Who a child's father is doesn't matter?"

"I loved the baby, then already. It and its mother."

Carney's friend Mot buzzed, Watch yourself.

"A few days ago the husband found us together. He beat her, hurt her badly. And there's not going to be a child. The beating caused her to abort."

"And how is she, the mother?"

Karl blinked but his eyes were too full, they overflowed. "The thing of it is, it's murder."

Carney remained silent. The cut-off back down was maybe fifty yards ahead.

"The mother's—okay as she can be. The baby had no chance. He took that life away."

Lighten this burden? How? "A few weeks ago? Still in the first trimester?"

"Weeks' and weeks' worth of experiences. There's amazing evidence how much a few weeks' old fetus feels and reacts to. You ever seen pictures of a fetus in the womb? He killed it. Sister Sarah won't kill ants and mosquitoes. They're a lot less human than this little thing was."

"Still, lots of abortions are performed on fetuses much more advanced."

Karl nodded. "I know. And that's a crime."

"Not here. Not now."

"It would have been a boy." Karl kicked at a stone.

Cauterize the pain. Carney spoke, slow and gently. "Maybe it wasn't yours."

Karl stopped, stared at him, unbelieving. "It doesn't matter, Carney."

Carney's head shook again. How can the father's identity not matter?

They walked in silence. Carney turned them down the cut-off. Karl didn't notice, he seemed absent now. Carney preferred to live among men and women who civilized their emotions, or acted as if they did. A world he'd chosen for himself, rational, damage control a large part of it. Now here was a certain Mrs. X not sure who the father of her child might be, and Mr. X pummeling the life out of his wife's womb. And Sarah, testing his preconceptions about the worth of many kinds of life. An insect, a fetus, an old woman hit by a stroke.

Silly though Karl could get, a part inside him had splintered and he needed solace. Tears ran down the man's face. He didn't try to hide or stop them. Carney put his hand on Karl's shoulder. It struck him that Milton's empathy for Karl's distress came closer to understanding his son than Milton realized.

They arrived at the farmhouse. Carney said, "I can give you some armagnac."

"I'll take it." Karl sat, drank down two ounces in three large sips. He squeezed his eyes shut and shook his head. "I'm not usually like this."

"We all have to let go sometimes." Ah, the strength of cliché.

"Yeah." He released a breath so long he might've been holding it since before the armagnac. "Thank you for letting me talk."

Carney waved him away.

"And for responding. My goddamn confessor sat behind the screen dead silent. I made it gory just to get him to react. He didn't."

"I guess he hears a lot of miserable stuff."

"I guess. Any advice?"

"Well, don't report it as murder, least not till after a long talk with Mrs. X."

"Yeah. Hard to do. She only had a couple of minutes when she called to tell me. About the baby. She's with her husband."

"John Cochan."

"How the hell—?"

"A reasonable guess." Carney shook his head. "You're an ass, Karl."

"Probably. Except I do love her."

"And I suppose she loves you."

"Very much."

Ah, romantic love. "And Cochan? How's she feel about him?"

"She loved him, she said."

"And now?"

Karl shook his head.

"But she's with him."

"She says he's calm."

"And contrite?"

"Withdrawn."

"What does she want?"

He thought a moment. "I'd guess, time."

Of which Carney had little left, it was getting on toward four. Sarah had said she'd arrive around five and he couldn't count on her not being early. "I have to go out, I'm already late."

Karl went to the door. "Look, Carney. Another favor?"

"I shouldn't tell your family about this."

Karl grinned, but without cheer. "Thanks."

○

It's at times like this I'm saddest that Lola isn't here. Down there she'll never get to see that side of Karl.

○

9.

Johnnie dreamed the camping trip, pitching the tent by the stream, laying out the sleeping bags, close. Only the place was wrong, no waterfall here. No Benjie, these people were Barney and Tick, Benjie's friends. They slept one on this side of Johnnie, one on that. They squeezed in tight, crushing him. These weren't kids anymore, they were too big, too strong. They pulled him up, one by his right arm, the other his left. Come on, you dumb bug-fweep, they said, and led him by both hands to a field, no grass. A cobblestone path to a house, two stories. The big wood door opened. The man there said, You're late, come in. The man was an engineer or a doctor, he wore a white coat, and Johnnie nearly recognized him. He went down a staircase, Tick in front, Barney in back. A cellar transformed to a laboratory, white tile walls, stainless steel sinks. Johnnie's crucible was ready. But he didn't need a crucible, the spiders were too big, white crab spiders. Everywhere. And wasps. Spiders fornicating with wasps! Webs in the air, in sinks, across the ceiling. The walls were white spiders and wasps, and each mouth's teeth grasped a butterfly, *Phoebis sennae eubule*, boy, never forget that name. Crushed butterflies released their odor, violets, musk. Johnnie cried out: "Not the butterflies, no!" The spiders heard. They looked up. "Not our pretty *Phoebis eubule*?" The spiders stared across at him, down at him. "If not butterflies, then what?" "Why anything, anything you want." "The wasps, then, all the wasps." The wasps drew themselves out of the spiders, they turned to Johnnie, advanced on him, an army. He couldn't call out, he couldn't move. They raced toward him from eighty directions. He slipped, his arm grabbed out, his fingers found the sink. On his feet and legs, his arms his crotch, in eyes through ears on tongue down throat. Spilling wasps took him low, his temple landed soft in a white pillow, wasp corpses. In choked silence he screamed, screamed. And woke to break his mute cry.

Twelve

BEST-LAID PLANS

1.

Sarah sat on the bank, just the rare mosquito today, and watched two shiny brown butterflies flit about dry moss on rocks jutting up at the water's edge. "And Carney and Company?"

"For a long time"—barely two weeks since Carney had hooked a solid trout in the pool upstream and been hit by a slingshot stone—"it was central."

"Not what I asked." She turned to face him.

"Now? Sure. But I own the company, and others work for me." He smiled.

Her eyebrow arched. "So you'll go back to it? Or not."

"What d'you mean?"

"Old habits." The butterflies on the rock took on its color. Water rippled. "Non-endings prevent new starts."

"I don't change easy."

"I was thinking about me. And Driscoll."

"Yeah?"

"You're way more enigmatic."

Carney stared at sunlight reflecting from the stream. He said, "You know, I'm not. I've done just one thing all my working life."

"One thing can make a first-class disguise."

"You push hard, lady."

"See those butterflies?" They were flying again, circling each other. "Monarchs?"

"Viceroys. They look like monarchs. But they're fine to eat."

"You've tried them?" Carney smiled.

"A little oil and garlic, some salt. Delicious."

"Next thing, you'll be eating cow."

"Just don't eat monarchs. They feed on latex. From milkweed. Know what's in latex? Digitalis. Which can be bad stuff. But it doesn't bother monarch caterpillars, they eat it up, they become chrysalides and soon there are monarchs again. New ones."

"The cycles of nature?"

"Swallows and jays and the like eat most kinds of butterflies. But they've learned something. Munch on a monarch, you retch till you die."

"Charming."

"Be quiet. At last I'm understanding you."

"What?"

"Carney the viceroy, Carney the orphan, Carney his aunt's ward, Carney the cellist, macho Carney of the fires, Carney the loner, Carney the contradiction with a single name."

"Parts of the above. Except maybe the viceroy."

"You'll tell me everything. When you're ready. But for now talking isn't on."

"And what is?"

"For me, you." She gazed into a middle distance. "And for you?"

"I'd like to take you fishing."

She turned, took his head gently with eight fingertips, kissed his mouth. "I'd like to go."

For an hour they swam in the pool and played bare-assed in the sun.

Lola would have loved it. But she didn't see them, no way could she catch sight of them from the middle of the down below.

2.

Stupid Priscilla. She wouldn't shut up. Stupid woman.

From nowhere she asked in her drivelly way: "But isn't it possible to feel so much love I can love more than just one? Love you, Johnnie, so much. Love Benjie and Dee and Lissa, love him too, my dear good friend?"

This was the moment, the closest he ever came to smashing her across that whiny face—

But her question caught him up, too. Because the answer helped him see everything in the sharpest white on black. No. No you cannot love more than one. For Johnnie, this one was Benjie. Always. And before Benjie was born? Well, Johnnie wasn't a metaphysician but he'd have to say, Yes, before too. Which meant, by clear subtraction, Johnnie could never have loved her. What's never been loved can never be lacking, right? So he didn't slug her, he smiled.

From her face, stupid pulpy tear-driven face, a staggered grin. As if she'd won or something. He said, "No." What sweet pleasure to see the gloat slide from that face, so much slush. "The one I love," he said, "you burned him up."

"I brought him back, Johnnie. To the farm." She reached her hand to him. "For you."

"You burned him. Till there was nothing. The one I love."

She nodded. Nodded? So did she finally understand? She went upstairs, nodding all the time. A revelation. To Johnnie, and surely to her as well, her head bobbing like a couple of neck vertebrae had gone loose or maybe some bouncy pith in her mushy brain. She locked their bedroom door. Deirdre and Melissa in with her? No matter, in Benjie's room all he needed, the small bed. He lay down and slept far away, deep, first time in a long while. A clear answer.

The sun came up too early, right through the window. Johnnie thought he heard a car start. He closed his eyes, turned, slept again. Less deeply. He dreamed he flew on wasp wings high above Terramac to the craggy mountaintop. He stayed for a long time, looking down, seeing everything. He watched everyone drive away. Only he remained. And the rock he sat on. And the spider-free air. Here at the pinnacle of the world, of all history, he felt at peace. He awoke again. The house was silent. He came downstairs. Her note lay on the table:

I've gone, Johnnie. You said it all last night. No. You can't love. I wonder if you ever loved. Even Benjie.

And more: arrangements, Melissa, Deirdre.

He breathed deeply. Cleansed. All that female fear, all gone. Upstairs again he washed his face. He shaved his mustache off. As he would clear away the shadow of his future. His life, scrubbed pure. She was gone.

Deirdre and Melissa? He would give chase! Rescue them— Not physical chase. Legal. He'd call that lawyer, that fellow in Burlington, local lawyer was important. Meanwhile the girls would be okay, sure. Even alone with the mother. As long as he, that one, didn't ill-use them. That would be unbearable. For now it was out of Johnnie's hands.

A new start. A few details to take care of.

She'd left so easily . . .

Unimportant. He was rid of her. He made his breakfast. His veins and bones felt clean.

Of course he'd loved. And had been loved. For her to doubt his love of Benjie, incredible.

He drove the Rolls to the church. So deliberately. So sweetly, hardly a sound from the engine. So early he sat alone at his desk, feet up, eyes closed, at peace.

3.

The new wheelchair arrived, more sensitive controls. Milton had asked Ti-Jean to put it together. He agreed. But remained wary. The finished conveyance, dull aluminum and black steel gloss, glowered tough and technological. He let Milton attach the charge for its double batteries. Once juiced, it could be dangerous. The charging took fourteen hours and would provide four hours of driving time. The salespeople had said to boost the batteries every night. And get an extra set.

Theresa had been using the old chair again, her good and steady friend she called it. But despite therapy and acupuncture treatments —stiletto needles lancing her flesh, she'd muttered—her better hand found the controls stiff. Damned weakness this, turning an ally into an adversary.

At four Theresa would try the new chair. They had lunch together, Feasie and Ti-Jean, Milton feeding Theresa as he had after the first stroke, Sarah and Carney, a couple clear to all. After lunch Theresa slept. Carney and Sarah sat in the garden, talking. Theresa woke up giving Milton orders; Carney's sympathy went to Milton. Milton argued with her, gave in to her. Twice her face contorted as if something weird were happening, something she couldn't deal with.

They loaded the new chair into the back of the van, Theresa strapped onto the front seat. Feasie and Ti-Jean followed in their pickup, Sarah and Carney in the Jag.

In a near-empty University of Vermont parking lot Theresa Magnussen tested her chair. Its acceleration and steering were more delicate. She over-compensated, she lurched and jerked. Still, after half an hour, she'd gained some mastery.

Ti-Jean said, "I don't like it."

Feasie nodded. "A rolling stone can kill two birds in a bush."

"Let's hope that's all it kills."

The chair's controls were set on a flat bar in front, not on the arm as before. The wheels wrenched left, and left again. Theresa, taking charge. She pulled in beside them. Feasie lay her hand on Theresa's shoulder. "Doing great." Milton leaned and kissed her cheek.

Theresa shook her head—twitched it to the right, the only direction her neck went—and powered herself away. She rolled fast, quicker than a woman could run. She slowed, stopped.

Nice chair, Theresa.

Glad you've come by. Hello.

You miss me?

You damn well know it. I keep looking for you.

Lola kissed her on the forehead. Let's see you drive that thing.

It's tricky.

I'll help.

A grin. Okay, let's go. She turned toward Milton, Sarah, and the rest. Lola sat on her lap.

They watched the chair execute a smooth rotation. It began threading its way between the white lines, up one set and down another, gentle arcs. For Milton it was lovely to see, a bulky water bird taking flight, all ease and grace. For Carney she was a cocoon opening, gold-brown wings stretching, drying, the butterfly aloft on the breeze. He grinned. Theresa's disguise?

A final arc and Theresa turned toward them, fast, still faster, then slower, slow, and she drew level. Her lip edge ticked up three-four times.

Milton put his hand on her neck, his eyelids beat quickly. Ti-Jean's head shook, he caught himself, shrugged. Carney wondered, maybe there are good demons too?

Milton and Carney walked behind Theresa, Sarah and Feasie on each side. Before they reached the Jag, Milton held Carney back. "Something I'd like your advice on. You have time?"

"Sure. I'm going to drop Sarah off at the lab. She's on evening shift. I'll come by."

○

Lola's okay. Except now she's gone again. Why can't I see her like I see the people down there, whenever I want? People don't see her either. No, I don't like the implications of that thought.

On the positive side, the Gods haven't returned.

○

At the Magnussen house Leonora let him in. "Hi," he said.

"Oh. Hello."

"Still want to set up a lunch?"

She looked at him, a squint, as if not understanding.

"To talk about whatever it was you wanted to talk about?"

She raised one eyebrow, Sarah-fashion. "Too late for that, isn't it."

"For what?"

"Forget it. Look, my next couple of weeks are extremely busy. I'll call you."

"Okay, good." Irritated with him? Jealous of Sarah? He sniffed a little laugh.

Milton found him, led him to the living room. "First I want to thank you. About Sarah."

"What about Sarah?"

"She's here so much more now."

"She's worried about her mother."

Milton grasped Carney's elbow. "Then you've changed her."

"She's been worried. All along."

"Well you've helped her show it."

Innocent action interpreted as good deeds. "Hardly me."

"Oh yes." He squeezed Carney's forearm. "Thanks." Then, embarrassed, he reached for a letter. "Look at this."

From John Cochan to John Milton Magnussen and Theresa Bonneherbe Magnussen, on letterhead proclaiming, in silvery Latin, that Intraterra represented Quality and Quantity, Quantity in Quality. A new offer to buy the Bonneherbe Magnussen land for $5.9 million. Carney said, "He makes an offer sound like a threat. But he can't do anything."

"Except destroy the land, make it worthless."

"Or more valuable."

"But in the wrong way." Milton folded the letter. "Theresa wants to go there."

371

"Don't do it."

"Leasie thinks it might be good for her. Theresa's got a big fat bumblebee in her bonnet about going. And now Leasie's written a letter over Theresa's name, asking to come out."

"A really rotten idea, Milton." Best way for Cochan to send her over the edge.

"Letter got sent before I knew about it."

"Theresa actually signed?"

"Leasie did, for her. What can we do?"

"When was this sent?"

"Couple of days ago."

Carney shrugged. "If Cochan says yes you can always refuse."

"Carney, do you— Would you talk to him again? Cochan?"

He patted Milton's arm. "Let me go say so long to Theresa."

Milton puffed a hard laugh. "Huh. She's becoming impossible. Said she wants to roar down the sidewalk. Like a kid on a dirt bike. She worries me."

"I'll go for a walk with her, keep her on a short leash."

He squeezed a one-sided smile. "I don't want her going batty."

Carney went up to the bedroom. Carney still needed to listen hard but her slur had decreased and her mouth muscles were tighter. "Look at this." She showed Carney a long stick.

"What is it?"

"Milton bought it. My foilpole."

Carney took it. About six feet long, lightweight. One end could grab with the heavy-duty pincers, the other with stiletto prongs. A spring-loaded stiletto point, thin blade, as for skewering. "Dangerous-looking item, that."

Theresa grinned. "Case I'm mugged." She reached up with it, it was telescopic too, and the pincers plucked a book off a shelf. She retracted and released the book onto his lap.

"Amazing."

"I saw a lot of films this week. And I'm reading again."

"Good. What?"

"Couple of biographies about Lola. You know, the actress. Remarkable life."

Carney shook his head. "Theresa Magnussen, the eminent moralist, concerned with a glamorous sex-kitten?"

She broke into a guffaw, she rumbled, choked. "A—a—" she wheezed, "a silver tiger!"

"What?"

She shook with laughter. Tears came to her eyes. Slowly she calmed.

"And what was so funny?"

With her right hand she waved Carney off. "No way can you understand."

Was Milton right, maybe Theresa's mind really was losing a couple of hinges? "Want to go for a roll, Theresa?"

"I'm on a roll!" And more chuckles. "Let's go into town."

So he loaded the chair once again into the van and drove her to Main Street. They rolled, along the sidewalks of Burlington. Carney started a fishing story but Theresa wasn't interested, she glanced about, accelerated, ripped ahead. Twenty feet away she stopped, stared across a lawn, pointed the stick at a front window. She held her hand in front of her mouth to hide a laugh.

Carney caught up. In silence they returned to Main Street. Theresa paused at a storefront, a dress boutique. She gazed at the display, suddenly raised her foilpole high and sliced the air. She pointed to a white-sheath evening gown, talking but not to Carney, the words gibberish.

"Theresa, we better head back."

"I'll get back alone. Leave me. I'm in good hands." She laughed again.

"Impossible, Theresa."

She glared at Carney. "Bhllarghgh—" She waved her foilpole and turned the chair, breathing a chatter-like nonsense.

Again Carney didn't understand, but he'd never seen her happier. He hoped there wouldn't come yet another fall. He grew stern. "We're going back now, Theresa."

"This time," she assented.

4.

Sarah and Carney took off in a Carney and Co. single-engine float plane from the southern end of Lake Champlain. They flew north, crossing the border, the St. Lawrence River, and over the Laurentians to waters of pike and walleye, doré they're called up there. They'd be away nearly five days, till Tuesday morning.

The plane followed the James Bay power lines, a scraped yellow scar fifty meters wide. Millions of kilowatts streamed down the transmission corridor.

Over the roar of the engine Sarah shouted, "They use herbicides to keep the ground under the lines plant-free! Contaminated half the wells in the bedrock two hundred miles to the dams!"

"Terrific!" Ever well-versed, was Sarah. Well, good for her.

As for Carney, right then he beseeched the demons in the plane's single engine to keep them aloft. Though he'd logged thousands of hours flying time and was a first-class pilot, small planes still scared him.

They came down on one of the thirty-plus arms of the Gouin Reservoir, a dammed and flooded river system. The banks had been Indian land, still were Sarah told him, but a lot of first nations acreage now sat under water. Politics aside, here lay a magnificent wilderness, heavily wooded in all directions, the Canada of Carney's childhood imagination. The sense of calm was pervasive. They located the cottage they'd rented, from the shoreline no other units visible. They also had a fifteen-foot aluminum boat with a 9.9-horse engine, good power given the potential for two- to three-foot swells.

The lake if not teeming with fish was at least rich enough to satisfy a greedy angler: sixteen walleye the first day, and five pike, the largest nine pounds, a majestic fighter. Carney used his barbless hooks and kept a couple of doré to eat. This far north and this late in the season only a few blackflies remained. Carney didn't kill many, Sarah none.

How about bringing back a water sample, Carney? But why know the worst when the beauty here was so wide-reaching.

He offered her a bite of doré fried in garlic butter. She stayed with her vegetables. Carney put a piece on her plate. She looked at it. She seemed tempted. A weak moment. He would try: "Don't be atoning for setting anthills on fire. Or your husband's death."

She stared at the fish. "Don't spoil it, Carney."

"Then tell me."

"It was such an—unnecessary accident."

"How do you know?"

Her eyes never left the fish. "So much of death is. Premature."

"I think you're doing penance." He hesitated. "A decade and a half of penance."

She looked his way at last. "A decade—" Crimson rushed to her cheeks. "What?"

"When you were seventeen."

She thought. "My abortion."

He nodded.

She stared at his face, searching again. Then at the cold fried fish. She sat that way a long time. He came up behind her, put his hand on her hair. No reaction, no resistance. He cleared the table but left her plate. He boiled water, washed dishes. She didn't move. She said, "Would you—heat up that piece of fish for me?"

It crackled lightly in the butter. The garlic came alive again. He gave her the crispy doré.

She ate it, five tiny bites. "I wonder how rich the mercury content is," she said.

They went to bed, made the best of love, held each other. Over the next days she ate no more fish. Nor mentioned the conversation.

The pervasive calm of the wilderness was replaced by a mighty storm, black sheets of rain. So they spent the afternoon in bed, hours of delicate exploration, responsible only to the moment and each other. Carney rediscovered, and discovered, some remarkable pleasures. The body even after the half-century mark was not too old to learn. Though it, at least Carney's, had come to feel the wear.

The next day from morning to night they trolled or cast. By late afternoon she admitted a fishy strike from the depths did send a thrill through her. Carney had her hooked, yes he did. They released all she caught. Including a pike longer and heavier than Carney's big one; at the end she let her line go slack and the fish, near three feet long, parallel to the side of the boat, shook his immense snout, spat out the red and white Dardevle and glided, peaceful, into black water.

The evenings too were fine. Even Sarah's beans and grains, cooked over a wood fire, tasted grand. They talked as if compensating for early silences. No one mentioned penance.

After the rainstorm, calm had returned. Monday morning, floating, the motor cut, the sun high overhead, a carnal urge came into their minds at the same instant and they committed, across the seat of their round-bottomed boat, lustful and voluptuous love. Without falling overboard. Three blackflies drew blood from Carney's butt.

Later Sarah covered the bloated bites with her special lotion. "A sexy horny new strain of blackfly coming into the world," she divined. Even with the goo, the bites itched.

In the evening they sat staring into the fire. She pulled close to him and took his hand. "I'm the world's biggest blackfly." She bit his neck, gently. "What's it like, Carney blood?"

He laughed. "Like Sarah blood."

She shook her head, "Nope," played with his fingers, her eyes examined his nails, his knuckles. "Blood with one name." His right thumb so fascinated her she had to taste it.

The wicked witch incarnate.

She stroked his cheek, testing it.

She wouldn't dare. "Sarah we could go—ow!"

"Carney blood." She nibbled his earlobe. Bit. An intake of breath, no other response. She stared.

He got up.

"Going somewhere?"

"For a bit of air."

She thought: almost okay. "Can I come with you?"

He nodded. She walked with him down to the water's edge. He stared out over the silent lake for a long time. At last he put his arm over her shoulder. She held him to her tight.

In bed the last morning Sarah said, "Fish or fuck?"

"How about putting both on the agenda?"

"And a little foretalk?"

Carney felt the tic of Mot. "Sure."

"When you first came to my cottage and you sat so silent, what were you thinking?"

"Oh, figuring out what you were thinking."

"All the time?"

"Till I gave up. You baffled me."

She laughed, pinched him.

"Ow! I've only got one of those."

"And then?"

"I let my mind take its own chaotic course."

She grinned. "Good."

"And you? What was in your silence?"

"You."

Carney pulled back and looked at her. "Already?"

"Not in that way. Just nice not to have to talk all the time."

"Hmm." He drew close again.

"Silence has gone out of style. You didn't mind being quiet. Even with someone you barely knew."

"Clever, right?"

"Very." She paused. "You know how to listen. Which isn't the same as staying quiet."

That stopped the conversation. They went on to item two. Calm hung misty about them.

They fished, they caught and released, they packed, they loaded the plane. "Next time let's go farther north, right up to Hudson Bay."

"Not if you want to eat what you catch."

Memory tickled. "Mercury?"

She nodded. "All that land flooded for the power dams. Chemicals from the drowned trees leach mercury out of the rock. Rock that's been stable millions of years, till now."

Tuesday afternoon they flew away, over hundreds of lakes looking virgin from the air, down the power-line corridor, passing Montreal, Burlington, to the Carney and Co. float plane dock. Sarah left for her lab.

5.

On his answering machine at the farmhouse Carney found a dozen messages, including one from Karl. "Give me a call, come up for lunch tomorrow." And one from Milton. He sounded upset. "You have time? I'd like to show you something."

Did he have time? Didn't he once have some other life? He called Milton. "What's up?"

"More Intraterra mail. I'll bring it over to you."

Serious, if Milton would leave Theresa for so long. Carney gave him directions.

Milton arrived, Carney poured them a Scotch. "All day Theresa was in a great mood, jovial. She talked and talked. Slow, but what an improvement." Milton, right now happy.

"Good." Carney sipped.

"And she's reading. She asked Feasie for books. Those movies she's been watching, remember that actress Lola? Theresa reread two Lola biographies." He grinned weakly.

"Long as it cheers her up."

Milton showed Carney two letters, one another offer, but fifty thousand less. The second a response from Aristide Boce, beneath the quality/quantity piety: We fear it will be inappropriate to invite you to Terramac. Thank you for your interest. Sincerely.

Carney handed them back. "Okay, so it's okay."

"Theresa was furious. So bad for her. Why won't Cochan stop these offers?"

"Why don't you just ignore them? Come September, the hearing'll take place. We'll know what's going on down there, and everything will change."

Milton sighed, and gazed at Carney. Like Sarah's exploring stare. Milton said, "I even asked Karl to talk to Cochan. But he refuses. He says Cochan and he have personal differences. I didn't know they'd ever met."

Carney shook his head.

"If Theresa learned about the new offer she'd grab the shotgun, ride her chair all the way there."

Theresa roaring down the highway, grunting, firing in the air on the road to Terramac. Carney felt what Milton wanted, go back to Richmond, say to Handy Johnnie blunt and clear, Back off! "When you asked me before to talk to Cochan again—"

"Could you?"

So innocently asked. He expected, on Milton's face, a smile: Thanks for volunteering. What Carney saw was fear.

Milton left. The Gouin foreboding calm was back, double-bite. Carney tried to repress it by scratching at the cello. He slept but was haunted by dreams of multi-ton steamrollers driven by demons, of a man in an airplane, a small Cochan chasing a boy on the ground who wasn't quite Carney, of roach caverns under Bewdley's apartment willing him down, a plexiglass coal-chute plunging him into the bowels of Terramac.

He spent the morning catching up on Carney and Co. business. Remarkable how easily it ran on without him. An appointment with Cochan? No, just show up. He reached Richmond at three. Close to Sarah's cottage. But she'd be at her lab.

He entered the ex-church and spoke to a young woman with green fingernails. Yes, Mr. Cochan was in, he was busy. Carney gave his name, said he'd wait, could she inform Cochan, please?

Carney waited. Cochan at his desk picked up the phone. The receptionist pointed up the nave. Carney walked with care.

Beyond the glass Cochon waited, sitting behind his desk. He let Carney open the door. He waved Carney to the chair opposite. He said, "There's only one thing I want from you."

Carney waited.

"Tell me they accept my offer."

Carney's head shook. "It won't happen."

"Oh, it will." Cochan smiled. "One day very soon they'll understand my Terramac. Their love for it will be as great as mine."

Carney stood. "Drop it, Cochan. The water, the fish. You've messed up an ecology you swore to improve. The court order's on its way and the whole of your Terramac is at the brink of being closed down." What he had to say was spoken. "Unless you invite me to go down there. If there's nothing, I can tell them, and there'll be no need for the court order."

"Go down into our Terramac," said Cochan, but Carney was already standing, turning, by the door.

Carney stopped. "Yes?"

"Nothing. Nothing, nothing." But Cochan's mind whispered, If they come to Terramac I'll show them everything.

Carney passed down the old nave. Cochan's eyes bored ice through his shoulder blades.

Carney was gone. A good thing, changing one's notions. The Magnussens would observe with their own eyes, their very own eyes, why they would want to sell. He watched Carney close the church doors behind him. "Thank you," Cochan whispered at Carney's disappeared back.

6.

Milton saw a smile suggesting bright pleasure on Theresa's face. He wanted to share it but she, off in one of her private moments, ignored him.

Be gentler to him, Theresa.

I will, Lola. Real soon.

Don't wait, old woman. Very soon Handy Johnnie will be ours. We've nearly got him.

Yep. The slug in his hole.

And how will we do it? With your grabbin' foil, what delicate fast sword is that?

Leave me be, Lola. I've got to think. Create the chance.

How?

Remember the important, forget the trivial. Love old Milton, that's important. Ti-Jean and Feasie and the lodge, important. Both Noodles, yes. And Sarah, she's coming by today.

With Carney?

No. But he's important too. Advantage of getting old, with a stroke or two you separate what's valuable from the other stuff, little stuff. Never again deal with the rest, haha. Laughing, that's pretty good, why'd I used to laugh so little? Such questions when you get old.

Do you care?

No. Ha!

And what do you want?

What's most important? A little obliteration.

Sounds like fun.

Yeah, destruction's the perfect joke.

Yours, Theresa?

You got it.

Like in the earliest of days? When all of chaos roared as one? 'Twas massive laughter that gave birth to life itself. Before the first Immortal drew a breath.

Let's go for it.

How?

"Hello, Theresa."

"I'm in the middle of something, wait a minute." ("Aynheng an ilo ungheng, whay a ninihd.")

"Middle of what?"

"Shh. Sit down." ("Ghgh. Ghidh owhn.")

Sarah sat on the couch. Theresa, upright in her chair, truly looked as if someone were talking to her, describing wonders. Her face on the side that moved was so animated, lithe, the same half grin as while she watched her movies. A couple of times her shoulder wagged, laughter taking over whatever body parts could budge. What goes on in a mind after a stroke?

Strangest of all, she pursed her lips, the right side, and seemed to be kissing the air. Weird. Then tranquillity. In some curious way she was, yes, glowing. Ease, even peace, and a pleasure about her face. On the mend? Or going crazy.

She turned. "Hello, Sarah." ("Eho, Gharhh.")

"You're looking well."

"So are you." Sarah in jeans and a shirt. Good. Like she'd once worn.

"I'm feeling pretty good."

She knew that, could see it all. Wonderful. "How's Carney?"

"Oh, okay."

"A good man, Carney."

"Yes. He is."

"I like him. I like him a lot."

She'd see him later. "We all like him."

"You like him more than the rest of us do."

"I suppose, in my way." Nosy old woman. Sarah smiled. "Each of us, in our way."

"I wish you'd have met him fifteen years ago."

"What?" Sarah heard only, I wish oooghghghet him feten eehrz gho. Theresa tried differently. "I wish the two of you had met long ago."

She felt her cheeks warming. "Except I didn't."

"Even ten years ago. Instead of Dreec Skl."

She thought she heard Drip Skull. She giggled, she couldn't help herself. "What're you saying, Theresa?"

"We might've saved a lot of time, you and I."

"Saved?"

"Instead of the anger and the fighting. We could have had better times."

"You wouldn't take me as I was, that's all."

"I know. I blame myself."

She caught each word. Or thought she did. "I don't understand."

"Sure you do." Half Theresa's mouth twitched. "I'm sorry, Sarah. It could've been better, all these years."

Her head was shaking, hesitant. From Theresa Magnussen, an apology? A mistake conceded? Sarah tried to smile. Her eyes filled with water. "Lots of—years."

"No sense talking about might-have-beens." Theresa stared at her. "Tell me about after, after now."

She got up. Theresa touched the lever, the chair crept toward Sarah. She stood beside it, bent down, and embraced her mother's head, squeezed it to her chest, held it, felt her mother's arm around her waist. Felt her chest rock, little heaves.

Theresa had to laugh, such a strange embrace. She had to laugh, first time she'd been this close in years, till now just a peck on the cheek and that only recently, and now— She had to laugh, her tears tickled her neck. She had to laugh, they were her tears, where'd all that come from, both eyes? She had to laugh because the left eye could do more than stare, how about that.

She had to laugh, Sarah was laughing too. Sarah, standing in front of her, nose dripping, telling her mother yes she was in love with Theresa's friend Carney. Life-giving laughter.

Sarah shook her head, found a tissue, wiped her face, blew her nose. Found another, wiped her mother's cheeks.

"Like I used to wipe you. All over."

"Oh Theresa—" She laughed, couldn't keep her eyes dry.

"Never mind. Tell me, what are your intentions?"

"My what?"

"Intentions. With Carney."

"Oh, dishonorable."

"And his?"

"The same, I think."

Theresa nodded. "Then there's hope."

"Always."

When Sarah went off to meet Carney, she wondered could she be dishonorable to the extreme. Yes, she figured.

Your nose is running.

I think I spoke with Sarah right.

Not too much weakness. But a little.

For a confirmed anarchist, Lola, weakness too becomes a weapon.

Abstractions, abstractions.

Permit me a few.

A happy woman was Theresa Magnussen.

o

Relief. Even if Lola was plotting with Theresa. At least I can see Lola some of the time. The people can't see her at all. Except of course Theresa. Some of the time.

No. Stop. Refrain from metaphysics.

o

7.

Theresa's daughter Leonora, the solitary Noodle, was far from happy. She sat with Karl at the Frontier Café, couple of miles from Canada. "Why?" she whispered. "Why Priscilla Cochan?"

Karl took his sister's hand. "Would it matter who?"

"But John Cochan's wife!?" Tears, held in until now, welled out.

"You meet someone, another person, and usually nothing happens. This time something did." He squeezed Leonora's fingers. "Something wonderful, and the consequences were hideous. But the results of those consequences— Leasie, it's the best, being with Priscilla. It's that simple."

No it wasn't that simple, it was far from simple. "Simple?"

"Yes."

Inside her chest a hollow. Here was retribution for her link to John Cochan. She took from her mother and gave to John Cochan. The amazing ironies of coincidence. She should be laughing. But her heart ached. "I'm pleased you're—happy."

Karl smiled. "We are. I love her."

If she hadn't listened to Cochan four years ago maybe Terramac

383

wouldn't have happened, maybe he'd have taken his whole family and gotten the fuck out of here.

8.

John Cochan woke early. Today, first and at last: the rest of the Terramac land. With a flick of his mind he knew who he needed. Too early to call him at home? Nope.

A bad last couple of days for Henry Nottingham. He'd driven around the county serving writs, a deputy's job. People weren't in. What the hell, the time was shot anyway. Over those days he'd also talked with Rebecca a half-dozen times about his weird chat with John Cochan. Just close the Investigation office. What, it takes too much time? Conflict of interest? Discovered when? Or, more dangerously, the simplest truth: his nerves couldn't take any more dealing with Cochan.

Labored discussions. Rebecca was a good listener. They talked it through one way, the money was good, she liked the business, both the job and sharing the work with Henry; and the other, his doubts, the stress. Nothing decided.

They were finishing breakfast, last of the coffee. The phone rang. From where he sat the Sheriff reached up and lifted the receiver, "Hello?"

John Cochan himself. "Like to talk to you, Hank. Mind coming over, first thing?"

"It's kind of a busy morning, uh, John—"

"I'd appreciate it."

"Just a minute." Henry Nottingham cupped his palm over the mouthpiece. He looked over to Rebecca, his lips sucked in, his eyes asking the question. She shook her head. He nodded. "Two or three things I've got to do right off, be there quick as I can."

"Sooner's better, Hank." He broke the connection.

"Choose your time," said Rebecca.

9.

My time-below sister-in-law, Roberta Feyerlicht, is a clever woman. Yesterday Carney brought her two presents. He told her about Sarah, she had enchanted him when he thought no woman could ever again—one part of Carney fearing it impossible, another delighted. Yes, even better than producing rarely in-tune melodies on his cello.

Well. Bobbie adored Carney and would be there for him forever. Since his parents' deaths she had been, but knew that for full-time duty she was getting old. Her love for Ricardo was for twenty-one years their unhidden secret. Her only other long-term passion.

The second present was Carney's description of dragonflies he'd watched with Sarah, and Sarah's explanation. Bobbie realized she'd been handed a moment of exquisite clarity. For others too, if she could make it so. She heard Ricardo whisper, Set it down. Immediately.

SEX

A hazy sun. Flit of a breeze and water sparkle.
A dragonfly, sheen of black, wings banded silver-blue.
He sees her.
Darting.
Feeding.

He clasps a petal of a lily.
He curves his tail, tip out to belly.
He slides open his abdominal sac.
He inserts, such easy care, his tail's tip.
He releases, slow, the precious liquid,
droplet,
droplet.
And withdraws. A full pack.

His eyes, globes, follow her flight.
His territory. His right.

Her long body knows.

He spurts over water, blue sun in his wings.
He follows as she goes.
She hunts, darts, feeds, dares.

Behind her, now above, his legs grab on,
the deed dared.
She slows, she's here for this.
They fly, paired.
He carries her.

His abdomen loops high.
Tail-hooks clasp pits, groove behind her head. They fly.
His legs let go. His tail, her neck, a coupling.
They swoop, one thing.

A sun-warm swampgrass stem. No sound.
Tail-tip circles up to sperm sac mound.
She strokes its center.
His bore enters.
Under him she's curved around.
A wheel.

They clinch coital half an hour,
their artful ways.
The droplets fill her core.
They fly apart.

Some sticks, dead bark.
She finds a hollow, wind-free, soft mud, dark.
She pushes, squeezes, lays.

A new male swoops, ill-concealed.
Her partner surges up, abdomen a shield—
The interloper sails away, his plot undone.

She rises, hovers, streaks toward the sun.

Well now. Was it all of a piece? Thank you, Carney. And Sarah.
But most of all, Ricardo. As if his hand had guided hers. She laughed
aloud.

Carney and his cello, a tiny bit of order. What other order is there? We've made the world a mess, he'd say to Ricardo. The isms have fallen, Ricardo agreed, commune, capital, social, modern. All isms except those beginning with post-, the empty posts. And my job, Carney had said, is to clean up after them, post-pesticide and post-fungicide, post oil slops, post plutonium slops, post-herbicide.

With Sarah, Bobbie wondered, would he learn a different order? Because there is order, with the greatest clarity Bobbie affirmed this. Order in the growth of fruit, the pathways of ants, the cycle of seasons. True that in this century these smaller orders have for most people grown invisible. True as well, there are also larger orders. The purpose of her new poem-sequence? To show how these orders fit with each other. Which helped explain the reluctance of another poem, in memory of Ricardo. It had fought her for months.

TRIANGLES

a.)
Think of it this way.
At the base, under the ground, in the soil, bacteria.
In one square yard, ten trillion.
A 1 and 13 zeros.

Broaden the base.
4,840 square yards, an acre of
pasture, a billion arthropods, the largest animal group.
Mites, spiders, springtails, aphids, millipedes, beetles.
Arthropod: jointed leg.

Recall the triangle. Above
the arthropods, birds, reptiles, small mammals. Fewer.
Above, the larger animals.
On top, humans.

b.)
A survival triangle.
Those at the top eat those below.

The bottom knows nothing of the top.
　　The top, little of the bottom.
　　Destroy the bottom—

　　What did it still need? She didn't know. Perhaps nothing.
　　Thank you again, Sarah.

○

Thank you, Bobbie.

Thirteen

HIDDEN DEPTHS

1.

Rebecca Nottingham slid her plate aside, set her cup on the table, leaned his way. "We don't need the money, Henry."

"He'd push to keep me getting re-elected."

"I know."

"Maybe I'll tell him when I see him."

"Pick your time."

Henry Nottingham nodded. Then he stood and embraced his wife, held her tight.

He drove around for half an hour admiring Merrimac County. A glorious August morning. At a crest pull-off he stopped, got out. It'd be hot by eleven but right now everything smelled of pine and, from somewhere hidden, wild roses. So late in the season? He'd get another job, he knew the land, the people. Maybe this afternoon he'd head over to Lake Champlain, rent a boat at Wedge's Cove, try for some deep smallmouths. That felt right. Best idea all week.

He drove across to Richmond. John Cochan kept him waiting five minutes, then buzzed him in. Cochan looked sleek and ruddy. Something different about his face— Yes, the mustache was gone. Pleasantries. Let him get to his business. Then Henry Nottingham would state his.

"Sheriff, I need to contact those Magnussen people."

The Sheriff nodded, waited.

"Got to do it the right way. Proper, but pleasant. You know what I'm saying? So a registered letter wouldn't be it. They could refuse to sign for it, right?"

"Sorry sir, I don't know."

"No matter, I don't want that route. And they wouldn't sign for a courier message either, would they. Or listen on the phone. So we need someone they trust. You following me, Hank?"

"I'm not sure, sir."

"I think you are. You'll find someone they can trust. Think you can think of someone?"

"Well—"

"I'm sure you can." He reached for an envelope on his desk, folded down the adhesive seal, handed it to the Sheriff. "They ought to get it today."

Henry Nottingham glanced at it. "Another offer?"

"An invitation."

A white business envelope. Just, Mr. J.M. Magnussen, Professor T.B. Magnussen. No printed Intraterra emblem. No return address.

"That's all, Hank. Give a call when it's delivered, okay? Mind seeing yourself out?" Already John Cochan had punched numbers on the phone and was talking. "Yak, it's me."

He could sit and wait till Cochan finished, then a few words. But he got up and, closed the door behind him.

2.

Without Priscilla-the-wife, John Cochan was a man at ease. From behind his desk he smiled at Harry Clark. John, good at explaining clearly, said, "Because we have to break through is why."

"But what's it going to prove?"

"We'll see what's back there."

Harry shook his head, not saying no, just exasperated. As dumb a thing as John had insisted on in a long time. No merit to the idea, nothing to be gained. Go through, yes. But not in this way. And not now. Almost certainly illegal, that far over. And with that heavy a charge, bordering on hazardous. "That's not a good enough reason."

John leaned forward, a growing smile. "I don't give a damn if it's good enough, Harry. I think I know what's there. I need to be sure."

"Listen, that's not how we cooperate."

"We don't cooperate at all, Harry. You cooperate with me."

"Look. I know it must've been a terrible week, godawful, and I'm sorry. Let's not argue."

John Cochan's smile widened. "You have no idea. So don't put your nose where it can't tell shit from porridge."

"Maybe you should take a little time off, John. Give yourself a bit of a break from all this."

"Harry, would you like a lot of time off? Give yourself a total break from this?"

Clark's head shook again. "I'm saying I worry about you."

"Well don't, Harry." The sweetest smile. "Worry about Terramac instead. Worry about showing me what's back behind there."

"I don't understand."

"I know you don't. That's why I'm telling you. Get Bang to worry about how to set the charge. Worry how to set the remote."

"It could be dangerous, blasting right there with only the one charge."

"It's a wall of stone like any other."

"It's thicker. And from the soundings the cavern out back there is way deeper."

"Just do it. And do it right. Okay, Harry?"

"And if I refuse?"

John pressed an intercom button. "Steed, can you come in for a minute?"

They watched Aristide Bocc came out of his office, into John Cochan's. "What's up?"

"Tell Harry what happens if Bang doesn't set the charge in the wall."

"Then Intraterra wouldn't be certain what lies beyond it."

"Is that important, Steed?"

"If that chamber gives us potential to build more units, there could be a significant shift in profit margin in the second stage. Hence more flexibility elsewhere, hmm? It's what you're hoping for, Harry, higher unit space."

"In a way." Harold Clark had been hoping for all kinds of eventualities. Some had come along, others not. The deep fissure for one, that was intriguing, he'd enjoyed planning around that. A large, even an immense, cavern was only one possible hoped-for eventuality.

"And Steed, what happens if we don't build additional units."

"Something would have to go. Say, the golf courses."

Some kind of catechism, these guys back-and-forthing. "If I concede the golf courses?"

"It would make Terramac less than we'd hoped. And H.M. Clark could end up designing four-family apartment units for the next quarter century."

"Oh, come on."

Boce smiled. "John Cochan knows many people."

"I'm not sure. I'd need the best part of the week to work it out."

"You have two days. My guests are coming Friday evening. We'll clear the distant cavern in the late afternoon. We'll blast at 6:00 PM."

"I'll have to work straight through. Day and night."

"It's all the same down there, Harry."

Clark nodded.

"Not too soon to start, right now."

"See you later." Clark got up, left the office, walked slowly down the nave.

Boce said, "He'll get it done. He's good."

Without looking up Cochan said, "Yes."

Aristide Boce would back John Cochan in anything. He returned to his office. But it was true, he too felt uncomfortable about this one.

John put his feet up on the desk. Harry'd get it done. Magnussen and his wife must see. After the blast they'd know this was a natural extension of Terramac's Underland, the future for all the children.

Underland, the pinnacle. Johnnie smiled, delighted with his little irony.

3.

Friday Carney drove up to Burlington for lunch, the odd invitation from Karl. Then three days with Sarah. Could she possibly really alter his life? This far along?

Karl's home despite the view of the lake felt cramped, suburban. Carney met Priscilla Cochan, a woman with red hair and a soft face gone tight. Her two daughters ignored Carney's attention, they fussed through the meal, chicken in an orange sauce. Karl handled the small ones well. A young woman named Diana who ate with them took the girls away for a separate dessert.

"Must be convenient, having a nanny."

"Yep." Karl nodded. "Suddenly I'm part of a ménage of five." He grinned.

Too bright and positive, thought Carney. "A large shift."

Priscilla smiled. "You married, Carney?"

Carney passed lightly over his long-ago divorce.

Karl smiled. "Going to marry again?"

"Lots of ways to be, right?"

The phone rang. Karl excused himself. Carney felt a strained urge to ask Priscilla Cochan about her husband. If he spoke that'd be the first question out of his mouth. He said nothing.

Priscilla began talking. Anger tumbled out, and fear—words, paragraphs, a self-scouring. She saw it clearly; in retrospect, they'd been rising to the break all last year. They'd lost their boy, Benjamin, drowned, right on their property. Johnnie hadn't been the same since.

"I'm very sorry."

"I've been trying to think it through." She stared at the tablecloth. She played with her dessert spoon. "But my mind's not too clear these days."

She wanted to smile, Carney thought. "A terrible thing like that, it can be a catalyst."

"I guess so. Last couple of weeks, that was a catalyst, sure was." She set the spoon down and faced Carney square on. "He killed the baby I was carrying."

Carney held her stare, sighed audibly, shook his head. How to react? "Terrible." He looked down at the tablecloth. "Awful." And Sarah thinks I know how to listen.

"I'd never go back. And for sure he doesn't want me back, it's done." She shook her head. "But you know, I still love him. I've asked myself so many times, how is it possible? Is it because, if I hated him, I'd have to hate all the years I spent with him? And hate all we had."

Here lay Karl's professional ground. Maybe he could in fact help her. Carney wouldn't say this to Priscilla Cochan. When at a loss for intelligent words, embrace the banal. "Hard questions."

She dropped her eyes. A small nod.

"What will you do?"

"Go somewhere. Away from here."

"You know where?"

"A city. I'm from Boston. Around Boston, that's all I can think of. It depends on Karl."

"You'll both go?"

Again she looked over to Carney.

○

In her eyes that curious human desire: If I look hard into both your eyes I can be totally honest. I've learned it can't be done. It's a physical impossibility to look at two things at the same time.

○

Priscilla's stare shifted from one of Carney's eyes to the other, then chose the bridge of his nose. For a moment her eyes crossed. "All of us, Diana too, if she'll come." Priscilla Cochan released a long breath, and looked away. "The girls love her and trust her."

"It'll be a big change."

"It's been a big change."

"I can imagine."

"Karl's been so wonderful with the girls—"

Karl returned. He stared at Priscilla, then at Carney. "Amazing, that call. A first."

"Who was it?" she said.

"My mother." Karl sat. "I don't think I've ever talked to her on the phone. She doesn't talk on the phone." His voice quavered. "She didn't even when I was a kid."

"She's changed a lot," Carney platituded. "Since the last stroke."

Priscilla took Karl's hand. "What did she say?"

He looked down at her, tears in his eyes.

Carney thought, Damn, but I've been privy recently to lots of crying.

"She's not easy to make sense of. Even when you're right there with her." Karl shook his head. "That's a fierce slur she's got."

Carney asked, "Could you make out what the words were?"

"I think—" Karl looked from Priscilla to Carney, and back to Priscilla. "I think she—was telling me she loved me." His words launched a tear down each cheek.

"Well"—Priscilla, now so sensible—"and why shouldn't she tell you?"

"She never has." His head shook. "Not in so many words." He forced a laugh. "And on the phone—" He shook his head, found a tissue, and wiped his eyes. "She called me—I think she called me—her little clinker."

Priscilla said, "What does that mean?"

"I have no idea."

"Sounds affectionate," said Carney.

Karl dabbed his nose. "Sorry, Carney. You haven't seen me at my best."

"You've had a lot to bear." Full to bursting with helpful homilies, Carney.

"Maybe she's gone soppy in the head."

"She's alert when I visit."

"It makes me miss her ranting."

"I'd bet she goes on saying what she wants." Carney smiled.

They let Karl talk, he telling them about Theresa in earlier days, blasting out at the dinner table against the stupidities of the day, verbally fencing with friends.

Carney had to leave. He'd be seeing Sarah, likely Feasie too. Any messages?

None. Yesterday Karl had told Feasie about Priscilla by phone, he'd confided in Leasie a few days ago, he'd asked them both not to tell Milton, he wanted to himself. Sarah could know.

"Feasie reacted okay?"

"Oh, you know her, she'll tell Ti-Jean first, then figure out what she feels."

That didn't sound right to Carney, but he didn't comment. He left Burlington and headed north toward the Grange, to be there to meet Sarah and her Jeep. His Jag wouldn't take to her road.

4.

Sarah drove slowly from Richmond. She was tired but felt herself swinging between joy and reservation. Along the way some amusement, a little hesitation and a touch of doubt. The dry air was thin, a cloudless sky, and mid-afternoon promised a chilly night. Okay by her, Carney was coming out, he'd stay the weekend. The week's shopping was done. No time to straighten the cabin before picking him up? Too bad.

Halfway home by some low-lying fields the Jeep passed through a hatch of late mayflies. In half a minute five dozen bugspots had spattered her windshield. She sprayed window-wash and set the wipers whirring but only smeared the mess, nearly impossible to see out. She hated killing them. She stopped the car, found a rag, the water bottle. Mayflies everywhere, millions of them, landing on the seat, the dashboard, her arms and hair. She flicked at them, and stopped. She held out her hand. Two landed. Long narrow wings, a grace of curving thorax and abdomen and a feathery sweep of tail. Magnificent.

Never in her life had she seen so many mayflies. And never so late in the season. She decided to take the hatch as an omen. The best of omens.

She watched them, awe replacing the earlier weariness. She'd worked half a day in the lab, then had a check-up appointment for herself that finished late. She preferred her own doctor; too many of those guys, which of late included women, treat you like so much meat. But at the county, personal preference meant waiting. It had all taken longer than she expected.

She sped past the Grange turn-off and threaded the Jeep down her dirt track. Would Carney buy a four-wheel drive so she wouldn't have to pick him up? This ease of being with him, the sensual luxurious back-and-forth understanding, is that what gets called love? Would she miss him if he disappeared tomorrow, would her heart break? Yes, there'd be a good-size hole. A segment of her, unshaped till Carney came along, would be empty. Now she knew it'd be impossible to live without him, he'd always remain some elusive part of her.

Theresa his reason to come into their lives, Sarah his reason for staying: he'd said that to her a few days ago. Love with Carney, if that's what it was, was going to have to get made day by day.

The dozens of lovers, too many to remember, and then Driscoll, battles in an unending war. And during Driscoll— Poor Nate, he'd deserved better, but she'd been incapable of giving better. Was the family's great dislike of Driscoll the reason she married him? Bemused, she concentrated on the road.

Her patchwork history with men left this attraction to Carney, her feelings for him, hard to give name to. The family liked him, he came ready-approved. But clear flaws, limits; despite the years of damage control, he was fragile. His urge for privacy, his shield that kept women—men too, likely—from entering his life.

But he did attract Sarah as no one before. Not even Nate.

She put away the pastas and beans, and stored the vegetables and salmon steaks in the ice house. Yes, salmon. She'd eaten fish again since the nibble of doré up at Gouin, in a restaurant, by herself. She admitted she found it as delicious as once it had been. Maybe Theresa was right, if she'd met Carney years earlier, the time so much better used—

She stared at her pond, poor silent dying pond. Would she ice-farm this winter? For chunks of frozen chemical glop to melt into her Scotch come next summer?

She should be cleaning up the cabin. Instead she sat on her porch steps and marveled at Theresa's transformation. The shock of that outright apology still made Sarah shiver. Theresa had leaned back, looked over at her, grinned with such pleasure—

Sure, Theresa had known. Sarah laughed aloud. Dear old woman. Dear mother Theresa, the old clairvoyant. Sarah laughed, sitting on the steps she laughed, a loud laughter that suddenly hacked and she found she was crying.

A new thing, this crying. She wiped her face. She'd not cried when Driscoll died. Now the tears wouldn't stop. A wellspring, bursting out. She let it flow.

5.

Carney drove quickly. A soft afternoon, warm and still, the road curving north. After the lunch with Karl and Priscilla, the Mot sense of things had started prickling down his back like July mosquitoes. A straight stretch. He accelerated hard. At faster than eighty he noted a County Sheriff's Department cruiser lurking on a dirt road. It pulled out, red and blue flashers blazing, the siren whining. Ah Mot, perceived and neglected. Carney slowed. Some day he'd get smart.

A uniformed officer left his vehicle. He walked toward Carney. Sheriff, his uniform pocket said. The Sheriff asked for driver's license, registration. Carney handed them over. The Sheriff looked at the license, at Carney, back to the license. "You're Carney?"

Carney acknowledged he was. And, curious, here's Mot, his work done but still present.

"Mr. Carney, you see that moose across the river maybe half a mile back?"

"Moose? No."

"You might have, sir, if you'd been doing forty-five."

Carney sighed. "I wish I had. Both."

"There's reasons for these speed limits, you know. At times there's no reason for some laws, but for speed limits there is."

Carney nodded.

"Anybody's allowed to kill themselves, they want to. Sometimes they don't want to. But the bad thing is, sometimes they kill somebody else."

A philosopher, a Vermont sage. Outsiders should feel privileged being given such insight, ought to take a tad of wisdom from the experience. Today Mot itches seemed hard to scratch.

He got the ticket. The Sheriff rounded his speed off to seventy-five. Carney didn't argue. He drove away and kept to forty-four the rest of the way.

Just as well. The air was full of insects. His wipers smeared the bug juice. Twice he stopped to clean his windscreen. Tiny blue damselflies. Go back into the swamp, guys, feed the frogs. He laughed. A plague of damselflies. Must be a huge major solunar period.

He drove on. The itch irritated, it localized in his throat. Or some grizzle from the chicken at lunch? A bone? He stopped at the gas station in Richmond, sipped a soft drink. "Shit." He said it so loud the man pumping gas glanced his way. Of course the bone wouldn't go down. Carney shook his head; no, nothing wrong with the drink. The first time in months, globus hystericus. What did he know he didn't know he knew? What did Mot know?

He stuck the bottle three-quarters full on the rack and drove slowly to the Grange.

6.

Theresa had insisted on breaking up the trip. "Been a long time, Milton, who knows when I'll be up that way again."

But at the Grange agreement on the question was complete. Milton had no business taking Theresa to Terramac.

"Stupid that I wrote that letter," Leonora said, her voice a thin edge. "John Cochan can be one mean parcel."

"You hit the nail on a hole in the head," said Feasie.

Leonora shook her head. "Couple of weeks ago he beat up his wife and she lost the baby she was carrying."

"How do you know that?" Gossip from Leonora?

"I have my sources."

"Theresa wants to see the place," Milton said, "so we're going."

"I wish you wouldn't."

Leonora had recommended against telling Karl about the visit. "He's in the middle of some professional problem, let's not bother him." Sarah couldn't be reached.

Ti-Jean joined his wife and sister-in-law in trying to keep Milton and Theresa from going.

Theresa said, "I got me a new suit of armor" and shook with laughter. Only tying her down would keep her at the Grange.

Feasie must have reached deep into her aphorism sack for the supporting declaration, "I suppose you can't make an omelette without opening the whole can of worms."

Theresa in her right-sided way shook her head, proclaimed Feasie correct, and thanked her so warmly she blushed. Years ago, Milton remembered, Theresa often made Feasie blush.

Theresa asked to sit out back for a few minutes, she wanted to breathe some cool air.

Ti-Jean said, "Get on some bug stuff. Mosquitoes are restless today."

Milton walked and Theresa rolled over the rough ground to the grass. She'd maneuver from there, she insisted. Milton returned to the house but watched her through the window. A long while since Theresa had been so pleased with herself. At one point she shifted the direction her chair faced and with her good hand shoved up the sleeve of her left arm. Milton wondered at this but let her be.

You set, Theresa?

Just about. What's going on?

Why, preparations everywhere.

I don't see a thing.

Of course not. You're mortal.

Tell me about it. Keep me entertained. While we wait.

Well, the termite's loosening his jaws. And in the stream, against a splinter of granite, the hellgrammite's whetting its pincers.

What's that got to do with us?

Nothing. And everything.

And me? With my sleeve up?

The wasp, he's transformed his ovipositor, he's ground it to a fine lance point.

What's that mean?

The mosquitoes are mulching saliva, there's mayflies all over the place, out of season but they want to be around. And you should see the damselflies. My faves.

We're ready, you mean?

Barbs. Stilettoes. Hooks.

We've each got our weapon. Let's head out.

Relax, Theresa. Close your eyes a while. Good. Here, I'll stroke your brow.

After a few minutes Milton came to get her. "Time to be off." He saw her arm. "Tessa?"

Her bare left arm had been stung half a dozen times, little red welts. And another bite, yellow, bigger. She shook her head. "Doesn't itch at all." She pulled her sleeve back down.

"You sure?"

"Sure I'm sure."

"Good." He walked beside her to the van. "That big one looks angry."

Theresa asked for a large hug from Feasie. Unusual. But little had been normal since the stroke. "Think us luck with the slimeslug— Oh, I mean our host, Handy Johnnie."

"Great good luck."

"That's it."

Luck. Theresa, accepting the possibility of luck. Milton marvelled. She rolled her chair onto the lift platform, Milton dropped the arm, raised the chair, and slid Theresa onto the seat in the van. He strapped the belt about her. He swung the rear door open, worked the wheelchair up the ramp, set her foilpole out of the way, rolled the chair in and fastened it in place. He sat behind the wheel and drove from the Grange. He glanced over. The outing was doing her good.

Theresa remained silent till they angled onto the Terramac road. She asked him to pull off. He crunched onto the shoulder, stopped, and turned to face her.

With her right hand she reached for his left wrist, grabbed it, squeezed it tight. She released him, with her good hand brought her left to the knob of the shift stick rising from the floor. Then her left hand alone lay on the knob. Slowly her fingers began to bend, they closed around it. They were white, as if congealing in place. She set her right hand on top of her left and, the two a forked extension of the shift, turned her shoulders and chest about to face him. "The muscles have gone soft in there. But they move."

He put both his hands on top of hers, his grin locked in place. "They'll come back."

She nodded twice. "They'll do what they have to. When they have to."

Her slur had grown stronger but he understood everything. He raised her hands one by one from the knob, slid over close beside her, brought his arms around her neck, leaned his head on her chest. They sat this way a couple of minutes, he with his face against her shirt, she staring through the window toward Terramac.

She said, "Maybe it was the bites."

"What bites? The mosquitoes?"

"All of them. Lances. I felt something move inside my arm. Not move, more like flow, I don't know. Something happened. Back on the grass."

He touched her cheek and shook his head. "Extraordinary."

"Out there, sitting, it was a moment of peace. I realized a bunch of things, Milton."

"Like?" He watched her face. Could a full smile ever come to it again? Her eyes held steady on his, back, forth, not blinking.

"What we've done in the last forty years. I sat there, I saw pieces of the forty years. Like pictures on the TV. Except the screen was the

401

sky. From us in Europe back then, to right now, this summer. A few miracles."

He smiled. "Carney coming to us this summer, that was some kind of miracle."

"Miracles are organized coincidence."

"A lucky chance."

"Yeah." A bare nod.

"Do you think he and Sarah will stay together?"

"I hope so." On her lips the twitch was stronger now. Her eyes filled with mirth, as at some delightful private joke. He knew she wouldn't tell him.

"Milton, here's what I figured."

He waited. He tried to help. "When you were over on the grass?"

"Yeah. I think, near all our life together you've been between me and the kids. You know? All of them. Including Sarah. For certain the last twenty years."

"Between?"

"Like, a magnet. Holding them close. They've stayed close. To me, now. I'm glad. That I'm still near them. I might have—just let them go. You held us together. I never understood."

He stroked her cheek again. "I was just being there."

"That's what I mean."

"Little enough."

"Everything."

"You're dramatizing again, Tessa."

Her head quivered right, back, right. "You kept them close."

"They're closer now."

"I could've been closer to them all the time. A waste."

"You will be. You'll like that."

"We both will."

"Each in our way." He smiled again. "Like it's been for forty years, right?"

She looked away again, down the road. "More."

For half a minute neither spoke. Milton pulled back. "We should be heading along."

She nodded. "Would you make my hair clip a little tighter?"

Milton reached behind her head and pulled the clip taut.

Then her left hand rose, millimeters of slowness, by itself. Her fingers took his forearm, worked up to his elbow, with infinite determination to his shoulder, touched his neck, at last his cheek. "Thank you, Milton."

He kissed her, a gentle breath, and pulled away. "Come on. We don't want to keep John Cochan waiting."

"No." Theresa panted her small laugh. "That would not do."

BUGS

The termite loosens his jaws, tightens his face.

The crab-louse marches, onward, to the pubic joints.

The mosquito mulches her saliva, seeps it down to her lancet base.

The wasp grinds his ovipositor to a skewer point.

The sucking cone-nose, that assassin bug, hones her orifice.

Against a granite splinter the hellgrammite whets its curving pincers.

Barbs, stilettoes, hooks. Prepared for the crisis
with many answers.

Roberta Feyerlicht, Jan. 13, 2004

7.

John Cochan waited alone, ready for his guests. Steed and Yak and Harry would be there already.

In the end each man is alone. All along he had known this. But he'd hidden from this knowledge. He wanted to believe in collaboration with good men, canny men. A few women too. Except they could never truly unite with him, not in Terramac, his econovum. But is it not inherent in the very nature of a perfected vision that only one man can see it truly, grasp it in all its shapes and forms? Believe in it, apply it, stand one day at its peak, yet see it still as the play of light and shadow it once was, its first flash and its final manifestation become a unity?

Alone now, and alone this morning, before dawn. It had still been dark when he'd driven in the silence of his Silver Cloud to the farmhouse, sealed, abandoned. First light streaked across the sky to the east. He marched along the little path, across the field, by the hill, into the wood. Here in deeper dark he followed the path, untraveled this summer, overgrown, his flashlight beam keeping him on track. He heard the stream before he saw it. He worked his way along, bending low, downhill, the brush thick again, and found the muddy bank where the stream divided. Here, the sluice walls; over there the opening, the cave, water flowing in. He took off his shoes, waded in, stood at the mouth. He folded his arms and stared into impenetrable darkness. He closed his eyes. He breathed, "Benjie."

On the inside of his eyelids he saw Benjie. Benjie, happy, running across the field. Johnnie called his name. Did Benjie hear? Benjie? Want to go camping? By ourselves, and leave the others. Later she, the one gone now, laughed, mockery: You, going camping? Johnnie hated her then, already.

Benjie? Why did you ride the waterchute?

Benjie didn't hear. John Cochan opened his eyes. The chute, thick, black. Specks of dirty white foam. He was alone.

Yak, Steed, Harry. They'd never understand being alone. From Harry he expected little more than measurements, equations. But that little was loyalty. To have his way, Harry had whispered poison in the ears of the others; for a wall he'd maligned John Cochan.

Steed, what a surprise he was. Steed who only days ago had explained to Harry the wondrous implications of the final blast. Now Aristide Boce argued, this very afternoon, they should await the final survey, unclear under whose land this wall of calcium, granite, limestone, descended. Oh Steed, how your eminence withers.

Worse, far worse, was Yak, as close a friend as a man could enjoy, hinting at doubts and legality. Why must they bore John Cochan with legalities? He'd played at the edge of the legal all his life, defining it, creating it. Goddamn it, the edge *was* his life. And Yak knew this, yet here he comes now, the danger of the blast, the danger of Magnussen and his wife as witnesses. Tries to argue from how the layers sit, the striations, Harry-talk from Yak's mouth. No, no danger, John had seen all the projections. No problem.

Not in the projections. But deep inside Yak, a man who believed in the caverns. Except, had Yak's belief been whole-hearted? But Yak had pretended too. To find such betrayal of friendship, after so many years. A disease, festering.

The blast would go forward. Dr. Magnussen had to be there, such a fine antagonist. The husband too. Oh they'd see why they had to sell, at last. He'd go back to his offer of $10 million. When they saw what lay back there, they'd understand. He thought then, Maybe not sell, maybe in the end ownership wasn't necessary, maybe a thousand-year lease. They would see for themselves why he had to proceed.

8.

Sarah in her Jeep and Carney from Richmond arrived at the Grange turn-off moments apart. Gentleman that he was, open vehicle that she had, he let her go first. So he drove down the road chewing dust. They pulled up, got out, she came toward him grinning with pleasure and, first things first, they kissed. His throat hadn't loosened up.

Ti-Jean ambled down the steps. His face was out of joint, his brow so crimped it might have gone corrugated. Behind him stood Feasie, arms folded, eyes to the ground.

"What's wrong, Fease?" No answer. "Ti-Jean?"

Ti-Jean scratched his hair. "Theresa and Milton." He shook his head. "They were acting weird."

"What?" Sarah grabbed Ti-Jean's arm. "They okay?"

"Oh sure, I guess so. They've gone off to Terramac."

A stab in Carney's throat. "When?"

"Maybe"—Feasie shrugged—"forty, forty-five minutes ago?"

"You let them? Just like that?" Sarah stared at Feasie.

"Am I going to stop Theresa? Milton figured it was okay. Anyway, they had an invitation."

Because of Carney? Damn! "From who?" Mot pulled hard. And whispered Theresa's words, He'll kill me. Unless I kill him first.

"The Sheriff, Nottingham, he delivered it. From Handy Johnnie."

"Come on." Carney grabbed Sarah's arm. They ran to the Jeep, jumped in. Sarah revved the engine.

Ti-Jean and Feasie caught up. "What're you doing?"

"Getting them out of there." Carney saw Mot nodding. "Come on, Sarah, move it!"

The tires screamed on gravel, back, out. Feasie yelled, "We'll come too!"

They wound up the dirt road and screeched along Fortier Creek. Sarah glanced to Carney. "What're you thinking?"

"He'll take them down there, Cochan will, I mean. Theresa thinks she's got to kill him."

"What?!"

"We have to get them out."

Miles ahead Milton drew up in front of a trailer, stopped the engine, stepped out of the van. He was in guarded shock from his first view of the razed land. Theresa had nodded merely. As if she'd seen it before.

John Cochan received them. "Welcome, welcome. Delighted to have you here." He marched around and opened the door for Theresa.

"I'll get that." Milton swung the rear door wide, rolled the chair back, down the ramp and around, slid Theresa onto it, lowered her, handed her her pole.

Cochan understood the problem. He called two men over, explained, and within minutes they, three others, a forklift, and a back-hoe had improvised a ramp up to the trailer porch, four sheets of Québois Fina end to end supported by sacks of cement. Two burley men tested it with their weight.

"Will that be too steep, Mr. Magnussen?" Cochan looked to Theresa, who scowled, lined herself up with the ramp base, accelerated, and zipped up to the porch platform. Cochan smiled. "Very impressive." They followed Theresa. Cochan opened the trailer door. They went inside. "Would you care for some tea? Or coffee?"

Theresa's head twitched, no.

"Something stronger?"

"No, thanks." Milton smiled, his lips tight.

"Well. We'll go down in a few minutes. You'll see the future that links our destinies."

Theresa glanced up at Milton, caught his eye, touched her throat, mockery of Cochan's scarlet necktie. Black suit, black shoes.

"In the meantime, let me show you the models." He did, and checked his watch every couple of minutes. He left them. They could examine the maquettes of surface Terramac at their leisure. "I'll just call ahead, we'll organize a little trailer rig for Dr. Magnussen's wheelchair."

Theresa watched Milton. He glanced at the maquettes, shrugged. His head shook, she saw him bite the insides of his cheeks. She touched his arm with her foilpole, smiled, nodded, "It'll be okay."

Cochan returned, grinning. "You'll be fascinated, John. Appropriate, isn't it, our sharing not only this land but first names as well."

Theresa said, "He doesn't use that name." She could feel Milton grasping tight on the back of her chair.

"I'm sorry, what did she say?" Cochan sounded interested.

Milton answered, "Nothing important."

9.

Sarah turned down the Terramac highway. A minute later the hut stood ahead, bar over the road, spikes gleaming. She stopped.

A tall guard strode to Sarah's side. "Yes, ma'am?"

"We have an appointment with John Cochan."

"Your name?"

"Magnussen."

"Well now, the Magnussen party came through some little while ago."

"Mr. Cochan invited all of us. I'm the daughter. We're late."

He squinted at Sarah. "You got some identification?"

She showed him her driver's license, two credit cards. "Come on, open the gate. Mr. Cochan won't be happy."

The guard pointed to Carney. "Who's the gentleman?"

"For godsake, man, he's my husband. Just open up!"

Another slow perusal. He meandered back to the guardhouse. The pike rose, the spikes retracted. They roared through. Carney glanced back. Just coming into view, Ti-Jean's and Feasie's truck. But the pike was lowering.

On. And on. The rise. The wasted plain of Terramac below. Sarah whispered, "Un-be-lievable." She stepped hard on the gas and they sped down. "What shit."

"We can go now. Everything's ready and waiting for us." John Cochan reached for Theresa Magnussen's chair.

"No." With her right hand Theresa moved her left arm, left hand holding the foilpole flat against the chair's bar, if necessary to wipe Cochan away. Cochan pulled back. Milton held the door open. Theresa's right hand worked the controls. With care she propelled the chair out, down the trailer ramp, on past a shiny gray Rolls-Royce.

Cochan strode ahead, to lead.

Theresa's little twelve-horsepower engine rolled her through the cooling air past construction material and dozens of men in overalls and hard hats, and many large machines. She thought, Where are Ti-Jean's demons when you need them?

John Cochan described the forthcoming function of near-complete buildings. He detailed their construction, in cement, steel, brick, stone, wood, glass. He noted the choice settings of the condominiums of Terramac, their fine views. And he made much of the hollow beyond, soon to be flooded, Lake Fortier. They arrived at the elevator building. Cochan held open the door.

Theresa looked around. A naked land. She stared up at the sky, a few clouds, sun nearing the horizon. That would be the west, then. She nodded, and rode through the doorway.

○

I shifted my focus and watched them descend. And yes, it was Lola, exquisite in silver, riding on Theresa's lap. What now?

○

They dropped some fifteen hundred feet, a trip of less than two minutes, Cochan tour-guiding the whole while. They got out. Thick warm air hit them. Yakahama Stevenson met them. John Cochan glared. "Well?"

"Everything's ready, John."

A four-seater golf cart. "We've got about a mile to go." Milton strapped Theresa onto a back seat, her chair to the flatcar trailer. "We'll be dropping an additional three hundred feet here, feel the slant? It's all natural, built the way the cavern slopes. We've kept it like we found it, completely natural."

A momentary rush of claustrophobia took Milton. Too humid. Too sticky.

"In about four months these golf carts will be replaced by an electric tramway. Right over there, that's where the casino will be." And a couple of minutes later: "Along here, this is the boutique district, over a hundred shops. We're very selective."

Lola grinned. You ready, Theresa?

Have to see what it looks like, when we get there.

A quarter mile beyond: "Now here we've got three blocks of elegant homes planned. Two, three, and four bedrooms. But that'll be in the next stage. Oh, look over on your left, that'll be the gymnasium there."

A thick wall of granite, patched at the peaks with concrete. "It looks immense." Milton touched Theresa's left arm.

"It is." The response cheered John Cochan. They deserved the preliminary special treat. "Yak. Up ahead, please, a brief stop."

"Sure thing, John." Yak slowed, drove close to the railing, and cut the motor's hum. As planned.

"Hear the roar? It comes from deep below, the clear sparkling waters. One of the bits of magic Terramac abounds in, two flashing streams. They meet deep in the flume. We believe it's a cut-back from the Sabrevois River."

Milton said, "How do you figure that?"

John Cochan nodded happily. "With these waters and no doubt others we haven't located yet, Terramac connects to the St. Lawrence and from there of course to the sea. Some day it might be possible to sail from Terramac directly into the ocean."

Milton said, "My god."

His exclamation delighted Johnnie.

It's close, Theresa. Very close.

Yep.

Any thoughts?

A hug, Lola. I need a hug.

Yes, Theresa. I think you need a kiss too.

John Cochan watched Theresa Magnussen's arms spread, and squeeze. As if the woman was embracing air! Clearly senile. Which meant he'd be dealing only with the husband. Good.

○

I knew! In that instant I grasped what they'd do, Lola and Theresa. I didn't think. I pressed my eyes tight shut, let go. Yes, I stepped off the edge. It felt a bit like falling. Once again. I forced my eyes open, and landed on my feet. A cinch.

○

Milton thought: Convince Theresa to leave right now. He pressed her arm. But she wouldn't respond. The golf cart stopped beside two smaller ones. Here yet more construction had begun, shattered and crumbled rock, cement foundations. Milton got off, unstrapped Theresa and her chair, and sat her in it.

"We go this way." Cochan led them to a rounded opening in the rock face, twenty-five feet in diameter, some eight feet up the wall. The opening was reached by a long steel ramp. Its slant, a few degrees less steep than the makeshift one to the trailer, showed muddy tractor treads.

"Theresa, you sure you can get up?"

"It's a good chair." She rolled up fast, an easy glide to the lip.

Milton followed. He was trembling. He squeezed his hands tight around the back of the chair. At the ramp's summit stood a platform, straddling the opening, constructed from twenty four-by-eight Québois Fina sheets.

Theresa glanced around. On a horseshoe of tables sat a lot of technology, computers and whatnot. She understood nothing. On the far side another ramp led down into what looked like a large empty space, dark, a chill rising from the thick air. Somewhere water burbled and gurgled.

John Cochan waited. The company assembled on the platform. Cochan said, "Okay, Yak." Yak pressed a button. The dark space flooded with lights: green, blue, yellow, red.

A dream of rapturous illumination. To the left, massive stalactites, stalagmites, speleothons, sparkling red, gold, and silver. At the center, six fountains playing glossy colors, a hundred thousand diamonds, rubies, emeralds in soft motion, their waters connected by rivulets of blue and gold.

Along the right wall, deep below, its rim twelve feet from the platform, a flume raced the fifty-yard length of the space. Above the chasm hung mirrors angled for a platform view, the reflection revealing waters frolicking a hundred feet down. Down there too the lights played their magic, soft golds, purple, silver, rose. Only the distant wall stood blank, a dull gray-brown.

Milton shook his head. He grasped Theresa's shoulder. She nodded.

Cochan gave them a grand smile. "Wonderful, isn't it?"

"It's very—complex."

"Yes. I know."

Two more men joined them. Cochan introduced one as somebody Clark, the architect of much of what they'd seen, the other as his assistant Bang something. The second man's face was held in a permanent scowl.

"We all set, Harry?"

"As much as we can be."

"Good." Cochan turned to his guests. "What we're going to do now— You see that wall of rock directly across?"

Milton nodded.

"We're going to blast through it."

"Why?"

"Beyond it lies a cavern. It's beneath what's now your land."

"Beneath the Grange?"

"Which, as you'll see before you leave, must be part of Terramac."

"We're leaving now. Let's go, Theresa." He grabbed her chair, began to turn it—

Cochan stayed his hand. "Please. You have to see. To know why this must happen."

412

Milton couldn't help himself: "And why is that."

Cochan smiled. "It won't do you any good, what's back there."

Milton shivered, his fear surely visible now. "Theresa doesn't like explosions. She wants to leave. Right now." With his free hand he released the brake on the chair.

Cochan held his elbow as in a vice. "What Mr. Clark has done, he and Mr. Steele have placed a dynamite charge against that wall. Look with care and you can see it, we circled it in white. Over there." He pointed. "In a moment Bang will set the timing. Then we'll step down from the ramp and walk around the corner."

"Never mind. I don't want any blasting when I'm down here." He couldn't make Cochan let go.

"The blast will be clean. When we return you'll see what lies beyond." His voice went soft, reverent. "What heights and depths."

Milton didn't understand this heights business but knew Cochan made him good and mad. He looked from the man called Yak to the architect, Clark. They were both staring at Cochan. "What—heights?"

Johnnie gazed at the wall, the circle. He spoke with great respect. "Our future history."

Milton's eyes widened.

"The future. Yours. Mine. My son's."

Milton said, "You feeling okay, Mr. Cochan?"

"Bang, set the remote."

"Look, Mr. Cochan, I think we shouldn't—"

"Set it."

Bang Steele turned to his boss. "Harry?"

Harold Clark stared at the playing lights.

John Cochan whispered, "Do it!"

From the passage they'd come along, Milton heard a shout.

Clark nodded.

Milton saw Theresa staring at Clark. He watched Steele type a series of numbers and tap the Enter key. He saw the hands on two of the dials leap, one the whole way, one a few degrees. He swung around—"Theresa! Tessa!!"

Her chair was rushing down the ramp into the bright cavern. It picked up speed, lurched ahead, on the flat now, her pole brandished high, her voice intoning sounds, words, impossible to make out what.

"Get back here, you fool!" Clark, the architect.

Milton leapt after the speeding chair—"Tessa!"—but one of them had him around the waist, another grabbed his shoulder—

"Lola!" I had to make them stop. "Don't! Please go back!"

"You're here!" She grinned at me. Then her pleasure turned to taunt. "So come along for the ride!"

What's the shouting, Lola?

Keep your eye on the steerin', Theresa— Lola reached behind Theresa and pulled off her hair clip. Here, Theresa, chew on this. Lola handed her a greenish pastille. Chew on this.

What is it? Theresa took it.

Powdered bloodstone. For strength.

Theresa chewed. Time for one more fine special thing.

"Lola! For heaven's sake, and eternity's!"

"Come with us!"

I could do no more than watch.

Sarah and Carney reached the platform. Everywhere hands and faces in confusion, a dozen feet cavorting on a tiny stage. Beyond, below, the wheelchair rushed through a chamber lit up like a hundred Christmas trees. Sarah grabbed a man hanging on to Milton, the three struggled together, Sarah's fist caught the side of the man's head, he let go, turned on her, Milton grabbed him—

Cochan recognized Carney. Someone he'd met. A man who'd lied to him.

Yak stared at Carney. "It's going to blow."

"What?"

He pointed, beyond Theresa, to the far wall. Carney shot down the ramp after Theresa, Theresa all aglow in ten thousand lights. Her hair had come loose, a sea of white cloud behind her head. Carney heard a hollow voice yell from behind—"less than a minute"—and he pumped his feet like a crazy man but the chair was too powerful. For a second he thought he saw a white-gold demon riding with the chair—

Cochan shouted, "Abort, you ass! Abort! Abort!"

Clark's head quivered. "I can't, once it's set—"

Come on, Theresa, faster! To the wall, tolerate nothing! This is it, this is us, now!

"Lola! Come back!"

You and me, Theresa, push, there's the white circle, grab the thing!

Here we go, Lola!

You should see them back there, all frozen in place, icicles among the stalactites, so funny! No, don't look, faster!

—embracing hope upon the fields of danger, the ancient gods rejoice, and death no stranger!

Reach out, Theresa, the pole, the circle, you got it! Hold on, off off off we go, a splendid grand abandon!

Here we go, Lola, down the middle, hahahahahahaha!

Carney heard a voice shrieking, "Off! Off! Off! Off! Off!" And Sarah's shout, "Carney! Too late!"

He didn't hear, ran on. I couldn't help myself, I flew off after him, caught up and tackled him. He crashed to the ground. Now how did I do that?

Theresa reached the far wall, she'd turned her chair, her pole thrust high, the tip grasping some kind of package, speeding now to the right, the chasm, and Carney heard Theresa's laughter, the whole chamber filled with laughter, a life in laughter, laughter from the glistening stalactites, laughter far huger than Theresa's voice could produce, laughter from the spew of sparkling fountains, echoes of laughter, laughter in spasms, laughter from the flume, the walls laughing, the ceiling and far beyond the ceiling laughter, laughter, roars of laughter, the chair lunged forward— Carney bellowed, "Theresa! No!"

I screamed, "Lola! No!"

They disappeared over the edge. The tiniest tickle of a laugh, silver, mixing with, faraway, a hoarse, Off, off . . .

And the blast. A wall of air hit Carney. He might have flown fifteen feet. He landed in water, on his shoulder, he heard it crunch. Since I have no earthly substance, the explosion didn't bother me. Then Sarah and Milton were next to Carney, pulling him from a fountain, sopping wet, standing, dragging him away, up the ramp, to the platform.

John Cochan stared at the chamber. I remember his eyes, wide, white, their focus far beyond the wall.

A voice said, "Holy shit." An arm pointed.

Rising from the chasm, a spurt, a single narrow spume.

Someone said, "Harry?"

Another voice: "I don't know."

Then a second spurt, and another, it became a shaft of water a yard thick. And the roar. A highway of water, spewing, churning, flooding— Over the chasm's edge a curve of water, more, pumping— Waves.

The chamber went black. "It's a short!" Sarah grabbed Carney, pulled Milton, dragged him, shoved toward the golf carts and the light.

Behind them a voice: "Johnnie, come on, come on!"

Johnnie's head nodded. Yes, he stood at the pinnacle. Below him, water fell everywhere, rose, fell again, dark diamonds of water. Playing among the diamonds, Benjie.

Why, boy?

How far down, Daddy?

Why did you ride the waterchute?

To save you, Daddy.

You saved me?

No, Daddy.

EPILOGUE
AUTUMN EQUINOX
2003

I can't say the explosion finished Theresa. A sense of her lingers in the down below, in the water and on the sunbeams. No, she's not been seen up here in the eternal infinite realm.

They pulled Carney out, and Cochan. Sarah forced Milton to help drag Carney off. Milton had been ready to wade out and follow his wife.

Carney blamed himself for tripping up while chasing Theresa. But he wouldn't take her choice of death away from her, not for the world. He prized Theresa's wild laughter.

Terramac is gone. The explosion measured 3.1 Richter, not that violent but it built on itself. Belowground it tore into the wall of ancient rock, its shock waves shot miles along schists and striations, its force brought fragile crust crashing down, leaving rifts and two immense crevices. The caverns are flooded. A damage control team from the University of Vermont—not including Carney and Co.—has hypothesized the greatest harm was caused when the blast's reverberations tore a hole under the Sabrevois River, draining near a third of its flow down to Terramac depth. Then the hole plugged up, no adequate theories as to why or how. But for nearly two days the river did in effect run backward. A new sea, dark and silent, lies below the shorn square miles of the old Fortier Farm, under the Magnussen land as well. The water level has settled, forever or for now, no way of telling, its highest point 1,180 feet below ground. Part of Ginette Seymour's inheritance.

Aboveground, structural damage has made even the near-complete condos unsafe. They will be dynamited. Summerclime, like Underland, all done with.

Handy Johnnie Cochan is gone as well, from Vermont anyway. He's resigned as head of Intraterra and lives now in the Caribbean, on an island with a high hill in the middle. He's bought a big house. He climbs the hill each morning. From there he can see in all directions, 360 degrees of perspective. If he'd taken Benjie camping that one time, would it have made a difference? But events that don't take place cannot be understood.

Johnnie's friend Yak feels great compassion—the Handyman lost his son, his wife, and Deirdre and Melissa, as well as the majesty of

Terramac, all in one year. But there's a shade of enmity there too—why, why that one last cavern?

Insurance will cover some of the Terramac disaster. How much?

"We'll never find out," Ti-Jean muttered. "It's not a public company."

Or, as Feasie said, "Hell is paved with happy clams."

The Sheriff of the county, Henry Nottingham, has launched a campaign for private and government money to reseed the scraped area with conifers, birch, and maple. This will take a while, both the raising of funds and the regrowth of trees. How the new ecology there will compare with the old is hard to predict.

Milton wouldn't leave the Grange. When Carney, arm in a sling, shoulder set but the pain still bad, saw Milton a few days after the explosion, he looked years older. His kids had convinced him, he said, that Theresa had been fully aware of her actions. Talking to him this way, Leasie, Feasie, Sarah, and Karl softened their own loss.

Sarah's pond filled again, a long blast of water from the spring. After half a day it ran clear. The muck tore apart and was washed away, down Gambade Brook on its way to the sea. Right away she put in two hundred trout, fingerlings. When the pond is still, in the early morning or when the sun sets and there's a hatch, ripples form as the fish come up to feed. A year from now, Carney figures, they'll be approaching keeper size. But unless the acidity goes down they'll never breed.

Bobbie's new poem hopped out of nowhere. Or rather from somewhere but a place she'd not been to till now. Last night, going to bed, she felt the compulsion to write. Now she took a sheet of paper from the desk drawer where she'd carefully concealed it, didn't want some casual anybody to see it. Way unlike her other stuff to now, not even the nature poems. She reread it.

> When I was young I wanted fame,
> The world to know me by my name.
> To brand each plague, ordain its cure;
> I wanted to make literature.

When I was in my middle age
I tried to dazzle, page by page,
To celebrate each setting day.
I had a thing or two to say.

I'm old now and I've nearly found
The limits of my world around:
To make a little public time,
To make my poem, word by line.

Maybe she'd call it *Three Women for Robert Frost*.

A week after the explosion, early evening, the sun going down, Sarah and Carney were sitting on the cabin's porch. They listened to water from the spring gurgling in, watched bats swoop for mosquitoes, and, in the way they'd gotten used to, kept their silence. He felt her eyes then, watching and memorizing. What more to know? he wondered. He glanced over to her.

Her face didn't change. "Hi," she said.

"Hello," he said. "How are you?"

She said, "Pregnant. How about you?"

○

And Lola? Why, she's come home. Getting back meant reaching for the edge, leaping up and free. And yes, the Gods can't remember ever missing her. No one missed me. And nothing's changed between us.

"Sure it has." Lola smiles, but charming sin shines in her eyes. "I've seen their joy and fear, I've felt their juices flow." Her right eyebrow rises, a new talent. "Yours too."

"From now on, be discreet."

"Here and below, there's lots of tricks to try."

"Lola. When you meddle with mortals—"

"Me? Theresa planned it all. Anyway, leave guilt to the living. We're too far away from that world." She thinks for a moment. "And too dead." She shakes her head. "Proud of your boy?"

I am indeed. Except, and here's my one regret, I'll never get to hold my grandkid, not in the world's way. Though I did go down there once. We'll see.

Sarah wants to call the kid Teddy. For Theodore, or Theodora.

Think of this: my son, Carney, in his fifties, me thirty-six forever, and soon a tiny baby. With Milton and me as co-grandfathers.

Lola says, "Let's go play."

Sometimes I shrug and say, "Why not?"

She grins. Sometimes I say I need to keep an eye on the down below, find more stories to tell her. Sometimes she grabs the hem of my robe, that lustrous magenta, and trips me off my feet.

ACKNOWLEDGMENTS

Great thanks to those who have read one or another of the several drafts of the *Lola* manuscript and commented on it—you have greatly helped focus and clarify my intentions: Rhonda Bailey, Robert Barsky, Sandy Frances Duncan, Marie-Christine Leps, Alison Szanto, David Szanto. Thanks as well to my erstwhile publisher at Brindle & Glass, Ruth Linka, for her appreciation of *Whatever Lola Wants*. And Leah Fowler, my editor, with whom I had not worked before, was brilliant in helping me cut and pare. Thank you, Leah.

A National Magazine Award recipient and winner of the Hugh MacLennan Prize for fiction, George Szanto is the author of several books of essays and half a dozen novels. His most recent novel prior to *Whatever Lola Wants* is *The Tartarus House on Crab*. A fellow of the Royal Society of Canada, Szanto is the co-author (with Sandy Frances Duncan) of the Island Investigations International mystery series, which includes *Never Sleep with a Suspect on Gabriola Island*, *Always Kiss the Corpse on Whidbey Island*, *Never Hug a Mugger on Quadra Island*, and *Always Love a Villain on San Juan Island*. In 2013 he published a chronicle/memoir, *Bog Tender: Coming Home to Nature and Memory*. Please visit his website at georgeszanto.com.